THE ACCIDENTAL WAR

ALSO BY WALTER JON WILLIAMS

THE SECOND BOOKS OF THE PRAXIS

The Accidental War

THE FIRST BOOKS OF THE PRAXIS
DREAD EMPIRE'S FALL

The Praxis
The Sundering
Conventions of War
Investments
Impersonations

NOVELS

Hardwired
Knight Moves
Voice of the Whirlwind
Days of Atonement
Aristoi
Metropolitan
City on Fire
Ambassador of Progress
Angel Station
The Rift
Implied Spaces

QUILLIFER

Quillifer
Quillifer the Knight (forthcoming)

DIVERTIMENTI

The Crown Jewels
House of Shards
Rock of Ages

DAGMAR SHAW THRILLERS

This Is Not a Game
Deep State
The Fourth Wall
Diamonds for Tequila

HISTORICAL FICTION

To Glory Arise
Brig of War
The Macedonian
The Tern Schooner
Cat Island

COLLECTIONS

Facets
Frankensteins & Foreign Devils
The Green Leopard Plague and Other Stories

THE ACCIDENTAL WAR

WALTER JON WILLIAMS

This is a work of fiction. Names, characters, places, and incidents are products of the author's imagination or are used fictitiously and are not to be construed as real. Any resemblance to actual events, locales, organizations, or persons, living or dead, is entirely coincidental.

FIRST EDITION

Designed by Paula Russell Szafranski

Library of Congress Cataloging-in-Publication Data has been applied for.

ISBN 978-0-06-246702-7

18 19 20 21 22 LSC 10 9 8 7 6 5 4 3 2 1

For Kathy Hedges

The author would like to thank Steve Howe for details of antimatter containment, Oz Drummond for economics lessons, and the 2017 edition of the Rio Hondo Workshop for their accustomed intelligence and advice.

DRAMATIS PERSONAE

MARTINEZ FAMILY AND DEPENDENTS

MARCUS, LORD MARTINEZ: Terran, patriarch of Clan Martinez, patron to Laredo, Chee, and Parkhurst.

LADY MARTINEZ: Terran, wife to Lord Martinez.

LORD ROLAND MARTINEZ: Terran, Lord Martinez's eldest son and heir. Convocate.

GIRASOLE MARTINEZ: Terran, Roland's daughter.

SENIOR CAPTAIN LORD GARETH MARTINEZ: Terran, second son of Lord Martinez, awarded the Golden Orb for conduct during the Naxid War.

LADY TERZA CHEN: Terran, daughter and heir of Lord Chen, wife of Gareth Martinez.

GARETH THE YOUNGER ("CHAI-CHAI"): Terran, son of Gareth Martinez and Terza Chen.

YALING ("MEI-MEI"): Terran, daughter of Gareth Martinez and Terza Chen.

LADY VIPSANIA MARTINEZ: Terran, daughter of Lord and Lady Martinez, married to Lord Convocate Oda Yoshitoshi and head of Imperial Broadcasting.

LADY WALPURGA MARTINEZ: Terran, daughter of Lord and Lady Martinez, widow of PJ Ngeni.

LADY SEMPRONIA MARTINEZ: Terran, daughter of Lord and Lady Martinez, estranged from her family. Married to Nikkul Shankaracharya.

KHALID ALIKHAN: Terran, weaponer first class (retired). Orderly to Gareth Martinez.

DOSHTRA: Daimong, butler to Gareth Martinez.

MISS SAPERSTEIN: Vipsania's assistant in video production.

FRAN: Lady Terza's maidservant.

LADY SULA, HER DEPENDENTS AND ASSOCIATES

SENIOR CAPTAIN CAROLINE, LADY SULA: Terran, head of Clan Sula, Fleet officer and former head of the Secret Army. Former leader of Action Team 491.

CONSTABLE FIRST CLASS GAVIN MACNAMARA: Terran, detailed as servant to Lady Sula, former member of the Secret Army and Action Team 491.

ENGINEER FIRST CLASS SHAWNA SPENCE: Terran, detailed as servant to Lady Sula, former member of the Secret Army and Action Team 491.

MASTER CLERK TY-FRAN: Lai-own, Fleet veteran detailed as Sula's personal secretary.

FER TUGA: Daimong, "the Axtattle Sniper," veteran of the Secret Army.

SIDNEY: Terran, weapons designer and owner of Sidney's Superior Firearms.

MING LIN: Terran, veteran of the Secret Army, graduate student in economics, and Sula's economic adviser.

ASHOK SURESH: Terran, veteran of the Secret Army, law professor, and Sula's legal adviser.

MAHRU TIFFINWALA: Terran, a baker.

THE FLEET

LORD TORK: Daimong, Supreme Commander of the Fleet.

FLEET COMMANDER LORD IVAN SNOW: Terran, Inspector General of the Fleet, head of Investigative Service and military police.

FLEET COMMANDER LORD PA DO-FAQ: Lai-own, commander of the Third Fleet at Felarus, Gareth Martinez's former commander.

FLEET COMMANDER PEZZINI: Terran, member of the Fleet Control Board.

JUNIOR FLEET COMMANDER LADY MICHI CHEN: Terran, commanding Fleet ring station at Harzapid. Sister of Lord Chen, aunt to Terza Chen, and Gareth Martinez's former commander.

JUNIOR FLEET COMMANDER LORD ALTASZ: Torminel, commander of Altasz Force during the Naxid War.

SENIOR SQUADRON COMMANDER NGUYEN: Terran, commanding a squadron under Do-faq at Felarus.

SQUADRON COMMANDER LORD SORI ORGHODER: Torminel, commanding Force Orghoder. Veteran of the Naxid War, the Second Battle of Magaria, and the Battle of Naxas. Nephew of Lord Orghoder. A yachtsman.

JUNIOR CAPTAIN LORD JEREMY FOOTE: Terran, commanding light cruiser *Vigilant* and Light Squadron Eight. Veteran of the Naxid War, the First and Second Battles of Magaria, and racing pilot for the Apogee Club.

SENIOR CAPTAIN LORD OH DERINUUS: Daimong, commanding cruiser *Beacon.*

SENIOR CAPTAIN AN-SOL: Lai-own, commanding cruiser *Conformance.*

LIEUTENANT LADY BENEDICTA KELLY: Terran, formerly of Martinez's frigate *Corona,* yacht captain of Corona Club.

LIEUTENANT-CAPTAIN LORD NAAZ VIJANA: Terran, commanding frigate stationed at Esley.

LIEUTENANT-CAPTAIN LADY ELISSA DALKEITH: Terran, former premiere lieutenant on Martinez's command *Corona.*

LIEUTENANT-CAPTAIN ARI ABACHA: Terran, a friend of Gareth Martinez, and a sporting enthusiast.

LIEUTENANT-CAPTAIN LADY ALANA HAZ: Terran, former premiere lieutenant on Sula's frigate *Confidence.*

LIEUTENANT LADY REBECCA GIOVE: Terran, formerly second lieutenant on Sula's frigate *Confidence.*

LORD PAVEL IKUHARA: Terran, former third officer on Sula's frigate *Confidence.*

LIEUTENANT LADY CHANDRA PRASAD: Terran, formerly of Martinez's command *Illustrious.*

LIEUTENANT LORD SABIR MERSENNE: Terran, formerly of Martinez's command *Illustrious.*

LIEUTENANT LORD AHMAD HUSAYN: Terran, formerly of Martinez's command *Illustrious.*

LIEUTENANT LADY KOSCH ALTASZ: Torminel, pilot in the Corona Club.

LIEUTENANT VONDERHEYDTE: Terran, formerly of Martinez's command *Corona.*

LIEUTENANT GARCIA: Terran, former prisoner of the Naxids.

LIEUTENANT RATNA: Terran, aide to Fleet Commander Ivan Snow.

LIEUTENANT SODAK: Torminel, pilot in Corona Club.

WARRANT OFFICER FIRST CLASS MAITLAND: Terran, former sensor specialist on Sula's frigate *Confidence.*

ENGINEER FIRST CLASS MARKIOS: Terran, formerly of Sula's frigate *Confidence.*

EXPLORATION SERVICE

CAPTAIN SHUSHANIK SEVERIN ("NIKKI"): Terran, captain of *Expedition* and puppeteer.

LIEUTENANT LORD CHUNGSUN CLEGHORNE: Terran, premiere lieutenant of *Expedition.*

LIEUTENANT CRESSIDA TOUPAL: Terran, second lieutenant of *Expedition.*

PILOT FIRST CLASS LIU: Terran, crew on *Expedition.*

WARRANT OFFICER FALYAZ: Terran, crew on *Expedition.*

PEERS

MAURICE, LORD CHEN: Terran. A convocate, member of the Fleet Control Board, and father-in-law of Gareth Martinez.

LORD SAÏD: Terran, Lord Senior of the Convocation and head of Clan Saïd.

LORD MEHRANG: Terran, patron to Esley, home planet of the Yormaks.

LADY KORIDUN: Torminel, the young head of the Koridun clan.

LORD CONVOCATE MONDI: Torminel, former Fleet captain and member of Fleet Control Board.

LORD TCHAI RIDUR: Torminel spokesman for Imperial Bank.

LADY KANNITHA SEANG: Terran, head of the Imperial Bank.

LADY DISTCHIN: Torminel, absentee patron to Spannan.

LADY GRUUM: Daimong, patron to the newly settled world Rol-mar.

LADY TU-HON: Lai-own, presiding judge of the Court of Honor in the Convocation.

LORD ORGHODER: Torminel, president of the Yachting Association.

LORD GONIHU: Daimong, a wealthy and respected Peer.

LORD PYTE GONIHU: Daimong, Lord Gonihu's grandson, representing the Gonihu clan in the Convocation.

LORD MINNO: Cree, a banker.

LORD ODA YOSHITOSHI: Terran, heir to Yoshitoshi clan and husband of Vipsania Martinez.

LORD DURWARD LI: Terran, former client of the Sulas, now client of the Chens.

CAPTAIN LORD RICHARD LI: Terran, son of Lord Durward Li and Lady Amita. Terza Chen's fiancé, killed at the First Battle of Magaria.

LADY AMITA: Terran, Lord Durward's first wife.

LADY MARIETTA: Terran, Lord Durward's second wife.

LORD NGENI: Terran, member of the Convocation, former patron to the Martinez clan.

LORD PIERRE NGENI: Terran, Lord Ngeni's son, member of the Convocation.

LADY CASSILDA ZYKOV: Terran, former wife of Roland Martinez and mother of Girasole.

LORD ZYKOV: Terran, Lady Cassilda's father.

LORD ELDEY: Torminel, a convocate and former governor of Zanshaa.

LADY FITZPATRICK: Terran, steward of the Apogee Club.

LORD ARRUN SAFISTA: Torminel, officer in the Legion of Diligence.

CAPTAIN EHRLER BLITSHARTS: Legendary yacht captain who died with his dog, Orange, during the Vandrith Challenge Cup.

CLIQUEMEN

HECTOR BRAGA ("LAMEY"): Terran, sometime gangster from Spannan, now lobbyist.

JULIEN BAKSHI: Terran, head of the Riverside Clique, member of the Commission.

SERGIUS BAKSHI: Terran, Julien's father, a retired gangster.

NAVEEN PATEL: Terran, a member of the Commission.

GREDEL ("EARTHGIRL"): Terran, a street girl from Spannan.

OTHERS

COSGROVE: Terran, an entrepreneur.

TARN-NA: Lai-own, Lord Chen's elderly servant.

CHESKO: Daimong, clothes designer in Petty Mount.

TI-CAR: Lai-own, maître d'hotel of the Corona Club.

MOCK: Daimong, waitron at the Corona Club.

SEKALOG: Cree, bartender at the Corona Club.

CAPTAIN KLARVASH: Naxid, officer in the Urban Patrol.
NETTRUKU: Daimong, sous-chef at the Corona Club.
CAPTAIN SOR-TAN: Lai-own, captain of the yacht carrier *Corona.*
FIRST OFFICER ANDERSON: Terran, Naxid War veteran, first officer of the yacht carrier *Corona.*
KO-DON: Lai-own, a journalist.

THE ACCIDENTAL WAR

PROLOGUE

The wind coming down from the glacier seemed to cut right through Lord Mehrang's Devajjo-fur coat. Ice crystals stung his cheek. He moved heavily across the tundra and gestured for Lieutenant-Captain Lord Naaz Vijana to follow. The young officer climbed out of the VTOL craft, and surprise showed on his face as he encountered the full force of the freezing wind. He pulled up the collar of his viridian-green Fleet great-coat, then jammed his cap far down his forehead, partly for warmth, partly to keep the cap from flying away.

Mehrang adjusted his hood to keep the ice crystals away from his face. A hot exhaust port on the aircraft gave a metallic ping as it cooled.

When Vijana joined him, Lord Mehrang raised his mittened hand and gestured to the camp huddled next to the long lake below the glacier. "There they are," he said. "The true lords of this world."

Hide tents seemed to crouch before the wind. Hundreds of shaggy brown cattle drank from the lake or grazed on the mosses and grasses. Humanoids, equally shaggy, walked among the tents and the cattle.

"Extraordinary color," said Vijana. The lake was teal green and laced with silver as the wind tore at its surface.

"It's rock flour from the glacier," he said. "Changes the way the water refracts. You can look up the science later, if you're interested." Lord Mehrang had not brought Vijana here to discuss the color of lakes.

"I will, my lord, thank you."

Vijana had a cunning, pointed face, caramel skin, bright, alert black eyes, and a pencil mustache that Mehrang considered unfortunate. Lord Mehrang knew that Vijana also had a gambling habit, little or no patronage in the Fleet, and no hope of promotion. Vijana had only managed a promotion to lieutenant-captain because of a need for officers during the war, but now the war was long over, and Vijana's career had stalled. Not only was he in debt and with no chance of advancement, but his little frigate had been stationed here at Esley, a world as sad and pathetic as his own hopes.

Lord Mehrang shifted his large, heavy body and began his trudge toward the camp. "Glaciers cover almost a quarter of the planet's surface," he said. "And nearly half of what's left is reserved for the Yormaks." He gestured toward the camp in disgust. "There are only a couple hundred thousand of them, and they get half a world!"

And between the frigid, dry climate and the Yormak reserves, there wasn't a lot of room left for settlers, or—more importantly—developing a proper economy. Only forty-six million people had settled the planet under Clan Mehrang's patronage, and it was hard for the current lord to scrape his proper share from the scant profits. Of all those Peers who served as patrons to settled worlds, he was by far the poorest. His family could barely afford a third-rate palace in Zanshaa High City, and no Mehrang had ever been co-opted into the Convocation. It was a situation that filled him with fury.

"And it doesn't have to be like this! My family drew up plans generations ago," he said. "Seed lampblack over the glaciers to reduce the planet's albedo, as well as absorb heat to melt the ice. Giant mirrors put in space to reflect even more light and heat onto the planet to speed the process. The consultants say we'd have a green, warm world in under thirty years. Even if that's too optimistic, we can still manage it in under fifty. But generation after generation, century after century, the government on Zanshaa has turned down our every application."

"That's a shame, my lord," said Vijana. He shivered as the wind blasted down his neck, and with a gloved hand he drew his collar closer around his throat. "This place could certainly be warmer."

"And it's all because of *them,*" Mehrang said, pointing again at the camp. "It's all because of the Yormaks."

Esley had been discovered eighteen hundred years before, along with the humanoid Yormaks, tool-using natives who followed their herds of cattle from one pastureland to the next. When the then Lady Mehrang was first appointed patron of the new world, she must have been skipping with joy. She would settle this world, adjust its climate, take a piece of every profitable enterprise, and raise the Yormaks to become full citizens of the empire, subject only to the will of the conquering Shaa. After all, races such as the Naxids and the Torminel had been advanced from a primitive state and were now obedient, productive citizens.

Except it had all gone wrong. The Yormaks ignored Lady Mehrang and her settlers and would only pay attention if they were somehow compelled. They were disinclined to learn the language of the Shaa, and again used it only under compulsion. Further, they never tried to teach the newcomers their own language, and it was only learned by dedicated researchers who followed them over the frigid world, recorded their speech, and made educated guesses as to what the words meant. When provided with useful technology—wagons or sleds, modern stoves, simple tools—the Yormaks simply abandoned them on the tundra and continued using the crude implements they crafted themselves.

Lady Mehrang tried to find the dominant personalities in each band, appointed them chieftains over each group, and tried to use these to control the native population, but the chieftains were uninterested in being in charge of anything, and they refused to participate in any of Lady Mehrang's schemes for advancing them. When Lady Mehrang separated Yormaks from their families and herds in order to subject them to a concentrated education in modern civilization, they had simply lain down, stopped eating, wasted away, and died.

Delegations of chieftains had been sent to the capital at Zanshaa so that the Shaa could explain to them their responsibilities under the Praxis, but the first group wasted away before the Great Masters could even see them. Subsequent delegations were better supervised and had a lower mortality rate, but all they did was stand listlessly and ask to go home.

Eventually even the Shaa were forced to concede defeat. They announced that they had granted the Yormaks' petition to live on their home world, and they subsequently made arrangements for them to continue their traditional life. Enormous tracts of land were reserved for them along their established migration routes, and a branch of the Ministry of Forestry and Fisheries was dedicated to studying the Yormaks, protecting their way of life, and mitigating any conflict with Esley's new settlers.

"All because the Shaa could never admit they'd made a mistake," said Lord Mehrang. "They misclassified the Yormaks as *people,* when in fact they're just clever animals."

Vijana didn't reply, as by this point they were walking through the herd of cattle, and he was eying them nervously. An adult bull or cow stood as high as Vijana at the shoulder, and its massive, shaggy head alone probably outweighed him. Vijana was treading cautiously past one of the animals, a vast gray-backed creature, and when the animal turned its head to view him with all its four eyes, Vijana nearly jumped out of his skin.

"They're harmless," Lord Mehrang said. "They might step on you by accident, but they won't deliberately do you harm." One cow loomed up in front of him, walking on enormous spade-shaped feet that were used to dig through winter snow to find grasses. "Just prod them out of the way," Mehrang said, and did exactly that. The cow moved without any sense of resentment.

The animals' smell was overpowering, and the scent seemed somehow to clot at the back of Lord Mehrang's throat: he hawked and spat.

They walked around the cow and came face-to-face with a Yormak. It was built like a short, stocky human, but with a leathery muzzle full of yellow teeth and four eyes distributed evenly around the circumference of its head. The Yormak was covered in long brown fur, and it wore a shaggy coat made from the pelt of one of the cattle. Over one shoulder was a leather strap from which dangled a furry leather bag. A handmade wooden tool was carried in one three-fingered hand.

The Yormak and the two Terrans gazed at one another for a few seconds, and then the Yormak, without changing expression, altered course to walk around Lord Mehrang. Mehrang took a step to block the Yormak's path. The Yormak altered course again, and again Lord Mehrang blocked it. The Yormak gave a kind of sneeze from slitted nostrils, then stood completely still. This time it waited for Mehrang and Vijana to move out of its way and then walked past them, again without acknowledging their existence. It paused, then used the tool to scoop up a patty of cattle dung and dump it in its furry sack.

"They burn dung for fuel," Mehrang said in disgust. "We give them *stoves,* but . . ." He waved a hand helplessly.

"Burning dung?" said Vijana. "That would account for the *smell.*"

Mehrang walked on in the direction of a drumlin, a glacial-formed ridge running parallel to the lake. "And that scoop it carried?" he said. "The design hasn't changed in millennia. All their tools, the clothes, the tents . . . it's all identical as far back as we can go through the archaeological record. Eighty thousand years, they've been making the exact same spear point, the same cattle goads, the same snowshoes, the same cradleboards for their young."

The smell had caught in his throat again, and again he spat. "They don't *evolve*. They're a dead end." He made a broad gesture that encompassed the entire world of Esley. "The Praxis is all *about* evolution. When we encounter a new world, we import new plants, new crops, new animals, and let them all compete with the native life-forms. The best life-form wins. Except we can't do it *here*." Disgust welled in him. "Even if we started absolutely level, with the same primitive technology, in a hundred years *any* of the other species under the Praxis would outcompete the Yormaks. They'd be *extinct*."

Vijana shivered in his greatcoat. "*I* might be extinct if I stay out here much longer."

Mehrang ignored the complaint and strode on through the camp, into the smoke of the dung fires and the stink of hides and unwashed bodies, past the Yormaks, who barely glanced at him. He came to a kind of cove carved into the flank of the drumlin and paused to watch a group of Yormaks sitting or kneeling there. Before them was a natural shelf on which sat some objects—stones, a bundle of twigs wrapped with grassy twine, the shoulder bone of some creature with glyphs carved into it. One of the Yormaks was holding another object—some sticks lashed together with rawhide into a kind of asterisk shape, with stones and bits of bone tied to it all with strands of sinew. The Yormak was speaking rapidly, apparently to the thing itself, with other Yormaks chiming in, as if in agreement, or offering further clarification.

It was the most animated, Mehrang thought, that he'd ever seen these creatures.

Vijana seemed bewildered. "What are they *doing*?" he asked.

"It's classified as 'undefined ritual behavior,'" Mehrang said. "But it sure looks like religion to me."

"Religion?" Vijana was appalled.

"They're calling on these *things*—these fetishes—for some kind of supernatural aid." Mehrang spat again. "This is a *shrine,* except you can't get the government to admit that. Officially, these aren't gods or fetishes, they're 'traditional ritual objects of uncertain utility.'" He laughed. "What kind of lawyer gibberish is that? They're bending over backwards not to see what's happening right in front of us."

Vijana was confused. "But if it's actually *religion*—" He shook his head. "Well, that can't be, right? Because if it *were*—"

"If you or I practiced religion openly," Lord Mehrang said, "we'd be arrested and very possibly executed." He flapped a hand at the Yormaks. "But these—*creatures*—are allowed to flout the Praxis in the most egregious way. Explain to me how that's even possible!"

Vijana spread his hands. "I'm in the Fleet," he said. "All manner of orders are given that I'm obliged to carry out, whether they make sense or not."

"You understand, then." Lord Mehrang nodded. "Someone decided ages ago that the Yormaks were going to be protected, and now they're protected no matter what madness they do." He stepped closer to Vijana, looming over the younger, smaller man. "The only way that would change," he said, "is if the Yormaks rebelled."

"Rebelled?" Vijana was dubious. "Why would they rebel? They seem to have everything exactly the way they want it."

Lord Mehrang took Vijana by the arm. "Let's not go into that right now," he said. "Let's just assume that the Yormaks rebel for whatever reason gets into their thick heads. What would you do if the lord governor asked for your assistance to end a revolt? How would you do it?"

Vijana considered this and spoke through lips blue with the cold. "Firing antimatter missiles from orbit would be far too destructive. Still, Yormaks would best be attacked from the air, I imagine. Arm aircraft with automatic weapons." His brows knit. "How many aircraft do you have on Esley?"

"The administration has been generous with licenses. There's such a lack of infrastructure on my poor planet that aircraft are necessary to knit the settlements together."

"And weapons?"

"We'd have to make most of them, but we have enough industrial capacity to turn out what we'd need in short order."

"Bombs? Incendiaries?"

Lord Mehrang smiled. "Entirely within our capacity."

Calculations flickered across Vijana's face. He seemed wholly absorbed in the problem. "How dependent are the Yormaks on their cattle?"

"Completely. For food, clothing, shelter, bone for tools, and dung for their fires."

"Yormaks might be able to hide, I suppose, but they can't hide whole cattle herds." He looked up in query. "Kill the cattle, and the Yormaks will starve?"

"They fish and hunt, but they won't survive on that alone, not in this climate."

"Well then. Just mow the cattle down, along with any Yormaks we find. Either way the rebels die."

Lord Mehrang gave a satisfied smile. "Let's say you take command of suppressing the rebellion. How far away is your nearest superior?"

"I'm an independent command, so I report directly to the Commandery on Zanshaa. If they detailed someone from the Home Fleet to supervise me, it would be at least three months before he arrived. But more likely they'd order a squadron out from the Fourth Fleet at Harzapid, and that's six to eight weeks out, depending on how soon they could leave and how many gravities their commander piles on to get here. Since it's a chance to command in the suppression of a revolt, they'd almost certainly be here sooner rather than later."

"It sounds as if someone would want to steal your credit for suppressing the rebels."

Vijana shrugged. "It's the Fleet, my lord. You'd be surprised how often the credit goes where it doesn't belong."

"Your possible supersession concerns me." Mehrang patted Vijana on the arm. "If anything as regrettable as a rebellion were to occur, I would have to make certain that you received proper credit for a successful action. A promotion, decorations . . ."

"Beg pardon, my lord. But these are not within your purview."

Mehrang straightened. "I am not without influence. I am patron to an entire world, and my own patron is Lord Convocate Mondi, on the Fleet Control Board. Which *is* in charge of decorations and promotions."

"Mondi is most influential," Vijana agreed.

"And of course Esley itself would express its appreciation. There would be cash rewards, and grants of land. *Choice* grants, too, taken from the Yormak reserves, and full of resources, or perhaps in strategic locations certain to be developed within your lifetime. You would be patron to a city, perhaps more than one."

Vijana smiled. "A gratifying picture, my lord. But of course there is no rebellion, and the lord governor has not summoned me to his aid."

"The lord governor is my cousin. We agree on many matters."

Vijana's thin little mustache twitched. "And the rebellion? The Yormaks have no reputation for violence."

Mehrang smiled. "Watch," he said. He turned and walked into the midst of the dialogue between the Yormaks and their totem, and then he snatched the talisman from the hand of the speaker and brandished it high above his head. The Yormaks yelped in surprise, or gave deep coughs of apparent disgust, then sprang to their feet and clustered around Mehrang, all of them shouting, or howling in warning. Some snatched stone knives from their belts or brandished other implements.

Alarmed by the threats and the noise, Vijana patted his greatcoat for a weapon he knew was not there.

Just as the howling peaked, just as it seemed the Yormaks were about to tear Lord Mehrang limb from limb, he returned the totem to the Yormak who had been holding it. The shouts and shrieks died away almost to nothing. After patting the creature and speaking soothing words, Lord Mehrang left the group and returned to Vijana. The Yormaks resumed their dialogue with the talisman as if nothing had happened.

"See?" Mehrang said. "Those fetishes are the only things they really seem to care about. It's not hard to get them stirred up."

Vijana nodded. "I'm impressed, my lord. Impressed by all the . . ." He hesitated. "The *planning* you've put into this."

Mehrang took Vijana's arm again and steered him out of the camp. "Shall we go to some warm place and have a drink?" he said. "We should give further thought to your future."

"I should like nothing better, my lord," said Vijana. They walked through the herd again, then up the slope toward Mehrang's aircraft. Vijana flapped his arms for warmth. He gave Mehrang a thoughtful look.

"It would be better if the rebellion happened in winter. You could track the Yormaks through the snow."

Mehrang nodded. "I'll bear that in mind."

"Have you ever considered fuel-air explosives? If we could get them built, they'd wipe out a whole herd of cattle at a single go, along with any Yormaks in company."

Lord Mehrang smiled even as the cutting wind blew sharp

ice crystals into his face. "You'll have to tell me all about them, Lieutenant-Captain," he said. "They sound most useful."

THE FIRST VIDEOS of the rebellion were jittery and incomplete and were supposed to have been shot by the employees of Forestry and Fisheries assigned to supervise and protect the Yormaks. They showed a howling mob of Yormaks brandishing weapons, and over the soundtrack you could hear the custodians shouting in alarm before the video abruptly cut off. Some of the videos ended with the thud of blows, or the screams of wounded.

Rescue parties found only the bodies of the custodians, beaten and stabbed with primitive weapons, and lying adjacent to the camps of the Yormaks, who by now were showing no interest whatever.

The scenes hadn't been difficult to arrange. There were plenty of people on Esley who hated the Yormaks and their guardians both, and Lord Mehrang had been careful to encourage and reward that hatred.

The videos provided enough evidence for the lord governor to declare the Yormaks in a state of rebellion, and to call for assistance from the Fleet. Police forces descended on the remaining guardians, rounded them up, and escorted them to the towns, where they would be safe.

Along the way, the police killed any Yormaks they encountered.

The governor also called for volunteers to form a militia,

and within days well-armed hunters were speeding out onto the winter tundra in their tracked snow machines, following the trails of the herds.

A few weeks later, the fuel-air explosives began to prove their worth.

Lord Mehrang amused himself with the thought of the last few Yormaks being rounded up to live in zoos. Though he very much doubted that, once confined, they would long survive.

CHAPTER 1

Lord Chen, wearing the wine-red coat of a convocate, walked among the purple lu-doi blossoms in his courtyard. The spring day was unseasonably hot and sultry, and he felt prickles of sweat beneath his collar.

Around him on all four sides loomed the tall Nayanid-style gables of the Chen Palace, the center of the power, money, privilege, and duty that had surrounded Maurice Chen from the hour of his birth. A tangible reminder of his status, his importance, and his position within the empire.

Gravel crunched beneath his mirror-polished shoes. The beige stone of the palace glowed in the bright sun. Birds called from overhead. The heavy, sweet scent of the flowers oppressed him.

He rehearsed his arguments in his head. Then he rehearsed them again.

Lord Chen approached a bronze statue of a maiden wearing an elaborate, formal gown of a fashion that had gone out of style a millennium ago. Near the statue was an old Lai-own servant with a tray, laying out the refreshments Chen had ordered: a pot of tea with two cups, alongside a dish of muffins, pastries, and sweets.

Suddenly Chen felt the need for something stronger.

"Bring me mig brandy," he said.

The Lai-own bowed, his feathery hair waving in the spring air. "Do you wish me to bring the bottle, my lord?"

Lord Chen fought impatience. Did the creature think he'd be swigging a whole bottle of brandy in his garden, in the middle of the afternoon?

"Bring it to me in a glass."

"Right away, my lord."

The servant brought him the drink on a salver, and Lord Chen tossed it off in a single gulp. A pleasing fire coursed its way down his gullet. He returned the glass to the salver and looked up to see his daughter, Terza, approaching from amid the blossoms.

Terza seemed to float over the path in an air of unhurried tranquility. On the sunny, sultry day she wore a lacy white summer dress that contrasted with the long black river of hair that fell past her shoulders. Her expression was serene without being insipid, her almond eyes acute without being intrusive.

Besides which, she was quite frankly beautiful. Because, Lord Chen thought, she was a *Chen*—the product of millennia of breeding, of education, of taste, now gliding toward him through the palace garden of her ancestors.

She looked at the glass he'd placed on the salver. "It is a hard day?" she asked.

Not yet, he thought. But he gestured with one hand in an

equivocal way. "Not worth discussing," he said. "You weren't at the Ministry today?"

Terza held a post in the Ministry of Right and Dominion, the civilian bureaucracy that served the Fleet. If she'd come from work, she'd have worn the brown tunic of a civil servant.

"I did some work from home," she said. She was not only a high-ranking official but a high-ranking Peer, and there was little pressure to spend time in the office.

The servant drew a chair back from the small table and offered it to Terza, and she thanked him and seated herself. Then the Lai-own helped Chen to his seat.

"I have tea," he said. "Unless you'd prefer something stronger."

"Tea would be lovely."

The servant poured. A rich, smoky odor filled the air, the scent of the first cutting from the family tea plantation in the To-bai-to Highlands. Terza opened a napkin, and the fine linen wafted over her lap.

"Thank you, Tarn-na," Chen said, and the servant ambled back into the house.

"How is Mother?" Terza asked.

"I've heard no complaints from Sandama," Chen said, "so I suppose she's doing well."

She cocked her head and looked at him. "Are you lonely?"

He was, actually, and had been for years, ever since his wife had left Zanshaa rather than live with the family tragedy. But he smiled and took her hand. "Not as long as you're here."

Terza smiled and squeezed his hand. "And you have grandchildren to keep you young."

The grandchildren, he thought. *Who are part of the problem.* But he smiled again.

"Yes. And I have the affairs of the clan to keep me busy," he said. "I had a meeting with the directors just this morning."

She withdrew her hand and took a cup of tea. "Good news?"

"Better than good," Chen said. "Our businesses are reaping record profits. Particularly shipping."

She nodded. "Yes. Of course."

"We are completely free of debt and obligation. We own the ships outright, and we own much of the cargo. We—"

He was interrupted by blaring music, trumpets of some sort, that floated over the Nayanid gables. He looked up and scowled.

"What's that?" Terza asked, as the fanfare was joined by what sounded like kettledrums.

"Cosgrove the financier," Chen said. "Our new neighbor. His children and their friends have some kind of . . . *brass band* . . . and they rehearse at every hour of the day."

Cymbals crashed. Birds rose alarmed into the sky.

"Oh, they are *unspeakable,*" Chen continued. "They throw enormous parties that disturb the entire neighborhood. The other night they all spilled out into the street and began a game of zephyrball, outside and in the middle of the night. We were lucky any of our windows survived."

The music came to a clattering, stuttering halt. Then started all over again, more discordant, but with even more enthusiasm.

"It might be different if they could actually *play,*" Chen said.

"Is this the Cosgrove from Hy-Oso?" Terza asked. "Shipping and finance?"

"And gold. He's got some kind of corner on those gold-bearing seaweeds they have there." He grimaced. "They're *new*. Like so many of the people I see in Zanshaa these days."

Terza took a bite of pastry, dabbed with her napkin at the corner of her mouth.

"The war made some people rich," she said delicately.

"All the wrong people, if you ask me."

She smiled. "You were just telling me how wealthy we are."

"We didn't profit from the *war*," Chen said. "We almost lost everything. But with the years of peace, we've finally worked our way out from under."

From under your in-laws, he thought.

From their earliest days in the Hone Reach, the Chen family had always been strong in shipping, but the outbreak of the Naxid War had been a disaster. A significant number of Chen ships had found themselves in parts of the empire controlled by the Naxid rebels and had been confiscated by the enemy. Loyalist ships had wiped out many of these in raids, and the Naxid rebels had used the survivors so hard that they all needed refitting. Others were cut off in remote areas where they could only sit in dock and await the end of the war.

Other Chen assets had been similarly compromised. Clan Chen had been facing ruin, until Lord Roland Martinez had approached him with a business arrangement. The Martinez clan would rent all his cargo ships, even the ones cut off or in enemy hands, for a period of five years. In return, Lord Roland expected Chen to steer military contracts his way, favors that Lord Chen—a member of the Fleet Control Board—was in a good position to grant.

Lord Chen had no problem shifting government business toward his financial savior. Trading favors was a long-established element of the system by which the Convocation, the Peers, and the empire itself functioned. Clan Martinez was ridiculously rich even by Chen standards, and they were useful allies. All had worked out well for Chen until Lord Roland turned up at the Chen Palace one morning with a demand—Roland Martinez wanted his daughter.

Not for himself, but for his younger brother, Gareth. Who was, admittedly, a clever man and a hero of the war, but who was still a Martinez. A provincial Peer from the distant world of Laredo, with a ghastly backwater accent that all the training in the world had not polished from his palate.

Laredo had not been settled—had not even been *discovered*—when the Chen Palace first rose in Zanshaa's High City. What right had this clan of arrivistes to demand a Chen—and not only a Chen, but the Chen *heir*?

In vain Lord Chen argued against the match. Terza barely knew Lord Gareth Martinez, he explained. She had only recently lost her fiancé in battle, her mourning period should be respected. The war had unsettled everything, perhaps they could discuss the young couple's future after the peace . . .

But Roland had beaten him down with the simplest of arguments: Clan Chen would take Gareth Martinez, or Clan Chen could go down to ruin.

And so Lord Chen had given—had *sold*—his daughter.

His wife had been so mortified by the match that she'd left Zanshaa permanently and now traveled aimlessly from one world to the next, visiting old friends and relations and spending months at a time at spas and exclusive resorts. Spending Chen's money, or, as if adding insult to injury, sometimes the money that Clan Martinez had loaned him.

Terza, still wearing in her hair the white mourning threads for her lost fiancé, Lord Richard Li, had taken the news of her fate with a calm resolution that bespoke her breeding, and she submitted herself to the tragic marriage that must have cut short all her hopes. Lord Chen had never so admired his daughter as at that moment.

Chen had submitted to Roland's demands, but he had no intention of remaining under Roland's thumb forever. Once Clan Chen was on its feet, it would have no need of Lord Roland, Gareth Martinez, or any other member of their parvenu breed.

It had taken longer than expected for Lord Chen to free himself from Roland's clutches. The agreement over the ships expired after five years, leaving Chen with a profit, but Chen still needed to replace what was lost during the war, and that required more borrowing. Only now, with strong profits in shipping and his other enterprises, had Lord Chen been able to pay off the last of the loans.

Lord Roland had been surprised that he'd wanted to pay them off at all. He hadn't been pressing for reimbursement. And when Lord Chen had made the last repayment, Lord Roland had made a point of telling him that if he ever ran short, he could call upon Martinez funds at any time.

I will no longer be your puppet, Lord Chen had thought. *And Terza will no longer be your prize.*

"Yes," Chen said. "We've repaired all the damage done by the war. The economy is booming. And . . . we are no longer under obligation to anybody."

Terza sipped her tea. "I'm very pleased," she said.

"To *anybody,*" Chen repeated. "And of course—" Again he sought her hand. "*You* are no longer obliged to anyone."

A slight frown crossed her perfect, serene brow. "Financially, you mean?"

"In any way."

"I have children. I imagine I'm obliged to *them.*"

"Yes. That's true." Lord Chen began to sense that his point was beginning to be lost in digression. He let go of Terza's hand, reached for his teacup, and tried to compose his thoughts. He decided to opt for confession.

"I've always been uneasy," he said, "over the way your marriage was arranged."

There was a flicker of intensity in Terza's dark eyes, a flicker there and then gone, to be replaced by her usual tranquil gaze.

"It was war," she said. "There was no time for the usual formalities."

"There is time *now.*"

A crooked smile quirked the corner of her mouth. "It's a little late for a betrothal party, don't you think?"

"No," said Lord Chen. "No, it's *not.*" He said the last word with, he thought, too much emphasis.

Composing himself, he said, "You should consider yourself free to choose the life you wish. You're still young, and we aren't obliged to anyone, not any longer."

Terza said nothing, only frowned into her teacup. Lord Chen decided to view this as encouragement, and he went on.

"Gareth Martinez is a worthy fellow," he said. "Brilliant in his sphere, I'll grant you that. But in *your* sphere—*our* sphere—his limitations must be obvious." He tugged at his collar and found it damp with sweat. "As Lady Chen, you'll have a brilliant future ahead of you. You'll be a member of the Convocation, you'll be among the highest in the land. I can see you chairing one of the important committees, or becoming governor of someplace important, like Seizho or even Zanshaa itself."

Lord Chen raised his palms. "How can Gareth help you in any of this? And what can he do that is meaningful while you are rising? He'd just be someone *attached* to you, with nothing to do. It would drive him mad, an active man like that."

A look of deep concentration settled onto Terza's face. She spoke slowly, as if each word had taken a great deal of thought.

"You wish me to preserve my husband's sanity . . . by *divorcing* him?"

Chen sighed. "There are many more suitable men in the High City—surely you realize that?"

"He's the father of my children. He's the father of my—of *our*—heir."

"You're *young,*" Chen insisted. "You can have more children with another man. A man with whom you could be an *equal.*"

And who will provide you with another heir, he thought. *An heir with more suitable ancestors.*

Trumpets and kettledrums sounded in the air. Lord Chen glanced in the direction of the Cosgrove Palace and snarled. Then he turned back to Terza.

"Our bloodlines are immaculate," he said. "We go back almost to the beginning of human history."

"You mean almost to the conquest of Earth."

Chen flapped an impatient hand. "There *was* no history before that, just barbarian tribes slaughtering each other." He leaned toward his daughter. "Once there was a reason for your marriage to Gareth Martinez. I wish only to say that the reason no longer exists, and you should be free to attach yourself to a man with ancestry as illustrious as your own, and a future as brilliant as yours can be."

Terza placed her cup in her saucer, and her saucer on the table. The look of concentration had faded, and her face now bore its usual serenity. A smile touched her lips.

"I'm perfectly happy in my marriage, Father."

"But surely you can see—"

"You say I should be free," she said. "I *am* free, and I choose freely. I choose Gareth."

Lord Chen felt his heart sink. "But, Terza," he said, "you can do so much better."

"I think I have done very well." She removed the napkin from her lap. "If you'll excuse me," she said, "I should go home. Gareth is highly favored in the Vandrith race, and it will be broadcast live tonight, and the children are very excited. I should make sure they have their tea, otherwise they'll be too keyed up to eat."

"But, Terza . . ." It was all Lord Chen could do to keep from wailing in despair. *That* accent! he thought. *I'll have to listen to that dreadful accent for the rest of my life.*

"Thank you for your concern," Terza said. "I know that you want the best for me, but I assure you that the best has already happened."

She bent to kiss his cheek and drifted away, a pale erect figure amid the lu-doi blossoms, the tranquility of her slow, measured walk immune to the provocations of the brass band next door.

Lord Chen leaned back in his chair and looked at his cooling tea in its porcelain cup. He looked at the walls of the Chen Palace around him, and he imagined their ancient halls sullied for centuries by Martinez accents, by Martinez brats. He turned and signaled for Tarn-na, who was waiting in silence on the other side of the glass doors that led to the pantry.

"Another brandy," he said. Loss and despair seemed to howl in his soul like a cold north wind around the eaves of his palace.

"This time," he added, "you may as well bring the bottle."

CHAPTER 2

The gas giant Vandrith, with its bands of cinnabar and ochre, loomed close on the overhead display, so vast it seemed just a little bit threatening. Some of its larger moons appeared as crescents, and the rest were brilliant dots, brighter than anything in the starry background.

The people below, dressed in finery and standing at the glossy, exquisitely appointed table, were slightly diminished by the grandeur over their heads.

"My lords and ladies," said Lord Orghoder, as he raised a glass. "I give you the Vandrith Challenge Cup."

Orghoder, thought Lord Gareth Martinez, had taken very good care with his diction and had avoided lisping around his fangs. Martinez preferred not to know what was in Orghoder's glass, though he knew it would be served at the temperature of fresh blood. Because Torminel—squat, powerful, and furred—were descended from solitary carnivores and still liked their meat raw.

Martinez tried not to shudder as he raised his glass and

drank. White wine of some sort. No doubt it was of the finest vintage, though it tasted to Martinez much like other white wine.

"My lords and ladies," Orghoder said. "Please be seated."

There was a general shuffle as everyone—racing yacht owners, pilots, race officials, relatives, friends—took their seats. Terrans, Torminel, Daimong, and Cree were each at separate tables, arranged in a rectangle beneath the ghostly holographic form of Vandrith. Lai-own, whose hollow bones couldn't withstand high gravities, didn't participate in yacht racing, and Naxids—those who had survived the rebellion—refrained out of discretion.

The dinner was being held on the transport *Seven Stars,* which was the property of the Seven Stars Yacht Club and carried its members' racing yachts to competitions. For the last fourteen days, *Seven Stars* had been flying toward Vandrith in the company of three other transports belonging to the three other yacht clubs competing in the Vandrith Challenge race. Of the four clubs, Seven Stars, the Ion Yacht Club, and the Apogee Club were venerable institutions going back millennia, and with a membership drawn from the most exclusive families in the High City. In fact, the Apogee was so exclusive that it accepted only descendants of previous members whose genetics were verified by the Peers' Gene Bank.

The fourth club, Corona, was a newcomer and had been entering races only for the past three years. Its membership was composed exclusively of those who would have been blackballed from the High City clubs if they had ever been so rash as to apply, and during the club's brief existence the outsiders had made a substantial impact. First, because they existed at all.

And second, because they kept *winning*.

There were two barriers to anyone wishing to enter the world of yacht racing. The first was money, and the second was birth. And the Corona Yacht Club didn't much care about either.

That was the way Gareth Martinez had intended it when he founded the club. He had plenty of money with his access to his family's enormous wealth, and he was as unimpressed by the lineage of the High City Peers as they were impressed with each other.

Prior to the Naxid War, piloting a small, agile Fleet pinnace had often served as an entry to the world of yacht racing, and high-ranking Peers had competed for the few piloting slots available. The Fleet had held regular regattas and gymkhanas and developed excellent racing pilots. But during the war, casualties among pinnace pilots had reached something like 80 percent, and Peers for the most part decided to let the honor pass to lesser mortals.

Which was neither here nor there—the desire to avoid dangerous duty was not the sole province of Peers—but it did mean that there was a large well of expertly trained, experienced pinnace pilots who were either commoners or lower-status Peers, and who could be recruited by Martinez for his racing team.

The soup course arrived—some sort of squash, with a

splash of white foam—accompanied by a different white wine that Martinez couldn't tell from the first white wine.

"This is absolutely splendid, don't you think?" said Lady Fitzpatrick. She sat on Martinez's left; she was a large, hearty, white-haired woman, and a steward of the Apogee Club. "There's just the right touch of nutmeg—and it's so easy to overdo the nutmeg, don't you think?"

Martinez murmured agreement.

"I wish we'd been able to get Boutros for the Apogee kitchens," she said. "But Orghoder snatched him up from under our very noses."

The clubs competed in cuisine as well as in racing, and their chefs were renowned. The trip from Zanshaa to Vandrith was one formal banquet after another, as each yacht club entertained the others in turn, and the presentation of a bad dish could be perilous to a club's prestige.

Martinez had known better than to trust his own taste in finding staff for Corona's kitchen, and so he'd relied on his sisters—the two who were still speaking to him—and his wife, Terza. The results had been more than satisfactory, if the praise of the other clubs' members was to be trusted.

Martinez ate enough of the soup to reveal the club's crest on the bottom of the bowl, and then the bowl was swept away, replaced with a small platter that featured three small ochoba beans ringed by a green sauce. Lady Fitzpatrick gave a sigh of pleasure at the sight.

They're only beans, Martinez wanted to say.

Lady Fitzpatrick had never, so far as Martinez knew, piloted a racing yacht. The High City clubs were full of those who gained entry because of celebrity, amusement value, talent in some other sphere, or because some ancestor had won a race eight hundred years ago.

Possibly one of the qualifications for membership was proper appreciation of beans. Martinez couldn't say.

Martinez ate his beans and waited for one of the waitrons to take his plate away.

"Gareth, dear," his sister Vipsania called from across the table, to his right. Vipsania shared with Martinez the family genetic inheritance: olive complexion, dark hair and eyes, and—he liked to think—a vast, subtle, and flexible intelligence. Vipsania, though, had managed to polish away her native Laredo accent, and Martinez hadn't, which made her considerably more acceptable in this company than he.

Vipsania wasn't a racing captain but had been accepted into the club because Martinez was too frightened of her to keep her out.

"Yes?" Martinez said.

"I was talking to Lieutenant Lam here." Lam was a fresh-faced young man whose jacket bore the badge of the Ion Club. "He's on Fleet Commander Pezzini's staff, and he says that the official Fleet history of the war is about to be released."

Martinez raised an eyebrow. "Am I in it?"

Lam looked a little uneasy. Martinez's part in the war was the subject of controversy, and he suspected that both Fleet Commander Pezzini and Supreme Commander Tork would write him out of the history if they possibly could.

The lieutenant made an effort to be tactful. "Your exploits

on the *Corona* are mentioned, my lord, as is your part in the battle at Hone-bar."

"Second Magaria? Naxas?"

"Well..." Lam flushed. "You served under other officers at those battles, my lord."

Martinez smiled thinly. "So I did."

"Since the war is now under review," Vipsania said, "perhaps it's time to release our own documentary on the Empire stations."

"Ah." Martinez considered this. "Perhaps you're right."

One of Vipsania's achievements was her marriage to Lord Oda Yoshitoshi, the nephew and presumed heir of Lord Yoshitoshi. Clan Yoshitoshi owned a majority of Empire Broadcasting, seven channels viewed by the populations of eighty-odd planetary systems, and the family was content to let Vipsania run it. They thought being a media titan was an eccentric hobby for her, but they were willing to indulge her. That she'd increased profits every year since she'd taken over helped her case.

It was no surprise, then, that Empire's two sports channels were being very thorough in their coverage of yacht racing, and they emphasized the challenge that the upstart Coronas were mounting to the established clubs. In fact, Empire reporters and cameramen were a constant presence on this trip, interviewing, analyzing, and reporting every possible variation and every possible outcome.

Nothing like blatant favoritism, Martinez thought, to boost one's public profile.

Or to contradict a biased official history.

But, he thought, Vipsania was mentioning this possible documentary in public, in front of a member of Pezzini's staff. Which meant she *wanted* Pezzini to know that Martinez's sister was prepared to release her very own version of the war, particularly if the official history slighted a member of her family in any way.

After all, if you were an average citizen of the empire, would you rather read a dry official history, or watch a video documentary filled with action, heroes, villains, and a guaranteed happy ending, where peace and order were restored? With an emphasis, perhaps, on the handsome, brilliant, lantern-jawed young officer who had turned the tide?

And what could Tork, Pezzini, and the Fleet Control Board do about it? They ran the Fleet, not the Office of the Censor, and Vipsania was intelligent enough not to run afoul of the latter.

He supposed that the Fleet could forbid any of its officers from cooperating with the project, but that would merely give Vipsania more freedom to speculate—or simply to invent the stories she liked.

Indeed, Lieutenant Lam's face was already showing a degree of alarm at the knowledge of Vipsania's project. Martinez would be very interested to view the contents of Lam's next transmission to his superior, but it wasn't too hard to guess.

Martinez raised his glass to Vipsania. "I'll be happy to cooperate, of course."

She raised her glass in reply. Lieutenant Lam smiled weakly.

Martinez looked down and saw that his beans had been replaced by the paw of a sweet trynti, a fruit-eating nocturnal marsupial, adorable but edible, native to Zanshaa's southern hemisphere. Trying not to think of the big-eyed plush trynti doll that slept with his daughter every night, he employed his knife and fork to remove the claws and ate the paw whole. Whatever fruit had sustained the trynti during its brief lifetime had given the flesh a distinct sweetish flavor, familiar but somehow elusive.

"Figs," Lady Fitzpatrick said, sighing with rapture. "The trynti's been fed exclusively on *figs*."

"Quite," said Martinez.

"My lord captain." Martinez looked at the speaker, on his far left, whom he recognized as Lord Jeremy Foote. Foote was a tall, imposing blond specimen, with a distinctive cowlick on the right side of his head, and had been an annoying presence in Martinez's life for years. The most annoying thing about him was that he was a very good racing pilot, the best the Apogee Club had.

"I wonder, Captain Martinez," Foote went on, in his insufferable aristocratic drawl. "I wonder if the sight of Vandrith is a cause of nostalgia for you?"

Martinez didn't understand the question and had the sense that Foote was luring him into some kind of trap.

"No," he said. "Why would it be?"

"Because it was the occasion of your first step upon the public stage." Foote turned to Lady Fitzpatrick. "Lord Captain Martinez commanded the attempted rescue of Ehrler Blitsharts, you know."

"Ah yes." Lady Fitzpatrick nodded. "A terrible tragedy. I knew Lord Ehrler well." She shook her head. "His poor dog."

Ehrler Blitsharts had been one of the most celebrated pilots of his day, always accompanied in races by his loyal dog, Orange, who was at least as popular as he was. During the Vandrith Challenge seven years ago, his yacht had inexplicably accelerated into the void on a day when Martinez happened to be on duty.

"I supervised the rescue from the Commandery," Martinez clarified. "I was on Fleet Commander Enderby's staff at the time."

"Yes," Foote said. "It was of course Lady Sula who performed the actual rescue. Blitsharts and the dog were dead, naturally, but that was hardly Lady Sula's fault."

Martinez tried to keep his face impassive. He hardly wanted to think of Caroline Sula at this moment, in this company.

"I knew her parents," said Lady Fitzpatrick. "Quite lovely people, the handsomest couple imaginable. I was so surprised when they were arrested and executed in that dreadful way."

"I served with Lady Sula briefly during the war," Foote said. "A very sharp intelligence, and of course the most beautiful young woman I'd ever seen. Such a presence!" He smiled at the memory. "But rather a prickly personality—I wished to know her better, but she kept me at arm's length."

"Shows her good taste," Martinez said, and plastered a completely false smile on his face as an indication to bystanders that he didn't mean it.

Foote nodded in easy agreement. "Captain Martinez had

better luck, I believe." He turned to Lady Fitzpatrick and took a deliberate taste of wine. "During the war I had the duty of censoring the correspondence that Lady Sula had with Lord Captain Martinez—and such a passionate correspondence it was! Such fervor! A true meeting of minds."

Lady Fitzpatrick gave Martinez a sidelong glance. "Indeed," she murmured.

"But then of course the Chen heir lost her fiancé at First Magaria, and Captain Martinez maneuvered to secure the prize like the bold captain he is," Foote said. He turned to Martinez. "Do you hear much from Lady Sula these days?"

The moment awkward, Martinez thought quickly. Foote had made him look like a complete unprincipled mercenary, deserting Sula for a richer, better connected heiress. As if Sula hadn't walked out on him. As if she hadn't—well, he couldn't discuss that here, not without seeming a complete cad.

"You forget that Lady Sula and I served together," Martinez said. "At Second Magaria, and Naxas."

"But separate squadrons, though, eh?"

Not really, he wanted to say. Because though she commanded a light squadron and he served as tactical officer aboard another vessel, they had fought brilliantly together, their ships moving as if they were parts of a single organism. As if they were in telepathic contact. As if they were in some kind of mystical union.

Martinez feigned confusion. "I'm not quite sure what you mean," he said. "We're both captains—we can hardly serve on the same ship. Our appointments were 'as the service requires,' as we say."

"Quite," said Foote. He leaned back, content to have blackguarded Martinez in front of this select company. "And speaking of captains," he added, "I've just been promoted to that august rank myself."

Martinez murmured congratulations. Foote was among the exclusive breed of aristocratic officers whose career path had been determined long before they entered the academy, each promotion and posting arranged by relatives, friends, and clients in the service. The family had planned for him to ascend to fleet commander as soon as decency and Fleet regulations permitted.

But war had interrupted what should have been Foote's smooth rise. The uncle who had taken Foote on as a sublieutenant had been killed at First Magaria, and various other patrons were killed, captured, or shifted away from posts where they could help him.

"I'm getting a command as well," Foote said. "They're giving me *Vigilance,* rebuilding at Comador, and attached to Light Squadron Eight."

Vigilance was a light cruiser, Martinez knew. Foote, as a junior captain, would outrank the lieutenant-captains on the frigates that made up the rest of the squadron. Which meant that Foote would be a squadron commander, for all that he didn't yet have the rank.

Apparently Foote's inevitable rise to high command was back on track. Jealousy clawed at Martinez with adamantine talons.

"Congratulations, my lord," he managed.

"Thank you, Lord Captain!" Foote said cheerfully.

And then somebody down the table, one of Foote's many toadies undoubtedly, began to sing the "Congratulations" round from "Lord Fizz Takes a Holiday," and everyone had to join in. Foote just sat back and beamed, accepting the commendation as if it was entirely his due—which, according to law and custom, it certainly was.

Soak it up, Foote. Because winning the Challenge Cup won't be so easy for you, Martinez thought. *Tomorrow, I'm going to fry the nose off your boat.*

As the song died away Martinez felt a soft touch on his shoulder, and he turned to discover a tall Daimong looming over him, and behind him Lord Orghoder.

"Lord Captain," said Orghoder. "May we speak to you privately for a moment?"

"I'm at your service."

The conversation took place in a small salon off the banquet room, paneled and carpeted and made comfortable by aesa-leather furniture. There was a heavy smell of tobacco in the room, and cigar cutters, matches, and a hookah waited on a table, above which were placed the blazoned private humidors of the club's members. The Daimong commandeered the wall display and brought up an image of a yacht blasting past a satellite, the latter a blazing beacon in the reflected light of the yacht's streaming plasma tail.

Martinez had been trying to remember the Daimong's name. Like all Daimong she was tall and cadaverous, hairless and with a fixed, round-eyed expression that a human might read equally as horror, surprise, or fury. *Ichtha,* Martinez thought. *Lady Ichtha* . . . Something. He knew she was one of the stewards of the Ion Club.

"I regret to say that the Apogee Club has filed a protest about the Crucible race," Lady Ichtha said. Like all Daimong, her voice was sonorous, like chiming bells.

"The Crucible race was two months ago," Martinez pointed out.

"Unfortunately, the Apogee is within their rights," Orghoder said. "The protest involves your Captain Kelly, and the Apogee maintains they have only now discovered the violation."

"The Apogee Club has nothing better to do than to obsessively examine recordings of past races?"

"I'm sure you have been viewing past races yourself, Lord Captain," said Orghoder. "We all study our opponents' tactics, do we not?"

Which was true, so Martinez turned to the display. "What does Apogee claim to have discovered?"

Lady Ichtha's sonorous voice made the other club's accusation sound like a song. "They say that Captain Kelly failed to properly tag Satellite 11."

During the race, all the competitors had to speed past a number of satellites, and they were required to pass within a certain distance of them.

"That makes no sense at all," Martinez said. "The satellite itself registered Kelly's pass."

"Apogee maintains that the satellite was in error," chimed Lady Ichtha. "They have analyzed the parallax of the background stars in this video, and they claim that their computations show that Captain Kelly passed outside the allowable limit. We have reviewed their calculations and have found no"—she offered a diffident chime—"no error."

"I protest this underhanded attempt to disqualify one of Corona's captains," Martinez said. "Has this method ever been used in the past?"

"It seems to be an innovation," Orghoder admitted. "But the stewards and I will meet later this evening to review the data. Your protest is noted and will receive equal consideration with that of the Apogee Club."

"Thank you," Martinez said, as his heart began drifting toward his boots. He knew perfectly well what was going on—the upstart Coronas were being sabotaged by the established clubs. They were disqualifying Corona's most successful captain at the last minute in hopes of causing chaos in the club's organization and putting a less experienced captain in Kelly's place.

If you can't win, cheat. He really shouldn't have expected anything else.

"In any case," Orghoder continued, "I thought it only fair to give you warning, so that you could inform Captain Kelly that she may be scratched tomorrow. And you should also inform your next in line, ah—"

"Captain Severin," Martinez said.

"Severin? Oh dear." Orghoder shook his furry head. "Well, I understand he is very promising."

Martinez eyed Orghoder narrowly. "He is. I would also like a copy of Apogee's protest. I have friends who are astronomers and mathematicians, and I would like them to review this data."

Orghoder hesitated. "Ah," he said. "It would be a shame if this controversy were paraded before people outside our circle."

I'm already *outside your circle,* Martinez thought. "If this protest succeeds," he said, "you'll have to release the data in any case. There are a dozen or more representatives from sports networks and the sporting press on this ship, and they'll all want to know why one of the most successful captains was disqualified on the eve of the race."

"Ah. Yes." Orghoder licked his fangs. "Yes, I suppose that's true." He gestured at Lady Ichtha, who sent a copy of the data to Martinez's hand comm.

"Thank you," Martinez said. And then he returned to the banquet room to make his grim preparations for the next day's race.

He had no doubt that Apogee's protest would be upheld.

His only consolation was that he planned to beat them anyway.

"MY LORDS AND ladies," said Lord Orghoder. "I present today's challenge course!"

Holographic displays flashed into existence above each of twelve tall, round tables, and a much larger hologram appeared overhead. Martinez looked at the course, then gestured at the image to tilt it at a better angle.

"Interesting," said Kelly, as she leaned forward with her

elbows on the table. She was a long-limbed, black-eyed young woman with a bright, blazing smile. Technically she was Lieutenant Lady Benedicta Kelly, but she disliked her forename and never used it. During the war, she had served as a cadet and pinnace pilot under Martinez. They had even been lovers, for at least an hour, during the breathless escape after Martinez had stolen the frigate *Corona* during the mutiny at Magaria. The proprieties had been restored shortly thereafter, but Martinez had retained an affection for Kelly that he hoped came across as completely disinterested. Still, when he'd heard that Kelly's career had stalled due to her single patron having been killed in the war, he'd been pleased to recruit her as one of the Coronas.

She had more than fulfilled his trust, becoming over three seasons the best pilot in the club, and the captain most likely to win this year's Captains' Championship, as the pilot with the highest score.

Until, of course, the unfair disqualification, which had been duly reported that morning—the timing perfectly coordinated so Martinez couldn't make an appeal before the race. Kelly had taken the news philosophically, and Martinez promptly snared her for his support team. For which he felt a pang of guilt, since Severin surely needed the help more than he did.

He cast a glance in Severin's direction and saw the young officer frowning at his display, while the three members of his support team spoke animatedly around him. Shushanik Severin had done well in the races in which he'd been entered, but as he was also a captain in the Exploration Service, he'd been on active duty for part of the season and missed several races.

Well. Martinez would have to do the job himself, along with Lady Kosch Altasz, Corona's third pilot in the race. Altasz was a Torminel from a provincial family whose Fleet career had stalled due to lack of influence. She was a ferocious competitor, though, and stood just behind Kelly in Corona's rankings. Martinez could count on her to help punish the Apogees for their outrageous protest.

He turned his attention back to his own display. The rules allowed him to study the course for exactly one hour, and to plot his track along with the help of three members of his support team. This year's Challenge Cup race would consist of three complete orbits of Vandrith, with the racers required to pass within range of a host of satellites placed around the gas giant. Each satellite had to be passed at least once. But the path from satellite to satellite was strewn with Vandrith's twelve moons, which could either be obstacles or provide a gravity assist for acceleration or deceleration. And in order to make the whole business even more challenging, the satellites were programmed to maneuver randomly.

All of which was meant to keep the pilots alert and improvising.

Of course the colossal accelerations and decelerations did the opposite, exhausting the pilots and dulling their minds and reactions. Even the most skilled yachtsman could suffer a blackout or miscalculate a course, and this unpredictability—and inherent danger for the pilot—was why yacht racing had a vast audience throughout the imperium, even among people who had never left the planet of their birth.

He saw that the race would start and end at Vandrith's twelfth moon, romantically named V12. So long as he tagged every satellite, his precise course was up to him. Mentally he threaded a path through the tangle of satellites—he dared not point, for fear someone on another team would be able to work out his plans.

"Oh look," said Kelly. Her black eyes were shining. "V3."

Martinez's eyes traced a path to the moon.

"Ah," he said. "I see."

"ELEVEN-SECOND WARNING!"

The call came just as Martinez's racing boat *Laredo* flew out of the shadow of the moon and into the light of Shaamah. Ahead the sun winked off the skins of other racing yachts, all in an arc stretching around the moon.

The moon's bright terminator scrolled beneath Martinez, black on one side, wispy green on the other. Displays flared around him. Calculations sped through his mind.

The twelve racing yachts, three from each club, were in orbit around Vandrith's twelfth moon. They had been waiting for the eleven-second warning, which was triggered randomly in the Timekeeper's boat by the unpredictable decay of a minute amount of radium-226 into radon-222. The yachts, which had been spaced evenly in their orbits, were now free to maneuver; but none could actually break orbit until the eleven seconds had expired and the race was officially on its way.

Impatience urged Martinez to add delta-vee, but he knew that he couldn't just yet—it would risk breaking orbit too early and being forced to return to swing around V12 again.

In the rearward display he saw engine flares. Boats coming up from behind him.

Precious seconds ticked by while his own eagerness warred in his mind with calculation. Then, finally, he felt free to shove the throttle forward with his left hand, and he felt the kick of acceleration as antimatter flared into gamma rays and pi-mesons. The pale green atmosphere of V12 scrolled rapidly under him. He saw engine flares ahead.

A computer could have made the calculation for him, but those sorts of computers were forbidden in this kind of race. He and the other pilots would have to plot their courses on the jump, based on whatever plans they had made during the hour-long view of the course.

A tone sounded in his headphones. "The race is on! No false starts! No foul!" Kelly's voice was loud in his earphones.

Martinez didn't answer: his attention was focused on his next target and the acceleration that was dragging against his mind. His suit clamped down on his extremities to keep blood from draining from his brain, and his breath was laboring against the increasing weight that piled on his chest.

Laredo's course was taking him across the orbits of four of Vandrith's moons, to V6, a small moon with a meteor-scarred face and no atmosphere to speak of.

"You're in sixth place," Kelly informed him. He already knew that. Right in the middle of the pack.

Gravities piled on Martinez like smothering blankets of heavy wool, and his heart boomed in his chest as it fought against increasing acceleration. His breath came in deep grunts forced up from his belly. Three-quarters of the way to V6 he cut the engines and pitched the *Laredo* over—he panted with relief in the brief moment of weightlessness—then began a deceleration that would send him past the moon and on a steep curve toward his next objective, a satellite placed ahead of V6 in its orbit.

The deep craters of V6 flashed on his displays like yawning mouths reaching to swallow him, his periapsis so close that he was straining one of the very few safety features of the race—computer control of the yacht was forbidden unless the plotted course would result in actual collision with a planet, in which case the computer would take over and swing the yacht wide.

This time the computer did not intervene. Martinez used a reverse gravity assist to aid the braking, his torch burning the entire time, and skipped away from V6 and on toward the satellite, which was already maneuvering. His vision narrowed, turning dark around the edges. He adjusted his course and fought for consciousness.

"You're overtaking Elmay," Kelly reported. "Don't let him burn you."

Martinez overtook without colliding or bathing *Laredo* in Elmay's antimatter tail, and that put him in fifth. The satellite scudded past, but by that point Martinez was already burning for V7, his next target.

"You are in fifth place," Kelly said. "Lamanai is first. Altasz is in second."

And Foote is third, Martinez thought. He had some catching up to do.

AND SO IT went for nearly two orbits, gravities piling hard on Martinez's body and mind as he fought for every objective. In a moment of inattention, Lamanai of the Apogee Club failed to anticipate the maneuvering of a satellite and missed her mark by a hand's breadth; and though she was still technically ahead of the others, she'd have to detour to tag the satellite again on the final orbit, and that would take her out of the running.

Martinez used a gravity assist from the rocky moon V9 to add a burst of speed and jump one spot ahead. He was on Foote's tail.

Lady Kosch Altasz, Martinez's teammate, would inherit first place once Lamanai made her detour on the next orbit. Two other racing boats missed their targets and were out of the running. That left nine in the race.

"Where's Severin?" Martinez asked.

"I'm . . . not sure," Kelly said. "He's in last place . . . I *think*. His track is wandering all over the place, I can't work it out. His crew can't figure out what he's doing either."

Martinez didn't have the luxury of contemplating Severin's course: he was engaged in a massive deceleration in order to swing around V5. His vision narrowed, and he had the sense that ocean breakers were crashing inside his skull, one thunderous boom after another . . .

The tawny bands of V5 swept past, and there was a moment of blessed weightlessness as he pitched the ship to its new heading. His moment, he thought, had just come.

His left fist slammed the throttle forward, and he dived toward V3. Now he was on the far side of Vandrith from Kelly and his transport ship *Corona,* and out of direct contact—communication would be routed through a satellite on this side of the gas giant, but it would add a three-second delay each way, and any news Kelly sent him would be out of date by the time it arrived.

The red-and-ochre mass of Vandrith completely filled his vision. Another engine flare burned close, and Martinez saw that it was Foote, aiming for V3 on a slightly different heading. That blond ninny had worked out the same trick Martinez planned to employ—or more probably he'd paid one of his crew to work these things out for him.

Martinez would just have to do the maneuver more precisely than Foote. After which the lead would be his.

Accordingly he maintained his burn for V3 even after he prudently should have rotated his ship and started a deceleration—clenching his teeth, fighting for every breath, his vision narrowed to a mere dot. He waited until he saw Foote cut his own engines, and then he held on for a couple more seconds before he cut power and spun the ship over. Unable to properly read the displays, he performed the maneuver by feel alone and then rammed the throttle forward again.

His vision slowly returned, and he saw Foote's boat hovering in the display, its engines aimed at him like the barrels of a gun, and then Foote's antimatter fire lit again, and gamma rays promptly fried every sensor on the forward part of *Laredo*.

Screens went black.

Martinez himself was safe: *Laredo*'s crew compartment was surrounded by thick slabs of antiradiation armor. And he could replace the sensors on the fly: yacht designers anticipated these problems. But he wouldn't replace them for the moment, as any new sensors would be cooked as soon as they were deployed.

Fortunately Martinez didn't need to look forward: he was flying stern-first, aiming for V3, the blue dot visible against the striped surface of Vandrith. He stared at V3 as his vision faded again, and his right hand on the joystick made minute adjustments to his course. This took him out of Foote's gamma ray plume just as he jammed the throttle all the way forward and his vision faded completely beneath an avalanche of gees.

There was a crash and Martinez's helmet snapped back against his headrest. It felt as if someone had just dropped a ton of boulders onto his solar plexus. He tasted blood. His stern sensors showed nothing but a brilliant flash of ions.

Laredo had just encountered the methane-rich blue atmosphere of V3. It wasn't at a steep enough angle to dive through the methane to an impact with the planet—instead *Laredo* would skip off the topmost layer of the atmosphere. But contact with the atmosphere would brake the yacht, and also, since Martinez's direction was opposite to that of the moon's rotation, he would be slowed by a negative gravity assist.

Leaving a brilliant trail of ionized radiation across the blue surface of V3, Martinez bounced off the moon like a rubber ball, his momentum considerably reduced. That enabled him to safely cut the corner in the race for a satellite placed in the orbit of V7, a target that Altasz and the others were heading for directly, their boats standing on tails of flame as they decelerated the hard way.

In that moment of inspiration while looking at the course, Kelly had found a way for him to leap to the head of the queue.

Foote and his *Cockerel,* trailing ions, followed *Laredo* three seconds behind. Martinez cut his engines, replaced his burned sensors, and oriented his boat to nip close to the target satellite and then head on to the next via a slingshot at V8. Then, head swimming, he took a breath and shoved the throttle forward again.

"You're in the LEAD you're you're LEAD LEAD the LEAD!" *Laredo* had just flown into direct communication with *Corona* again, and Kelly's jubilant cry was echoed by the very same transmission chasing Martinez around the back of Vandrith.

Martinez flashed by the satellite a good fifteen seconds ahead of Altasz, but by then he was accelerating again, burning for V8. Foote was still a scant few seconds behind, and Martinez was pleased in the knowledge that this time it was *his* gamma ray tail that was cooking his rival's sensors.

They were very near the end of the race. From here it was a straightforward burn to V8, then on to a satellite, then back to V12 and the finish line. Hardly challenging at all, except in terms of how much punishment the pilots could stand. It was no longer a test of maneuver and intelligence, but of stamina, conditioning, and physiology.

And Foote showed every sign of rising to the challenge. His engines burned at maximum thrust, and the gravities were piling on. Martinez matched Foote's acceleration exactly, knowing that all he had to do was keep his lead, and that Foote's loss of his forward sensors wasn't going to help him much.

V8, with its ruddy atmosphere and drifts of carbon dioxide snow, loomed closer. Martinez's thoughts crawled beneath the gravities weighing them down. He locked his track exactly where he wanted it and watched as blackness invaded his vision.

The encounter with V8 lasted only a few seconds and was in the direction of the moon's rotation. The slingshot added a burst of acceleration, and Martinez slammed back in his seat and felt darkness smother his mind.

When he woke, he was in a weightless cabin. The throttle had slipped from his unconscious grip and snapped back to the neutral position, shutting off the engine. This new spring-loaded throttle was a reform that had come about as a result of the Blitsharts disaster, when Captain Blitsharts's dead hand on the throttle kept his boat accelerating into the void for hours.

Martinez slammed the throttle forward again and was promptly punched into his seat. He had to take a few moments to orient himself with regard to his displays, and just as he found the target satellite and corrected his course, Foote's *Cockerel* slipped past him.

"You're in second!" Kelly called. "Damn damn damn!"

Not for long, Martinez thought, and clenched his teeth against gravity. There was no way he would allow one of the Apogees to snatch first place from him, not after their disgusting protest.

He passed out once more on the way to the satellite, but apparently so did Foote, and the relative position remained unchanged. Martinez came so close to the satellite that he almost obliterated it, and now he had V12 in his sights. Foote had taken a slightly different line and was now off Martinez's bow, antimatter tail brilliant in the night.

This time Foote passed out first, and Martinez passed him in the seconds it took him to recover, only to lose the seconds all over again when it was Martinez's turn to lose consciousness. And then, as he regained his vision and clenched his teeth in anticipation for the final acceleration, he saw something flash across his displays far ahead of him, something that looked like a star that had broken free and shot like a skyrocket for V12.

"What was *that*?" he managed, every word a battle against gravity.

Kelly was stunned. "That was—that was *Severin*. He just won! He's in first!"

"How?" Martinez demanded.

"I don't know! I don't see how it's possible! The stewards are conferring, but the computer says he won!"

Martinez came in third, with Foote ahead of him literally by a nose.

"What the hell just happened?" Martinez demanded.

SHUSHANIK SEVERIN HAD spent the first three-quarters of the race tagging satellites on a path uniquely his own, and to all appearances in a very inefficient way. The scoring computer had counted him in last place.

The point of all his wanderings was to end far from Vandrith at V11, from which he turned and then dove at full acceleration for the surface of the gas giant, tagging two of his last three satellites but accelerating almost the entire way. When he hit Vandrith's atmosphere, he kept his engines lit, and his boat entered at such an angle as to form an aerodynamic projectile, which meant that—instead of braking—he actually *gained* speed. But more importantly, as he was traveling in the same direction as Vandrith's rotation, he benefited from a gravity assist, and—as the gas giant exerted enormous gravitational force compared to its moons—the gravity assist was *colossal.* Severin was fired out of Vandrith's atmosphere at an enormous velocity, as if from the empire's most prodigious cannon.

Naturally Severin was rendered unconscious by the acceleration, but he recovered in time to tag the very last satellite on his way to the finish line at V12. He was traveling at such a velocity that it took him four and a half hours to decelerate and return to *Corona,* by which time the party had already started.

By this time *Corona* and the other transports were already on their return journey to Zanshaa, traveling at a steady one gravity so that plates would stay on tables and drinks in cups. Pilots, friends, and support crew roistered back and forth between the dinner tables. Vipsania's camera crews dragged various people off for interviews.

Severin turned up looking a bit dazed. As he had all along, he wore his blue Exploration Service uniform, Martinez suspected because he really couldn't afford the grand wardrobe displayed by most of the yacht captains present.

To be sure, Martinez hadn't enjoyed being upstaged by Severin at the climax of the race, but after a few drinks he'd grown philosophical. The Corona Club's pilots had taken three of the four top places at the finish, and even though Martinez hadn't personally won the Vandrith Challenge Cup, the object itself would still look very good in the club trophy case for the next six years—for the Vandrith Challenge wasn't held annually, but only when Vandrith's orbit took it close enough to Zanshaa to make the trip conveniently short.

And if Martinez couldn't win himself, he would just as soon the winner be someone he liked.

When Martinez saw Severin enter *Corona*'s banqueting hall, he rushed to hand him a glass and to shake his hand. Vipsania's cameras caught everything. Severin's face—high cheekbones, narrow eyes, straight black hair—shook off its befuddled look as the assembled company began the "Congratulations" round from "Lord Fizz," and a grin slowly worked its way onto his features.

There followed the formal presentation of the cup by Lord Orghoder. It was a hideous thing, half a man's height, solid gold, and with reliefs of allegorical figures like the Spirit of Competition, the Wings of Speed, and the Glory of Friendship. Severin offered polite thanks to Lord Orghoder and to his boat's support staff and was then rushed off to be interviewed by one of Vipsania's broadcasters.

Martinez sent one of the waitrons to take him some food. The poor man deserved to eat.

Martinez found Lady Fitzpatrick standing next to him. "Is it true," she said, "that our new champion is a commoner?"

"He is," Martinez said. "But at least he didn't file a sneaky little last-second protest."

Lady Fitzpatrick, the steward of the Apogee Club, gave him an accusing look. "It's bad enough that you permit a commoner to compete. But to *win*?"

Martinez fought off an unjustified urge to apologize. "Who am I to refuse the man who shut off a pulsar?"

Lady Fitzpatrick's eyes narrowed. She looked at the door beyond which Severin had vanished. "He is *that* gentleman?" she said.

"He is."

She looked at him. "Clearly an original mind," she snarled.

Exit, muttering, Martinez thought as she wandered off. Martinez took himself to the punch bowl for a refill, where he encountered Foote, whose fair flushed face suggested he had taken a fair-sized load of alcohol on board.

"I crossed ahead of you by one eight-hundredth of a second," Foote said. "Aren't you going to congratulate me?"

"I'd be happy to," said Martinez, "so long as I don't have to sing that damned song again."

Foote seemed a trifle morose. "Your explorer friend has eclipsed us."

"You'll have to settle," Martinez said, "for the glory of commanding Light Squadron Eight."

The thought cheered Foote. "And what will *you* do by way of compensation?" he asked.

Martinez refilled his punch cup. "This," he said, "for starters."

He wandered back into the throng and found Severin heading for the buffet, having finally escaped Vipsania's interviewers. "Thanks for sending dinner after me," he said.

"How do you feel?" Martinez asked.

Severin's hands probed his torso. "My ribs aren't happy," he said. "I'm trying to walk without bending over. And I'm seeing flashes in both eyes."

"See the race doctor."

Severin nodded. "After the puppet show."

Martinez stared at him. "The puppet show," he repeated.

"I was scheduled to perform tonight," Severin said. "I'm just not sure where I fit on the revised schedule."

Martinez looked at Severin in amazement. Severin—a commoner, promoted for his war service into a milieu to which he could not normally aspire—had found a unique way to enter a society for which he had not been prepared by either birth or training. He had devised a sort of career for himself as an entertainer, a creator of puppet shows for a sophisticated, adult audience. He had become the pet of a number of high-status Peers, mostly women, and performed his entertainments in their parlors, for a choice audience.

What other entertainments might follow, in certain bedrooms, were only rumored.

Whatever they were, his talent as a performer had gained

him access to high-ranking society, and in a situation in which all parties could be comfortable. His status as an entertainer had not been the least of Severin's achievements.

"Tonight," Martinez said, "you're the cynosure of all eyes. Your job is just to be at this party and enjoy yourself, and to accept the worship of your genius."

"Oh? That would be all right, then?" Severin seemed genuinely curious.

"Yes," Martinez said firmly. "You are completely forgiven."

A FEW HOURS later, Martinez and Vipsania stood on one of the balconies above the dining room and watched their celebration roll on. The weak and faint of heart had long since fled, and the heavy drinkers had settled in for the long haul. A group was clustered in a corner watching a sports feed from Zanshaa, and another group was rewatching the race, stopping the replay every so often for analysis. Music rose from the grand stairway that led down to the ballroom, where a few aerobically fit diehards were still dancing.

No puppet show was in evidence.

Water cascaded from a nearby waterfall—*Corona* was celebrated for its elaborately engineered water features. The transports belonging to the other yacht clubs were museums of their heritage: their paneled walls displayed portraits or memorabilia of racing pilots who had died centuries ago, and their cabinets displayed trophies that had belonged to the club for millennia.

Martinez had known that *Corona* couldn't compete with

the others on the grounds of history, and so he had opted for practicality mixed with spectacle. The furniture wasn't historic, it was merely well-made, comfortable, and stylish. The kitchen produced fine food, the bars fine vintages. The betting parlor featured a tote and the opportunity for interesting side bets. And water flowed in every public room, sometimes inhabited by rare and interesting fish.

Flowing water was a challenge on a ship that was required, on occasion, to experience zero gravity, but complex engineering enabled the ship, on receipt of a zero-gee warning, to rapidly swallow the water into its internal tanks, then regurgitate it when gravity was restored. And in case the system failed, Martinez had tried to waterproof as much of the ship as he could.

At the moment Martinez felt as if he'd been swallowed and regurgitated more than once. His body ached, his bones creaked, and his head felt as if it had been stuffed with cotton rags. He badly wanted everyone to leave so that he could go to bed, but he was the host here, and good form required him to stay with the party till the end.

"How did you do on the tote?" Vipsania asked him. "Did you lose much?"

"I don't bet the tote," Martinez said. "I make private bets with people from the other clubs, because nobody from that lot of snobs really wants to bet on the Corona Club, and I can get good odds."

"So are you up or down?"

"I'm slightly in the black," Martinez said. "I bet myself to win, and lost there, but I also bet myself to show in the top three, and there I won. I also bet the Coronas to place two pilots in the top three, and I got good odds there. Wish I'd put more money down."

"Who bet on Severin, I wonder?"

"Whoever they are, they're very happy."

There was a moment of silence, filled only by the sound of water falling and some shrieking laughter from one of the partygoers.

"Well," Vipsania said. "I'm for bed."

Martinez yawned. "I'm envious."

Vipsania shrugged without much sympathy and left in the direction of the trunk elevator that would take her to the living quarters. Martinez looked down at the revelers and saw the Vandrith Challenge Cup standing tall and gold on a table, where Severin had left it. Some energetic attendees were trying to fill it with wine so they could use it as a punch bowl.

Well, Martinez thought, *maybe I'll win it in six years.*

His eyes turned to the group that was replaying the race. The vast tawny stripes of Vandrith filled the display.

Foote asked if this reminded me of Sula. The phantom thought strayed into his head from he knew not where.

Ridiculous, he thought. *I haven't thought of Sula in ages.*

But the pang in his heart told him that his thought was a lie.

CHAPTER 3

The Petty Mount rose partway up the granite cliffs of the High City like a social climber in search of loftier status, trying but failing to rise to the glittering world of palaces and politicians that occupied the great plateau. Instead the Petty Mount made the best of its failed aspirations and rejoiced in its position as a meeting place of high and low. There were restaurants, boutiques, bars, hairdressers, smoking dens, theaters, and a myriad of little stores that sold vintage clothing, old porcelain, reupholstered furniture, antiques, bric-a-brac, books, maps, and anonymous portraits of ancestors that could be sold to anyone who needed a boost to their bloodlines.

The Petty Mount featured Peers whose ancestors stretched back thousands of years. There were people who slept on the street. There were exquisites who paraded in fashion, inebriates who staggered from bar to bar, musicians who performed in alcoves. Partygoers, party crashers, and certain other sinister parties whose existence was strictly off the record.

Directly above the Petty Mount was the Couch of Eternity, where the ashes of the Shaa Great Masters were entombed. The Shaa had conquered the other races of the empire and forced them to conform to the unforgiving rule of the Praxis, but the Shaa had died, and now the subject species—and the Praxis—were on their own.

On its own or not, the Petty Mount found itself overshadowed by the empire's most celebrated mausoleum.

The woman called Caroline Sula preferred the Petty Mount's lack of pretension to the ordered hierarchies of the High City, and she didn't mind her existence being supervised by a posse of dead aliens. That was restful, if anything.

Sometimes she thought she had more in common with the dead than with the living.

Sula had spent the hot spring afternoon at the Commandery, tucked beneath the Great Refuge on the other side of the High City. She was looking for employment. Sula was an officer in the Fleet and had been decorated for her activities in the war. With her record, and the rank of senior captain, she could normally expect command of one of the new cruisers being built to expand the Fleet after the war.

Instead, for the last six years, there had been nothing. During the war she'd fallen afoul of Lord Tork, the elderly Daimong commander of the Fleet, and she could feel his pale, rotting hand tipping the scales of her life. Sula would have no meaningful job until after Tork died or retired, and at the moment he showed no sign of doing either.

If she'd had patronage in the Fleet or on the Fleet Control Board, Tork's baleful influence might have been mitigated. But the closest person she had to a patron, her former squadron commander Michi Chen, had likewise felt Tork's displeasure.

She hadn't received a promotion since the war and had spent most of the time in command of a dockyard.

The only consolation Sula could find in this situation was that Tork hated Gareth Martinez, too. So there was *some* justice in the world.

In order to pay her courtesy call in the Commandery, she'd worn her medals and her dress uniform, the viridian-green tunic with its two rows of silver buttons. She'd been treated courteously by the staff officers she'd met, who agreed to forward her applications to the Fleet Control Board and to various flag officers.

She knew beforehand that nothing would come of it. But still she traveled to the Commandery every month or so, just so that one of her applications might pass before Lord Tork, and the sight of her name might bring him just a little pain.

The war had left her a public figure, and her blond hair, green eyes, and pale skin were too recognizable, especially if she was in uniform. This wasn't a day when she wanted to be buttonholed by some old comrade who wanted to take her to a club and buy her drinks and reminisce about the battle she'd fought here, in the High City itself, so she rented a car and driver for the trip. The driver was a Cree, with primitive eye-spots, and wore an elaborate apparatus that gave him a sonar picture of the road.

Sula couldn't help but appreciate the irony that she had been taken to and from the Commandery, on a pointless mission, by a driver who might as well have been blind.

The driver returned Sula to the Petty Mount and let her off in front of her apartment, where she was immediately enveloped by the combined scents of hot pavement and meats being cooked on skewers. The Lai-own doorman, dressed in a uniform more elaborate even than that of the Supreme Commander Tork, swung open the door.

And then she caught movement out of the corner of her eye, and she froze in a cold, stunning flash of recognition.

It had been thirteen years since she'd seen that gliding walk, but she knew it at once. It was the walk of someone who'd been born lame but who'd had it fixed as soon as he got money, and who'd taught himself to move in a distinctive, elegant, light-footed style, as if he were walking on rice paper and wanted not to tear it.

Halfway through the lobby door, Sula turned in disbelief, and a second shock of recognition. He had been young when she knew him, but he was a mature man now, with a face and body fuller than she remembered. Too, he dressed in a more mature style, a deep blue coat with gold braid, the blue and gold accented again in a cravat. But no matter how glossy his boots, he retained that gliding, purposeful walk as he ghosted toward her along the baking pavement.

A voice she recognized. And a name she thought she'd drowned years ago.

"Earthgirl," he said, and laughed.

HER FIRST INSTINCT was to run, pelt as fast as she could through the late-afternoon crowds. Her second impulse was to deny she'd ever known him. But neither was possible, or practical.

He wasn't quite the man she knew; but she wasn't the girl she had been either.

If need be, she could have him killed. The thought comforted her. But in the meantime, she needed to engage.

"Ah. Hah," Sula said. "Lamey. I thought you were dead."

He smiled. "That would have been the way to bet."

His lameness had given him his nickname, and the name stayed even after he'd had his gait fixed. He glided to Sula and stood just a little too close, so that she could sense the heat that radiated from his skin.

Her heart beat high in her throat. She sensed a yelp, or a shriek, trembling on the edge of release, and she tried to force her voice into its normal register.

"Did you come to Zanshaa just to see me?"

"No. I have business here. But I knew you were living on the Petty Mount and I thought . . ." His voice trailed away. He looked her up and down. "By the all, Earthgirl, you look beautiful. But you were always beautiful." His eyes traveled over her again, absorbing the uniform, the medals, the rows of silver buttons. "Every inch the Peer," he breathed. "I would never have believed—"

"Perhaps you should come in," Sula said quickly. She didn't want the Lai-own doorman to hear Lamey voice his next thought.

He smiled again. His teeth were brilliant white.

"That would be lovely, Earthgirl, thank you."

Sula turned and entered the cool lobby with its red-and-yellow tiles and its Devajjo stylings and took off her peaked uniform cap as she crossed the floor and summoned the elevator by flipping the cap toward the sensor. The door rolled open and she entered and turned to face front. Lamey followed like a dutiful staff officer, standing slightly behind her. The door closed in perfect silence. His voice came softly from over her shoulder.

"I don't know what to call you. Is it Caroline? Caro? Margaux?" The voice took on a knowing tone. *"Gredel?"*

"I'm a Peer," Sula said. "The correct form of address is 'my lady.'"

"Of course." Agreeably enough. "My lady."

The elevator reached the top floor, and Sula's reception area opened before them. Her heels clacked on parquet, an echo to the urgent knocking of her heart. Niches on the walls held porcelain plates, jars, urns, pots. Sula put her cap on a side table and walked into the living area with its broad curved window that wrapped around a corner of the building—which she owned—and provided a view of the Lower Town.

In the living area there was more porcelain on display, and irises and hyacinths in celadon vases. Antique books sat in airtight, climate-controlled display cases, and cheap collections of mathematical puzzles were laid neatly on a low table, next to a rank of sharpened pencils.

Otherwise the furniture and decor were simple, almost spartan. The elaborate furnishings, the precious woods and inlays so common in the High City, did not interest her. She kept everything obsessively tidy, and a faint whiff of lemon polish assured her that someone had tended to the room that day.

Lamey prowled the room, shook his head at the porcelain. "You like pots?" he said, half in surprise.

"It's old porcelain, from Earth. I spent three years there, commanding the ring station."

"So Earthgirl actually went to Earth? And went collecting, it seems."

"I did a lot of . . . inspecting. It took me all over the planet."

Many of her treasures were, frankly, bribes, given in hope of contracts or other favors. She hadn't wanted to give the impression that she could be bought, so she'd accepted the gifts and then done whatever the hell she wanted.

Oddly enough, though, the gifts hadn't stopped coming. Apparently corrupt contractors lived forever in hope.

Lamey reached out to touch a light blue bowl with a greenish, crackled glaze. He hesitated. Sula smiled.

"Ru ware," Sula said. "Song Dynasty. You can touch it if you like—it's survived thousands of years, so odds are it'll survive *you*."

Instead of touching the bowl he turned to look at her. "You probably know all about the Song Dynasty, whoever they were. I remember how you used to love history."

"The Song chose their officials by competitive examinations instead of by heredity."

Lamey's eyebrows rose in surprise. "How . . . how unlike our own perfect system."

They turned at the sound of footsteps. A tall man entered the room. He wore the undress uniform of the Fleet, and his curly hair formed a light brown halo around his head. Lamey seemed surprised to find a man here at all.

"I heard voices, my lady," said the newcomer.

Sula nodded at Lamey. "Macnamara," she said, "this is an

old friend from Spannan." She looked at Lamey and realized that she couldn't introduce him by his nickname, and that she didn't know what name he was using. He had been a young hunted gangster when she'd last seen him, and he might have adopted a new identity.

After a moment of silence, Lamey seemed to realize her difficulty.

"Hector Braga," he said. Which Sula knew to be his birth name, which in turn meant he wasn't traveling under an alias.

"Can Macnamara bring you anything?" Sula asked. "A drink?"

"Kyowan and Spacey," he said.

"I'll have a lemonade," said Sula.

"My lady," said Macnamara. "Sir."

He gave Lamey an appraising look from beneath his brows, then left the room. Lamey hadn't made a good impression with him, or so Sula surmised.

Constable First Class Macnamara was one of the servants that the Fleet permitted her to take from one posting to the next, and he'd been with her in Action Team 491 during the Naxid War, when he'd helped her kill a great many rebels. But Sula had found he was a little possessive of her, and that he sometimes disapproved of her male friends.

Usually, it had to be admitted, with good reason.

Still, it was good to know that Macnamara was in the apartment, in case she had to throw Lamey out.

Sula looked at her guest. Her panic had faded once she'd brought Lamey onto her home ground, and now she felt as if she could exert a little more control over the situation.

"Sit down," she invited. Lamey gracefully flowed onto a sofa, where he carefully left room for her. Sula chose an armchair. He looked at her with appreciation.

"You've really got the manner, you know," he said. "You've really perfected it. You always had the voice, but the rest . . . would have needed polish."

"You're more polished yourself," Sula said.

He smiled, tweaked the knees of his braided trousers. "I suppose we've both earned our places."

Sula gave him a sharp look. "What *is* your place?" she asked.

Lamey made an equivocal gesture with his hands. "I'm a lobbyist, I suppose. For Spannan. Ultimately we hope to remove the Distchin family as the planet's patrons, but we need allies first, so that's why we're here."

The Distchin clan—high-ranked Torminel Peers—had been the chief patrons of Spannan since it was first settled. They were infamously absentee landlords, living in the High City while running things on Spannan through a series of appointees. Lady Distchin had never been on Spannan in her life, nor had her last two predecessors.

"You're awfully candid about your objectives," Sula said.

Lamey shrugged. "It's not as if the Distchins don't know the delegation is here."

"That's quite a task you've set for yourselves. You'll need a vote in Convocation."

"That's why we need as many convocates on our side as we can find."

Macnamara returned with a tray. Ice tinkled in glasses

as he handed out drinks and placed coasters and napkins on polished side tables. He straightened.

"Will there be anything else, my lady?"

"No, thank you. You can go."

Macnamara withdrew, casting another suspicious look at Lamey over his shoulder as he went. He had never managed the imperturbable countenance so desirable in a servant.

She turned her gaze back to Lamey and found him looking at her with frank calculation.

"I knew you at once, when I saw that video." Admiration suddenly flooded his face. "There you were, straight as an arrow in your uniform. Beautiful as a sunrise. And I thought, *That's my Earthgirl!*"

Sula cast a glance after Macnamara to make sure he'd gone into the kitchen and closed the door behind him. The conversation was getting onto dangerous ground.

"What video was this?" she asked finally.

"You were getting a decoration, during the war. We didn't have a lot of heroes then, and you'd destroyed those six Naxid ships at First Magaria."

"Five," she said. She could remember the reek of Lord Tork's rotting flesh as he leaned close to pin the Nebula Medal on her tunic.

"Five, then," Lamey said. "And then of course there was a lot of video of you when you captured the High City with your army. I knew damned well that Caro couldn't have pulled *that* off."

Again Sula glanced toward the kitchen door to make certain it was still shut. Lamey looked at her with a frown.

"Whatever happened to Caro, anyway?" he asked.

His tone was light, but there was a dangerous edge beneath the words, one that sent a chill along her nerves. It occurred to her that he might be an informer, that he might have survived on Spannan by betraying his friends—and that he might be recording this, or broadcasting to a third party.

Sula pressed two fingers to her throat and mimed triggering a med injector to fire a dose into her carotid. Lamey nodded.

"Overdose," he said. "She was headed that way, sure enough."

Sula didn't want Lamey to know her part in that overdose, of the way she'd encouraged Caro Sula to consume hit after hit of endorphin that night. Or the fight to get the limp, dead body onto the cart so that it could be shuttled to the river and weighted down so that it would never see Spannan's sun again.

Sula didn't want Lamey to know of the calculations that she'd made, the way she'd carefully planned to step into the shoes of a sad, lonely, self-destructive young girl who was absolutely no harm to anybody, and no good, either. A girl who happened to be Lady Sula, heir to one of the greatest names in the empire.

A young Peer, blond and green-eyed, doomed by the fact that she happened to look just like her best friend, the gangster's girl named Gredel.

Sula rubbed the pad of scar tissue on her right thumb. "I'm sure you haven't looked me up just to relive old times," she said.

He cocked his head as he looked at her, and a ridiculous grin spread across his face. It was a grin that spoke of self-satisfaction at his own cleverness.

"You've obviously done well for yourself," he said.

"I made some good investments during the war."

"But you're not in the High City."

"I don't *like* the High City." Which was truthful enough.

"But you really can't afford to shine there. The late Lord and Lady Sula lost all that before you even came on the scene, didn't they?"

Sula wanted to laugh. She remembered Lamey taking her into boutiques and buying her all the most expensive things he could find, the aesa-leather bags and the jackets with all the zips and the thick-soled boots and the clunky jewelry that all the kids were wearing back then.

"Are you thinking of setting me up in an apartment in the High City?" she asked. "I'm to be your mistress now?"

"You mean *again,*" he said. "And it wouldn't be such a bad idea, would it?" He pushed out a hand and made a patting gesture, as if reassuring her. "But no, I plan to set you up all right, but not in the way you're thinking."

Sula made no response, only lifted an eyebrow. He laughed.

"That's the manner, all right! By the all, no one would believe you weren't born to it!"

Sula was irritated. "You're going to come to the point sooner or later, aren't you?"

He sighed and twitched again at the fabric over his knees. "The Sulas are an ancient family. As good as Peers get. They had birth, status, money, and vast patronage. But the previous generation got caught defrauding the government, and Lord and Lady Sula were skinned alive and all their money and property confiscated. *But*"—he held up a finger—"their brilliant daughter"—here he made a generous gesture toward Sula—"redeemed the family name in the war, killed scads of rebels, blew up enemy ships, got decorated, liberated the High City from the Naxids . . ."

He spread his hands. "Why should she be punished for the faults of her parents? Why shouldn't she"—he sat up straight—"why shouldn't the name of Sula be restored to the honors and privileges enjoyed by her ancestors?"

She stared at him in speechless disbelief. She tried to find words in the chaos that was her mind and managed to stammer a few.

"You'll," she said. "You'll—you'll have to—"

"I'll have to arrange a vote in Convocation," Lamey said. "It won't be as hard as you think. We have our friends, but for *this* all we need is tradition. The most conservative Peers in the assembly will remember Clan Sula in its glory and will want those days to return." He frowned, tapped his chin. "But we'll need the right person to introduce the motion. Someone unimpeachable, of a bloodline comparable to the Sulas themselves." He raised his eyebrows. "Do you know anyone like that?"

Lord Chen. Names flashed through her dazzled mind, faces rising one after the other in a kind of mental parade, all without conscious thought. *Lord Durward Li. Lord Eldey . . .*

"I—I might," Sula said. She tried to force logic into her

astonished brain and took a deliberate sip of her lemonade. The astringent taste awakened her palate, her mind. She gave Lamey a look that she hoped was critical.

"Assuming you can make this happen," she said, "what do I have to do in return?"

"You'll have to become a convocate, of course," Lamey said. "The head of the Sula clan always does. And once you're in Convocation, you could vote for, say, Spannan's getting rid of Lady Distchin and replacing her with someone who actually knows how to run a planet. Perhaps even yourself."

She laughed, just a bit scornful. "Don't try to hypnotize me. You know Spannan will go to someone more important."

"It'll be years before that happens," Lamey said. "Who knows how important you'll be then?" He leaned forward, the ice rattling in his drink. "I have confidence in you, Earthgirl. Absolute confidence."

"Stop calling me that," she said.

"Very well." He smiled. "My lady."

"And you haven't told me how I'm going to be able to—I believe the word was *shine*—in the High City."

"You'll be a convocate, and you'll have a vote."

"Hah. One out of six hundred."

"You'll sit on a committee or two, and you'll have a vote there as well. And maybe you'll have a chairmanship, because you're a Sula, and Sulas have always been in charge of one thing or another. And even if in general Convocation you're only one in six hundred, that's one of the six hundred *who run the entire empire*. Six hundred out of *hundreds of bil-*

lions. That's *power*." He shrugged. "Money adheres to power, Earthgi—my lady."

Sula said nothing. She was thinking hard. Lamey rattled the ice in his drink and looked over his shoulder for a refill.

Conspiracy was thirsty work, apparently.

"We each know things about the other," Sula said. "Things that could get us in trouble."

"All the more reason," said Lamey, "to trust each other. Don't you think?"

He had an answer for everything. She had obviously been a part of his plans for some time.

But that didn't mean she wanted him in hers.

Lamey rattled his ice cubes again. "Can you call what's-his-name? Get me another drink?"

Sula rose abruptly from her chair, stood before him with straight-spine military posture. "No, I don't think so. I think you should leave now."

His eyes widened. "You're turning me down?"

"I didn't say that. But I'm going to have to think."

Lamey carefully put his drink on the side table, then rose. He was very close to her. She smelled the earthy tones of his hair, felt his heat prickling on her skin.

"Is there anything I could do," he said, "to convince you?"

She tried to make her voice brusque. "Not right now. Tell me where I can find you, and I'll be in touch."

He looked at her intently, his lips going thin, his eyes hooded in anger and frustration. She sensed danger, and she remembered his moods, his anger. His fists.

I'm not seventeen anymore, she told herself. She wasn't vulnerable to Lamey's brand of intimidation any longer.

The moment of tension broke, and it was Lamey who broke it.

"I'm at the Imperial Hotel," he said.

She had tried to blow up the Imperial Hotel during the war, and failed.

Maybe I should try again, she thought.

"I'll be in touch," she repeated.

He turned and made his way to the entry hall. Frustration had caused him to abandon his usual gliding step, and his walk had a jerky, mechanical quality. Sula followed him and summoned the elevator. By the time it arrived, his humor had returned. He stepped into the elevator, turned, and gave a slight bow.

"My lady," he said.

"Sir."

The doors closed, and Sula returned to the living area. She looked out the window into the Lower Town and reached for her lemonade with fingers that trembled.

CHAPTER 4

Sula invited Lamey to join her at a club on her thirtieth birthday. She supposed surviving to thirty was something worthy of a celebration—the odds had been very much in favor of her dying on a scaffold or finding herself reduced to atoms in the vacuum of space.

The club was constructed along the lines of an amphitheater, with the patrons stacked in rising tiers around the small stage. Lamey entered the club with his usual smooth glide, then paused while his eyes adjusted to the dim light. He saw Sula perched on the second tier and climbed the creaking wooden stairs. He looked at the small table in surprise.

"Are we alone tonight?" he asked. "I thought this was a birthday party."

"It is."

"And in a place called 'The Heart and Dagger.' I wondered if I should bring brass knuckles, but it seems to be peaceful enough."

"The entertainment's good."

Lamey helped himself to a chair. The fact of their being

alone with each other seemed to please him. "You're thirty now? It doesn't make you feel old, does it?"

"Not at all," said Sula. "In Earth years, I'm still only twenty-five."

"I have—" But Sula held up a hand to silence him as the entertainers stepped onto the stage.

"Listen," she said.

"Oh," said Lamey, as Sula began to applaud. *"Derivoo."*

The derivoo was a Terran woman with face and hands whitened, and high spots of color painted on her cheeks. She wore the traditional flounced skirts, and her dark blond hair was pulled back in a severe style. As she and her two accompanists took their places, the small crowd responded with enthusiasm.

A lone chord rang out, and the derivoo began to sing, the song of a woman who had left her husband for a lover, only to have the lover desert her. The singer enacted the woman's shattered life, the husband who turned her away, the children who now were strangers. But the song was *defiant;* the woman scorned the anguish that consumed her and remained unbent even in the face of catastrophe. After the song came to its bitter conclusion, there was a moment of hushed silence in the amphitheater, and then the crowd burst into applause.

Lamey signaled the waitron. "I'm going to need a few drinks if I'm going to listen to any more of this."

"Hush," Sula said. The derivoo began again.

She sang of terror and desolation, desertion and violence,

the loss of love, the betrayal of hope, death's final separation. Her whitened hands fluttered to draw raw emotion from the air. Sula watched the performance in rapture, felt the woman's terror in her losing battle with fate, felt also the defiance that would never permit her to surrender even though her cause was hopeless.

After half an hour of nerve-searing performance, the singer paused and bowed and left the stage for an intermission. Lamey finished his third drink and grinned.

"Now let's do something fun!" he said.

"This *is* fun," said Sula.

Lamey shook his head. "No wonder you're alone on your birthday." He reached into his pocket and withdrew a brightly wrapped package. "For you, Earthgirl."

Sula plucked at the wrapping. "May I?"

"Of course." He was unable to restrain his enthusiasm. "It's something called a lion dog. From someplace called Newporn, or something."

She looked at him. "Nippon, you mean?"

He shrugged. "Maybe. From before the conquest, that's all I really know."

The package held a fine, small piece of porcelain, a guardian lion playing with a ball, its mouth open in a snarl. Sula looked for the maker's mark on the underside but couldn't read it in the dim light.

"Okimoko," she said. "These were often in pairs—this is the male, with the ball and the open mouth. The female would have a lion pup under its paw, and its mouth closed. Between them the lions are saying 'Om,' which has to do with religion, though I don't know exactly what."

"You like it then? Even though the girl lion is lost?"

"It's lovely. Thank you."

Lamey preened. "I thought you might like it."

Applause rang out as the singer and her accompanists returned to the stage. Lamey's face fell. Sula wanted to laugh.

"I like derivoo," she said, "because it's *true*. It's about death, and desire, and—"

"It's depressing," said Lamey.

"Quiet now."

As the derivoo began to sing of another confrontation with the fates, Sula looked sidelong at Lamey and considered her situation. Anything she did, she thought, anything public, was a risk, and there was nothing more public than being a member of the Convocation. The more she appeared in the public eye, the greater the chance that she—that Gredel—could be exposed as an impostor.

But on the other hand, she was sick of hiding. She'd been doing little other than hiding since her return from Terra to Zanshaa.

Hiding in her tidy little apartment built up against the side of the High City. A comfortable refuge filled with her porcelain, her books, her puzzles and games.

Her *hobbies*. Hobbies that filled her life, because there was nothing else. Nothing but the ritual trip to the Commandery, every month or so, in hopes of finding a posting that might give a little purpose to her life.

Lamey signaled the waitron for another drink. *Blackmail,* she thought. *He's trying to blackmail me.*

But why? To gain one vote in six hundred? What else could Lamey be up to?

She didn't trust him. She didn't trust his offer.

But still something in it spoke to her. She yearned for something other than amusements.

She wondered if she was like one of the women in a song by a derivoo, enticed by a temptation that would destroy her.

Though Sula knew that, as a high-ranking Peer and Lady Convocate, she could be dangerous to more than just herself. She'd had experience with how useless and hidebound the denizens of the High City could be, how locked they were in a world of caste and privilege that amounted to little more than a delusion. It was so strong a delusion that they'd convinced the rest of the empire to share it with them, but Sula figured reality would break in sooner rather than later.

The highest caste would remain in power only so long as they managed to convince others that they deserved it, and then—once the illusion was gone—so long as they were willing to employ violence to stay in power. As soon as their will failed, they were finished.

And when they were gone, who would replace them?

Sula, perhaps. Maybe even Lamey. Why not?

She'd stormed the High City once. Maybe she could do it again.

When the derivoo left for another intermission, she leaned close to Lamey.

"I'm in," she said. "If you still want me in Convocation."

She watched delight blossom in his face. "You won't regret this," he said.

"Don't be ridiculous," she said. "Of course I will."

THE CONVOCATION'S MORNING business had been to vote its thanks to Lord Naaz Vijana, Lord Mehrang, and Lord Governor Rao Mehrang for the successful suppression of the Yormak Rebellion. Along with its thanks, the Convocation voted in new arrangements for Esley, opening to exploitation vast areas that had previously been held in trust for the ungrateful Yormaks, who would now be penned into reserves much smaller than their native ranges.

Another world, Sula thought, had been opened to speculators. Generally she was all in favor of such speculation, since she had a financial interest in the development of three new worlds near Terra, worlds discovered when she was in command of the Fleet dockyards there.

Though it might take years, decades even, before the newly settled worlds began to return profits to their investors. Sula wouldn't be building palaces on the newly discovered worlds anytime soon.

After the vote, Sula felt an air of self-congratulation settle over the Convocation. They had, after all, just settled the affairs of millions of citizens, along with an entire species. Just the moment for the Lord Senior to allow himself to make a small digression.

Lord Saïd rose to his feet and made a gentle, beneficent

gesture with the copper-and-silver wand that marked his status as the Lord Senior, the presiding officer of the Convocation. First among equals, he wielded the wand of authority with a firm impartiality and managed debates with an economy that the other convocates appreciated. Nothing, they all knew, was more tedious than one of their number who could not manage to bring himself to the point, and if a convocate wandered too much from the matter at hand, Lord Saïd would cut him off and find someone else to make the argument for him.

Lord Saïd was the most important and powerful Lord Senior in the history of the empire. He was an impressive man, with a swordlike nose, bright eyes, a magnificent gray mane of hair, and a bushy mustache. He was over a hundred years old but carried himself with the firm, erect carriage of a man of eighty. The scarlet brocade cloak that marked his office was worn with a ceremonial grandeur that only underlined his authority.

But it was not Lord Saïd's appearance that gave him the authority that led the empire so effortlessly, but the prestige that had come with his actions during the Naxid Rebellion. During the very first minutes of the conflict, Saïd had acted against the rebels who were trying to seize control of the chamber of the Convocation. Despite his age he'd thrown a chair at Akzad, the rebel Lord Senior, and led the loyalists in a straight-up brawl, fists and feet and furniture, that resulted in the insurgents being hurled from the cliff behind the Convocation terrace. Then, elected to his current post, he had led the government in the fight against the traitors until the loyalists had finally triumphed.

Since then, radiant in his majestic halo of victory, he had continued unchallenged as Lord Senior and would probably hold the office until he died.

And now the most powerful man in the Convocation was going to speak. And he would speak for Sula.

"Before the Convocation resumes its business this afternoon," he said, "I should like to raise a point of personal privilege."

Despite the fact that she had known approximately what Lord Saïd would say, Sula felt a shimmer of anticipation at the Lord Senior's words.

"I should like to direct the attention of this assembly to a certain officer of the Fleet," he said. "This officer bears a great name, which, though lately eclipsed, has provided the empire with many generations of brilliant leaders and faithful servants. She fought in the late war with great distinction and has earned the commendations of her superiors for her actions at Magaria, Naxas, and elsewhere."

Sula, in her full dress uniform with its double row of silver buttons, sat in the small visitors' gallery above the assembly and heard the murmuring from the convocates as they tried to guess of whom the Lord Senior spoke. The six-hundred-odd desks of the convocates were laid out in graceful half circles centered on the Lord Senior's dais and rose in tiers, each half circle higher than the one before it. Behind the Lord Senior was the glass wall that led onto the terrace of infamous memory, the terrace from which the Naxid rebels had been flung to their deaths; but against the strong afternoon sunlight the wall had been darkened, so that Lord Saïd would be more than just a silhouette against the bright background.

"In fact," Lord Saïd continued, "this assembly owes her a debt of gratitude, for after circumstances compelled us to abandon the capital, it was she who led the forces that recaptured the High City and scourged from this chamber the rebels who had fouled it for so long."

A stir ran through the amphitheater as the convocates realized the subject of Saïd's address. A few faces turned up to the gallery to see if Sula was present. Sula felt the touch of their interest, and she felt her spine straighten and her chin rise as she presented herself to their gaze.

The Lord Senior went on to praise her ancestors, who had served the Praxis as high-ranking Peers for hundreds of years, dating almost to the Shaa conquest of Earth, and then he wound up his address. "While the late Lord and Lady Sula were judged guilty of a crime against the Praxis, and paid for their crime with their lives, their punishment was not only directed against them, but against their descendants. Members of Clan Sula are forbidden to serve in the Convocation or in the civil service. Only a military career was open to Lady Sula.

"But that career has been astounding, marked with nothing but success. Captain the Lady Sula has redeemed her name and her clan by her brilliant actions against the enemies of the Praxis, and in response I would like to conclude by moving that this assembly, in thanks to the champion of the High City, immediately restore Clan Sula to its ancient privileges."

There was some applause in the chamber as Lord Saïd fell silent, adjusted his brocade cloak, and sat on his chair. Several convocates had bounded to their feet in order to be recognized, and the Lord Senior recognized Lord Eldey.

Eldey, an elderly Torminel with gray-and-brown fur and lamplike, night-adapted eyes, had followed Sula as governor of Zanshaa after the reconquest and had proven both able and sympathetic to the problems Sula had encountered at fighting a highly irregular ground war on her own, a war the very nature of which her superiors were bound to disapprove of. He spoke with admiration of Sula's abilities and then seconded the Lord Senior's motion.

Eldey then surrendered some of his time to Lord Durward Li, whose son, Lord Richard, had been Sula's commander on the heavy cruiser *Dauntless* before both he and *Dauntless* had been lost at First Magaria. Lord Durward was not a convocate himself and couldn't have spoken without the cooperation of Eldey and Saïd. But with their permission, he spoke of his son's admiration for Sula and her abilities and reminded the convocates that she had taken a First in the exams for lieutenant held just before the outbreak of war.

After Lord Durward came Lord Chen, who served on the Fleet Control Board, and Chen was followed by Lord Roland Martinez. Sula viewed Roland with distaste—with his wide shoulders, long arms, and big hands, he resembled his younger brother, Gareth, and he spoke with the same provincial Laredo accent.

She hadn't asked Roland to speak, and she wondered who had, and if Lamey's influence extended as far as Clan Martinez.

What could Lamey have to do with Roland Martinez, or anyone else in the Martinez family? If they were in some kind of alliance, an alliance to accomplish what? For a moment, even as Roland praised her to the Convocation, she felt a strong, sudden sense of her own helplessness—she was caught up in a web of relationships and objectives that she clearly didn't understand, and that meant that she was someone's pawn. Possibly not even Lamey's pawn, but that of the person behind him.

Roland was followed by Lord Ngeni, who had been Roland's patron before his own rise to the Convocation, and then by Lord Yoshitoshi, who like Lord Chen was a Martinez in-law. Others rose to speak, strangers whose connection to any of the others was not apparent, and as yet there was no dissent. Not one spoke in favor of continuing the ban on Clan Sula.

And then members of the Convocation began to rise from their seats, first a few scattered members, then whole groups. Eventually everyone rose, including Sula in the gallery, and she knew this would be a fight after all.

Lord Tork entered the room in silence. The gray-skinned and cadaverous Daimong was approaching the age of ninety, but despite his advanced age, he had organized the loyalist Fleet and then led it to victory at the Second Battle of Magaria, and afterward he had been awarded the unprecedented title of Supreme Commander of the Fleet.

That his tactics had been clumsy and wasteful, and resulted in more casualties among the loyalist forces than were necessary, was a minority opinion shared by Sula and other younger officers. Tork was perfectly aware of this and viewed

Sula with distaste when he did not view her with hatred. He looked at her unorthodox behavior in the war as a threat to the perfect ways of his ancestors; and he had done his best to keep her unemployed, and her part in the war obscure. Tork's malevolence would last a long time, since victory had so secured his grip on the Fleet that, like the Lord Senior, he would probably only leave office when carried out in his coffin.

What had caused the Convocation to rise to its feet was not Tork's rank, but the baton in his gray, ever-dying hand. This was the Golden Orb, the empire's highest military decoration. It consisted of an ornate golden baton topped by a crystal sphere filled with a golden liquid that swirled in layers and bands, like the clouds of a gas giant. So prestigious was the award that every person in government service, civilian and military, was required to rise to their feet in the Orb's presence. Only two Orbs had been awarded during the entire war, one to Tork, and the other to Gareth Martinez.

Sula couldn't claim to be a fan of either.

Tork may have been Supreme Commander, but he was a professional officer of the Fleet, not a member of the Convocation. If Sula succeeded in becoming a convocate, she could end up his boss.

Maybe, she thought, she could keep *him* waiting in an anteroom for a long afternoon.

At any rate, that prospect was clearly not to Tork's taste. No doubt he'd heard of the motion before the Convocation and hurried over from the Commandery as quickly as his ancient legs could propel him.

"My Lord Senior," Tork said, in the bell-like tones of his

species. "I respectfully request permission to address the Convocation."

Lord Saïd, standing in the Orb's presence, waved his wand of office gracefully. "The Supreme Commander is always welcome to address this assembly."

"I wish to offer a few remarks on the Lord Senior's motion," Tork said. His beautiful voice seemed to shimmer in the air. "I prefer not to comment on the details of Lady Sula's career, but to remark generally on the morale and tradition of the service."

Tork's black, unblinking eyes scanned left and right at the standing ranks of convocates in their wine-red jackets. He had not given them permission to sit, and under his blank gaze the assembly shifted uncomfortably on their feet.

"There were many in the Fleet who served bravely and capably," Tork said. "They did so without hope of reward or favor, united as they were by the knowledge that all who served would be rewarded equally by the preservation of the Praxis and the restoration of a way of life built by the Great Masters together with our ancestors. The morale of the Fleet was sustained by shared hardship and danger, and the knowledge of the great purpose that drove them."

The tone of Tork's melodious voice shifted, became more insistent. "But what will become of that morale, that unity, when this assembly chooses to honor only a single officer, while offering the others no awards at all? I offer no disparagement of Captain the Lady Sula, but I would like to state firmly that offering her rewards beyond those she has already earned will, in my opinion, certainly damage the service."

Sula wondered if her sneer was visible from the dais below. What damage had been done to Fleet morale, she wondered, when the Convocation had given Tork, a single officer, not only the Golden Orb, but the unprecedented rank of Supreme Commander?

The Lord Senior offered a lazy wave of his wand. "I would like to offer a clarification to my friend the Supreme Commander," he said. "My motion was not to offer Lady Sula any extraordinary reward. The motion offers her no commands, no promotions or decorations, but rather intends to restore the ancient rights that have long attached to her family."

Lord Tork hesitated. The ancient rights of established Peer families were a part of the tradition for which he had fought. Without them, without the privilege that had enfolded him from the day of his birth, the Praxis would hardly have been worth defending at all.

"The officers of the Fleet may not understand your lordship's distinction," Tork said. "They would, however, know that it is the prerogative of the Supreme Commander to approve awards."

Saïd's orator's voice seemed to offer nothing but understanding and sympathy. "I have every confidence that the officers of the Fleet have the intelligence and understanding to know that your prerogative is in no way being usurped," he said.

While Saïd's voice had grown silky, Tork's timbre now grew discordant. "I strongly advise against this motion! This will not be received well!"

Not by Tork, anyway, Sula thought. She was enjoying the debate, not only because her side was winning, but because her enemy Tork was getting a thumping. She had served under Tork and knew he was a bully in debate, repeating his views over and over, with ever-increasing stridency, until he overwhelmed all opposition. But never before had he taken on the full Convocation, hundreds of able orators whose noble antecedents equaled or exceeded his own.

"I'm sure this assembly will give full weight to the Supreme Commander's views," Saïd said.

"I wish also to make a correction!" Tork said. His voice sounded like tortured metal. "Lady Sula was *not* commended by her superiors after the Battle of Magaria, as the Lord Senior stated!"

Now *that,* Sula thought, was just petty. There was a moment of silence in the chamber as the convocates absorbed Tork's small-minded retort.

It was Roland Martinez who begged then to be recognized, and then shot the Supreme Commander's feet out from under him. "I'm sure the Lord Senior referred not to your lordship's victory at the Second Battle of Magaria," he said, "but to the *First,* in which Lady Sula in her pinnace succeeded in destroying no less than five enemy warships. I believe, Lord Tork, that you decorated her personally."

Which completed the rout. Lord Tork begged permission to withdraw, and permission was duly granted. The Convocation gratefully returned to their seats. A half-hearted debate followed, in which Tork's clients and adherents duly registered their support for the Supreme Commander's views, but the debate died away, and the Lord Senior called the question. The motion passed overwhelmingly on a voice vote.

On the instant, Roland Martinez sprang to his feet, turned to face Sula in the gallery, and began to applaud. The applause spread through the chamber, and the convocates who had stood for the Golden Orb now stood for Sula.

Sula rose to her feet, smiling, and for a tingling instant bathed in the warmth of the chamber's approval. Her heart lifted, but she knew that *she* was not the object of the Convocation's approval. *She* was not a member of an ancient Peer family, *she* had not been raised in a mansion in Zanshaa's acropolis, *she* had never been swaddled in an atmosphere of privilege, and the only right her ancestors had ever possessed was the right to toe the line or die. If the Convocation knew her true identity, they would have ordered her torture and execution with the same enthusiasm with which they now applauded her.

As she turned to the different corners of the chamber with her arm raised, she noticed a message of congratulations shining on the sleeve display of her uniform tunic. It was from Lamey.

She managed to keep herself from scowling just in time, but the thought had already entered her mind. *What does he* really *want?*

CHAPTER 5

The reception hall at the Martinez Palace echoed with the sounds of servants preparing the afternoon's fete. Encountering his brother by the drinks counter, Martinez paused to ask the question that had been occupying his mind.

"Why does Sula get to be a convocate? Why not, for example, myself?"

"Our family already has a convocate," Roland said.

"Other families have more than one," Martinez said. "The Ngenis, for example. The Yoshitoshis. Or the Akzads."

Roland picked up a crystal goblet and viewed it against the light shining in from the clerestory. "The Akzads were traitors who were thrown off a cliff at the end of the war."

"True, but irrelevant to my point."

Roland put down the goblet and patted Martinez on the arm. "Your day will come, Gareth."

"When?" Martinez spread his hands. "Not only am I a war hero and a brilliant yacht captain with a following throughout the empire, but I'm married to the future Lady Chen, who is almost certain to become a convocate on her father's death."

"And that would make *three* of you." Roland sighed. "If you can convince Lord Saïd to bring your candidacy before the Convocation, then I'm sure I and all your friends will be happy to vote for the motion."

Suspicion entered Martinez's mind. "How *did* you get the Lord Senior to back your Sula scheme?"

"I didn't. That was your father-in-law."

Martinez felt taken aback. "It's more than he's ever done for *me*."

"Lord Chen's an old friend and ally of Lord Saïd, and Saïd was also a particular friend of Lady Sula's grandmother and remembers little baby Sula fondly. Once prompted, the Lord Senior was happy to do the family a favor."

Martinez raised an eyebrow. "Little baby Sula? How adorable she must have been, crawling about the nursery with a knife in her teeth and a grenade in her tiny fist."

There was a stir by the door to indicate the arrival of the first guests.

"I don't suppose Sula's going to be here today?" Martinez asked. At the thought he felt an invisible hand close, just slightly, on his windpipe.

Roland peered over his brother's shoulder to see who had arrived. "No," he said shortly. "She doesn't have enough money. We're here to raise funds, after all."

You're *here to raise funds,* Martinez thought. I'm *here because I have nothing else to do.*

He had been unemployed since the war, save for an appointment as Lord Inspector of the Fleet for Laredo, Chee, and Parkhurst, an appointment intended as meaningless, but which had enabled him to do some useful work after all. But there had been nothing since then. He had been promoted from junior to senior captain, but that happened automatically after five years and could only have been prevented by his resignation or his conviction for treason or some other serious crime.

And all that while his wife, Terza, had been rising at the Ministry of Right and Dominion, the civilian agency that supported the Fleet.

Because of his wife's prominence, he'd been obliged to join Terza in a long series of receptions, balls, dinners, and entertainments—and when she wasn't so occupied, his brother and sisters were always inviting him to one event or another. Most of the events had one thing in common, which was that Martinez envied almost everyone else present. They all seemed to have work, or if not work exactly, some meaningful way to spend their time. If they were not serving in the government or the Convocation, they were hardworking merchants or financiers or builders; and if they were so rich or well placed or lucky they had no job at all, they occupied themselves with bankrolling theater or ballet companies, with amateur sports, with collecting art or supporting concert halls.

Martinez had founded the Corona Club out of desperation—racing gave him both an occupation and the public recognition that helped him to convince himself that he hadn't ceased to exist.

The new arrivals at the Martinez Palace turned out to be Vipsania and her husband, Lord Convocate Oda Yoshitoshi, a distinguished-looking, white-haired man a couple decades older than his wife. Though he was now a perfectly respectable figure in the top echelon of the High City, Martinez knew enough about him to guess at depravities somewhere in his past, enough to run up a considerable amount of debt. Roland had purchased the debt, and with it Lord Oda, who was now a faithful and indulgent husband and compliant member of Roland's faction in the Convocation. Should Lord Oda step out of line, Roland would bring the debt to the attention of Oda's uncle, Lord Yoshitoshi, who would almost certainly disinherit him.

Roland preferred his in-laws tractable, and for that he was willing to spend money. He'd purchased Lord Oda, he'd saved Lord Chen from bankruptcy, and he'd stripped his one-time father-in-law, Lord Zykov, of his considerable fortune—but then Zykov had been trying to do the same to him, so that was perfectly all right.

Martinez greeted Lord Oda and kissed his sister on the cheek. She gave him a businesslike look. "We're wrapping up our war series," she said. "I'd like you interviewed again—just a few questions to clear up a few last-minute issues."

"Certainly."

"The Fleet's official history is going through what is supposed to be a final revision, and we've heard some of the changes that are being made. So we thought we'd have you address them—head off Tork and his minions."

Martinez felt a flush of pleasure. "I'd be delighted to

thwart the Supreme Commander in any way. Can you send me the questions?"

"It'll look better if your answers don't seem rehearsed. And you should wear the same uniform as last time, and we'll interview you in the same room at your palace."

He nodded. "With the racing season over I'm reasonably free, not to say indolent. Send Miss Saperstein around whenever is convenient, and I'll try to sound as unrehearsed as I can."

Echoing from the high ceiling came the sound of an orchestra tuning. Martinez walked with his sister and Lord Oda in the direction of Roland, who was frowning at something on his hand comm. Roland dictated a brief message in reply, then put the device away.

The Martinez Palace bustled around them. It was a new structure, built on the footprint of an older palace owned by Lord Akthan, a Naxid rebel who with most of his family was executed after the war.

The Martinez family, when they had first arrived in Zanshaa City, had been cautious about the way they intruded upon the stately rituals of the capital. They knew they were interlopers, and they didn't want to call too much attention to themselves too early in the game. Therefore they had rented an old palace in one of the less fashionable districts of the High City. Carefully they probed the crust of the city, looking for cracks.

But the war had, for a while, changed all the rules and thrown the whole family into prominence. Four of the five siblings had married into the highest strata of the Peer hierarchy. Roland had become a convocate, and his brother a successful military leader. For Roland, the future Lord Martinez, to build his own palace no longer seemed presumptuous.

Still, the palace wasn't on the Boulevard of the Praxis, where the most elite clans resided, but one street to the south, on the Street of Righteous Peace. Roland preferred not to push himself too far forward, especially as his brother, with the Corona Club, was garnering massive amounts of attention throughout the empire, and equally massive amounts of disapproval.

The building was in the conservative but monumental Tanyl style, the same architectural school chosen by the Shaa overlords for the Great Refuge and the Couch of Eternity, possibly because it reflected the proportions of their own towering, massive bodies. Square, rather squat pillars supported a portico in front, and the main body of the building hunched beneath a roof that overflowed the walls like the cap of a mushroom. Gazing upon the street were windows that weren't quite rectangular, and weren't quite oval, either. Martinez thought the windows reminded him uncomfortably of eyes. The palace as a whole seemed to crouch beneath its shadowing roof, ready to spring upon the unwary world—not unlike his family, now that he came to think of it.

The building had been constructed of pink limestone imported all the way from Chee, a planet the Martinez family were developing. The polished limestone resembled marble and served as a massive, public, unavoidable advertisement for Chee's exports. Indoors, the rooms were tall and proportioned more to humans than to the vast, slack-skinned frames of the Shaa conquerors. In the reception room the eyelike windows brought the light of Shaamah in to the sparkling crystal glasses, the softly glowing porcelain, the polished parquet floors, and the fine wood veneers on the wainscoting. Fine art occupied the walls or stood on pedestals.

Though they might be found in a private study or two, there were no portraits of ancestors on the walls of the public rooms. There were no Martinez ancestors the High City would have considered important enough to look at.

Guests began to arrive, Lady Gruum among them. She was a Daimong of the highest caste and had been named by the Convocation the patron of Rol-mar, one of the new worlds open to settlement. During the long centuries of the Shaa decline, exploration and settlement had fallen to nothing; but now inhabitable planets that had been discovered ages ago were being opened, and an expanded Exploration Service was venturing through wormhole gates to discover new worlds.

Lady Gruum normally lived in a sphere so rarefied that she would never have crossed the threshold of a palace as inconsequential as that of the Martinez family; but as it happened Clan Martinez was in a position to make her a great deal of money, and in order to multiply her colossal fortune she was willing to unbend. Truth was, the Martinez clan were the only people in the empire who had any practical experience in settling new worlds. Lady Gruum had hired the Chee Company as a planning executive and Meridian as prime contractors, and these were both owned in large part by Clan Martinez.

And so she graciously deigned to make an appearance, accompanied by a loyal entourage of friends, aides, and relations. She was dressed in silken robes of violet and mauve and moved with a faint rustle on tall heels. Her face was fixed in what a human would have thought an expression of round-eyed surprise, and perhaps it was fortunate for all concerned that nature had masked her true feelings at having to visit the home of a social inferior and hustle her fellow guests for money.

Martinez greeted Lady Gruum as she entered the room, and she answered in gracious, musical Daimong tones. Baths and scent had masked the odor of her ever-rotting flesh, though he observed that one strip of dead skin hung off her chin like a little beard. She made a stately progress through the guests and then stationed herself near the drinks table, where everyone would have to encounter her sooner or later.

The orchestra began to play, effervescent tunes suitable for dancing, though no one danced. Martinez greeted Lord Chen as he arrived, and Lord Durward Li and his new, vivacious wife, Lady Marietta.

Lord Durward was a distinguished older Peer who had suffered two profound tragedies in his life: the loss of his son, Richard, at First Magaria, and then his subsequent remarriage. The second had proceeded from the first: Richard was his only heir, and his relatives had nagged him into divorcing his first wife, whom he loved, and marrying another, whom he didn't, for the sole purpose of carrying on his line. Ordinary families might have used a surrogate to carry a child, but families as old and traditional as the Lis would never consider such a thing.

Lord Durward had surrendered to his clan's wishes and made himself miserable with a bride thirty years his junior—though at least Marietta had provided him with a set of twin girls before setting forth on an enthusiastic, zigzag voyage from one lover to the next.

"I'm pleased to have spoken in Convocation for your friend Lady Sula," Lord Durward said.

Martinez clenched his teeth. "It was very good of you," he said.

"It's only a matter of time before she's co-opted into the Convocation," Lord Durward continued. "It should happen as soon as the Credentials Committee issues its report, and that's a mere formality."

"Very good to know."

Lord Durward raised his ginger eyebrows. "Did you hear about the new Lord Koridun? Held the title for less than two months, and now he's dead. Another accident—apparently he slipped on a staircase down on the Petty Mount."

Martinez absorbed the news with interest. The Koridun clan had suffered an unprecedented number of losses over the last few years, all to a series of accidents, including half a dozen lost in a tragic fire.

"I'm tempted to start a sports book offering odds on the next Lord Koridun," he said.

"*Lady* Koridun. The last lord's sister. Though if she has any sense, she'll resign the title before she's formally invested." Lord Durward shook his head. "First a Koridun gets blown up by a volcano on Terra, and then they start dropping dead here on Zanshaa. It's as if the whole family's cursed."

"Excuse me, Captain Martinez," interrupted Lady Marietta. She was a tall young woman with a mass of pale curls and a spray of impish freckles over the bridge of her snub nose. "Do you happen to know if Captain Severin is here?"

"I believe he said he'd attend, but I haven't seen him yet."

"Thank you." She looked at her husband. "I'm going to get a drink. Can I bring you anything, darling?"

"Kyowan and Spacey, thank you."

"Of course." She kissed her husband's cheek, then sped away. Martinez and Lord Durward watched her go, each lost in his own reflections.

A few minutes later Martinez welcomed Junior Fleet Commander Lord Altasz, an aggressive officer who during the war had successfully commanded a long, devastating raid into Naxid territory. Altasz was a squat Torminel with thick fur, brown shading into black, and a pair of dark bubble lenses over his nocturnal eyes, to shade the daylight. To avoid overheating he wore shorts and a vest, but these were far from casual clothes and were brilliant with braid and gemstones. Jeweled billiments were braided into his fur.

Lord Altasz was also a distant cousin of Lady Kosch Altasz, the Corona Club captain who had come in fourth in the Vandrith Challenge race. The career of Lady Kosch had suffered because of lack of patronage in the service, and Lord Altasz would normally have been expected to provide such backing, but apparently the two branches of the family were estranged and had been for generations.

Martinez wished he could somehow bring the two officers into some kind of reconciliation, but he knew better than to get involved in a feud between Torminel. If he were lucky he'd be the victim of only a lashing verbal assault—but if unlucky, he might lose body parts.

If only Lord Altasz weren't such a yachting enthusiast. Discussing the races without bringing Lady Kosch into the conversation was trying on the nerves.

Altasz didn't open with a hello but went straight to his favorite subject. "At least you won your appeal on Orghoder's ridiculous ruling!" he said. He made a disgusted hacking sound deep in his throat. "*Parallax!* Even a cretin like Orghoder should have known that the video in question didn't offer sufficient movement against the background stars to be able to work out parallax!"

"The protest wasn't about parallax," said Martinez.

Again the hacking sound. "Yes, it was about Apogee keeping your best captain out of the match! And now your Captain Kelly has her victory back, Severin won a brilliant triumph, and Apogee got what it deserved."

Martinez smiled. "I cannot but agree with you, my lord."

Even though he was a member of the Ion Club, Lord Altasz was unusually free of the elitism that was so common among the Peers who dominated the racing world. He cared more about the captains' piloting skills than their ancestry, and he spoke admiringly of any Corona captains who didn't happen to be his cousin.

Perhaps, Martinez thought, the war had broadened Lord Altasz's point of view. He would have seen talented pinnace pilots drawn from other than the highest-ranking Peer families, and he might have come out of battle thinking their talent deserved recognition.

"I'm afraid the poor old Ion Club had a wretched season," Altasz continued. "But Fenthag is promising, don't you think? If only we could give her a decent backfield."

Martinez agreed with his lordship, and the two discussed racing for a while. "I'd like to recommend a young sublieutenant to your Coronas," Altasz said. "Sodak. Very talented, has won a couple of Fleet gymkhanas, but has no chance of getting into the traditional clubs."

"I've heard of her. You can sponsor her directly, if you like."

The fur on Altasz's forehead shifted in what Martinez somehow knew was a benign way. "May I? That's very good of you."

"Corona's new," Martinez said. "We don't have a back bench of older members to sponsor new ones. So we're very happy to take your recommendation."

An approving growl issued from Altasz's throat. He touched Martinez's arm. "Do you know," he said, "the other day I heard some of our members complain about how the Coronas were just a gang of mercenary pilots . . ."

Martinez stiffened with indignation. "That's not even remotely true," he said. "We don't pay the pilots a minim, we just enable talented people to race."

Altasz touched Martinez's arm again. "I know, I know. You're going to get that sort of thing for a while, till people get used to you." Altasz's voice was as soothing as a Torminel voice was ever likely to be. "Be that as it may, Lord Captain . . .

one of the people complaining to me was a high-ranking officer in the Fleet—I shan't mention which—and I pointed out that all the Corona pilots are Fleet officers on inactive status, and if he wanted to be rid of competition, all that would be necessary is to employ all of you on some duty that takes you out of Zanshaa's system."

Martinez's mind whirled. *Would they actually* do *that*? he wondered.

Of course, he'd desperately wanted a new posting for years. But how would he feel if he received an assignment not because his talents were appreciated and judged worthy of reward, but as an underhanded means of fixing yacht races? And if he were offered such a posting, would he accept?

Depends, he supposed, on how good the assignment actually was.

Command of a squadron at least, he decided.

"But," Altasz continued, "the officer pointed out that Tork would never give you a real assignment no matter how many yacht races you won. Which of course is true, isn't it?"

Even though he knew that Altasz meant no offense, the words seemed to stab Martinez like a knife. "I won't disagree with your officer friend," he said.

"We shouldn't let talented officers go to waste, not when the Fleet's being expanded," Altasz said. "It's absurd that the service is so given to these feuds!"

One might mention your feud with your cousin, Martinez thought. But he smiled pleasantly and agreed, and then saw someone approaching. "Ah," he said. "Do you know Lord Minno?"

"I have not had the pleasure."

Lord Minno approached. He was a Cree, short and randomly wrinkled, with large prehensile ears capable of funneling the subtlest sound into his aural cortex. His deep purple skin featured darkish patches that sensed light and shade, but other than this crude optical apparatus he was blind and lived entirely in a world of sound. The Cree had evolved on a dark, warm, heavily forested world a long distance from its dim star, but with a greenhouse atmosphere that kept the temperature suitable for life and produced heavy clouds that made the dim star even dimmer. In such an environment a highly evolved sonar was more practical than vision. Martinez had been on Fleet warships optimized for Cree crews, and their control spaces were filled with a bewildering sonic barrage that informed the crew about the status of their ship and the universe outside but were incomprehensible to anyone else.

What disturbed him most was the lack of eyes. Martinez was used to being able to look into the eyes of people to make some kind of basic contact, individual to individual, and more importantly to make certain he was being understood. Talking to a Cree was like talking on an audio link, with no visual feedback, and he never knew whether he was making an impact or not.

"I am pleased to make your acquaintance," said Lord Altasz. It was considered polite to speak first when introduced to a Cree, so that he could hear your voice and be able to recognize you when you spoke. In Martinez's experience that politeness was hardly necessary, since the Cree had a virtuoso memory for voices and sounds and probably could recognize Lord Altasz's distinctive voice from across the reception hall.

"I am happy to know you," Minno said. His voice burbled with good humor. "I hope you will pass on my hearty congratulations to your cousin Lady Kosch on her successful season with the Corona Club."

Altasz's lips twitched, and Martinez caught a flash of fang before his lordship mastered himself. "Should I ever see her," he said, "I will faithfully convey your message."

Martinez intervened to change the subject before Lord Minno could begin an analysis of Lady Kosch's performance during the last season. "Lord Minno," he said, "is here on behalf of the Bank of the High City. The bank is aiding Lady Gruum's efforts to pioneer Rol-mar."

Junior Fleet Commander Altasz was suddenly quite alert. As blunt as if he were addressing a junior lieutenant, he got straight to the point. "What dividends are your bonds currently paying?"

"There are several series available," said Minno, "with yields ranging from three to seven and a half percent. Plus of course there is the opportunity to have yourself, your family, or any designee immortalized by having a city, district, mountain, or other feature on Rol-mar named after them."

"My family has quite enough mountains named after them," said Altasz. "As well as lakes, townships, cities, and at least one glacier covering half a continent. I'm pleased to say I've never seen it." He took Lord Minno's arm. "No, I'm interested in a less symbolic reward."

"Then let us discuss your options, by all means!" The

blind, pointed face turned toward Martinez. "Captain Martinez, would you excuse us?"

"Of course."

The two lords walked away, and Martinez decided that he had earned a drink. He drifted across the room to the drinks table and ordered a Delta whisky from Laredo, an export he was duty bound to drink in public. Next to him, a Terran was drinking a hairy roger.

"You're Captain Martinez, aren't you?" he asked. He was a thick-bodied man with a truly impressive set of side whiskers, so woolly they looked like carpet glued to his face. The whiskers were many shades darker than the curly fair hair on his head, which added to the impression of artificiality.

"I'm Martinez. I don't believe we've met."

"My name is Cosgrove." Which explained the gold rings on his fingers and thumbs, each with its set of winking gemstones, and the thick gold rope around his neck. He was the man who had cornered the market on the gold-bearing seaweeds of Hy-Oso, and everything he wore advertised his product.

"Pleased to meet you," Martinez said. "You live next to Lord Chen, don't you?" He had heard his father-in-law complain, more than once, about his tranquil afternoons being disturbed by Cosgrove's brass band.

"I'm Chen's neighbor, yes. Not that he's ever spoken to me or would cross my threshold." Cosgrove shook his head, then smiled. "You and the Corona Club made me a packet in that Vandrith race. I had you across the board, and once

I saw the odds on Severin I bet him to win and collected thirty-two to one."

"I wish I'd thought to do that."

Cosgrove brandished his glass. "Anyone ever offers you thirty-two to one, take it. Tiny risk, giant reward."

"I'll certainly bear that in mind."

Cosgrove finished his hairy roger and returned the glass to the bar. "Another," he told the waitron. "And at the right temperature this time."

"Are you here to invest?" Martinez asked.

"Depends on the return I can get."

"It won't be thirty-two to one," Martinez said, "but then you're betting on an entire habitable world, so you can't lose over the long run. It's about as safe an investment as you can make."

Cosgrove ran a thick, hairy finger along his furry jawline. "The long run, ye-es," he said. "But if I can make more money by investing right here in Zanshaa, where I can keep an eye on it, then why should I invest in some far-off planet that might not be profitable for fifty years?"

"Chee's starting to turn profits now," Martinez said. "But the real reason to invest in Rol-mar is that the bonds are absolutely safe. Nobody's going to abscond with an entire world. Plus, of course, you could have a city named after yourself, or an ocean, or a mountain."

Cosgrove seemed as uninterested in eponymous mountains and cities as Lord Altasz. "I wonder," he said, "if the bonds are so safe, what percentage I'd get for borrowing against them."

"I don't know why you shouldn't do that," said Martinez. "I could introduce you to Lord Minno, who could answer your quest—" But Cosgrove was already changing the subject.

"You know," Cosgrove said, "I've been meaning to ask you about your house."

Martinez was taken aback. "My house?"

Enlightenment had to wait as Cosgrove's hairy roger appeared. He took a goodly swallow and was apparently satisfied with the temperature. Finally he said, "You have that house on the north side, yes?"

Martinez, Terza, and their family shared a small, cube-shaped palace on the north edge of the High City, perched on a cliff on the northern edge of the granite escarpment. The house was unpretentious as High City palaces went, twelve rooms, pale marble contrasted inside and out by brilliant scarlet carnelian pillars, but it had a beautiful terrace overlooking the Lower Town, with the verdant lawn of a park stretching off into the distance like their own personal bowling green.

The palace was a little small for the sort of entertaining indulged in by prominent Peers, but then he and Terza could always use the Chen Palace, the Corona Club, or for that matter the Martinez Palace, provided they didn't mind subjecting their guests to Roland's schemes.

"Yes," Martinez said, "that's our palace."

"I'll give you seventy thousand for it," Cosgrove said.

Martinez blinked in surprise. He and Terza had paid thirty-two thousand for their home—but then it had suffered during the Battle of the High City from the effects of machine guns, grenades, and a small but fierce fire that had consumed the kitchens and pantry. The repairs and upgrades had cost thousands.

Even so, Martinez had hardly thought it worth more than forty or forty-five thousand. Still . . .

"We're not interested in selling," Martinez said.

"You will if the price is right," Cosgrove said confidently. "How about seventy-five?"

"Do you plan to live in it?" Martinez asked. "You already have a much larger place."

"I'd knock yours down," Cosgrove said. "Then build a newer, bigger palace. A place with real distinction, if you know what I mean."

Martinez felt a little shock at this, shock followed by indignation as he realized that his home did not meet the financier's standards.

"If we wanted a new palace," he said, "we could knock it down and build one ourselves."

"You could," Cosgrove said. "But if you don't do it right, you'd lose a bundle, while if I buy your place, you're guaranteed a profit and any risk is mine." He took a gulp of his drink. "Tell you what," he said. "I'll offer you eighty."

"I'm not interested in selling."

"I won't go higher," Cosgrove warned.

"Thank you," said Martinez, "but I'm really not interested. Would you like to meet Lord Minno? I see that he's free."

Martinez left Cosgrove and Minno together, then remembered the drink in his hand. He finished it in three swallows, then decided he needed another. On the way he encountered an old friend, Lieutenant-Captain Ari Abacha.

"Drink?" he asked.

"Drink?" Abacha said, as if the notion hadn't ever occurred to him in his life. "By all means, Gare."

Abacha was a tall, elegant Terran, with deep black skin and an architecturally perfect mustache. He had risen in the Fleet through efficient use of patronage, which was lucky, because he was so naturally indolent that he would never have been promoted on his own merits. He was superb at anything he actually cared about, but he cared only about sports, women, liquor, entertainment, and clothes. These might be viewed as frivolous pursuits, but Abacha didn't view them frivolously, but with the deep seriousness of a connoisseur.

And he was sometimes useful. Years ago he'd recommended his tailor to Martinez, and the result had been a series of beautiful uniforms that had helped to minimize the anthropoid silhouette caused by Martinez's short trunk and long arms. Martinez hadn't been called "troglodyte" in a long time, at least not to his face.

Martinez got Abacha a cocktail and himself another whisky. "What do you think of Andiron's chances now they've lost Tiana?" Abacha asked.

They discussed football for a while, and then Martinez asked if Abacha was here to invest in Rol-mar.

"Virtues, no," Abacha said. "I have a fellow who handles all that—all I do is sign the papers he sends over."

"Then why are you here?"

Abacha raised an eyebrow. "Well, you *did* send me an invitation. And besides, I'm in hope of meeting—ah, here she is!"

Bearing his cocktail, Abacha ambled over to the side of his paramour of the moment, someone Martinez didn't recognize. Martinez sipped his whisky, stared into the amber depths of his glass, then felt enveloped by a strange sensation of serenity. He wondered for a moment where this perception had come from, and then realized that he'd detected, from several paces away, the scent of vetiver—the "heart notes" of his wife's perfume. He turned and kissed Terza hello. Her scent caressed his senses. She was dressed in the brown tunic of the civil service, with her long black hair coiled like a sleeping serpent at the back of her neck.

"Meeting run long?" he asked.

"Cost overruns at the shipyards at Comador," Terza said. "A whole new set this time. We need an inspector general to sort it out, but one of Ong-at's in-laws is in charge at Comador, and she's resisting sending anyone."

"You know," Martinez said, "if the Ministry would just let my father build *all* their new ships, they wouldn't have these problems."

The Fleet had gone into the Naxid War with under four hundred warships, most of which had been crewed, seized, or destroyed by the Naxids on the first day. Despite a frantic building program, after the last battles the Fleet had been reduced to less than a hundred warships, many of which had been severely damaged.

The Convocation, the Fleet Control Board, and the Ministry of Right and Dominion had decided to increase the Fleet to more than eleven hundred warships, not because they were needed to fight an enemy—there wasn't one—but because organizing another large mutiny amid an expanded fleet would be exponentially more difficult for a subversive to accomplish. Before the war, ships had spent most of their time in dock, which was very convenient for the officers' social schedules, with their receptions, balls, parties, sporting events, hunting or shopping trips to the planet below, and familial duties. Now many of the ships would spend their time in transit from one station to another, again to minimize the chance of subversion within each unit and the Fleet as a whole. Of course, the older officers very much resented being torn away from the comfortable lives they felt they'd earned in the war, and ship duty had become the least popular requirement of the service, though apparently there were still enough balls, receptions, and sport to keep the officer caste at full strength.

Building the new warships, along with the hundreds of support craft necessary to service their needs, was keeping many shipyards busy, happy, and profitable. Though, with the Fleet now consisting of over a thousand ships, the end of this happy time was now in sight, and competition for the last few contracts was fierce. Fortunately, postwar commerce was expanding so rapidly that the dockyards were expected to keep their profits high by building merchant vessels.

Terza approached the bar. "Will I be penalized," she asked, "if I don't order something from your father's distilleries on Laredo?"

"I will quietly disapprove," said Martinez. "But I will remain silent."

Terza ordered a wine from Zanshaa. “Have you been enjoying your afternoon?” she asked.

“I’ve discovered that I’m not cut out for a career in bond sales. The job requires an unrelenting optimism that’s completely exhausting.”

“Have you sold any bonds?” Collecting her wine.

He shrugged. “Who knows?” He glanced out over the room, saw Cosgrove and Lord Minno still in conversation, and frowned. “I see that some of the bonds are offering seven and a half percent. That seems high.”

“There’s a lot of competition for investment these days. Lady Gruum has to attract the investor with higher rates—though I imagine those particular bonds have a very long term.”

“Speaking of investment, I was offered eighty thousand zeniths for our house just now.”

Martinez had expected surprise, but Terza’s expression was thoughtful. “Who made the offer?”

“Your father’s neighbor. Mister Cosgrove.”

She looked across the room, in the direction of Cosgrove’s curly head. “I was offered sixty-five the other day, from Lla-la.”

Martinez blinked at her. “Our contractor?” Lla-la ran a construction company that was working for the Meridian Company on Chee, Parkhurst, and now Rol-mar.

“Apparently she’s got a business renovating homes in Zanshaa City,” Terza said.

“Why didn’t you tell me?”

“It was a casual conversation, and besides, I had no intention of selling.”

Martinez sipped his whisky. "Maybe we ought to sell, if the prices are that high."

"Then we'd have to buy a new place at these high prices," Terza said. "We'd lose a packet. Much better to keep our current home and let it appreciate."

"I suppose."

"And for all's sake avoid these bonds."

Martinez laughed. "I'm the last person to be tempted by my own salesmanship. We learned on Chee who makes the real money from pioneering."

Patronage of a world might be profitable over time, but when a world was developed, it was the contractors, not the patron, who raked in the cash. All the money from Lady Gruum's bond sales would go straight to the Chee Company, and from there to Meridian, and from Meridian to all the subcontractors. And when money went from the Chee Company to Meridian, it was the right hand of Clan Martinez paying the left hand, and the family took its cut at every stage.

If the contractors weren't paid, they sat on their equipment, the planet didn't get its infrastructure, and the whole venture collapsed. Pay the contractors, and all was possible.

"Gareth. Lady Terza."

Severin appeared, wearing his blue Exploration Service uniform and carrying a cup of tea.

"Hello, Nikki." Amusement touched Terza's lips. "I was just advising Gareth not to buy those bonds he's selling."

"Oh." Lifting the tea to his lips. "I know better than *that*. I've got my money with Meridian."

"Very wise," said Terza.

"Lady Marietta was looking for you," Martinez said.

"I saw her. She wanted to invite me to supper after the puppet show."

Terza and Martinez exchanged glances. Severin had a knack for appealing to married women of the upper caste who were, if not exactly unhappy in their marriage, certainly restless within its confines. Together these ladies formed a kind of clique of hostesses who had helped him rise in the world of the High City and contributed to making his puppet shows fashionable.

Poor Lord Durward, Martinez thought.

"I also wanted to mention," Severin said, "that I've been given command of the *Expedition*. I'll be leaving in a few weeks for Harzapid to supervise the final stages of her construction, so I won't be flying for Corona in the next season."

The Fleet wasn't the only service to be expanded after the war. The Exploration Service was building ship after ship and sending them through wormholes to conduct surveys, find new worlds, and expand the empire.

Martinez found himself intrigued by the news. "Do you know," he said, "Lord Altasz just told me that he mentioned to a friend that the best way to keep the Coronas from winning in the next season was to put us on active duty. Do you think that's what happened?"

Severin's narrow eyes grew narrower still. "If it's true, we should start winning more races and put the pressure on."

Martinez raised his glass. "Well. Here's to your new posting."

Severin raised his tea. "Thank you."

"Are you sure you don't want something stronger?"

"Not till after the puppet show."

"Of course."

Martinez looked up over the room and saw Lady Gruum speaking with Lord Altasz and another potential investor whom Martinez didn't recognize, a Lai-own in a convocate's wine-red coat. Nearby, he saw his brother, Roland, talking earnestly to a man named Hector Braga. Braga was a new arrival from Spannan, and he dressed with elegance and walked with a distinctive gliding gait. He had the air of someone with a lot of money, so perhaps he was here to invest in Rol-mar.

Braga and Roland seemed to be deep in each other's counsels. *Do I really want to know what they're up to?* Martinez wondered.

He decided that he probably didn't and turned to order another drink.

CHAPTER 6

"Well, princess," said Naveen Patel, "we've put another Koridun in his tomb for you."

"Much appreciated," said Sula.

Julien Bakshi's hand made a quick little movement toward a pack of cigarillos, then he remembered Sula hated smoking and retracted his hand. "We're happy to do these little errands for you," he said. "But it would be good to know how many more you're going to ask us to put away. There's a risk associated with each one, after all."

Sula wanted to tell them to eradicate the whole family, root and branch. After all, they had tried to kill *her,* or at least some of them had, and she didn't know which ones. Best not to take chances.

But she said nothing, because she wanted to find out what Julien and Patel were thinking.

"If I were with the police, I'd begin to wonder about the death toll," Patel said.

"They've all been pronounced accidents," said Sula.

"Cases can be reopened," said Julien. "But either way, we

can handle the cops. It's an investigation by the Legion of Diligence we want to avoid."

That brought Sula up short. The Legion of Diligence were black-clad fanatics who enforced the strictures of the Praxis, and they had little problem with sweeping up the innocent as well as the guilty.

Not that Sula was precisely innocent, in this case.

"How does any of this fall under the Legion's remit?" she asked.

They sat in Julien's office above his restaurant, conducting a little private business before going downstairs to attend a reunion of a unit of the Secret Army that Sula had commanded during the war. The room wasn't styled so much as *upholstered,* with red leather pinned to the walls and ceiling by brass medallions and echoed by the slightly darker leather of the tall chairs. The brass was echoed as well, by the lamps that sat on Julien's desk and hung from the ceiling. A window allowed him to view the restaurant below. Even though Julien wasn't smoking, a harsh tobacco odor tainted the air.

Julien and Patel were leaders of the cliquemen, gangs whose businesses lived in the twilight zone between law and necessity, and members of an unofficial commission that ruled Zanshaa's underworld. During the war, Sula had needed soldiers unafraid of mayhem and experienced in delivering violence, and the cliquemen had provided the Secret Army's shock troops. In Julien's case, his position had been inherited from his father, Sergius, who had taken Sula's amnesty after the war and retired. Julien had not been given the opportunity to retire: Sergius had made sure that his son was invested with all his own authority before he left.

As for Naveen Patel, he'd been raised to his current prominence at a young age by virtue of everyone senior to him being arrested and executed. Very few cliquemen survived long enough to die in bed.

Patel shook the glossy black hair that fell over the back of his collar. "The Legion make their own rules, of course," he said.

Chair leather creaked as Julien leaned forward. "But more than that," he added, "an old Peer family with so many casualties . . . accidents or not, people are talking about it. There was even a piece on the Empire Three broadcast last night. I wouldn't be surprised if some ambitious Legion investigator took an interest. Aren't they supposed to be charged with upholding the establishment?"

Julien's hand made a dance toward the cigarillos again, then again withdrew. His pointed face betrayed a degree of longing.

"You didn't used to smoke so much," Sula said.

"I've got more responsibilities now."

"Go ahead and light up. It couldn't smell any worse in here."

Julien rolled his chair toward the window, opened some panes, then returned to his desk. The sounds of assertive voices and clattering glassware came through the window. Julien reached for the packet of cigarillos and a desk lighter in the shape of a stylized Torminel head, the look of relief on his face profound.

"Look, princess," said Patel, "we accounted for the Lord Koridun who was leading the charge against you. You took care of the sister yourself. We've worked outward from the immediate family into the cousins, at least a couple steps in all directions. We even had to reach into a mental hospital to find one of them. Who knows if the survivors ever learned of the family's vendetta against you."

The Koridun family displayed extreme behavior even for Torminel, and their history was full of madness and violence. Their grudge against Sula had been obscure, and their attempted revenge had been baroque and expensive and had pursued her as far as her posting on Terra. So she couldn't expect the Koriduns to behave rationally, not even under threat.

"What you're asking me to do," Sula said, "is wait around to see if one of them tries to kill me."

"Princess," said Patel, "we're not asking you to do anything."

Julien blew smoke in the direction of the open window. "We'll do whatever you want us to do," he said. "You know that. We'd just like to suggest that you weigh the odds carefully before any further action."

"After all," said Patel, "you're going to be a convocate now. You've got to be careful."

Julien grinned, and he gave an expansive wave of his cigarillo. "Our own convocate! Whoever expected that to happen, back when we were all hiding in Riverside from the Urban Patrol?"

"I'll be one vote in over six hundred," Sula said.

Patel laughed. "Hardly worth bribing, then!" he said.

Calculations spun through Sula's mind. She mentally reviewed the family tree of the Koriduns, the dangers of illicit action, the chances of an investigation by the Legion of Diligence. She didn't think the Legion's intervention was likely, but it was significant that Patel and Julien had brought it up. They were looking for reasons to reconsider the vendetta against the Koriduns.

That, not the possibility of Legion intervention, loomed in Sula's calculations as the most important fact.

"All right," she said finally. "Why don't we let the new Lady Koridun continue to breathe for a while."

Julien nodded. "I think it's for the best. She probably has no idea what her—third cousin, was he?—was up to."

"But if they kill me," Sula said, "you'll finish them all, won't you?"

"It's a promise!" Patel laughed. "But it won't come to that. You've got more to worry about from your fellow convocates than from the Koriduns."

Probably true, Sula thought. The Convocation had never impressed her with their collective intelligence, but they were very good at maintaining their own privileges and sniffing out anyone who seemed out of place in their world, and Sula was certainly in that category. If anyone was likely to catch a whiff of her past, it would be those who were born to the role that Sula had only assumed.

"Shall we go down?" Julien said. "It sounds as if everyone's here."

Sula rose from her creaking leather chair. She had worn her undress uniform without her medals, not wanting to be too formal for this crowd, and she tugged her tunic into place as Patel opened the door for her.

They went down the stairs, and a cheer rose as they came into the main dining room. This was a reunion of the Bogo Boys, a unit named after an indestructible toy. They were her most deadly unit, one she'd saved for missions requiring large-scale mayhem. Most of them were cliquemen drawn from Terrans and other species, with the rest being folk who were simply very good at violence, or who had a specialty that was very useful, such as the ability to improvise munitions.

She was never going to introduce Lamey to any of these people. She was too afraid they might get along.

Sula walked among them and greeted them all by name and felt a rising sense of comfort and affinity. She had fought with these warriors, and stormed the High City, and shared tragedy, peril, and triumph.

She felt more at home among the Bogo Boys than she ever would in the Convocation.

THE LORD SENIOR'S chambers had a sweet woody scent, something like sandalwood. Or perhaps the scent drifted from Lord Saïd himself, the result of some strange botanical longevity treatment—for now that Sula saw the Lord Senior at close range, she saw how ancient the man truly was. His skin was the color of teak and covered by a webwork of fine lines that seemed to be incised across and inside one another, so that no piece of skin larger than a pinhead remained unmarked. He appeared so frail that it seemed a miracle that he could bear the weight of his red ceremonial cloak, and he was so shrunken that his big, beaklike nose seemed not to quite belong to him, but rather to someone far more imposing.

"Will you have tea with me, Lady Sula?" His voice was soft, very different from the authoritative tones he used when he sat in the Lord Senior's seat. Sula wondered which of the two was a performance, the gentle host or the powerful leader, and then considered the possibility that they both were.

"I would be honored, Lord Senior," she said.

Lord Saïd waved a hand over a desk carved with fruits and other symbols of abundance. A Cree servant appeared to take the order for tea, and a decrepit Daimong, nearly as old as the Lord Senior himself, came to lift the heavy cloak from Saïd's shoulders and place it on a stand nearby.

"Please sit down, my lady." Saïd sat behind his desk, and the chair adjusted to his body with a soft hydraulic hiss. Sula chose another chair suitable to the Terran physique and faced Saïd across his desk. The Lord Senior leaned forward and folded his hands in front of him.

"I'm very pleased to report that the Credentials Committee has reported and found no obstacle to your becoming a member of the assembly," he said. "You will be officially co-opted into the Convocation in three or four days' time, depending on how quickly we can conclude the debate on Lord Tork's proposal to build new battleships."

Sula wanted to burst into astounded laughter. "*Battleships?* I hadn't heard anything about this."

She'd seen the Fleet's battleship squadron die in fire at First Magaria, lost along with thousands of crew, and she had emerged from the battle convinced that the very size of the vessels simply made them bigger targets. While their armament was formidable, a single hit would destroy them just as surely as it destroyed a smaller vessel.

"The Fleet Control Board issued a recommendation last month," said the Lord Senior. "They suggest a single battleship at each major Fleet concentration, and a squadron of four here on Zanshaa."

Disgust warred in Sula with amusement. She suppressed a bitter laugh. "I'm sure the senior officers would find them very comfortable," she said. "Luxurious quarters, dining rooms, gymnasiums, steam baths, ballrooms . . . practically a world of their own, a little High City they can carry with them from one post to the next."

A smile touched the corners of Saïd's eyes. "Are you suggesting that the Praxis II-class ships are intended not for a military purpose, but only to feed the fleet commanders' vanity?"

"Your lordship expresses my thoughts so well."

The Lord Senior shook his head. "Ah. A shame you won't be able to express your views in Convocation, since you won't become a member until afterward."

"Should your lordship desire it, I can testify as an expert witness."

Lord Saïd spread his ancient hands before him on the desk and directed his gaze downward, as if he found his cuticles to be of sudden interest. "I shouldn't want you to begin your career with *two* wrangles with the Supreme Commander. Convocates might wonder if they truly want to admit a quarrelsome member. And while others might find these disputes entertaining, I have to watch such things from the podium, and it quickly grows tiresome."

Sula shrugged. Lord Saïd might have found it tedious, but *she* would have enjoyed scuppering Lord Tork's plans. "I hope *someone* will speak against the idea."

The Lord Senior gave a sigh. "A number will, I'm sure. And you have friends in the assembly—you can give them whatever information you possess."

"I will do that, thank you."

"Bear in mind, though, that the Control Board asks for no new funds, merely that the funds already in the budget be reallocated. That will make the Convocation less likely to question the measure. Ah. Here is our tea."

The tea arrived in a distinctive eight-sided teapot, cobalt blue on a creamy tin oxide glaze, and painted with pictures of languid Terran ladies in centuries-old fashions. The teacups had a different woman's elegant profile on each of their eight sides. The tea's smoky aroma, rising into the air as the Cree servant poured, complemented the room's sandalwood scent.

"I hope you like the tea," Saïd said. "A first cutting from my estates in the Lossing Highlands. I find it relaxing after a long day."

Sula looked at her cup with interest. "This is an old Guraware pattern, isn't it?"

The Lord Senior gave a sagacious nod. "Indeed, yes."

"Guraware hasn't used this pattern in ages. What is it—five or six hundred years old?"

Saïd's eyes widened in surprise. "Seven hundred. You are quite the authority."

"I have a small collection of old Terran porcelain."

"From your posting on Earth, then?"

"Yes." She turned to the Cree servant. "More of the honey, please. Unless you have cane syrup?"

The Cree answered in musical tones. "I'm afraid not, my lady."

"Honey then, and lots of it."

Sula had to prompt the Cree once more before the tea was sweetened to her satisfaction. Also on offer were two shelves well laden with a variety of pastry. Lord Saïd looked at it in appreciation. "I believe I can recommend the lemon cake," he said.

Sula had lemon cake with her tea and expressed appreciation of both. The Cree servant departed, leaving the tea trolley behind.

Lord Saïd put down his fork with a decisive air. "The reason I asked you to join me," he said, "is that I wanted to discuss your committee assignments."

Sula likewise set down her fork and thereby signified her willingness to engage in serious business. "It seems to me," she said, "that I could be useful on the Fleet Control Board."

Which would be a direct invasion of Supreme Commander Tork's domain, a challenge to the unquestioned authority he'd assumed since the war. Taking him on in person was something she'd very much enjoy.

Again the smile touched the corners of Lord Saïd's eyes.

"I'm afraid there are no vacancies on the Control Board at present."

"Anything else to do with the Fleet?"

Lord Saïd made an equivocal motion of his hands. "There are technology subcommittees and so on, but our technology is so standardized, and has been for so many centuries, that the subcommittees meet only once or twice each year. No, I was thinking of the Court of Honor."

Sula blinked at him. "I'm afraid I'm unfamiliar . . ."

"It's similar to the Credentials Committee, but for those who have already been issued credentials. The court investigates accusations against convocates and can expel them from the Convocation if the charges are serious enough."

Sula probed the idea carefully. "Wouldn't you want—I don't know—lawyers? Judges? Legal scholars?"

"I thought your experience with military courts of inquiry might be of use."

"I'm afraid I have no such experience." She had been promoted so quickly during her service that she'd never had the opportunity to sit on a formal court. In her commands any offenses were straightforward—inebriation and fighting being the two most common—and her summary judgments were equally forthright and included shooting two people in the head and arranging the assassination of the military governor of Zanshaa, her immediate superior. Which was what had led to the problems with the Koridun clan, which in turn had required her to shoot the sister of Lord Koridun, then ask her friends in the cliques to finish off the others.

All of which, come to think of it, would make interesting charges should *she* ever be brought up before the Court of Honor.

She didn't think she wanted the Court of Honor—it seemed like a good way to make new enemies, for one thing, and for another she didn't fancy spending her days sorting through reports detailing the squalid doings of convocates.

Unless, of course, she could catch Tork at something. *That* could be fun.

"I think you would be ideal for the court," Saïd said. "It's quite informal, and it's not a court of law, so legal knowledge isn't necessary—though of course we have legal advisers on staff."

Sula decided she might as well concede. "Very well," she said. "If you think I would suit."

"Splendid! I think you'll do very well." Saïd looked down at his empty desk as if he were reading the contents of a paper. "Now as for further assignments, I don't suppose you know anything about agriculture? There's a vacancy on that committee. Also the Oceanographic and Forestry Committee."

"I'm already on one board for which I have no qualifications," Sula pointed out. "Is there something on ring stations, antimatter and power generation, satellites, or wormholes?"

"Nothing available, unfortunately." He raised his eyebrows. "Banking and Exchange?"

Sula spread her hands. "I suppose I know a little bit more about money than I know about agriculture."

Lord Saïd smiled in satisfaction. "The committee doesn't meet very often, usually only to receive reports from the Imperial Bank. That and the Court of Honor should serve to acquaint you with the workings of the Convocation and give you a little seasoning—and afterwards, as vacancies become available, perhaps we will be better able to take advantage of your expertise."

"I'll look forward to that." In the last few years Sula had got used to meaningless activity, and now it appeared her work at the Convocation would be equally pointless. At least it would have the virtue of novelty.

Until it got boring, that is.

None of this, she thought, was anything like the war. Then, her every decision *mattered,* and life and death, victory and defeat, hung in the balance.

In the Convocation, nothing actually seemed to matter. The deliberative body that ruled hundreds of billions of souls seemed to be detached from the reality of the empire it governed, floating in an unreal world of custom, protocol, and privilege. Even to the Lord Senior, the useful employment of a new member was of less importance than the quality of lemon cake.

It was as if she found herself in a room filled with sleepwalkers.

But, she thought, it was useful being awake in a room of sleepwalkers. She could get away with a lot.

Saïd regarded her with his solemn brown eyes and smiled. "I would like to take an old man's privilege," he said, "and raise an issue that you might consider impertinent."

"My lord," said Sula, "I can't imagine you being impertinent. Not ever."

Saïd's smile turned impish. "You be the judge, my lady," he said. "I would like to raise the issue of your marriage."

An astonished laugh burst from Sula. This was the absolute last thing she had expected.

"Am I getting married?" she asked. "No one told me."

"Your duties as a convocate will raise your profile," Saïd said. "I may be the first to raise this issue, but I will scarcely be the last. And of course you bear also the duty to have children and continue the Sula line. Normally a husband is required in these circumstances."

Sula did not give a damn about the line of the Sula clan, or a husband either. "Your interest in these matters is . . . flattering, I suppose," she began, "but—"

"If you will bear with me," said Lord Saïd. "I have a grand-nephew, Eveleth, whose prospects are good and whose financial situation is secure, in fact nothing short of exemplary." He cleared his throat and continued in a measured, tactful tone. "I believe your own fortune is, well, not the equal of many in the Convocation, and an alliance with Eveleth would establish your future, and that of your clan—"

Sula was not willing to be purchased by someone's grand-nephew, not even if he were the richest lord in the empire. "Lord Senior," she said. "I have absolutely no interest in marriage at this time."

Lord Saïd inclined his head gracefully. "I apologize for any intrusion into your private affairs, Lady Sula. You know best, I'm sure."

Sula left the Lord Senior's office with her head spinning. She had never imagined Lord Saïd as a marriage broker, nor that he would pimp some sad relation of his . . . Did he think her that desperate, that she'd consider such an offer?

She had hidden herself and her private life away in the Petty Mount, and no one had cared; but now she was going to be a public figure. *I may be the first to raise this issue, but I will scarcely be the last . . .*

She would have to give this matter greater thought.

But not now. She had other worries.

TWO DAYS LATER, as she listened on her console to a languid debate about Lord Tork's battleships, she saw Lady Tu-hon walk past her office door. Lord Saïd had assigned Sula an office even though she wasn't technically a convocate yet, but then it wasn't much of an office: two airless, sunless rooms in the back of the Convocation complex, equipped with two desks and two terminals. The paneling was scarred, and the carpet smelled of mildew. On the walls were a pair of undistinguished paintings drawn from the imperial collection, one a still life of a platter of food with a roasted Hone-bar phoenix at its center, the other some planet or other viewed from its moon. Neither moon nor planet looked particularly hospitable.

Sula had been surprised to discover that she would have to pay for her staff out of her own resources. Convocates were supposed to be rich and easily able to afford a suite of servants and assistants. While Sula could afford a staff, it still bothered her that she would get precisely as much information and access as she was willing to pay for.

She wondered if she could hire experts part-time. Zanshaa City had more than a dozen universities, and surely some of the professors, or their more promising students, would be willing to consult. Lawyers for cases before the Court of Honor, and economists for Banking and Exchange. The latter especially—she'd looked at a few of the Banking and Exchange reports, and they were written in a bewildering, arcane language that seemed designed to baffle comprehension. There were references to *multitier practitioner-oriented collaboration on economic resilience and hyperbolic discounting* and *nonparametrics*. A translation would seem to be in order.

Or she could do the work herself, something few other convocates would have considered. But she had nothing better to do with her time, and she had always enjoyed research. The Banking and Exchange reports were too baffling, but the Court of Honor seemed to conduct its business in nonspecialized language. The archives were available, and so she'd spent the better part of two days trying to find out exactly what it was that got someone expelled from the Convocation.

Not bribery, apparently. Numerous accusations were made that convocates had been offered money or gifts in order to sway their votes, but most of the cases had been dismissed. The majority of the remaining cases were so egregious that the convocates had often been caught, tried, and executed by the Legion of Diligence before the Court of Honor had got around to removing the accused from the rolls.

Insolvency, on the other hand, would get a convocate ejected with relative speed. The one thing that alarmed the Convocation more than anything else was the sight of one of their number absolutely without money. Most of the fortunes behind the great families were so immense that it was hard to picture it all vanishing within a single lifetime, but the Naxid War had flattened the finances of at least sixteen convocates, all of whom were deprived of their seats. As for the rest who lost their money, Sula assumed that gambling on a vast scale was involved. She at least could understand the principle the Convocation seemed to invoke in these cases: if you couldn't manage the colossal sums you inherited, surely you wouldn't be much use in managing an empire.

Convocates could also be ejected for lesser crimes that embarrassed their peers and endangered the dignity of the assembly. Assault. Intoxication to the point of losing your clothing and staggering in broad daylight down the Boulevard of the Praxis. Killing your children's nanny with a shotgun while actually aiming at your spouse. Calling a fellow convocate a "lying sack of pus" on the floor of the assembly. Hiring an underage prostitute as your administrative assistant. Visiting a High City Peers' academy and paying the boys to flog you, then after being discovered by the school's chancellor, claiming you'd been kidnapped by a gang of twelve-year-olds. Filing false expense reports. Stealing from the Treasury, which of course also got you killed.

Such actions, however, remained fairly rare. Most convocates who were purged were removed for "illness"—which seemed a polite euphemism for senility, madness, hopeless addiction, or catatonia. Convocates served for life, Sula found, or until they lost their minds. Or their livers.

These researches explained why she was in her office to see

Lady Tu-hon pass by her door. Lady Tu-hon was the presiding judge of the Court of Honor, and Sula thought she might as well introduce herself, and so she followed the Lai-own convocate down the corridor to another office. Sula was about to follow Tu-hon through the door when she heard a voice from the office, and the voice froze Sula in her tracks and set her nerves leaping in panic. She restrained the impulse to bolt.

Gareth Martinez.

Her feelings for Martinez were so very strong, and so very conflicted, that by far the easiest course was to never hear the voice again. He had made her love him, and then abandoned her for a command and the opportunity to be the next Lord Chen.

Fury and frustration throbbed high in her throat, a deep ache with every beat of her heart. She despised him. Yet she had not found anyone who compared to him, and she could not stop thinking about him.

"I'm pleased to see your ladyship," said that familiar Laredo accent. "I know you spoke to Lady Gruum and Lord Minno."

"Yes," said Tu-hon. "And I've spoken to my banker."

"May I offer your ladyship refreshment?"

"Thank you. Perhaps a tisane?"

And then the realization came: the Laredo accent belonged not to Gareth Martinez, but to his brother, Roland. Who not only resembled him physically but had nearly the same speaking voice and provincial accent. And, as a convocate, would of course have an office here.

Now Sula directed the fury at herself. Mortification

flamed across her face at the realization that she had allowed herself to be frightened by a phantom.

"I have come here to express a deep personal chagrin," said Lady Tu-hon. "While I should love to invest in Lady Gruum's Rol-mar enterprise, and while my banker tells me that my finances are otherwise healthy, at present I am embarrassed for cash. *Illiquid* was a term he used, in my opinion a dreadfully vulgar word."

"I'm extremely disappointed to hear it," said Roland. "Did your banker suggest remedies?"

"I could take out a loan, of course. Though my interest payments would be so terribly close to the interest paid by the bonds that there would be precious little in the way of profit."

"Is there no friend to whom you might apply?"

An herbal odor wafted from the door, accompanied by the clink of porcelain: Lady Tu-hon's tisane was being poured. "I am desolated to report," said Tu-hon, "that this *illiquidity,* if I may so term it, has become very common among my friends. All their cash reserves are employed in speculation. Some are experiencing difficulties in meeting their bills, not from want of resources, but because their resources are all . . . taken up."

There was a moment of silence while Roland and Tu-hon contemplated this desperate picture. Porcelain clinked. Sula fought to suppress the alarm and terror that had so foolishly seized her.

"I hope I am not being presumptuous in suggesting a remedy," Roland said finally.

The throbbing pulse faded from Sula's ears as she listened to what came next, a proposal by which Roland offered to loan Lady Tu-hon eighty-three thousand zeniths in order for her to purchase, at a special discount, a hundred and three thousand zeniths' worth of Rol-mar bonds, the loan to be repaid when Tu-hon was in funds. The mathematician in Sula appreciated the employment of prime numbers, but what truly intrigued her was that the arrangement was an oral agreement only. Nothing was being written down, there were no terms for interest or repayment. There was only the word of the head of the Tu-hon clan that the loan existed, and that she would sooner or later have to pay it back.

So that's how it's done, Sula thought. She knew that bribery existed, and she'd accepted presents herself from those who wanted to do business with the dockyard on Terra when she was in command there. But even though she'd accepted presents, she hadn't considered herself under any obligation to do what her donors asked.

But a hundred thousand gold-rated bonds, Sula imagined, were not handed out free of obligation. Roland had bought Lady Tu-hon's vote, just as Lamey had bought Sula's.

As the chief judge of the Court of Honor offered well-bred thanks, Sula ghosted back down the hall to her own office, where she considered the matter while the debate over Tork's battleships played over her console. After a few moments she saw Tu-hon pass by her door again, and again she rose and followed.

"Lady Tu-hon?" she called.

"Yes?"

Lady Tu-hon was short for a Lai-own, and perhaps in compensation wore a tall hat on her flat, feathery head. Her eyes were orange, and she wore a matching body wrap beneath the gold-braided wine-red jacket of a convocate. Her jewelry was simple but exquisitely made, gold and rubies to echo the colors of her jacket.

"I'm Lady Sula. Lord Saïd is assigning me to the Court of Honor, and since we're going to be working together, I thought I'd introduce myself."

Tu-hon inclined her head. "I'm honored to meet such a celebrated warrior."

Sula looked at her. "I wonder if there's any current business before the court? I haven't been able to find any."

"There's none at all." She spoke in a tone of finality, as if she never expected any business to be brought before the court, ever.

"I'm pleased to hear that virtue and prosperity reign so completely in the Convocation," Sula said. *Along with bribery,* she thought.

There was a moment of silence as the orange eyes sharpened. "Come join me," Tu-hon said, and walked with Sula to her own office. Tu-hon rated an office of three large rooms, with soft lighting, furniture that gleamed softly with leather and metal, and yellow celadon vases that held the bright golden faces of marigolds—marigolds that formed a deliberate contrast with the lavender vases, over which drooped the exotic blossoms of irises. Sonorous chiming noises rang over the sound system. A staff of seven moved between the outer two rooms with silent efficiency.

"May I offer you something, my lady?" Tu-hon said. "Coffee, tea, wine?"

"Tea would be nice, thank you."

Tu-hon's personal office was decorated with more flowers and the usual portraits of ancestors. Tu-hon sat beneath a picture of an ancient, obese figure in a convocate's jacket. Behind the grandee were flowing draperies parted to reveal a tropical landscape, and on his lap was the plan of a city, presumably one he'd built or had named after him.

All this wealth on display . . . and yet none in Tu-hon's pocket.

Sula took it all in and decided she might as well make an effort to influence the upcoming vote.

"I was listening to the debate in the assembly," she said. "Lord Tork's battleships. A very bad idea."

"The *Fleet* is a bad idea," said Lady Tu-hon. "We're spending all this money, and for what?"

Sula was so surprised that it took her a moment to formulate a reply. "The Fleet managed to protect the empire from the Naxids," she said.

"The Naxids weren't invaders," said Tu-hon, "they were *mutineers*. They couldn't have seized any ships from the Fleet if there weren't a Fleet to begin with."

Again Sula hesitated. "That's an interesting point of view," she said finally.

"Please understand," said Lady Tu-hon, "that I say nothing against your own skill or courage, or those of the other brave officers who sacrificed so much in the name of the Praxis. I know enough about you to know that you earned every one of your decorations—the whole empire knows it."

All except Tork, Sula thought.

"But," Tu-hon said, "I find the Fleet to be a ridiculous, expensive anachronism. A thousand ships? To guard us against *what,* exactly?" She waved a hand. "Where does it end?"

Sula grinned. "With battleships, apparently."

Lady Tu-hon waved her hand again. Peg teeth flashed in her muzzle. "Let Tork have his ridiculous floating palaces. They're as useless as the rest. At least the expansion will soon be over, and we can try to bring things back to normal."

The tea arrived, wheeled into the room in a complicated metal machine that hissed and gave off a cloying herbal scent. The tea itself was green and frothy, and Sula tasted it cautiously. It was bitter, and she looked for sweetener but didn't find it.

Tu-hon sipped her tea, then placed her cup emphatically on her desk. "I will be very pleased to vote to bring you into the Convocation, Lady Sula," she said. "You bear one of the great old names, and I'm sure you are gratified that your traditional privileges have been restored."

"I am," said Sula, "though I seem to have been doing pretty well without them."

"Breeding tells," said Lady Tu-hon. "Your family's history is one of mastery and greatness. Of course you have been a success."

Sula rubbed the scar tissue on her right thumb. "Your ladyship is very kind," she said.

"And once the Fleet is built up to strength, I hope we can do without all the unnecessary emergency regulations."

Sula looked at her in surprise. "I'm sorry," she said, "but of course I was with the Fleet during the war, and I don't know what ordinances were passed. Are any of the emergency regulations still in effect?"

"They mainly have to do with commerce," Tu-hon said. "So much of our trade was captured or destroyed by the Naxids that the Convocation wished to rebuild. So as an emergency measure, and in large part to cover the expenses of the rearmament, the Convocation removed the tax on commerce and replaced it with a tax on equity."

"Yes," Sula said. And she understood immediately: *This bitch just doesn't want to pay her taxes.* Her taxes, which would include any profit on her hundred-thousand-zenith bribe.

"One percent," Sula said. "A tax of one percent."

"An outrage," said Lady Tu-hon. "Where in the Praxis does it authorize such a tax? No such tax was ever permitted by the Great Masters while they lived."

Sula strove to recall the Praxis Theory she had studied for the ideology section on her lieutenant's exams. "The Praxis says nothing about types of taxes," she said, "but only requires they fall on all citizens equally."

"It falls unjustly on Peers," Tu-hon said. "We are required to do so much as it is—we build roads, hospitals, schools. We are expected to support our clients, to look after them when they're sick or find them jobs when they're out of work."

"It seems to me that's an element of our privilege," Sula said. She was beginning to enjoy the debate, though she wished it were with a personage more substantial than this short-legged, overdressed whore. "We have the privilege of looking after our clients—much better than having the state doing it, after all."

"Even better if the taxes fall where they fell before," said Lady Tu-hon. "On the miserable peddlers who ship goods from one star system to the next. Fifteen percent on all, from the moment the cargo touches the ring station."

"Wouldn't that be taxing the people who contribute most to prosperity? It's not cheap, after all, to ship goods from one star to the next."

"Each world should be self-sufficient in goods anyway," Lady Tu-hon said. "That *is* in the Praxis. And if you ask me, interstellar commerce is generating far too many profits, and entirely for the wrong people." Her lips drew back from her peg teeth, a silent snarl. "Have you *seen* some of them? No breeding, no elegance. Some little jumped-up Cree approached me the other day with a ridiculous offer to buy my palace at an inflated sum—the palace that has belonged to my family for *twelve hundred years*."

"If imperial commerce is taxed into submission," Sula said, "then there are going to be a great many people out of work. I hope your ladyship will be willing to support them."

"Any who are my clients will receive my full attention," said Tu-hon. "And the rest can sell their overpriced High City palaces and go into some other line of work."

WELL,* THAT *WAS INTERESTING, Sula thought as she returned to her office. She wondered if Lady Tu-hon was quite stable, or whether the tea contained some kind of Lai-own intoxicant.

Probably, she thought, Tu-hon was just very passionate on the subject of conserving her money.

She decided she should find out as much as possible about Lady Tu-hon and had just made herself tea and settled into her office chair to begin her research when there was a knock on the door.

"Good afternoon, my lady," said Lamey. "I brought you a gift for your office."

He was dressed in white, with discreet gold braiding. He glided into the room and placed a vase on her desk.

"Meissen," Sula said.

"That's what the fellow at the salesroom said."

Her fingers itched to take hold of the vase, but she didn't want to lunge for it. Any gift from Lamey would of course come with strings attached, and she didn't want to get her fingers tangled up in those strings without knowing where they led.

Instead she told the terminal to lower the volume on the battleship debate.

"Go ahead," Lamey said, looking at the vase. "You know you want to touch it."

Sula leaned back in her chair and viewed him with what she hoped was cool objectivity. "What's this for?"

Lamey's brows arched. "I can't give you a simple present?"

"You don't give simple presents. Not that a vase millennia old is simple."

Lamey shrugged. "There's a vote coming up after your

swearing-in, concerning awarding contracts for cooling systems on the ring station on Zarafan. We'd be obliged if you'd vote in the affirmative."

Sula laughed. "The Convocation *votes* on that sort of thing? I would have imagined that the Ministry of Contracts and Works would let the contracts."

Lamey pulled a chair in front of Sula's desk and sat. "The minister has his favorites. We have ours."

"And if *our* side wins, the cooling systems will actually get built?"

Lamey's brows came together. "What do you mean?"

"I mean," Sula said, "the systems won't be substandard crap that will break down or poison anyone or cook them alive or kill them?"

"I—"

"Because I've been on those stations, and on ships, and my life has depended on whether such systems functioned as designed."

Lamey spread his hands. "The systems will be up to spec. They'll be inspected before and after. The question is whether a crony of the minister gets the job, or one of our friends."

"Well," said Sula, as she reached for the vase. "Long live friendship."

Not that she wouldn't research that contractor thoroughly before the vote came. Anything the least bit shady, and she'd vote the other way.

It would serve Lamey right for lying to her. If she were to be corrupted by a lobbyist, she needed him to be an honest one.

The vase was cool and smooth to the touch. White, with a

brilliant, eye-catching design of flowers and birds in a flaming color palette. Sula inverted the vase and viewed the Meissen crossed swords trademark. "Hard-paste," she said, "made in Germany, but in imitation of Japanese *Kakiemon*. The enamel paints were the first developed in Europe, by Johann Gregorius Höroldt. They called this style *Indianische Blume*."

Lamey gave an admiring smile. "See, the fellow in the salesroom called it 'Indian flowers,' whatever those are. And he didn't know that other stuff."

"Maybe I should become a dealer."

Lamey pointed at the vase. "Is that a bird? Do birds in Germany have antennae?"

"That's a quail, and they aren't antennae, they're a kind of feather crest."

"I knew you'd have the answer." The admiring grin broadened. "I love how you know these things."

Facts are easy, Sula thought. *Facts are easily learned, easily ordered, easily deployed when you need them.*

Life is the thing that's hard, she thought.

"I should take you out to dinner to celebrate your becoming a convocate," Lamey said. "Lots of great restaurants in the High City. Six or eight courses of the finest food, cocktails, five different kinds of wine . . ."

Sula was amused. Lamey had always mistaken quantity for quality, particularly if it came with a large price tag.

"You forget I don't drink," she said.

He waved a hand. "Whatever you want. Wine, hashish, fruit juice, doesn't matter. And then we go to the club, hear some music, go dancing."

It had to be admitted that Lamey was an excellent dancer. He'd made a point of learning after he'd got his limp fixed.

"Maybe," Sula said. Deliberately she stirred cane syrup into her tea. "But I don't know whether we should be seen too often in public."

Lamey raised his eyebrows. "Are you ashamed to be seen with me, Earthgirl?"

She looked at him levelly. "It's not about shame, it's about trust."

Lamey pretended astonishment and laughed. "You say that, and here I am with a whole other present for you!" he said.

She cocked an eyebrow at him. "What do I have to do in exchange?"

Lamey shrugged. "That's pretty much up to you. It's your first client."

"Ah. Hah." Sula was amused. "Who is he?"

"She. A Terran named Mahru Tiffinwala."

"And why is Miss Tiffinwala in need of a patron?"

"She's from our old neighborhood in Spannan. Her patron of record lives on Spannan, and so does *her* patron, and so on up to Lady Distchin, who lives here, but Lady Distchin won't see her, because when did Lady Distchin ever do anything for any of us?"

A suspicion began to settle in Sula. "Miss Tiffinwala doesn't need a job, does she?" Because she wasn't about to hire one of Lamey's spies for her office.

"No, she's a baker and is doing all right. What she needs is a *divorce,* but her husband is with the Urban Patrol and he and his mates have been harassing her ever since she moved out with the kids."

"How do *you* know her?"

A shrug. "I didn't till a few days ago. But my mom knows her mom, and my mom sent me a message. Said that since I was such an important politician now, I could have this taken care of."

Sula considered this. Word that Lady Sula was taking an interest in the case should convince the husband and his friends to back off, and if that didn't work out, there were always the Bogo Boys. In many parts of the Lower Town, police walked in fear of the gangsters and not the other way around.

"What's involved?" Sula asked.

"Changing patrons is a legal procedure—you have to get the old patron's agreement, and then the new client swears to accept you as a new patron, and you swear to do well by her. You need witnesses for that."

"Will the old patron agree?"

"Don't know why she wouldn't."

"Well." Sula surrendered. "Send Miss Tiffinwala here, and I'll talk to her."

Lamey grinned. "Very good! You'll be a grand Peer yet, with a lapdog and a thousand clients."

Sula sipped her tea. The aroma rose in her senses. "The problem is that I can't afford to offer my clients a lot of help, let alone give them jobs or set them up in business. I haven't got that much money."

Lamey gave a rippling shrug and made an equivocal gesture with one hand. "It can all be arranged, Earthgirl."

"My lady," Sula corrected.

"'My lady.'" Sula could hear the ironic quotes around the words. Lamey drummed his fingers on his knee. "Aren't you going to offer me tea?"

"I just poured the last of it. But the electric kettle is on the table in the corner."

"You don't have servants for that?"

"I don't *need* servants. I'd much rather do everything myself. That way I know it's done right."

She sipped her tea again. Lamey's lips formed a pout when he realized she wasn't going to make his tea for him, then he decided to forget about both the pout and the tea.

"How are your committee assignments?" he asked.

Sula looked at him narrowly. "How do you know I've *got* committee assignments?"

"Because it's on the Lord Senior's posted schedule for the day. '*Meeting with Lady Sula re: committee assignments.*'" He gestured at Sula's terminal. "You could learn a lot about the Convocation just by looking at where all the important people are during the course of the day."

Sula told him about the Court of Honor and the Committee on Banking and Exchange. He had to have the Court of Honor explained to him.

"Well, that's good, right?" he said. "If we can get Lady Distchin accused of something, maybe we can get her tossed out of the Convocation."

"It better be something good," Sula said. "The Court of Honor is lenient with common crimes such as bribery."

Lamey seemed impressed. "Yes? How do you know?"

"I just overheard Roland Martinez giving Lady Tu-hon a hundred-thousand-zenith bribe."

Lamey laughed out loud. "Well, she's on our side, then!"

"Our side?" Sula looked at him. "Maybe it's time you told me what 'our side' is."

"The side that wants to get rid of the Distchins and find patrons for Spannan who won't suck up all our wealth."

"Except," Sula pointed out, "that you seem to be allied with people who have nothing to do with the Distchins or Spannan and couldn't be expected to care. So what else are you up to?"

Lamey considered the question, then nodded. "One looks for allies, you know."

"One does," Sula said, her tone half mocking.

"You may have noticed that all sorts of people are making money now."

"There's a lot of it around," Sula said. "The other week I got a ridiculous offer for my building in the Petty Mount."

"During the war the tax law got changed," Lamey said. "It became a lot more profitable to engage in long-distance trade, and people in a position to do that got rich. So did the people who built their ships and who made the goods they were shipping from place to place. The government was also handing out a lot of money for war work, and the work was so urgent they didn't care so much who the money went to. Not all the money was made by the high-caste Peers, but by people further down the scale, like Clan Martinez." Lamey laughed. "A lot of it is even made by *commoners*."

"Lady Tu-hon wants to change all that."

Lamey laughed again. "I don't doubt it—though maybe being on the receiving end of Lord Roland's cash will change her mind."

"That's something I *do* doubt. She seemed very committed to her point of view."

"Well, maybe Roland's after her for some other project."

Sula decided she'd had quite enough of the Martinez clan. "And these moneyed people? What do they want, and why do they need *you* to get it for them?"

A pleased smile crossed Lamey's features. "They want the same thing you and I want," he said. "They want the old Peer families to get out of the way."

"Ah. Hah." Sula wasn't sure what degree of amusement was the proper response.

"See, whenever you want to pass through a door, there's some old Peer standing there with his hand out." Lamey illustrated with a cupped hand. "You pay a toll just to go about your own business."

Sula wanted to laugh. "I think you and Lady Tu-hon have a great deal in common. You both hate paying your taxes."

"When I pay a tax to the government," Lamey said, "I get services in return. When I have to pay off a Peer with a percentage of my business, I get nothing."

"What *is* your business, these days?"

Lamey waved a hand. "You're seeing it in front of you right now. I'm just a kind of agent for other people."

"So your indignation is secondhand." She considered

him, sitting opposite her in her dingy office, gleaming in his white suit. "And what's your plan for getting rid of the high-caste Peers, exactly?"

"We're trying a number of ideas," Lamey said. "We're not committed to a single course of action. Some Peers can be subverted, by making them a part of the program. If they have stock in a transport company, they'll want to see that company succeed."

"Wait a minute." Sula waved a hand. "Isn't that what you're complaining about—having to give Peers a piece of your business—and now you're doing just that, voluntarily?"

"In the first example," Lamey said, "I get nothing in return. In the second, I get a vote in the Convocation."

Sula was silent.

"Plus," Lamey continued, "it's not a bribe, it's an *investment*. They give *us* money, not the other way around, and get stock or bonds in return. The investment is worth nothing unless they help make it a success." He gave a reassuring nod. "And not all high-caste Peers oppose the program—Lord Chen, for example, makes a lot of money on shipping."

"True," Sula said, "but if you expect Lord Chen to join with you in sidelining his whole caste, I think you'll be very disappointed."

"Roland says that Lord Chen prefers money to class solidarity," said Lamey.

"Really?" At which point the gears of Sula's mind seemed to seize into a clashing halt. Because at Lamey's words an idea hurtled into her thoughts with the impact of a speeding bus: *Roland bought Terza Chen for his brother, Gareth.*

Which explained so much. Lord Chen must have been hard hit by the rebellion, with ships taken by the enemy or isolated by the Naxid expansion. It had become clear to Sula just that day that the most embarrassing thing possible for a Peer was to lose his money: the Convocation would have been so mortified that they'd have expelled him rather than have to look at him every day. It's one thing to be morally bankrupt, but financially—she could envision the shudders rippling throughout the Convocation. But if Roland appeared, checkbook in hand, to help him out? That would explain why Captain Gareth Martinez had gone, in a single day, from proposing to Sula to engaging himself to Terza. She wondered if Roland had given him any choice.

Of course *he had a choice,* she thought. *There was nothing stopping him from saying no.*

Nothing but Roland's money, and a father-in-law on the Fleet Control Board who could give him postings, and Lord Chen's sister, Michi, who promptly employed him as tactical officer. Plus a beautiful, accomplished wife who could bring him into the High City's most elite society.

"What's the matter?" Lamey said. "You look as if you've just been hit by a cannonball."

Sula's mind whirled. "I'm wondering. Lord Chen." She realized her words were as disconnected as her thoughts, and she tried to compose herself. "What you said makes sense."

Lamey's brows tented. "You know something?"

"Did Roland save Lord Chen's shipping business during the war?"

Lamey thought about it. "Roland didn't say. It didn't come up."

Sula took a drink of lukewarm tea while she tried to control her flailing thoughts . . . and her flailing heart. *Change the subject,* she thought. She gulped the tea, then blurted the first thing that came into her head.

"I've got to wonder how you're planning not to be killed," she said.

Lamey spread his hands. "I'm not killed yet," he said.

"But you're attempting a social revolution at the highest levels of the empire. One wrong step and the Legion of Diligence takes you and cuts off your head."

Lamey shrugged. "I've committed no crime."

Sula smiled. "I don't believe that's objectively true."

He offered an indulgent smile. "I've committed no crime *on Zanshaa.* And I won't. As you've pointed out, it's *normal* to cut high-caste Peers in on your businesses, and in this case it's not even *my* business, but those of my associates. As I said, I don't *have* a business. All I do is put friends together with other friends."

Sula found herself wanting to shake him out of his superiority, dent his invincible confidence. "Something bad happens, somebody reports a crime, who do you think the Legion is going to interrogate? Lord Chen? Lady Tu-hon? Or a suspicious-looking nobody from Spannan with lots of money and a background that won't stand up to investigation?"

He stiffened. One hand traced the braided seam of his trousers.

"It's to be hoped," he said, "that my powerful friends will intervene."

"I wouldn't count on anyone named Martinez. Or Chen. Or—" She smiled. "Who else do you know, exactly?"

Lamey scowled. "I know *you,* my lady," he said. "War hero, the heir to a great name a couple thousand years old, and perfectly placed to lead the charge against the old guard. After all, they can't accuse *you* of being a parvenu, can they?"

The smile froze to her face as Sula spoke through clenched teeth. "My background won't stand up to investigation, either."

"Who's going to even *think* to investigate it?" Lamey asked. "You're a far more perfect Sula than Caro ever was." He plucked at his braided trousers and smiled. "But if you're that concerned, you should take care that I'm not interrogated. The Legion plays rough, and though I'll do my best to keep your secret, I can't promise to hold out under torture."

Black rage settled onto Sula, and a savage response was poised on her lips. *Better not,* she warned herself, and instead adopted tones of dismissal. "Thank you for the lovely vase," she said. "Rest assured that the cooling systems on Zarafan are safe."

Lamey glared at her for a moment, then decided his message had been delivered.

"Always a pleasure, my lady," he said, and glided away, leaving Sula in her chair, an empty teacup in her hand.

CHAPTER 7

"Well, genius," said Martinez. "What do you have?"

"I made a picture!"

"Let's look at it, then."

Gareth Martinez the Younger, age seven, trotted to where Martinez was brushing his hair at his dressing table and handed the picture to his father. The paper was still warm from the printer. Martinez viewed the picture with the eye of a connoisseur.

"It's an excellent house," he said.

"It's not a house!" Young Gareth said. "It's a spaceship!"

Martinez held the picture at a slightly different angle. "Oh, of course!" He pointed at a figure in a corner of the structure. "Is that your handsome father?" he asked.

"It's me! It's me when I'm a captain!"

Martinez regarded the picture with unfeigned admiration. "And a very good likeness, Chai-chai. Does the picture have a name?"

"'Me When I'm a Captain,'" the boy repeated.

Martinez viewed his son with unconcealed admiration.

Young Gareth, he considered, had acquired the most attractive features of both parents. He had his father's olive skin and was tall for his age and thus stood fair to achieve his father's height without the unfortunate short legs of the Martinez family; but his face had a full measure of his mother's chiseled beauty. He was quite simply a lovely child.

Plus he'd inherited his father's brains, which was by far the most impressive thing about him.

Martinez returned the picture to his son. "Make sure you send it to me," he said. "I'll put it on my wrist display so I can admire it at my leisure."

He returned his attention to the mirror above the dressing table, gave his hair one last brush, and then did up the final buttons on his viridian-green dress uniform tunic. His medals rang lightly against one another. He brushed a bit of lint off his shoulder and then picked up his gloves from his chest of drawers and walked with Young Gareth to the palace entry hall.

There Terza awaited him, dressed in the brown tunic of the civil service, her long black hair drawn over one shoulder. Leaning against her was their daughter, Yaling, who had just enjoyed her third birthday. Young Gareth ran ahead.

"I want to show Mei-mei my picture!" he said.

Martinez crossed the floor and was enveloped in the scent of the flowers that brightened the hall in their tall vases. He kissed Terza's cheek while Yaling was shown her brother's drawing. Yaling had a round, ruddy face, and a smile that turned her lips into a perfect V shape, almost a caricature of delight. She was dressed in a fluffy jumpsuit with a pattern of birds in flight, and when she turned her eyes to Young Gareth's picture, she seemed properly impressed.

"Have you heard the news?" Terza said. "Cosgrove's gone smash."

Martinez looked at her. "What does 'gone smash' mean, exactly?"

"Bankrupt. Finished. Fled the High City just ahead of his creditors."

Martinez smiled. "Your father will be pleased. No more brass bands."

"Brass bands!" Yaling called in disapproval. "Brass bands!"

Martinez's smile broadened. "She's absorbed her grandfather's opinions."

"Brass bands!" Yaling stomped a foot, crushing all brass bands beneath it.

"Excellent!" Martinez approved. "Down with brass bands!"

"She's very vocal today," Terza said.

"Our genius has a new picture," Martinez said.

"Me when I'm a captain!"

Terza viewed the picture with harassed amusement and was about to offer praise when Yaling hurled herself bodily upon the paper and tore it from Young Gareth's hands. "Brass bands!" she shrieked. "Brass bands!" She flopped on top of the picture and began to tear at it with her hands.

"Mei-mei!" cried Young Gareth. Martinez bent and swept his daughter off the floor, but she retained the picture in one fist until her brother managed to snatch it away. Young Gareth was red with fury. Yaling pointed at him and chortled.

"Don't worry," Terza said to her son. "You can print another copy."

"I'm acrimonious!" Young Gareth said. Martinez had been trying to expand his son's vocabulary and took a brief moment to congratulate himself on his success.

"Brass bands!" Yaling laughed.

After a brief interval, order was restored. Young Gareth stalked off to print another copy of his picture, and Yaling's nurse was summoned and took possession of the child. Martinez and Terza were left alone in the entrance hall.

"Well"—Martinez offered a laugh—"Yaling's developed a fine sense of sibling rivalry."

Terza untangled the medals on Martinez's chest that had been disturbed by the squirming toddler. "Didn't Cosgrove buy Rol-mar bonds?" she said. "If Roland chases him down in time, maybe he can get them cheap."

"I seem to remember Cosgrove planned to borrow against them. Besides, what would Roland do with Rol-mar bonds?"

"Sell them at a profit, I imagine."

"It was hard enough to sell them the first time."

He turned at the sound of footsteps on the marble floor and saw Doshtra, the Daimong butler. "My lady," said Doshtra to Terza, "Lord Roland has sent a message to say he is very slightly delayed." His bell-like voice echoed slightly in the lofty space of the hall.

"Thank you, Mister Doshtra."

Doshtra made his way out, heels clicking, alternately passing through shadow and sunbeam as he moved through columns of light flooding through the clerestory. The palace was in the Devis mode, which featured long, functional, clean lines and interlocking geometrical shapes. In general Martinez found the Devis mode dull, but his own house was something of an exception: the polished scarlet of the carnelian pillars along the walls, with their blushing shades of red, made an interesting contrast to the pale gold marble and echoed both the sunset and the sunrise. Terza had found or commissioned artworks that provided splashes of brightness on the muted color of the walls. She had also provided the brilliantly colored cloisonné vases that filled the air with the scent of their flowers.

Bullet holes in the walls had been filled with gilded, star-shaped plugs and added a random element to the building's geometric perfection. Martinez thought of them as the constellation of uncertainty, a reminder that nothing was as solid as it seemed.

Terza had performed splendidly at creating a home, particularly as she'd started with a building wrecked during the war. Probably, Martinez thought, interior design was one of those things that Chens had been bred to do over countless generations.

Still, there were only so many long straight lines and right angles that Martinez could bear, and in his own office and study he'd equipped himself with comfortable, overstuffed furniture with barely a straight line to be seen. Above an oval, scalloped desk he'd placed his portrait by Montemar Jukes, who used to be the official artist aboard his cruiser *Illustrious*. He couldn't put himself or his ancestors on public display for fear of provoking mirth in well-bred Peers, but at least in private he could contemplate his past glories.

"You know, Gareth," Terza said, "I wish you wouldn't call Chai-chai a genius all the time, particularly when he's in the room. We don't want him to get a swelled head."

Martinez shrugged. "Well, he *is* a genius. And besides, I know *I'm* extremely gifted when it comes to brains, and *I* don't have a swelled head."

Terza raised an eyebrow. Martinez ignored it.

"If Gareth doesn't have a healthy ego," Martinez said, "he could be crushed. He's going to be insulted and despised simply for being my son. Just as I'm insulted practically every time I win a yacht race, or lose one, or make a suggestion to one of my social superiors, or for that matter open my mouth. No matter what Gareth does or who he is, his ancestors won't be good enough."

Despising their inferiors, he thought, was yet another thing the high-caste Peers were bred to do. Like interior decoration, like wearing clothes well and knowing the best wines, like retaining traditional pet names for family members, like "Chai-chai" for the eldest son and "Mei-mei" for the youngest daughter, retaining them even though the names were in a language that hadn't been spoken in thousands of years.

Like collecting a toll from everyone around them. Like treating their clients with condescension. Like dismissing talented inferiors by calling them "clever," as if displaying cleverness were a minor social embarrassment.

Terza's expression turned cold. "He's *my* son as well," she said.

Yes, he thought, *you're a Chen, and Chens aren't despised.*

But you're a Chen whose father sold her to a social inferior, and the other Peers might pity, but won't forget. Or forgive.

He knew better than to speak these thoughts aloud. Instead, "You know what people are like. They'll look for weakness to exploit, and my ancestors are Chai-chai's weakness."

"I think you're too sensitive."

"Sensitivity is a family trait," Martinez said. "It's from a lifetime of being insulted. And my father being insulted, and my brother and sisters being insulted, sometimes by the same folk who come to us for money."

"I had another call from Mister Yao at the academy," Terza said.

Nicely done, Martinez thought. Because he'd been feeling the rising tension that signaled the beginning of an argument, and he didn't want to argue with Terza, not least because she wasn't the problem.

"You know," he said, "perhaps it's time we considered taking Gareth out of that stuffy old school. Give him a private tutor who can take him along at his own pace."

"Mister Yao said that you'd contacted him to dispute one of Gareth's grades."

Martinez waved a hand. "I think that Yao has a limited imagination. I had to explain to him the originality of Chai-chai's concept."

"For all's sake, Gareth," Terza said. "It was an exercise about *vowel sounds*. There *aren't any new ones.*"

"Have you heard Chai-chai's sounds? They sounded pretty novel to me."

Terza gave him a serious look. "We don't want Gareth to

think everything's going to be easy for him. And we don't want to raise a conceited child."

"He's the Chen heir—conceited goes with the territory."

She looked at him, eyes imperceptibly narrowed. "I'm a Chen heir, too. You think I'm conceited?"

Careful, Martinez thought. Terza, he reminded himself, was not the problem.

"I think you do an admirable job of overcoming the disadvantages of your birth," he said. Turning away the argument, he hoped, with a joke.

In the pause that followed, a door opened and Khalid Alikhan entered. Alikhan was Martinez's orderly, one of the four servants allowed him by the Fleet, and wore the uniform of a master weaponer, which he had been before Martinez had snatched him out of his impending retirement. Alikhan offered Martinez the experience of his thirty years in the weapons bays and had in the past provided a conduit between Martinez and the enlisted personnel under his command. If Martinez ever had a command again, he hoped Alikhan would provide the same service.

Alikhan cut an erect figure with iron-gray hair, a goatee, and the waxed, curling mustachios favored by senior petty officers. He had a uniform cap under one arm and carried a polished mahogany casket in his gloved hands.

"Lord Roland's car is just turning the corner, my lord," he said. "I brought your Orb."

"Thank you, Alikhan." Martinez drew on his own gloves, then opened the casket and brought out the Golden Orb. When Martinez took the weighty object in his hand, both

Terza and Alikhan braced in salute, shoulders back, chins raised to expose the throat.

"At ease," Martinez said. For all that it was flattering to see a roomful of important people snap to the salute when he entered, it was more than a little embarrassing to be saluted in this family setting.

He closed the casket, and Alikhan tucked it away while offering the cap he'd carried under his arm.

"Your cap, my lord."

Martinez took the billed cap and placed it on his head. Alikhan surveyed his uniform critically and apparently found no flaw.

"Have a pleasant afternoon, my lord," he said.

"Hardly." Martinez sighed, and then Alikhan opened the front door and Martinez and Terza stepped into the sunlight. They walked through the front garden, ablaze with summer flowers, and the front gate just as Roland's chocolate-brown Hunhao limousine drew up to the curb and the passenger door rose with a smooth electric hum.

Roland reclined in the back, his convocate's tunic unbuttoned and a glass of Delta whisky in his hand. "Forgive me for not saluting," he said. "I've decided the only way to cope with the afternoon is with alcohol. Unless you prefer hashish, and I've got that, too."

"I don't want to melt down completely," Martinez said. "I'll stick with the whisky."

"Do you have any wine?" Terza asked.

Roland gestured toward the liquor cabinet. "I carry a surfeit of delights. There's also some pastry."

Martinez and Terza helped themselves. The door rolled down, and the car pulled away on silent electric wheels.

Roland lifted his glass. "So we'll have to endure paeans to the Supreme Commander for the whole afternoon and evening. Do we think we're up to it?"

"I'm hoping for a cloudburst," Martinez said.

Roland looked up at the clear viridian sky, with barely a wisp of cloud in sight. "I think you're going to be disappointed."

Martinez thought of the day devoted to the wisdom, leadership, and glory of Supreme Commander Tork and sighed.

"It's bound to be disappointing either way," he said.

"I WAS THINKING," said Martinez, "of arriving late, during Tork's address. That way things would come to a standstill while everyone saluted me."

"In front of an imperial audience?" Roland said. "People would think you're very rude."

"They think I'm rude anyway."

Terza's comment was incisive. "Best not confirm their suspicions, then."

Her husband sighed. "Best not."

Today was the seventh anniversary of the Second Battle of Magaria, the action that was viewed both as the pinnacle of Lord Tork's career and the climax of the Naxid Rebellion. That another battle at Naxas had been necessary before the end, and that Tork had not been present, was an element that had been minimized by Tork's partisans—according to them it was just a little mopping-up action. But the Battle of Naxas had been a desperate, hard-fought battle by two fleets at the ends of their tethers, and that the official account viewed it as merely a skirmish deeply offended Martinez, who remembered all too well how vicious the fight had been: antimatter blooms flaming in the night, squadrons darting like flights of birds, and the astounding synergy between him and Caroline Sula, maneuvering their squadrons independently but somehow together, as if they were linked by telepathy . . .

The Shaa conquerors had loved prime numbers, and so the seventh anniversary of the fight was bound to be well observed in any case, but this particular anniversary was grander than it might have been. Tork was putting on the biggest show of his postwar career, an enormous event taking place in Zanshaa's largest athletic stadium. And that, Martinez thought, was because for the first time since the end of the war he was on the defensive.

His sister Vipsania's documentary series *War of the Naxid Rebellion* had been broadcast to all the empire, and it had been a very thorough work indeed. So far as Martinez could tell, the series revealed as much of the truth as the censors permitted. Martinez had been interviewed, as had Sula, and Lord Chen, his sister Junior Fleet Commander Michi Chen, Lord Saïd, and Tork himself. Even Severin had his moment, explaining his decisions to shift the wormhole at Protipanu and remain behind to spy on the Naxid force. Each political decision had been recalled by those who had made it, with reference—when it existed—to the transcript of the meetings or the appropriate session of the Convocation. Between combat, executions, and suicide, none of the Naxid leaders had survived, but many records had, and the recollections of aides and surviving relatives made their actions comprehensible, if no less vicious.

Martinez had been on shipboard during much of the war and isolated from the political decisions that had sent him arrowing from one part of the empire to the next, and he found that part of the series fascinating.

But as interesting as that was, Martinez derived his greatest satisfaction from the beautifully realized combat scenes, in which both sides' tactics were lucidly drawn and then analyzed by officers and historians. Without explicitly saying so, Tork's celebrated victory at Second Magaria was shown to be a slugfest akin to a pair of drunken bar fighters windmilling at each other in a dark alley, a brawl redeemed only by Caroline Sula's disregard of orders to maneuver her own lead squadron brilliantly against the enemy. Tork's unimaginative performance was shown in contrast to the more innovative tactics used by Martinez at Hone-bar, Kangas at Antopone, and the triumvirate of Martinez, Sula, and Michi Chen during the final battle at Naxas.

Martinez had been deeply gratified by this, and more than a little surprised that his sister had actually bothered to notice he'd made any contribution at all.

War of the Naxid Rebellion was a superb work of history and had been watched by tens of billions of the empire's citizens. It had also brought Martinez and Sula to the public's attention once again, this time such that Martinez could no longer walk down the street without being stopped by admirers.

Another result of the series was a delay in the release of the Fleet's official history, as more and more rewrites were demanded in order to refute the video documentary. Martinez was perfectly confident that the history and rewrites were both doomed, since only a fraction of those who watched the video would read the dry history, and fewer still would be convinced by its arguments.

But still, Tork's prestige was enormous, at least among his own caste, and now Zanshaa was required to devote a day to celebrating his achievements, and such was his status that anyone of importance was obliged to attend whether Tork hated them or not. The Commandery would be emptied of Fleet officers, the Convocation was in recess to allow its members to attend, and the ministries were on holiday. After the official celebration, restaurants, theaters, clubs, and High City palaces would be open for a series of receptions.

As a decorated Fleet officer with the rank of senior captain, Martinez had been invited to the great stadium event and many of the receptions, a whole series of engraved invitations on exquisite creamy stock arriving over a series of weeks, and requiring handwritten replies written on equally well-engraved paper. Fleet and Peer politesse required that he attend, but at least he could spend the dreary day with his friends and family, in Roland's stadium box.

But first he had to get to the stadium, and since thousands of others were on their way there, the limousine was bogged in traffic almost from the moment it left the High City. During the long delay Martinez found himself drinking more whisky than he intended, and he felt a shimmer of vertigo as he stepped from the vehicle in the convocates' parking area. Terza took his arm, perhaps to steady him. With only a few minutes before the event was scheduled to begin, the party hurried to a tunnel that led to the exclusive boxes reserved for convocates. Vipsania waited at the tunnel entrance and favored Roland with an impatient glare that would have frozen him in his tracks if a lifetime's exposure to his sisters hadn't rendered him immune.

"You're late," Vipsania accused.

Roland buttoned his red convocate's jacket. "On the contrary," he said, "I'm just in time."

"Hold on." Vipsania raised a hand to stop them from entering the tunnel. They watched as she reached into her bag, produced a hand comm, and spoke a few words. Then she gestured them onward. "I've arranged a reception," she said, then gave Roland another glare. "Though you almost spoiled it."

Her pale, pearlescent gown shone like a beacon in the dark tunnel, and Vipsania held them to a deliberate pace until they entered the stadium and bright afternoon embraced them. Martinez blinked in the sunlight and found himself on the floor of the arena, surrounded by what—from his perspective—looked like near-vertical walls of seats climbing halfway into the sky, each tier aswarm with a population of bustling, ever-more-distant citizens. The stadium held two hundred thousand people, and it looked as if every seat was filled. Vaguely martial music played on the public address system and echoed with varying degrees of delay from different parts of the looming structure.

Still following Vipsania, Martinez and Terza walked on the grass past a series of enclosures set up for convocates and their guests, and separated by gated, breast-high wooden pickets. He had forgotten he was carrying the Orb until the convocates around him began leaping to their feet and bracing to attention. He gestured at them by way of giving them permission to sit, but more and more people were jumping to attention, and the stance spread out like a sea of dominoes falling in reverse, each tile picking itself up from a scattered pile and hopping into its assigned place. Only those in government service were required to salute, but others joined anyway.

Then the shouting and applause began, a vast sound that came roaring down like an avalanche from the highest rows of the stadium, a sound that seemed to snatch the air from Martinez's lungs . . . Martinez looked over his shoulder at the podium, to see if Lord Tork had made an appearance and they were cheering *him,* but he hadn't and they weren't. The great howl of the crowd went on and on, and Martinez felt his heart surge along with it. He raised his hand with the Orb and waved it, and the sound grew in volume. His heart raced, and he felt the blood blaze beneath his skin. Terza's hand tightened on his arm. He was aware that Vipsania had drifted to his side.

"You arranged this?" Martinez said.

Vipsania's eyes were wide. "I arranged for a claque to lead cheers when you entered the stadium. But there is no possible way I could have arranged *this.*"

Martinez kept waving and the crowd kept cheering. Terza held his arm and looked up at the crowd, her eyes ablaze with pride. After the cheers had gone on for several minutes, Martinez thought it might be time to try to put an end to the demonstration—the convocates standing braced in his vicinity were showing every sign of impatience at having to remain on their feet—and just as Martinez made up his mind to gesture for everyone to resume their seats the sky was shattered by a vast cracking explosion, and as his nerves leaped as he looked upward, half expecting to see the sky split asunder with antimatter fire . . .

The first report was followed by another, and then a third, and then Martinez realized the city was being overflown by shuttles dropping down from orbit, cracking overhead faster than the speed of sound. He leaned toward Vipsania.

"Now don't tell me you arranged *this*?"

She shook her head. He could see her startled pulse beating in her throat.

Cargo shuttles had been common on Zanshaa in the years after the war, for just before the Naxid occupation, the government had blown apart the world's antimatter-generation ring, which held the upper terminals for Zanshaa's space elevators. The ring had separated into pieces and floated into higher orbits, and loss of easy transport to and from the surface had severely handicapped the Naxid occupation. After the war, the largely undamaged components of the ring were steered back to their proper orbits and reassembled, and the elevator cables reconnected; but it had taken nearly three years, and during that time Zanshaa's commercial connections with the rest of the empire had been limited to the cargo capacity of the shuttles.

Before the skyhooks had been repaired, sonic booms were occasionally heard, but they were distant, the shuttles expending their velocity high in the atmosphere before coming to a landing at one of the five airfields surrounding Zanshaa

City. The city had never heard anything like *this*—nothing like these foundation-shaking, window-shattering blasts.

More sonic booms lashed out, seven altogether, one for each year of peace. The falling thunderbolts had stunned the crowd into silence, and Martinez took the opportunity to wave the convocates into their seats. They sat with expressions of relief, and the movement spread from there throughout the arena, the dominoes tumbling again . . . More booms crashed out, but this time it was drums, and a military band marched out onto the stage, Torminel in green uniforms with white piping and tall shakoes, and huge kettledrums on carts drawn by burly recruits, each thumped by three drummers at a time. The show had begun.

Can't escape the brass bands today, Martinez thought.

He followed Roland to his box, where one of Roland's aides greeted them and opened the gate to allow them to enter. There were servants to prepare food and drink, and an assortment of Martinez clients and allies. Also present was Martinez and Roland's second sister, Walpurga, whose presence only served to emphasize the similarities between the siblings: the olive skin, the dark hair and eyes, the sturdy bodies and long arms, and facial features rather more imposing than comely.

Martinez kissed Walpurga on the cheek and chose a chair near Roland. "It's been thirteen months since Lady Sula was accepted into the Convocation," he said.

Roland was looking at the band and its kettledrums. "I haven't been counting."

"Then, you said that my time would come." Martinez gestured at the vast crowd. "If not now, when?"

Roland was irritated and made a point of ordering a drink before replying. "They don't co-opt people based on popularity, you know. Popularity would mitigate *against*—"

"If not now," Martinez repeated, "when?"

"Even if you get in the Convocation," Roland said, "you'll be bored out of your mind in the first week. You have no idea how dull it is."

"I'm bored out of my mind *now*. I'd prefer a new way of being bored to any of the old ones."

Roland gave him an angry look. "You're a decorated hero known throughout the empire," he said, "your yacht club just won its third series trophy in a row, you were just cheered to the echo by two hundred thousand people, and all you can think of at this instant is that Lady Sula got into the Convocation before you?"

"This has nothing to do with Lady Sula," Martinez said virtuously. And then he looked up and saw the woman herself, Sula, walking past on the arm of Lord Durward Li. Her brilliant green eyes glittered from her pale face as she gazed at him, and his heart leaped into his throat and choked the words that lay poised on his lips.

The air between them seemed to shimmer, perhaps reflecting the light of history.

And then she was past, and Martinez stared after her, aware only of the blood that beat thick in his veins and the shackles of sorrow that had seized his mind with links of unbreakable steel.

CHAPTER 8

Sula managed not to break stride as her glance crossed with Martinez's. Heat flared suddenly beneath her collar. She managed a nod, and he half raised a hand in greeting, and then Sula was past.

She hadn't disgraced herself, Sula thought, because she'd expected to see Martinez here. He had the Golden Orb, after all, and she'd be expected to salute him. He would of course be here along with his grasping, pushing, scheming family, and it had been a matter of course that they might meet at some point.

Obviously Martinez had not given the matter equal consideration. She was gratified by the stunned look on his face, as if she'd just walloped him in the forehead with a mallet.

Reflecting on that moment as she walked with Lord Durward, she found more disquieting the reaction of Terza Chen, who had stood with a drink in her hand toward the back of the box, and whose dark eyes had turned from Sula to her husband, then back again as she absorbed the tableau that fate had spread before her. Terza's lovely, highly trained face betrayed no change of expression, let alone the gloating triumph that Sula imagined lurked behind her eyes.

"He's fled on his yacht," said Lord Durward, "though I can't imagine where he thinks he can run to."

Sula's mind tried to reel in the last few moments of conversation. "I'm sorry," she said. "The band drowned you out. Who are you talking about?"

"Cosgrove, the seaweed man," said Lord Durward. "He's bankrupt, and he's running for it." He snorted. "As if *that* will help. If you ask me, it's unfortunate that the tradition of honorable suicide seems to be falling into disuse."

"I'm afraid I don't know much about Cosgrove," Sula said. She was still thinking of Terza Chen's eyes, and what shadows might lie behind them.

"Not a lot to know. Pushy little beast, made a lot of money, then lost it all." Satisfaction glowed in Lord Durward's voice.

"Here we are," Sula said. Macnamara, in dress uniform as a constable first class, opened the gate to Sula's box and braced in salute as she entered. Her other three servants were present, led by Engineer First Class Shawna Spence, the third member of Action Team 491 that had formed the core of the Secret Army during the bitter ground war fought in the capital. Also on hand was Sula's Cree chef, offering a tray of canapés, and Master Clerk Ty-fran, a Lai-own veteran who served as her personal secretary.

Though Sula had a firm prejudice against having servants cluttering up her life, the last two had proved necessary as she'd eased into her existence as a convocate. Dinners and receptions were her new way of life, and a cook was a convenient accessory. A secretary had been required to handle, or at least supervise, the vast correspondence entailed by her new position, to file all the documents that passed across her desk, and to keep track of her appointments.

Because she was poor by High City standards and a little sensitive about having to fund her own staff, she was happy to draw the cook and secretary from the Fleet and let the Fleet pay their stipend. They allowed a captain four servants, after all.

The air smelled of sunlit grass and grilled meats. Her guests for the afternoon were largely from the military, though not always from the *regular* military. Fer Tuga, the elderly Daimong who during the war had achieved a deadly reputation as the Axtattle Sniper. The gaunt survivor Sidney, with his upturned mustachios, deep hacking cough, and his pipe of hashish, who had designed cheap, easily manufactured guns for Sula's Secret Army. Lieutenant Lady Rebecca Giove, who had served as second officer aboard Sula's frigate *Confidence,* and who—without the benefit of service patronage—had been unemployed since the Supreme Commander's malevolence had sent *Confidence* into dock for an unnecessary refit.

A new acquaintance was Ming Lin, who as a pigtailed teenager had been a half-crazed bomb thrower for the Secret Army and was now a graduate student at the Zanshaa College of Economics. She wore her pale rose-colored hair in a tangled updo and wore as well the commoner's black drill college gown with the soft round cap of a graduate student—had she been a Peer, the gown would have been silk and the cap would have had a pompon. The cap was tilted at a stylish angle, and she held a highball in one hand. Sula employed Lin part-time as an adviser for her work on the Committee for Banking and Exchange. She was most useful as a translator, rendering the specialized jargon used in economic reports into a language Sula could actually understand.

A counterpart to Ming Lin, Ashok Suresh served as Sula's legal adviser on the Court of Honor. He was a law professor who had joined the Secret Army early in the occupation, had been severely wounded escaping a hostage roundup, and had spent the rest of the occupation being shuttled from hospital to clinic to safe house, all under different identities, just ahead of the Urban Patrol. During the course of these wanderings he'd lost both legs to amputation, and his family to the executioner. His medical expenses were ongoing, and he appreciated the stipend Sula sent him for his contributions to her work on the committee.

For reasons of prudence Sula hadn't invited the cliquemen who had fought alongside her, or Lamey either. A public association with criminals would help her with neither the public nor her fellow convocates.

However, Sula had invited two guests who were not associated with her military career: her client Miss Tiffinwala, a robust and cheerful baker who provided pastry; and Lord Durward, simply because she liked him and at present he seemed very lost. Sula supposed most men of Durward's age would delight in a young, beautiful wife, but instead Lady Marietta seemed only to unmoor him. Both had answered Sula's invitation, but only Durward had turned up. Sula didn't know where Marietta was, and possibly Lord Durward didn't either.

Lord Durward and his wife—his *first* wife—had always been kind to Sula, and their son had been a captain whom Sula had admired, and one who (unlike the others) hadn't tried to get rid of her at the first opportunity, to replace her with relatives or the children of cronies. So, though human warmth wasn't really her specialty, she did her best to be kind in return.

Except for Lord Durward, everyone in Sula's box was a member of her official family. Each occupied an assigned orbit around her, and some of those orbits—those of Spence and Macnamara—were close indeed. With those invited within the pickets of her official enclosure, she could relax.

For everyone else she wore her dark red convocate's jacket, but otherwise cultivated a military appearance. The jacket was cut to resemble an officer's tunic, and she wore her senior captain's shoulder boards and—on a day as formal as this—her medals. The public knew her as a military leader, and she preferred to underline that fact rather than appear as a junior member of a body that had generally failed to earn her respect.

Sula got a ginger-and-lime from Spence, who was stationed at the bar, then dumped cane sugar into it until it was sweetened to her liking. Carbonation sparkled on her tongue. She greeted all her guests, then found a seat next to Ming Lin.

"Lord Durward tells me that Cosgrove has gone bankrupt," she said. "I'm sure that's a symptom of something, but I don't know what."

Lin grinned at her. "I don't know that much about Cosgrove," she said, speaking loudly over the blare of the band.

"But I imagine it's a symptom of Cosgrove's own miscalculation. By all reports he was an arch-speculator, and probably heavily leveraged. A man owing so much money, and with so many projects, wouldn't have to go very far wrong to have the whole enterprise collapse. But I can look into it, if you like."

"I'd be obliged," Sula said, and meant to add, *if you could have it before the committee meets in eight days,* but Ming Lin was already busy with her hand comm, and it was clear that she was pursuing her research without Sula's encouragement.

The Torminel band came to a triumphant, booming conclusion, and Sula applauded politely. A Lai-own host appeared on the stage—Sula knew him vaguely from video but couldn't recall his name—and reminded the audience of the solemnity and significance of the occasion, then turned the show over to an orchestra, which played an overture specially commissioned for the event. There followed a performance by a massed Daimong chorus, a Cree band playing tunes alleged to be popular in the Fleet, a Terran ballet in which dancers impersonated warships battling in elaborate formations, and a series of speakers extolling the Supreme Commander, most in exaggerated, florid terms.

One of the speakers was Lord Chen, who offered praise for Tork's ability at logistics. Sula knew that Chen was not one of Tork's admirers, and she had to appreciate his tact, as well as his strict adherence to fact. Tork, or at any rate his staff, had done a first-rate job organizing the Fleet that he'd nearly brought to disaster in battle.

Ming Lin reported that she had found little about Cosgrove's bankruptcy, but then banks were closed on the holiday, as were libraries and sources of data. She'd check first thing in the morning.

"Thank you," Sula said. "Ah—here's food."

Her chef served up a meal of egg dishes. Eggs were something all the species beneath the Praxis could eat, though some preferred theirs in malodorous sauces that Sula wished well downwind.

At a pause, when the orchestra was tuning in preparation for the next event, Lord Durward appeared. "Lady Koridun would like to meet you."

Adrenaline surged into Sula's blood. Her first thought was that Lady Koridun, bent on revenge for the loss of so many of her relatives, might have arranged for Sula's assassination right here at the greatest public event of the year. This was, after all, a scenario that would certainly suit the extravagant, demented, violent style of the Koridun family.

And then she thought: *Well, that would spoil Tork's day.* Grinning, she rose and walked with Lord Durward toward the gate, though she detoured to speak to Macnamara.

"Lady Koridun wants to meet me," she said. "If she tries anything, feel free to shoot her."

Macnamara was startled. "I don't have a sidearm," he said.

Sula laughed. "Throw a drink in her face, then."

She joined Lord Durward at the gate to her box. There she found a young Torminel female, barely an adult, with gray-and-cream fur and the unusual blue eyes of the Koridun family. She wore a short jacket in pale blue with a standing collar of lace, and elegant braided shorts.

"Lady Koridun," said Lord Durward, "may I present Lady Sula."

"I'm honored to meet you," said Lady Koridun. "I'm a very great admirer of yours."

This was not what Sula expected, and it took a moment for her to respond. "I knew your—cousin? Lady Tari."

She remembered the shriek that came from Lady Tari as she charged, the fangs that flashed within a finger-joint's length of Sula's throat . . .

"You very kindly recommended her for a decoration after she died," Lady Koridun said. *After I shot her in the face,* Sula thought.

"She worked very hard through the Manado crisis," Sula said. "She deserved the commendation." It had to be admitted, Sula thought, that Tari Koridun had been a hard worker. Just a demented and homicidal one.

"I wonder . . ." said Lady Koridun, and then her voice drifted away, her blue eyes losing focus. Then she gathered herself and asked her question. "Is it true what *War of the Naxid Rebellion* said about Light Squadron Seventeen?"

Sula wanted to break out into laughter. If this was some kind of revenge plot, it was clearly the most rococo conspiracy in all history.

"I'm not sure what you're referring to," she said, "but for something meant to be entertainment, *War of the Naxid Rebellion* was quite accurate."

Which had surprised her. She had cooperated with the project, though once she'd heard the Martinez family was involved she decided her cooperation had been a mistake, and that the purpose of the documentary had been to glorify Gareth Martinez and his kin. Which to be sure it did, but to her surprise the final product had been fair in reporting her contributions to the war, and it supplemented her own recollections with those of people who had fought alongside her, comrades like Fer Tuga, members of the Secret Army, and the Bogo Boys. The documentary had not exactly concealed the way that some of these people made their living but hadn't sensationalized it either.

"The way your squadron had to fight the enemy without support," said Lady Koridun, "and still you destroyed so many enemy ships!" She waved a hand and flashed her fangs. "This festival should be for you, not for Lord Tork!"

"I won't disagree with you," Sula said.

War of the Naxid Rebellion had made Sula an empirewide celebrity, giving her a status with which she was not at all comfortable. But the documentary had also been a platform for her ideas and exposed Tork's vindictiveness as well as the rift between the Fleet's conservatives and innovators. Some of the viewers had taken sides on the issues, and even argued them out in public—which was unusual, since they weren't officially entitled to an opinion.

And she had acquired fans, as any celebrity gathered fans and supporters. There was a group of amateur enthusiasts who dissected the battles and strategies of the war and who supported one officer or point of view over others. Apparently one of Sula's admirers was Lady Koridun.

Sula grinned. "Would you care to join me?"

And so she passed a pleasant hour with Lady Koridun, whose brother, uncles, and cousins she'd had murdered. Rebecca Giove offered her own impressions of the Battle of Magaria, not very complimentary toward Lord Tork. Outside the pales of Sula's box, Tork's great show went on, bombastic entertainment interleaved with bombastic speeches. The soft spring day turned dark and chill, the black night sky cut by the silver arc of the antimatter ring. The penultimate speech came from the Lord Senior, who came onto the stage with his ceremonial red cloak billowing out behind him. Lord Saïd paused for a dramatic moment while gazing over his beaky nose at the audience, and then he began an address that compared himself with Tork, one in charge of the civil administration, the other the military, both engaged in a desperate conflict to save the empire. "But all my efforts would have been in vain," he said, "had not the Fleet defeated the rebels in battle. And for that, I must give the Supreme Commander the supreme credit."

I may be supremely ill, Sula thought.

Lord Saïd then introduced the guest of honor, who came out to the thunder of kettledrums, his expressionless face glaring wide-eyed. Tork's Golden Orb was held firmly in his gray fist, and the silver buttons on his dress tunic glittered in the spotlights. Applause pummeled the air. Sula took her time rising to her feet and lifting her chin to the salute and was amused that Lady Koridun, who as a private individual was not obliged to stand, remained in her seat. Sula rocked back and forth on her heels to stretch her calf muscles as the applause went on, and when it began to die Tork gestured with the Orb, and the crowd resumed their seats.

Martinez must be pleased, Sula thought. His ovation had lasted a good deal longer than Tork's.

"It was my honor to build and command the Righteous and Orthodox Fleet of Vengeance," Tork said in his beautiful Daimong voice. "I led it to victory, but credit for the victory does not properly belong to me—it belongs to our ancestors, and to the Great Masters who in their wisdom gave us the gift of the Praxis. The Praxis gave us perfect government, good order, and a clear understanding of the lines of authority. Our ancestors bequeathed to us a faultless system of tactics that, properly employed, will guarantee victory in any circumstances. I was merely the ancestors' instrument in defeating the rebels and restoring the authority of the Convocation."

In that case, Sula thought, *why are we celebrating a mere instrument? Why not just proclaim Ancestor Day?*

"The rebels defied the Praxis," Tork continued. "They defied the example of their ancestors, and the memory of the Great Masters." Harsh overtones began to clang in his voice. "The rebels' defeat was *inevitable*—at least once the genius of our ancestors was properly employed against them. For our ancestors, living directly under the Shaa, constituted the epitome of civilization, and the further we fall from their example, the more failure will plague us, and the more wretched we shall be..

"Let us in all cases condemn the vice of *innovation.*" Tork's voice took on a braying quality. "*Innovation* may seem glamorous or exciting, and it may appear to solve a problem, but the glamor is false, the excitement misleading, and the solution of one problem will give rise to a host of new problems that mere innovation cannot solve. No—we must stand firm as a wall against such false solutions, and adhere without question to the perfection that is our heritage." He made a violent gesture with the Orb. *"Firm as a wall!* Firm in our orthodoxy, and sheltered by the rampart of our righteousness! Down with novelty and innovation! Up with the spirit of the Great Masters! And most important of all, long live the Praxis!" He gestured again with the Orb, and his voice took on a metallic shriek. *"Long live the Praxis!"*

At that cry, rockets launched from behind the stage, their glittering trails forming a shimmering silver wall behind the Supreme Commander. The rockets rose above the stadium and then detonated, shooting brilliant, multicolored sparks across the night sky. Additional volleys of fireworks followed the first. The Torminel band marched out with kettledrums thundering. Lord Tork stood alone on the stage, the actinic flashes illuminating his tall, gangling body and glittering on his silver buttons. The tang of explosive scented the air.

At the climax of the display, rockets were launched from the entire circuit of the stadium, surrounding the spectators with pillars of shimmering light. Detonations boomed overhead, flashes illuminating the upturned faces of the audience. Multicolored lasers cut through the sky and created shifting geometric forms in the billowing firework smoke.

Lord Durward was bent over in his chair with his hands over his ears. The show had begun with explosions, Sula thought, and it would end with explosions.

The last barrage exploded overhead, and silence fell over

the stadium. The scent of propellant and incendiaries drifted through the air like a light rain.

Sula's ears rang. "I feel as if I've been made war on," she said.

"Oh, I think you have been," said Ming Lin. "That's the beginning of Tork's counterattack."

Sula considered this. *What could he do, really?* she asked herself. But then a cold finger touched her neck as she realized that all Tork or his friends had to do was *investigate* her. She was vulnerable on too many fronts: her false identity, her association with cliquemen, the assassination of her superior during the war, and the deaths of so many Koriduns . . . she couldn't possibly keep *all* those secrets, not if someone were truly looking into her past.

But who would know to look? Anyone who had shared her secrets was dead or had his own reasons for silence. Tork had no reason to investigate her when he could just use his authority with the Fleet to silence her. If he wished truly to make her vanish, he had only to assign her to a remote post in a distant reach of the empire, so far away that Zanshaa would never again hear her voice.

As her mind worked on the problem, she gradually became aware that Lord Durward was still bent over, his hands still clasped over his ears even though the fireworks had ended. She saw the shine of tears on his cheeks, and she leaned close to him and touched his elbow.

"Are you all right, Lord Durward?"

He shook his head, but he straightened, and he looked at her with brimming eyes. "It made me think of Richard," he said.

"I understand," Sula said. Lord Durward's son had died in

a blaze of fire all too reminiscent of the barrage of fireworks that had just thundered over their heads.

Lord Durward shook his head again. "That was all nonsense, wasn't it?" he said. "Lord Tork's speech. We can't go back to the old ways now. It's all changed. It's all over." He bent his head again, put his hands to his face, and began to keen, a strangled whine rising from his throat.

Panic fluttered in Sula. She never knew what to do in situations like these. *Human warmth is not my specialty.* She gestured to bring Spence to her side, and then she turned back to Lord Durward.

"Can I get you something to drink?" she asked.

Durward made an effort to speak, and when the words came they were hoarse. "Just water," he said.

Spence had arrived, and Sula looked up at her. "Bring Lord Durward some water," she said.

"Right away, my lady."

Sula became aware of a half circle of her friends forming a wall between Lord Durward and the audience, the convocates and their guests, who were beginning to file out of the stadium. Standing, she saw the old Daimong sniper, the guncrafter Sidney with his pipe, Lady Rebecca in her dress tunic, Macnamara and Ming Lin and Ashok Suresh and Master Clerk Ty-fran. All veterans of the Fleet or the Secret Army, all acquainted firsthand with death and terror, all acting now to provide a curtain of privacy, and a modicum of dignity, for one of the war's victims.

Sula laid a hand on Lord Durward's back. "We'll wait for the crowd to leave," she said, "and then I'll take you home."

THE SOUND OF raucous celebration echoed from the Fleet Club's roof beams. Lieutenant Vonderheydte had to lean close to Martinez, and stand on his toes, in order to be heard. "Congratulations on your successful season, Lord Captain."

"Thank you."

"It was your best yet, in my opinion." Lieutenant Vonderheydte turned to Kelly. "And yours too, of course."

In the last year the Corona Club had scored a decisive victory over its rivals, with more points than in any previous season. Kelly had been the overall point winner, which helped to make up for her stolen win the previous season, and Martinez took second.

Though Martinez had been gratified by the result, he hadn't found the season as satisfying as in previous years. Severin had been away, shaking down his new frigate *Expedition*. And Martinez had to admit that he missed Jeremy Foote, if only for the pleasure of thrashing him in one race after another. The other clubs had fielded weaker teams than usual, and while Martinez enjoyed winning, he preferred his opponents to provide more of a challenge.

"And you, Vonderheydte?" Martinez asked. "You're not tempted to join us in the Corona Club?"

"I never was a pinnace pilot," said Vonderheydte. "I'll put up with high accelerations in the course of duty, but I'm not interested in undergoing high gee voluntarily." Though he seemed pleased enough to be asked.

Vonderheydte—small, blond, fine-boned—had been a cadet on *Corona* during the perilous escape from Magaria following the Naxid revolt, where he had experienced plenty of high gees, and Martinez had promoted him to sublieutenant afterward. He had been raised to lieutenant automatically after two years and had spent much of the time since with the Third Fleet at Felarus—not aboard a ship, but as a functionary in the Fleet's vast building program. That he'd been employed at all indicated that Tork hadn't viewed him as too dangerously close to Martinez. But now the building program was coming to a close, and Vonderheydte was kicking his heels at the Commandery, looking for a new assignment.

The Fleet Club rang with the boisterous elation of its members and their guests. In the aftermath of Tork's address and the exuberant fireworks finale, the members were happy to dispense with the service's accustomed formality and settle down to enjoying themselves. The odor of tobacco, leaking out from the overcrowded smoking room, tainted the air. The bar was packed five-deep, and food was flying up from the kitchens as fast as it could be readied. Drunken junior lieutenants offered advice to senior officers, who were just drunk enough to listen. Officers using borrowed instruments improvised dance music in the reception hall, and despite the crowding at least a few people were trying to dance.

In various nooks and corners, reunions were taking place. Kelly and Vonderheydte hadn't seen each other since they'd served together on *Corona,* and across the room Martinez had seen Elissa Dalkeith, who had been his flag captain, speaking with Khanh, who had been her first lieutenant. They, too closely identified with Martinez, had been unemployed since the end of the war.

I am a curse, Martinez thought. The price of his friendship was to lose all hope of advancement in the service.

"I'll be heading to the Corona Club later," Martinez said. "The drinks are at least as good, the food is better, and it won't be as crowded. You'll both be welcome."

"Thank you, Lord Captain!" Vonderheydte was cheered. "I haven't had anything to eat since noon. We were marched to our seats in the stadium, but the concessionaires were overwhelmed and out of food by the time I got hungry."

"I'll see you both later, then," said Martinez. "I have to say hello to a few people first."

Martinez made his way through the crowd toward Dalkeith and Khanh, but he was caught in a rush of Lai-own cadets charging the bar in a wedge formation, and when he extricated himself, he was seized by the arm, and a wet kiss was planted on his cheek. He turned in surprise to see a tall, long-eyed woman with hair dyed a metallic shade of auburn.

"Chandra," he said, repressing the urge to wipe his cheek.

"Gareth." Her eyes were bright. Her hands clutched his arm, and he felt her body's warmth as she pressed up against him. "I applauded you like anything this afternoon! And I didn't applaud Tork at all."

"You'd better hope you weren't seen by one of his minions."

She barked out a laugh. "Won't make any difference, I'm already on his list of unemployables. I was your lieutenant and Lady Michi's tactical officer, after all."

"Last I heard you were *still* Lady Michi's tactical officer."

"She's been rotated into a desk job and doesn't need a tactical officer anymore. No one else wanted me, so here I am, looking for work."

Chandra Prasad had been a passionate, turbulent force aboard *Illustrious* when he was its captain, and her relationship with Martinez had been complicated by the fact that they'd had a passionate, turbulent affaire when they were both junior lieutenants. Each had cheated furiously on the other, though they disagreed about whose fault that was. Chandra was the most ardent, high-strung person he knew, and being in her company could be exhilarating, at least until exhaustion set in.

And now here they were, talking as intimates in front of a couple hundred witnesses. Martinez was glad that Terza hadn't come to the Fleet Club and had instead chosen to attend a reception at the Oh-lo-ho Theater organized by her father.

A lie came easily to his lips. "I'd do something for you if I had a command of my own," Martinez said. "But of course I'm even more in Tork's bad books than you."

"I thought you might have friends," Chandra said. "You could write me a recommendation."

"I could," Martinez said. "But the only one who might be in need of a tactical officer is Pa Do-faq, and you can't be the only Terran on a Lai-own ship."

"I don't have to be a tactical officer," she pointed out. "I could serve as an ordinary lieutenant. Or conceivably be promoted to lieutenant-captain and given a frigate."

"Let me contact you once I've had time to think," he said. "I must know somebody."

Somebody, he thought, *at a faraway station.*

The front doors crashed as they were flung open, and over

mere seconds the room went from boisterous to absolutely silent, from chaos into disciplined order, and everyone was braced to attention. For Lord Tork had arrived, and he carried the Golden Orb.

In silence Tork entered the club, his expressionless black-on-black eyes panning left and right. Staff officers flanked him like wings. He marched past Martinez, then stopped and returned. The staff officers shuffled their formation to accommodate their chief's movements. The scent of Tork's dying flesh caught at the back of Martinez's throat.

"Captain Martinez, you do not carry your Orb," Tork said. His voice buzzed and crackled as if it came from a broken speaker.

"We are in an informal setting, my lord," Martinez said.

Tork's eyes again panned the room, then returned to Martinez. "Your reasoning is flawed," he said. "This is a day to celebrate the Fleet in all its pageantry and greatness. You wear the full-dress uniform, and part of that uniform is your Golden Orb." Martinez could see mouth parts moving behind the fixed, parted lips. "This is the sort of undisciplined behavior I have come to expect from you, Captain Martinez. Take care that this does not happen in the future."

"Yes, my lord."

Tork stood facing him for another few seconds, as if weighing another reprimand, and then he turned to Chandra, weighed perhaps another comment, then spun about and moved deeper into the silent club, his staff forming and re-forming as he moved among the uniformed statues on the club floor.

"Turns a party into an inspection," Chandra murmured. "That's our Supreme Commander."

"Maybe his title should be Supreme Killjoy."

After another ten or fifteen seconds Tork released the crowd from attention, and Martinez decided it was time to leave. He could send messages to Dalkeith and Khanh inviting them to join him at the Corona Club in Grandview.

"I'm escaping while I can," he told Chandra, but he had barely taken two paces through the crowd before he found himself facing a dark-furred Torminel with the shoulder boards of a senior squadron commander on his vest. "Lord Altasz," he said.

"Martinez!" said the squadcom. "Your Coronas gave us a good season!"

"Thanks in part to you, my lord," Martinez said. "You were good enough to sponsor Sodak into the club, and she had a very impressive debut year."

"I had better hopes for the Ions," Altasz said. "But we're still in a rebuilding phase. Next year I hope we'll give you a run for the trophy!"

"I hope so, my lord."

"Say, Martinez," Altasz said. "I wonder if what I've heard about the Chee Company is true."

Martinez felt a warning tingle somewhere in the back of his brain. "What have you heard, Lord Squadcom?"

"That you were connected somehow with that Cosgrove rascal, and now that he's gone smash, you're overextended and in trouble."

Martinez blinked. "We're not connected with Cosgrove

in any way." He sensed a glimmer of skepticism in Altasz's dark eyes, and so he added, "Cosgrove was a speculator. The Chee Company are *contractors*. He's never employed us in any of his projects." He frowned as another thought occurred to him. "Are you an investor in the Chee Company?"

Once Roland had outmaneuvered and outblackmailed Lord Zykov, his former father-in-law, almost all Chee Company shares were held by the Martinez family. Some had been sold to raise capital, but not enough to give anyone else anything like a controlling interest. These were traded openly, and Martinez didn't want anything to damage their value.

"I'm not in the Chee Company," said Altasz. "But I bought some of those Rol-mar bonds you were peddling, and if Chee Company goes in the ditch, it takes Rol-mar with it. So—"

"May I ask the source of your information?"

Altasz waved a hand. "The fellow who handles my business."

"And who is that?"

"Li-paq at Attfrag Associates."

Martinez had never heard of either Li-paq or Attfrag, but he thought that perhaps he should find out more about them, so he recorded the names on the sleeve display of his uniform tunic. Then, after he offered more reassurances to Altasz that the Chee Company was sound, he made his way out of the club and summoned his car. While waiting at the curb, he sent a message to Roland.

"Call me. I think we may be in trouble."

CHAPTER 9

"It is the Imperial Bank's view that the real estate market has grown overheated," said the banker, "and as a result too much capital is involved in investments offering no immediate return." The banker, Lord Tchai Ridur, was a Torminel with exquisite diction, careful not to lisp around his fangs, and he dressed in a sober gray suit that matched the color of his fur. "We feel that a contractionary policy will be necessary in order to provide a correction."

"My lord," said Sula. "May I ask what form this contractionary policy will take?"

The banker stared at Sula through the opaque bubble-glasses that encased his eyes. "Lady Convocate?" he asked.

Sula repeated her question. The banker looked at Lord Ngeni, the committee chair, for clarification.

"The witness is at liberty to answer the question," said Lord Ngeni. He was an elderly Terran with a large round black cannonball head set firmly on his shoulders. Crisp white hair and a deep bass voice added to an impression of effortless dignity and authority. He was the chief of the ancient and widespread Ngeni clan, and during the war one of his grandnephews had joined the Secret Army under Sula and died a hero's death. Possibly as a result of this, he had welcomed Sula to the committee and now tolerated her questions at a hearing that was expected to be nothing more than pro forma.

Lord Tchai paused a moment to consider his words. The hearing room was small, with the Banking and Exchange Committee brightly lit under spotlights and sitting behind a long slablike gray table, with a tall white wall behind. The wall could show video at need, but at the moment it looked very much like a wall. Lord Tchai and his aides sat at a somewhat less imposing desk set before the head table, also brightly lit, with a very few spectators in chairs in the comparative shadows behind.

One of those in the shadows was Ming Lin, Sula's economics adviser. Ming had apprenticed hurling bombs for the Secret Army and had prepared a few bombs for just this occasion. Her research into Cosgrove had borne explosive fruit. It would be Sula's pleasure and privilege to make a few prominent, privileged people look stupid, venal, and ridiculous.

The Lord Senior might in the end regret appointing her to the Committee on Banking and Exchange.

"Lady Convocate," said Lord Tchai, "there are a number of counterinflationary instruments available to us. We could cease to repurchase war bond debt at our current rate, which would have the effect of reducing the amount of money in circulation. We could increase the rate on discounts or overdrafts, which would have the end result of restricting the money supply. If this fails in its intended effect, we could increase the reserve requirements at our banks."

"Not simply at the Imperial Bank, but at all banks?"

"That is correct, Lady Convocate."

The banker looked down at his hand comm and prepared to continue his address. Sula interrupted him.

"May I ask, Lord Tchai, if this overheated real estate market is an empirewide phenomenon, or localized at Zanshaa?"

The banker licked his lips. "Inflation is a problem throughout the empire, Lady Convocate," he said. "It is particularly concentrated in the housing market, and most especially in the capital."

"You will be able to send the committee the statistics on which you base your analysis?"

"They are included in an appendix to my report, Lady Convocate."

"Thank you, Lord Tchai."

The banker gave a little huff of breath, perhaps to add an audible period to the interruption that had taken him from his narrative. His bubble-cased eyes returned to the text on his hand comm.

"I wonder, Lord Tchai," said Sula, "if you think the recent failure of the Cosgrove enterprise is symptomatic of a larger problem in the economy."

The banker was startled by the question, but responded firmly. "We have no reason to believe that."

"I am relieved to hear it," Sula said smoothly. In her mind, she lit Ming Lin's first bomb and prepared to hurl it. "Can you assure me, then, that the Imperial Bank's purchase from Cosgrove, eight days ago, of the entity called 'Render Six' was in the normal line of business, and not an extraordinary action on the part of the bank?"

Lord Tchai was frozen for a moment, then looked to the aides on either side of him. "I am not familiar with this entity, Lady Convocate," he said.

"I am informed that it is something called a 'Special Purpose Asset Vehicle, Class II,'" Sula added helpfully.

Tchai's aides were murmuring commands into their hand comms. "I am not a specialist in these vehicles," the banker said, "but I know that they are entities for the pooling of assets or to securitize asset-backed securities."

Sula grinned. "They *securitize securities*? Aren't securities securitized already? Isn't that why they're called *securities*?"

Tchai made an attempt to look stern. "Your ladyship is being facetious."

Sula's grin broadened. "I'm afraid so."

The banker made the huffing noise again. "Lady Convocate, I shall endeavor to respond more clearly. The purpose of an asset vehicle is to bundle assets into a single package, usually for a very specific purpose." The Lai-own aide on his right side directed his attention to his hand comm display. Lord Tchai took a moment to view the screen, then he gave that huff of air again.

"Your ladyship's information is correct," he said. "Render Six was purchased by the bank eight days ago."

"For what sum?"

Lord Tchai peered again at the screen. "A hundred and six million zeniths."

Sula was silent for a long moment, letting that vast sum sink in. "Was the bank in the habit of purchasing such vehicles from Cosgrove? Were there any more such purchases?"

She already knew the answer, but waited to see what the banker said. The fact was, Cosgrove's business was privately owned by Cosgrove himself, or by his immediate family, and much of its workings were opaque until the bankruptcy forced his creditors into the open. Now creditors were filing their claims in court, and there were a *lot* of them. Ming Lin had carefully looked at such filings, and she'd found a number of investment vehicles similar to Render Six that Cosgrove had sold, all in the last few months. Then she had looked more closely at how long these vehicles had been in existence, and some of them had been created *years* ago, and held by Cosgrove himself.

"There's no reason for Cosgrove to create these sorts of vehicles," Ming had told Sula that morning, over coffee and brioche in Sula's office, "no reason, unless it's to hide unprofitable investments. He controlled dozens of companies, and *some* of them had to be underperforming, or unprofitable. So he shifts them all into Render One through Six, which takes them off his own books. He then looks far more profitable than he is and is able to borrow more money. As long as the money keeps flowing from the profitable elements of his business, he's fine."

Sula had inhaled the fragrance of her tea. "So why would he sell Render Six? Wouldn't that give away his scheme?"

Ming Lin had laughed. "The money must have stopped flowing. Bills were coming due, and he dumped the parts of his empire that weren't making money."

"The Imperial Bank must have already had a ton of Cosgrove's debt," Sula had said. "Why would they buy his losing businesses?"

Lin had considered this, and then a wicked glimmer kindled in her eyes. "It's possible they didn't know what was in these vehicles," she had said. "Cosgrove may have hidden his losses somehow, or misrepresented the profitability of the Render vehicle. But it's also possible they bought it to hide their own exposure—Cosgrove created Render Six to hide his own losses, and then the bank bought it to hide how much Cosgrove owed *them*. It would give them time to sell Cosgrove's debt on to investors and to other institutions."

"Other banks?"

Lin had nodded eagerly. "Yes!"

"So they were likely selling Cosgrove's obligations to other banks knowing that they would soon be worthless?"

Lin had grinned and shaken her pale rose-colored hair. "It's certainly worth looking into."

Sula inhaled again the fragrance of her tea. "I believe I shall," she had said.

The memory of that fragrance tingled through Sula's senses as she listened to Lord Tchai's answer.

"According to what I've just learned," he said, "we purchased another vehicle called Render Two a little over two months ago."

Sula lit another one of Lin's bombs and hurled it. "Was

the bank aware that the Render vehicles seem to consist of Cosgrove's losing businesses and investments?" Which was something that was far from proved, but Ming Lin had made it seem likely.

Lord Tchai stared in surprise, then conferred with his aides. "I cannot speak to that," he said. "I don't have the necessary information at hand."

"Can you provide this committee with that information?"

"I will, Lady Convocate."

"Thank you, Lord Tchai. In the meantime, can you also inform us if the Imperial Bank has sold amounts of Cosgrove debt in the last few months?"

Sula had to admire Tchai's sangfroid. Even after she'd thrown Lin's third bomb, his immaculate diction didn't waver.

"I'm afraid I do not have that information available, Lady Convocate."

"But you'll share once you do?"

"Yes, Lady Convocate. Of course."

"WHY ARE YOU watching that?" Martinez asked. The video in Roland's lounge was turned to a hearing at the Convocation, at a well-dressed Torminel, in the glare of spotlights, being asked questions by a panel of convocates, all of them wavering shadows in the strong light.

Roland gave a wave of his hand. "It's very entertaining. I'm watching the Imperial Bank going down in flames."

Hector Braga gave a laugh. "Earthgirl's got them on the run!"

Martinez looked at him. "Who's Earthgirl?"

Braga seemed a little uncomfortable, as if he'd revealed something he hadn't intended. "I mean Lady Sula."

Martinez made an effort to overcome his surprise. "She's robbing the Imperial Bank? Characteristic."

"It's more like she's pointing out the bank's been robbed already," Roland said.

"I'm more worried that it's *us* being robbed," Martinez said. He went to the bar and helped himself to coffee. "Those rumors about the Chee Company are really hurting us."

"They can't hurt us," Roland pointed out. "The family owns a majority of the stock, and we can't be kicked out. The stock is worth a little less right now, but in time it will bounce back."

"It's hurting our good name," said Martinez.

"Our name is as good as ever it was," said Roland.

Martinez had been summoned to his brother's palace for what was described as a strategy session. What strategies were being discussed were unspecified, but Martinez had little enough to do and was pleased enough to be asked.

Roland's lounge featured the eye-shaped windows of the Tanyl style, golden paneling of chesz wood, and accents of wrought iron. There was a bar, leather armchairs and sofas, and soft carpeting. In one corner, lemon-scented water chimed in a fountain's scalloped bowl.

"I also wonder if it's the beginning of a more general attack," Martinez said. "This could be just the beginning." He took his coffee to a chair near Roland and sat. Pneumatics sighed and he felt the chair align itself with his lumbar region.

Roland frowned. "I've already headed off the likely source of damage," he said. "Lady Gruum contacted me—she's heard the rumors, too, and I was able to reassure her that there is no impediment to the Chee Company continuing its work on Rol-mar."

"Lady Gruum? Did she say where she heard the rumors?"

"From Lord Minno."

"Minno?" Martinez was outraged. "He's our *banker*!"

"He's not *our* banker," Roland said, "he's Lady Gruum's banker."

"So why is he scaring her?"

"It's his job to report anything that may affect the Rol-mar project," Roland said. "But my guess is that he's part of a syndicate deliberately trying to drive our price down. He may be shorting us, or hoping to pick up some of our stock cheap. The next step would be a pump-and-dump, where he spreads counterrumors to drive the stock price up, so that he can sell at a handsome profit."

"That's illegal, I hope," said Martinez.

"Of course," Roland said. "But it's very difficult to prove. He can say he was doing his duty to his clients by spreading the rumors."

"He's with the Bank of the High City, no?" said Hector Braga. "Pity he's not Imperial Bank—Earthgirl is going to keep them from thinking about anything but their own necks."

Martinez turned to him. "Why do you call Lady Sula 'Earthgirl'?"

Again an uncomfortable look crossed Braga's face. "She

was stationed on Earth, you know, a few years ago." This seemed an inadequate explanation even though this was true, but Martinez decided not to pursue it.

"And what is this about the Imperial Bank?"

The Cosgrove revelations were explained to Martinez. "So the bank bought all these—what's the term?"

"Special Purpose Asset Vehicles," said Roland.

"Class II," added Braga.

Martinez went to one of the room's desks and called up its computer. He adjusted the screen and asked it for information about Special Purpose Asset Vehicles and discovered that such funds had to be registered with something called the Imperial Securitization Section of the Ministry of Finance. From their files Martinez was able to call up the necessary information on the Render entities and learned that Cosgrove had created six such vehicles over the past five years and sold them all in recent months. He'd also created and sold two vehicles called Reaper, and another called Restore.

"The Bank of the High City bought one of the Renders, and also a Reaper," Martinez said. "And the Bank of the High City is publicly traded, is it not?" He laughed. "I believe we may have our vengeance on Lord Minno."

"Hardly seems worth our while," Roland muttered.

Martinez tracked the rest of Cosgrove's entities through the system and discovered that they had ended up in three banks, one of which was publicly traded and the other two of which were privately owned. All these banks had appeared as plaintiffs before the bankruptcy court concerned with the failure of Cosgrove's enterprises, and all were thus revealed to hold a considerable amount of Cosgrove's money-losing assets, with a few profitable businesses folded in to make the package seem more attractive. When Martinez looked at the dates on which the debt had been acquired, he whistled.

"The Imperial Bank *has* offloaded a good deal of the Cosgrove debt in the last two months," he said. "That tells me they knew it was worthless. And the Bank of the High City bought into that debt to the tune of—" He ran sums in his head. "Four hundred fifty million. And that's exclusive of the Render and Reaper, which set them back at least a hundred million each."

For once Martinez had the feeling that he had Roland's full attention.

"How many people know this?" Roland's voice was dreamy, as if he was speaking from somewhere in the interior of a lush fantasy that was scrolling before his eyes.

"We three. And people at the Imperial Bank *have* to know. Plus, if anyone was watching the hearings and paying attention, they might be able to work it out."

"I doubt there were many people watching," said Hector Braga. "It was a quarterly meeting for the Imperial Bank to deliver a routine report. Not even financial reporters turn up for it; they just read the report later. The only reason we knew to watch was because Lady Sula told me she was going to ask some unsettling questions."

Roland's eyes seemed still focused on his inner vision. "I think we should get our short positions in place," he said, "before it becomes a stampede."

The next half hour was filled with activity. Martinez and his brother placed large bets against the two publicly traded banks, and Hector Braga, caught up in the enthusiasm, made some bets of his own. Martinez's sisters Vipsania and Walpurga arrived while this was going on, and once the situation was explained, they made their own shorts.

"If only there was a way to short the Imperial Bank," Martinez said. "Not to mention the two privately held banks that bought Cosgrove's debt."

Roland strolled back from the bar carrying a tray with glasses and a bottle of mig brandy. "I think we should celebrate our good fortune," he said, "and not wish for windfalls that aren't possible."

Martinez looked at his cold cup of coffee, with its oily sheen, then withdrew his hand. "Oh, I know I can't short a privately held entity," he said, "but I might be able to bet against them in other ways—at a gambling club, for example. After all, the Corona Club runs its own tote. I'd just have to find someone willing to take my bet."

Roland sighed. "I realize that you're a Fleet officer, and you're used to pouncing on an enemy at the decisive moment, but you need to stay away from this. Making a side bet on the price of a stock, or on interest rates or market indexes, is called 'nonmarket derivative trading' and it's completely illegal. The Lai-own traders who invented those methods centuries ago made a packet at first, then lost their firms a colossal amount of money. As a consequence they were executed, and their methods outlawed."

Martinez frowned. "That just means I'll have to think a little harder about what I need to do," he said.

"Perhaps this brandy will aid your thoughts."

Martinez took the glass, brought it to his nose, and inhaled the sharp, spicy odor. Roland passed out the other glasses, and then raised his own.

"To an unexpected windfall," he said. He directed his toast to his brother. "Thank you, Gareth."

"My pleasure, I'm sure," said Martinez, and drank. The brandy burned down his throat.

Roland seated himself. "As interesting as the last hour has been, it's been a distraction from the issues I planned to raise at this meeting. The first explains why I've invited Mister Braga to join us—it involves Lady Tu-hon, and her reluctance to cooperate with us despite our having offered . . . inducements."

Martinez straightened in his chair, suddenly interested. It was very unusual for one of Roland's purchases to rebel, and it spoke to either unusual firmness of character or unbounded recklessness.

"What's she done?" Vipsania asked.

"Voted against our interest most of the time. I've spoken to her on occasion and reminded her that I had hoped she'd be more of a friend to us, but she just says that she is voting in accordance with her long-held principles."

"Can any more pressure be applied?"

Roland looked skeptical. "I loaned her eighty-three thousand zeniths for her to acquire Rol-mar bonds. I paid less than that for this *palace*. But the terms were that she would pay me back when she was in funds, and though I've spoken to her about it, she is still claiming to be cash-poor."

Vipsania gave a little sniff. "There's no record of this loan, is there?"

"No, it's all . . . off the books."

"Well," Vipsania said, "it appears you've given Lady Tu-hon a new palace, with nothing to show for it."

Hector Braga plucked at the knees of his braided trousers. "We could arrange for her to suffer a disappointment in the Convocation."

"Has she got a legislative program of some sort?" Walpurga said. "How do we defeat it?"

"Lady Sula is with Tu-hon on one of the committees," Braga said. "She says that all Lady Tu-hon cares about is money, and that she's one of the convocates planning to repeal the income tax and restore tariffs on interplanetary trade."

"We'd oppose that anyway," Roland said.

Walpurga looked at Vipsania. "I don't suppose Empire Broadcasting's news unit could do a piece on the Convocation? Mention that—I don't know—Lady Tu-hon is infamous for not repaying her debts."

Vipsania was skeptical. "The censors are very careful about what we say about the Convocation. And I don't know if you want to mention Lady Tu-hon and debt in the same breath—someone might accuse us of trying to bribe her."

Hector Braga grinned. "Can't have that," he said.

Martinez took a slow sip of his brandy and let it roll across his palate. He was carefully examining an idea that had floated up in his mind, examining it with careful mental fingers as he might examine a newborn child, testing it for soundness. It seemed sound enough.

"Let's just take a lot of her money," he said. "And Lord Minno's, too."

Roland looked at him. "You have a plan? A *legal* plan?"

"Yes. But first, let's thwart Minno on another level by stabilizing the price on Chee Company stock—our cash reserves are up to it, yes?"

"Possibly. But why? The price will return to normal in any case."

"I'd like to demonstrate to the syndicate that's manipulating our stock that we're willing to spoil their party. And also, I want Lord Minno to be just a little hungry for money."

Roland nodded. "Tell me what you're planning," he said, "and then I'll know whether or not I need to consult a lawyer."

THE BANK OF the High City was built of the same granite that made up the High City's acropolis and meant to suggest the same sort of permanence. The polished brass central door was flanked by bulbous eggplant-shaped towers that loomed over the mortals on the street below, as if to intimidate them with the bank's sheer power.

Martinez, who was not intimidated, passed through the brass doors with confidence. The interior featured beige paneling and more bright brass, and the air carried the scent of polished leather. Martinez asked for Lord Minno and was shown directly to Minno's office on one of the upper floors. The office was decorated in dark tile with patterns of bright golden starbursts, which probably featured enough contrast so that Minno could perceive them with his optical patches—the tiles would also reflect sound well, which would aid his echolocation.

"Lord Minno," he said as he entered.

Lord Minno was not at his desk but disposed on a sofa at one end of the room. "Welcome, Captain Martinez," he said. "I was about to take my wives out for our spa treatment."

The wives in question shared the couch with him, and at the sound of Martinez's voice they turned toward him with their large bat ears spread wide.

"I won't keep you for long," Martinez said. "I have only a question."

Both Lord Minno's wives got to their feet and loped toward Martinez to investigate him. Pointed faces sniffed at his legs and crotch. He patted each of them on her purple, hairless head.

"This one is Vetso," Lord Minno said, pointing. "The other is Desto."

"They're beautiful," Martinez lied. Minno's wives cavorted about his feet.

Blind and living in a world of sound and scent, Cree spent the first few years of existence as quadrupeds, gamboling about like puppies, and with about as much intelligence. The males later developed human-scale intelligence and upright posture, but the females remained four-legged and simple-minded. Martinez had to admit that the females' nearly hairless purple bodies, with their big ears, eyeless pointed faces, and dark optical patches, should have been repellent to the average Terran; but in fact the Cree females had such strong, cheerful personalities, and were so endearingly clumsy, that he found them strangely winsome.

Even though biologically speaking the females were little

more than mobile wombs, they and the males formed strong bonds with one another. The males lavished affection on the females, and Minno had given his wives jeweled collars, anklets, and clothing as elaborately purfled and ruched as the outfit he wore himself. Which was all the more generous, because the eyeless Minno couldn't even properly see or appreciate his wives' outfits.

Lord Minno rose to his feet and called his wives to him. They joined him happily, and he issued a set of clicks and gobbles that Martinez presumed were terms of affection. Then the sounds ceased, and Minno's ears focused on Martinez.

"You had a question, Captain?"

"It involves a retired petty officer of my acquaintance," Martinez said, "a man named Alikhan. I was at the Metropolitan Club this morning, and I saw that he was registering a bet with the tote."

"That is hardly unusual," said Minno. "I myself am a member, and I place bets there all the time."

"You normally don't see petty officers in a place like the Metropolitan Club, but it seems he's inherited some money and can afford a membership. But it was the subject of his bet that really raised a question in my mind."

"Yes?"

"He's offering a bet that Lady Kannitha Seang will lose her job within two months."

"The head of the Imperial Bank?" Minno was clearly puzzled. "Why does he think Lady Kannitha will be dismissed? Or does he think she'll resign for some reason?"

"He happened to see a picture of her somewhere eating a

bowl of stew made with hominy and potatoes. He says that anyone who eats hominy and potatoes in the same dish can't possibly prosper. He thinks she's doomed."

Lord Minno paused for a moment. "You are not joking?"

"I can assure you that *he* wasn't joking. And he's backing his bet with his entire savings—four thousand zeniths. Anyone who takes that bet and has the patience to wait two months will just be able to walk off with the money."

"It sounds as if your petty officer is disturbed in his mental processes. But you had a question, did you not?"

Martinez spread his hands. He found himself trying to make contact by looking for Minno's eyes, but of course Minno had none.

"Well—now it seems a little absurd even to ask. But I was wondering if you'd heard any disturbing rumors about Lady Kannitha, or any reason why she might be resigning anytime soon. Because if she isn't, then I've got to try to contact Alikhan and convince him to withdraw his bet."

"I have heard nothing derogatory about Lady Kannitha," said Minno, "and can conceive of no reason why she would resign. Heading the Imperial Bank puts her at the absolute peak of her profession."

Martinez sighed. "Alikhan is stubborn," he said, as if to himself. Then, to Minno, he added, "At least he was intelligent enough to demand high odds. That alone might deter anyone from taking the bet." He shrugged, then realized Minno probably would not be able to detect the gesture. "But if someone does bite, he'll have a very pretty payday in a couple of months."

"I hope the situation resolves itself to your satisfaction," Lord Minno said.

"Thank you for your counsel," Martinez said. "I won't detain you any further. Have a pleasant time at the spa."

"We shall! Thank you very much, Captain Martinez."

Martinez watched Lord Minno and his wives recede down the corridor and hoped he had been convincing, and that Minno's keen hearing had detected no trace of the mendacity in his words.

Martinez had bought Alikhan a membership in the Metropolitan Club and loaned him the money to make his bet. His plan took the chance that Minno might know how much of Cosgrove's debt Imperial Bank had sold his own firm and been privy to any complaints that High City might intend to lodge against Imperial and Lady Kannitha Seang—but years of working within the vast bureaucracy that was the Fleet had convinced Martinez that, when something went badly wrong, the instinct to cover up the mistake trumped any public airing of grievances. Those who had purchased the bad loans, and their supervisors, might now be sweating through a well-bred panic attack; but they would almost certainly not have shared their plight with Lord Minno, who after all worked in a different department, and whose job was not to purchase and manage debt, but to create and sell bonds.

Now, he thought, much would depend on how greedy Lord Minno was feeling this afternoon. For Alikhan was demanding formidable odds of twenty-three to one on his bet, which might give even Lord Minno pause. But Lord Minno's credit was good, and from Minno's point of view, all he had to do to earn four thousand zeniths was to sign a note at his club.

After all, hadn't Cosgrove said that when you encountered a bet at those sorts of outrageous odds, you took it? Though perhaps, Martinez thought, Cosgrove wasn't the best example to follow at this point in time . . .

And in any case there were other bets being laid today. One of Hector Braga's allies in the Convocation would even now be informing Lady Tu-hon of another extraordinary bet placed at the Ion Club, this one based on the future career prospects of the president of the Bank of the High City. And Lady Tu-hon's greed, as far as Martinez was concerned, was already proven.

The best part was that the bets did not fall under the illegal category of nonmarket trading. He wasn't betting on stocks or indexes, he was betting on whether a few prominent people kept their jobs. The bets were unusual, but they were hardly against the law.

His intuitions were proved right less than an hour later, when he found out that both bets had been accepted.

Strolling home through the Garden of Scents off the Boulevard of the Praxis, he decided that he should find out if any of his family's money was held at the Bank of the High City, or any other bank that had bought Render and Reaper, and make sure the cash was shifted to a safer harbor.

CHAPTER 10

From her position on the Committee for Banking and Exchange, Sula had a front-row seat for the catastrophe, beginning with Lord Tchai Ridur's return to the Convocation. Dressed in his beautiful gray suit and employing his perfect diction, he provided information about the Render vehicles purchased by the Imperial Bank, as well as details of the Cosgrove instruments that the Imperial Bank had sold to other banks. Sula and the committee asked for more information concerning exactly when the bank had known that Cosgrove would default, and if any of the debt had been sold after that determination was made. Lord Tchai testified that he didn't know the answer but would try to find out.

The committee jumped over Lord Tchai's head for the next meeting two days later and called Lady Kannitha Seang, the head of the bank, who brought a squad of assistants, including the account manager who had been assigned to Cosgrove. Lady Kannitha was a diminutive woman with long black hair that featured a pair of dramatic white stripes, colors that were echoed on her glittering beaded gown. Neither she nor the account manager admitted that they knew ahead of time that Cosgrove would default, but they conceded that they believed they were "overexposed" to his debt and decided to sell it.

That was the cue for the Bank of the High City, and several other banks, to file suit against the Imperial Bank for fraudulently selling them Cosgrove's debt. Then it was discovered that Cosgrove had bundled a special vehicle for the Imperial Bank to sell. Cosgrove had collected a large fee for creating the vehicle, which the bank then sold as its own, making it seem both safe and legitimate. The bundle was filled with Cosgrove's debt, along with some of Cosgrove's less successful businesses.

More lawsuits were filed. And right at this point of high drama, the Render and Reaper bombs went off.

But they didn't go off only at the Imperial Bank. Once they'd realized it was poison, the Bank of the High City and others had sold off much of Cosgrove's debt as well. The poison had then spread throughout the banking system, from those with more information to those without, and institutions that had never dealt with Cosgrove personally now began to totter.

The structures of Cosgrove's Special Purpose Asset Vehicles were complex, and it had taken the banks a while to unpack them and understand what it was they had actually bought. Render and Reaper had been worth roughly a hundred million each when purchased, but once Cosgrove defaulted, each of the vehicles turned out to be worth substantially *less than zero*—for one thing, they held a lot of Cosgrove's debt, which would never be repaid, and the cost of tracking down each element of the bundle, paying foreclosure costs, bank fees, legal fees, taxes, and the salaries of everyone involved, would in many cases be more than the assets were worth. And this, of course, was in addition to the millions these same banks had given Cosgrove in direct loans, many of which turned out to have been inadequately secured.

In fact, it seemed that toward the end, the banks had just *given* Cosgrove money, to keep his enterprises afloat and to avoid having to declare the enormous losses that a bankruptcy would entail. It was hard for Sula to imagine how anyone thought that strategy would end well.

Probably, she thought, because no one ever thought it would be questioned.

But someone—Sula herself—had questioned it, and in the aftermath, only the Imperial Bank survived the Render and Reaper crisis, and that was because the bank belonged to the same entity that printed the money. The other banks collapsed beneath the weight of debt, and then the rubble was submerged beneath waves of panicked depositors withdrawing their cash.

The Ministry of Finance, the Treasury, and the Imperial Bank worked overtime to find buyers for the bankrupt institutions, but this proved impossible as long as the banks were engulfed in Cosgrove's debt; and so the Convocation voted into existence a *new* entity, the Bureau of Arrears and Obligations, to which all Cosgrove's debt would be transferred until it could be wound up, thus taking it off the books of the affected banks.

"The government is packing all the bad investments into

a special instrument," Sula said during the debate. "Isn't this exactly what Cosgrove did with Render and Reaper? And wasn't it a bad idea *then*?"

At least shifting the debt to the government facilitated the purchase of the defunct banks and the installation of new management. Lady Kannitha had long ago resigned, as had Lord Tchai, who had probably done nothing wrong but who had become the public face of the scandal. The management teams of the other banks were gone as well. All were being investigated for fraud.

That was the good news.

The bad—or at least part of it—was that once the Bureau of Arrears and Obligations began to examine the vehicles it had acquired, they discovered that toward the end Cosgrove had put the same asset into more than one vehicle. The bureau might now possess 200 percent, sometimes 300 percent, of a single asset that was worth little or nothing.

Another round of lawsuits ensued, as those who had lost money on Cosgrove's assets now claimed they hadn't owned those assets at all, that the *real* assets had been previously sold to someone else, and that someone, preferably the government, should compensate them for their losses.

Plus the bureau was now plagued by a host of speculators. As soon as it was mooted that the government would acquire all Cosgrove's vehicles, speculators had stepped in to buy as much of Cosgrove's assets as they could find, paying the original investors a tiny percentage of their original value. Now these entrepreneurs flocked around the Bureau of Arrears and Obligations, demanding to be paid full value—and the bureau had a hard time saying no, because they had paid full value to the banks.

The departure of the Imperial Bank's management had delighted Lamey, who had made a fortune through some kind of side bet with Lady Tu-hon. He'd also sold some of the banks short and had collected on that as well.

"You should have bet along with me, Earthgirl," he said.

"It was too obvious, don't you think?" Sula said. "Betting based on information from my own committee hearings?"

"That's the best way to do it!" Lamey laughed. "That way you know you won't lose!"

Sula was wary of anything that might bring attention to her and lead to an investigation; but she *had* tried to short a pair of the banks after the scandal had broken. Unfortunately no one was left to take her bets, because it was impossible to sell a stock short when its value was already zero.

Ming Lin had a nose for what might happen next, and therefore Sula was not surprised when the Imperial Bank's new management announced themselves appalled at all the reckless lending that had been going on and increased the reserve requirements at every bank in the empire. Suddenly banks were required to increase their own cash reserves, and the only way to do that was to sell some of their investments, stocks and bonds as well as commercial and consumer loans. But since all the banks were in the same situation, it became difficult to sell to one another, and the result was too many sales chasing too little money. The value of stocks, bonds, and debt crashed. Much of it was sold to speculators, too many of whom were little Cosgroves operating heavily leveraged businesses on the fringes of the markets.

Another consequence of the increased reserve requirements was that there was less money available for lending, and therefore the cost of money rose as people competed for whatever financing was available. Businesses that depended on regular access to capital—transportation, foodstuffs, mineral exploitation, certain types of manufacturing—began to slow, and businesses that had been doing perfectly well began to run into trouble. Some failed, some slowed, some just closed their doors and waited for better times. The unemployed dunned their patrons, whose finances were already being stretched. Business failures rocked the banks even more. Many of the little Cosgroves crashed. Banks began to fail, banks that had never had anything to do with Cosgrove or his businesses.

Sula watched it all with the same horrified fascination with which bystanders view an auto crash. When she had first asked questions in committee, she'd intended to reveal fraud at the higher levels of finance and show how the most respectable institutions in the High City had been co-opted by a ruthless swindler.

But the situation had been far worse than that. Cosgrove hadn't operated on his own; he was a symptom of the whole shambling structure of postwar finance, where procedures and institutions intended to last only for the duration of the emergency had evolved into a half-hidden, shadow economy operating on the margins of finance and the law.

When she'd asked her questions, Sula had thought that a few incompetent bankers might lose their jobs, but now billions of the empire's citizens were out of work and growing more desperate by the day. She could see them from the windows of her apartment, wandering the streets of the Petty Mount looking for work, or maybe just a place to sleep.

Had *she* done this? she wondered. Would things have turned out differently if she hadn't asked questions?

No. The collapse would have happened anyway, but the insiders behind it would have had a much better chance to hide their tracks.

Ming Lin pored over financial reports and drank in whole floods of government statistics. She reasoned that it was possible to make money off the crisis, and Sula was willing to follow her recommendations if there wasn't too obvious a conflict of interest with her job on the committee.

Half the banks were for sale, and it seemed like these same banks had foreclosed on half the town and were now trying to sell it. Sula bought commercial property in the High City and apartment buildings in Grandview. She shorted a whole series of financial institutions. As she had during the war, she bought supplies of cocoa and coffee imported from other worlds and waited for the price to go up. She bought a hardwood forest in the southern hemisphere, a pecan farm, a fishing port, and a winery, each of which gave her certain tax advantages, as well as the unusual status of being a winery owner who didn't drink wine. She also bought the mortgage on Miss Tiffinwala's bakery and gave it to her as a gift.

The last was nothing—mortgages were cheap. But Sula's

feelings were eased at the thought of doing good for someone else, instead of just making money off the catastrophe, as if she were one of the rich insiders who seemed to make money off everything.

"Cost of goods is going up," Ming Lin told her. They were in Sula's office at the Convocation, much improved from her first view of it nineteen months earlier. Rare porcelain gleamed from display cabinets, and a handmade Preowyn carpet dazzled on the floor. The fragrant odor of golden Comador tea rose in the room, and Sula served it in cups made eight hundred years before in the Yangtze Valley, with matching plates that held pastry made just that morning by Miss Tiffinwala.

Lin looked at her. She still wore her student's gown, and the strands of her rose-pink updo were tipped with black. "Prices up," she said. "So what will the Imperial Bank do?"

"The wrong thing," Sula said. "I feel that almost goes without saying."

"True." Lin laughed, then took a luxurious taste of her pastry. "To the Imperial Bank, rising prices mean inflation, and they have only one response to inflation."

"Cut the money supply," said Sula. After nineteen months on the committee, she was beginning to develop a sense for these things.

"Which, as you point out, is absolutely the wrong thing," said Lin. "Prices are going up because there isn't enough money in circulation to manufacture and purchase goods, and if the Imperial Bank raises rates or increases bank reserve requirements again, that just makes the problem *worse*. But they'll never consider any other course of action."

At one time, perhaps, Sula might have felt a thread of pleasure at foreseeing a catastrophe that others had somehow not noticed, but now all it brought her was weariness. "How can we see this," she asked, "and they can't?"

"They all belong to the same families," said Ming Lin, "and go to the same schools. They all use the same playbook. You grew up in exile, and I'm a commoner who earned a scholarship based on my war service." She poured herself more tea. "We're looking at the world through a different set of assumptions. Assumptions based on the fact that neither of us could count on having money, not the way the top Peers do."

"Possibly so," Sula said. Her fellow convocates on the Committee for Banking and Exchange looked at her askance, as if she had somehow caused the disasters she foretold. Their own financial advisers were the people who handled the details of their businesses, and they shared the exalted views of their masters, in which all was well as long as the same families remained on top.

"And by now," Sula said, "the bankers and administrators are all afraid. They know their predecessors are being investigated. They know that if they do the most conventional thing possible, they can't be blamed."

Lin raised her hand comm and looked at the display. "The Guidance Committee of the Imperial Bank meets in two days," she said. "I have a list of firms you might want to short before their announcement."

"Here I go again," Sula said, "profiting off others' misfortune."

Though she supposed it could be argued that this was all she'd ever done.

AFTER THE MEETING of their Guidance Committee, the new president of the Imperial Bank announced that, in response to inflationary pressures, the bank was increasing its rates on loans, discounts, and overdrafts. Over the next months another wave of bankruptcies and bank failures swept through the empire, throwing billions out of work.

Cosgrove, who had been fleeing on his yacht the entire time, arrived in Hy-Oso, the gold-bearing seaweeds of which were the source of his fortune. But by the time he arrived he no longer owned the gold, or for that matter the weeds, and turned himself in to the authorities, along with his family and one or two mistresses. News of his incarceration went nearly unnoticed amid the long list of bankruptcies.

Those who were unemployed, disabled, or sick were supposed to rely on their patrons, who relied on *their* patrons, and so on up the social order to the topmost rank of Peers. But now bankruptcy was harvesting patrons, and many Peers were under pressure.

Lady Gruum and Lord Tork together announced the formation of the Steadfast League, an organization to help the unemployed. To Sula it seemed a way for Peers and patrons to share the costs of looking after their clients, by organizing the clients into units that might share resources such as food, housing, and child care. Tork offered retired or unemployed petty and warrant officers to organize things. The destitute were housed in barracklike accommodations and fed in street kitchens. Those who needed work were deployed in make-work battalions, cleaning and mending the streets, dredging and cleaning the canals, repairing and refurbishing buildings, and beautifying parks and neighborhoods, work for which they were paid a modest sum. Sula couldn't help but suspect this was a scheme to increase the value of buildings and districts for the benefit of property owners, but on the whole it seemed useful, and a better solution than depending on the erratic good intentions of patrons.

She had profited from the crisis and gave the League a modest donation, and in return the exterior of one of her apartment buildings in Grandview was cleaned, and nearby trees were pruned. She hadn't asked for a quid pro quo, but the organizers provided one anyway.

It seemed she couldn't escape the trading of favors.

More amusing were the Steadfast League's marches and demonstrations, in which they rallied for Public Sanitation or the Rule of Law or the Purity of the Praxis. Squares were filled, guest speakers offered bromides, and the League members were encouraged to maintain a Positive Attitude. A Positive Attitude, apparently, would cure the crisis.

Sula had to consider her own Positive Attitude a complete failure. It was a long time since she'd been very positive about anything.

Now that Peers were falling into financial difficulties, the Court of Honor became active. Sula had achieved nothing on the court in her first twenty-two months as a convocate. Lady Tu-hon never communicated with her about the business of the court, called no witnesses, viewed no documents, and analyzed no data. Anyone accused of collusion or bribery was found innocent without the necessity of a hearing, and those guilty of other offenses were allowed to resign before hearings were held. It was clear to Sula that Lady Tu-hon and her allies were ruling on the cases without involving anyone outside their circle. Sula considered being offended, but decided she couldn't bring herself to care about the cases one way or another. The Convocation was the Convocation, and Sula was unlikely to change it.

But now the Court of Honor was called upon to review the cases of several convocates who had committed what was for their class the ultimate crime: they had lost their money. Lamey, of course, was delighted. None of them were his allies, and there were a number of high-ranking Peers with whom he'd reached an understanding, and whose names could be put forward as replacements.

Some of the bankrupts were talked into resigning before their hearings were scheduled, but others maintained a deranged optimism and a belief that everything would somehow work out. They were in the process of being evicted from their homes in the High City, their debts stood at many times their net worth, and they could no longer pay their office staff, but they were full of plans that would assure their future and were convinced that soon the heavens would open up and shower them with money. They were maintaining a Positive Attitude. Some of these were friends and allies of Lady Tu-hon, and she was determined to save them.

The hearings were brutal. Sula had to keep pointing out

how the numbers submitted didn't add up, and that there was no hope of solvency for any of those brought before the court.

"You are well known for your prophecies of doom and despair," Lady Tu-hon said to Sula, "but I remind you these are not chiseling pawnbrokers or criminal financiers. Rather, these are Peers of unblemished ancestry and honor."

"I am not indicting their ancestry," Sula said. "Just their bank balance."

Lady Tu-hon's peg teeth clacked in anger. Her orange eyes glared at Sula, and Sula realized she was not about to be forgiven for opposing the committee chair. "And whose fault is it that they suffer financial embarrassment?" Tu-hon said. "They are the victims of economic crimes!"

"Very likely," Sula agreed. "If so, they may seek remedies in the law courts. But they are as insolvent as Cosgrove himself." She suppressed a smile. "But of course, there's no *law* that bankrupts may not serve in the Convocation—it is only a custom."

An elderly Torminel on the committee who dozed through most meetings was now brought to full alert by an apparent threat to tradition. "A *venerable* custom," he said. "A custom that has served us for millennia. Would we see convocates begging on the streets for marrowbones?"

In the end, Lady Tu-hon *did* manage to rally her allies on the court and save a pair of her friends, essentially by admitting that financial solvency was no longer a criterion for membership in the empire's highest body. Lamey, visiting Sula's office, burst into laughter when he heard. "I'll offer marrowbones for votes!" he said, and marched off to rally the destitute to his cause. Sula thought he might well succeed: Lady Tu-hon might have saved their seats in the Convocation, but she would hardly part with enough money to let them keep their palaces.

Lady Tu-hon had already shifted her energies to another forum, and now she introduced a motion in the Convocation. "The financial crisis is the greatest threat to order since the Naxid Rebellion," she said, "and it is time to restore to the empire the financial system imposed by the Great Masters, and under which we achieved our greatest height of peace and prosperity. I speak, of course, of ending the unjust tax on equity imposed during the late rebellion, and returning the burden of taxation to the exporters of goods, where it belongs."

Roland and Lamey rallied their own forces against the proposal, and Sula duly spoke against it with the authority of someone who had studied the numbers. "We can't afford the change," she said. "Coping with the crisis has already put a strain upon the Treasury. And in a moment of economic crisis we can't afford to increase taxes on those who are most responsible for our remaining prosperity."

Lady Tu-hon rose to reply, and her orange eyes blazed with rage. "It is the peddlers, moneylenders, and merchants who are responsible for the crisis!" she said. "We must keep their grasping hands away from our wealth and resources!"

Lord Saïd, who could read a budget, quietly had the motion sent to several committees for review, which effectively kept it bottled for the present.

"We can kiss any recovery good-bye," Ming Lin explained, the next morning in Sula's office. "Lady Tu-hon's just introduced uncertainty into the situation. People aren't going to invest in merchant ventures if they suspect they might be taxed out of existence. So we won't see new ships, or any new industries aimed at export, and the industries that already exist aren't going to be expanding anytime soon."

"I should consult my advisers," said Lady Koridun. She had come to Sula's office that morning to carry an invitation to a soiree and had been invited to join Lin and Sula in their morning meeting. They drank tea and ate pastry, while Lady Koridun lapped at a dish of blood warmed to body temperature and enjoyed some raw quail eggs topped with fish paste. Sula's office staff had stocked food acceptable to the palates of any member species of the Praxis, which was only courteous, but the reek of the fish paste would linger in her office for some time.

Lady Koridun had become a frequent visitor, and Sula had invited her to the dinners and receptions she was obliged by her position to host. Lady Koridun was a little too worshipful to become a true confidante—Sula preferred companions who weren't quite so completely impressed with her—but she was pleased to have found a friend, even though somewhere in an uneasy corner of her mind she retained the paranoid suspicion that Lady Koridun was enacting some impossibly baroque form of revenge.

"Consult your financial advisers if you like," Sula said, "but consult Miss Lin first. She's predicted almost every stage of the financial crisis."

Lin blinked. "Thank you. I try to do my homework."

Sula turned to Lady Koridun. "I hope your financial condition isn't too alarming?"

"The clan is basically sound," Koridun said. "But there are increasing outlays on behalf of our clients, and there's a certain amount of chaos in the accounts, after so many deaths in the family."

"Miss Lin can probably give you some good advice," Sula said, "but I'm beginning to find it depressing to so consistently profit off everyone else's misery."

"You're profiting off the people who are *creating* the misery," Lin pointed out.

"I hope so." Sula regarded Lin as she sipped her tea. "Are you sure you want to stay at the university?" she asked. "I could set you up in your own office as a financial consultant."

Lin was astonished. "Are you serious?"

"Certainly. Why not?"

Lin ran her fingers through her pale-rose hair. "Well," she said, "you're not my patron."

"I *could* be," Sula said. "If your own patron isn't willing to do right by you. Or I could speak with your patron and recommend that you be set up in business."

Lin looked thoughtful. "Will that offer hold in four or five months?"

"Of course."

"Because I'll be finishing my thesis soon, all about the crisis, and it's going to be . . . talked about. I've had extraordinary access to everything that's happened since the beginning." Her hands made nervous darting movements through the air. "It might even be . . . important."

Lady Koridun regarded Lin with her deep blue eyes. "If it's important," she said, "perhaps its audience shouldn't be confined entirely to the academy. Your work might deserve a larger readership."

"My lady," said Lin, "I don't know how to achieve that."

"My family owns a publishing house."

Ming Lin seemed stunned by her successive waves of good fortune. "I—don't know how to—"

"Thank me? Not necessary."

Lin was even more taken aback. "No, that's not what I meant—though I'm grateful, of course. What I meant was, I don't know how to write for a general audience. My thesis is very technical, with algorithms and charts and statistics . . ."

"Perhaps we can find a collaborator for you, Miss Lin. Or a very good editor. Your choice."

"I—" Words failed her.

"My advice," said Sula, "is to surrender."

Lin's hands fluttered once more, then subsided. "Yes," she said. "Of course."

Sula's hand comm gave a discreet chime, and she turned to view the message from her front office, forwarding a message from Lady Tu-hon. In two days' time, she learned, the Steadfast League would stage marches throughout Zanshaa, on the theme of Eternal Vigilance Against Subversion.

These marches, Sula decided, were growing less amusing.

CHAPTER 11

Autumn drizzle spattered the windows of the palace, and a gray mist obscured the view of the Lower Town. The star-shaped brass plugs, scattered over the walls and ceiling to fill the last war's bullet holes, were dull in the dim light. Martinez and Young Gareth, confined indoors, were spending the afternoon playing a tabletop game called *Barbarians of Terra*. Young Gareth advanced his chariots on the left, took fire from Martinez's field fortifications, and watched as the horses reared in panic and the chariots crashed.

"I'm *incandescent*!" Young Gareth proclaimed. "Incandescent with rage!"

Martinez paused for a moment to congratulate himself on the expansion of his son's vocabulary. "My archers were entrenched," he said. "Your chariots would have fared better on the other flank."

"Requital shall be mine," Young Gareth proclaimed, a phrase he had learned from a *Doctor An-ku* drama, and ordered forward his catapults to begin the bombardment of Martinez's redoubt.

Martinez ordered his archers to duck and sent some skirmishers forward to locate Young Gareth's main body. The skirmishers were promptly ridden down by cavalry, and Young Gareth chortled.

Martinez's sleeve display chimed. Martinez lifted his arm, saw it was Roland, and answered.

"The Rol-mar Company's gone under," he said. "This is going to mean trouble."

The bulletin ominous, Martinez thought. "And Lady Gruum?" he said.

"I don't know, I haven't been able to reach her. I need the family over here now."

"Right away." He broke the connection and looked across the table at Young Gareth, who was studying the board with utter concentration and probably hadn't heard a word that had been spoken.

"I'm disheartened, genius," Martinez told him. "You rode down my skirmishers, and I'm disheartened. So I'm going to surrender."

The boy's eyes widened. "Really? I've disheartened you?"

"Absolutely. I give up."

Young Gareth cackled about requital, and Martinez rose to leave and blundered into his son's cardboard castle, knocking it over and scattering toy men-at-arms over the floor. As Young Gareth rushed to restore order, Martinez apologized, then left for the Martinez Palace.

When he reached his brother's home, he let himself in, shaking water off his cap. He found Roland in the lounge, sitting in a leather armchair beneath one of the eye-shaped windows. His feet were stretched out in front of him, and he was scowling at the polished toes of his shoes.

"How did you find out?" Martinez said.

"I have friends on Rol-mar's board."

"What happened?"

Roland shrugged. "Investment money just dried up," he said. "Plus a lot of the investors ran into financial difficulties and put their bonds on the market, so the price fell off a cliff. No one is willing to invest in new planets any longer, not when they're worried about starving."

"You'd think new planets would be the safest investment possible. It's not as if planets are going to vanish in the night."

"People are more worried about the price of beans."

Are you disheartened? Martinez wanted to ask. He also wanted to tell Roland that his young genius had just used *disheartened, incandescent,* and *requital* in conversation, but he suspected that in his current mood Roland would not be impressed.

He looked up as Walpurga and Vipsania entered. The two sisters both wore elegant dresses, scarves, and jewelry, and had clearly been enjoying a long lunch with friends when Roland's call had taken them away.

"How bad is it?" Walpurga asked.

Roland scowled again at his toes. "The Rol-mar Company is bankrupt. Investors have lost everything. I don't know about Lady Gruum, but whether she's got money left or not, she's clearly out of the picture."

"This is what Lord Zykov and Allodorm tried to do to *us,*" Martinez said. "Remember?"

Roland was tart. "We didn't *do* this. Not to Lady Gruum or anyone."

"I never said we did."

"We don't profit from this, and we're badly damaged. Between the Chee Company and Meridian, we have more than sixty-five thousand employees down on Rol-mar, plus millions in supplies and equipment. And that's not counting the subcontractors' three hundred thousand workers, and all *their* gear."

"How long can we afford to pay them?" Vipsania asked.

"For some time, actually. Salaries are far from the largest element of our expenditure. But if we take our people off the planet—along with all the equipment and supplies—and ship them halfway across the empire to put them to work on Chee or Parkhurst—*that* will cost an absurd sum. I have our people working out exactly how much."

Walpurga walked to another armchair and sat. Vipsania went to the bar, found a soft drink, and poured it into a glass. Carbonation hissed faintly, and a lemon scent wafted into the room.

"And of course we're already under strain because so many of our clients are unemployed," Roland added. "All that extra money we made from shorting the banks—" He gave Martinez a significant look. "*And* the side bets—it may all be needed to keep our clients dry and fed."

"We had always intended most of the workers to *stay,*" Martinez said. They were intended to be the first wave of immigrants, building their own cities, homes, and infrastructure. "Maybe," he said hopefully, "they won't have to leave at all."

"They have no title to anything," Walpurga said. "They had to work for seven years in order to qualify for land and a home, and that time hasn't expired."

Vipsania made a sour face. "So they're out of work and they're homeless, but we have to pay them anyway."

"Well," Martinez said to Roland, "you *are* a convocate. Shouldn't you be talking to Lord Saïd and arranging for another Peer to take up the patronage of the planet? Or arranging to take it on yourself?"

"Our father is already patron to three planets," Roland said. "They're not going to give him another one."

"But still."

Roland gave Martinez a stony look. "I've tried to reach the Lord Senior. Also the chair of the Committee for Planetary Settlement. But the Convocation's adjourned for the Autumn Festival, and the Lord Senior's off in the south at his estate. No one's returned my calls."

"So why are we meeting?" Martinez asked.

"Because," Vipsania said, "we must decide what we need, and how to ask for it, and who to ask, and the earlier we decide that, the better." She settled onto a sofa with her soft drink.

Martinez conceded the point. "Obviously the best result is for another Peer to take Lady Gruum's place as patron, and leave us in place."

"Obviously," Walpurga said. "But likely?"

"Normally the Convocation would stampede over one another for the chance to be patron to a new world," Roland said. "But in the current financial crisis, and with Lady Gruum's example before them, they might well hesitate."

"Lord Chen," said Martinez. There was a moment of silence.

Roland spoke thoughtfully. "I believe he may suit."

Walpurga looked at him. "His financial condition is very healthy, I believe?"

Roland looked at his brother, who spread his hands. "So far as I know," he said. "Maurice doesn't confide in me." He looked from one to the other. "He's at the house in the Tobai-to Highlands for the holiday. Terza and I and the children were to join him tomorrow."

The other three considered this. "Could you contact him now?" Vipsania asked. "It would be useful to have his agreement before we end our meeting."

Martinez sighed, then lifted his left arm to view his sleeve display. "I'll talk to Terza first," he said.

Roland's hand comm went off as Martinez completed his order to his display. He paused while Roland glanced at his message, then turned to give verbal commands to the video display above the bar.

"My office tells me there's something I have to view," he said, and then Lady Tu-hon appeared on the screen. She stood outdoors in a high-collared dark overcoat, and someone held an umbrella over her head to ward off the drizzle.

"How often must we lament the conspiracies and calumnies before the administration takes action?" she demanded. An invisible throng roared its approval, and then the screen switched to a view of the crowd filling a tree-lined space that Martinez recognized as Loo Park in the Old Third district of the Lower Town. The swarm filled the park and overflowed its boundaries, and they held signs and banners that wilted in the rain. A rally of the Steadfast League, clearly. The picture cut back to Tu-hon, and her orange eyes flashed.

"The gang of criminals responsible for the financial catastrophe is known to the authorities!" she proclaimed. "And now they have claimed another victim—a Peer of the first rank, a Peer who was trying to open an entire world for her clients and for the benefit of millions of hardworking emigrants." Lady Tu-hon made an abrupt gesture, as if she were throwing away the hopes of those emigrants. "We must ask ourselves why the authorities refuse to act, and why they allow this gang of Terrans to continue their depredations!"

The crowd roared, and the four members of the Martinez family looked at one another. "Gang of Terrans?" Walpurga said. "What gang do you think she has in mind?"

"*Us*," said Vipsania.

"Us, yes," said Roland. He frowned in thought. "But ultimately, I think, she's aiming much, much higher."

"Gareth?" Terza said. Her image appeared in Martinez's sleeve display, and when she saw his expression her face took on one of concern.

"Gareth. What's wrong?"

He looked at her and took a breath. "I'm afraid there's rather a lot of news."

AFTER THE AUTUMN Festival holiday, the Convocation resumed a debate regarding a proposed amendment to the budget reducing funding for local arts and cultural services.

This was viewed as a temporary measure in view of a budget shortfall and wasn't considered particularly controversial, but many convocates felt they should put it on record that they generally supported arts and culture despite the upcoming vote. Sula didn't bother with any assurances and spent the debate working mathematical puzzles and sending messages back and forth to her office, and she paid little attention to the argument until she recognized the voice of Lady Tu-hon.

Sula looked up from her puzzle and saw Tu-hon rising from her seat halfway across the amphitheater of the Convocation. A jeweled collar glittered about her neck. Her amplified voice was pitched to ring from the roofbeams. "These painful reductions would hardly be necessary if the economy had not been plundered by Terrans!" she said. "Criminals who have yet to be punished by the authorities."

Sula jumped to her feet at once, but it was Lord Saïd who first took action. He rose from his chair and adjusted the rings on his wand of office, reducing Lady Tu-hon's amplification and allowing his own rhetorician's voice to rise in the chamber.

"I trust the distinguished lady convocate is not impugning the entire Terran species," he said. "Such a sentiment is expressly forbidden by the Praxis, as I'm sure the lady convocate is aware."

"I wish to reassure the Lord Senior that I do not condemn all Terrans," Lady Tu-hon replied, once she had her amplification back. "I refer only to the Terran criminal conspiracy who make their fortunes off the current economic distress. Cosgrove, for example, and his coconspirator Lady Kannitha

Seang. And of course the Martinez clan, who not only profited off the bank failures, but who have driven the Rol-mar Company into receivership and ruined the hopes of the millions who had hoped to immigrate to this promising new world."

Pure astonishment snatched the breath from Sula's lungs. Lady Tu-hon's audacity had electrified the sleepy assembly and provided a startling contrast to Sula's two years of dull conclaves and uninspired debate.

Roland Martinez was already on his feet, but now furiously waved an arm to be recognized. Lord Saïd spoke first.

"It is customary that such serious accusations be backed with evidence," he said. "I trust the distinguished lady convocate can substantiate her allegations?"

"The administration already *possesses* the evidence," said Lady Tu-hon. "Cosgrove is in custody, and the man is clearly guilty, but there has been neither trial nor execution. The Imperial Bank during Kannitha Seang's administration conspired with Cosgrove and committed numerous frauds, but there have been no indictments and Lady Kannitha walks freely among us. Clan Martinez's development companies remain profitable, even as they've bankrupted the Rol-mar Company that employed them—and the trades of the individual members of the Martinez family, which helped to drive two banks into financial ruin, are available in the records of the Exchange, for all the empire to view." She cast a serene glance over the room. "I say nothing of other Terrans—shadowy figures haunting the vestibules of the Convocation—who act as agents and messengers for the conspirators and their clique."

Sula made a mental note to tell Lamey to make himself scarce until this situation was somehow resolved.

Roland Martinez was boiling with rage and continued to call for recognition, but Lord Saïd passed him over in favor of the Minister of Justice, who was asked to report on the progress of the prosecutions against Cosgrove and any others suspected of fraud and bad dealing. The minister reported that Cosgrove's finances were so complex and baffling that his trial had been delayed until he could help the investigators make better sense out of them. As for Lady Kannitha, the investigators had no evidence that she had any dealings with Cosgrove whatever, or any knowledge of the bank's Cosgrove account until after the financier's emprise had collapsed.

"The bank committed fraud, and Lady Kannitha was in charge of the bank," Tu-hon proclaimed. "What more evidence is necessary? And as for Cosgrove—the authorities are now asking for his *assistance*? His bones should be broken with hammers, and then he should be strung from a scaffold and skinned alive!"

The justice minister hastened to assure the Convocation that gruesome punishment awaited Cosgrove, but that a better understanding of his finances was desirable in order that new commercial regulation, aimed at preventing any future Cosgroves disturbing the fiscal peace, might best be promulgated. Lady Tu-hon treated this reply with scorn.

Lord Saïd finally permitted Roland Martinez to speak. Roland decried the slanders inflicted on his family and the Terran species and insisted that the Chee Company and Meridian had been severely damaged by Rol-mar's failure, which had stranded hundreds of thousands of workers on a barely inhabited world far from help.

"If you had not driven banks into receivership with your destructive trades," Tu-hon replied, "perhaps the crisis wouldn't have reached as far as Rol-mar, and you could have continued to bilk investors out of their fortunes."

"Bilking? The Chee Company billed Rol-mar for work done on Rol-mar's behalf. Does anyone allege that the work was not done?"

"I will defer to Lady Gruum to answer that question."

Lady Gruum rose from her seat, looking strangely fragile with her pale face, round staring eyes, black velvet gown, and tall heels. She spoke of extortionate and ruinous demands from the Chee Company, and how she had sacrificed much of her own personal fortune to meet them, only to fail to keep up.

Lady Gruum drew herself up and spoke with the ringing tone of a symphony. "I regret extremely that I have disgraced my ancestors by failing as patron to Rol-mar," she said. "But I have only one piece of advice to offer to my successor—*avoid the Martinez family!*"

That had Roland on his feet again, along with his allies like Lord Chen, Lord Ngeni, and Oda Yoshitoshi, all of them ready to bear witness to the essential virtue and probity of the Martinez family and the defamatory character of the allegations against them. Sula was not entirely willing to agree with them, but she was more than willing to defend her species. And besides, she knew perfectly well the reasons the economy had faltered and was willing to testify to that in open

Convocation if given the opportunity. But instead the Lord Senior chose to refocus the debate.

"Perhaps we should return this assembly to its proper topic," he said, "and consider once more the matter of funding for cultural services."

Sula sat, having nothing to say on the budget discussion. She was thinking about Lady Tu-hon and the Steadfast League, which was beginning to look something like a private army.

Well, she thought, Lady Tu-hon wasn't the only person in the room with a private army, and maybe it was time for Sula to talk to her own.

CHAPTER 12

Martinez came down the stairs at the Corona Club, looked through the glass panes at the front of the building, and saw the street packed with marchers plodding along through the evening, probably on their way to the Grandview Arena for a rally of the Steadfast League. There was no way his car would get through the mob: he'd have to call Alikhan to pick him up behind the building, on Gearing Street.

"I'll join you," Kelly said, "if you can drop me off at the Petty Mount."

"Can I offer anyone else a ride?" he asked.

"I have a car waiting," said Lady Kosch Altasz. "And Sodak lives near me."

"You'll have to tell your driver to pick you up on Gearing, behind us."

Martinez had followed the news of the financial collapse, and once he'd realized the authorities and the banks were hopeless he'd amused himself by betting against them, but whatever excitement lay in speculation had long since faded. Boredom hovered in the air around him, but fortunately the yachting season would begin in a month, and the pilots and administrators had met to plan their strategy for the upcoming races. Only three pilots could fly in each race, and veterans had to be balanced against newcomers. Support teams and alternates had to be chosen, and strategies contemplated. The meeting had gone on all afternoon in the study, and then several of the pilots had adjourned to the bar for drinks and snacks sent up from the kitchen. Now only four remained.

Lady Kosch, the feuding cousin of Lord Altasz, was a burly Torminel with powerful arms and shoulders and blue-gray fur. Lieutenant Sodak, the newcomer recommended by Lord Altasz, was another female Torminel, short and sharp-faced, with fur of mixed black and gray. Over several seasons Lady Kosch had proved a reliable racer, and Sodak had settled into the team very well, and only needed seasoning to become one of Corona's stars.

Martinez looked up at Ti-car, the Lai-own maître d', who stood by the front door in a splendid dark green uniform distinguished from that of the Fleet by its gold buttons and braid, and by the badge of the club: an eclipsed sun and glowing corona with stylized loops and prominences. Ti-car's pale feathery hair, floating about his head, was itself reminiscent of a corona.

"Are we the last?" Martinez asked.

"Yes, my lord."

"And no one's staying in the apartments?"

"We have no guests at present."

Martinez looked at his sleeve display and called up a chronometer. It was later than he'd thought. "You might as well close the kitchen, lock up, and go home," he said.

Ti-car bowed. "Thank you, my lord."

Wine curled up in Martinez's skull like a warm, sleepy, contented cat. It was a night, he thought, for stretching out before the fire with a comic novel by Hoi-tun and maybe—no, *definitely*—another glass of wine.

He used the sleeve display to call Alikhan, who had been meeting nearby in a coffee shop, or perhaps a bar, with some retired petty officer friends. He told Alikhan to bring the car to Gearing Street.

"Right away, my lord."

Ti-car took Martinez's overcoat from the rack and held it open for him. Martinez looked through the window at the crowd marching past, and they seemed warm enough in the autumn night, so he reached out a hand for the coat.

"I'll just carry it, thanks."

He put the coat over his arm, and Ti-car opened the front door, with its glass panels featuring the club badge. They passed outside into the crisp autumn air and began their stroll up the sidewalk. The marchers, walking in the other direction, passed in a long column to their left. Somewhere ahead a Daimong chorus was vocalizing on "May Your Thoughts Be Ever Guided by the Praxis."

"Say," said Lady Kosch, "did you hear that Cosgrove's to be executed tomorrow?" Her breath frosted before her face, and her night-adapted eyes reflected the yellow tint of the streetlights.

"No," Martinez said. "I thought they were keeping him alive so he'd give up his hidden bank accounts, or something."

"Political pressure," Kosch said. "The government's decided on a splashy execution. I'm not sure when the broadcast will get here from Hy-Oso, but I may just tune in the Punishment Channel and watch. The bastard cost me thirty grand at least—and they said those bonds were rock-solid!"

"The only punishment channel I need is to look at my investments," Martinez said. Kosch made a throaty cough of amusement.

Wine purred in Martinez's blood. The Daimong chorus approached. Martinez saw they were marching beneath a sign that read DOWN WITH THE TERRAN CRIMINALS. A cold warning finger touched his spine, and his warm contentment vanished like the misty breath before his face. He walked on, but turned his head away from the crowd, toward the dark storefronts on his right.

"It's Martinez!" A threadbare Lai-own pointed from out of the crowd. "It's the criminal Martinez!"

Great, Martinez thought. For the first time in his life, he regretted being so easily recognized. And he regretted what had doubtless contributed to the recognition, his undress uniform, which he'd worn because the convenience of the sleeve display meant he didn't have to carry a hand comm when accessing the yachting simulations in the Corona Club study.

"It's Martinez!" The Lai-own was insistent. "It's Martinez the Terran! Martinez the thief!"

The Daimong harmonies stumbled and fell into discord. Lady Kosch snarled at the Lai-own marcher. "Be silent, you imbecile!"

"It's Martinez and his accomplices!"

Martinez heard Kelly's urgent whisper. "Maybe we'd better get back to the club."

Part of the crowd surged onto the sidewalk. One of the Daimong singers reeled up in front of Martinez, bringing with him the scent of grain alcohol and rotting flesh. He seized Martinez's arm and pulled him around to face him. Lady Kosch growled and tore the Daimong's hand away. "It's Martinez!" the Daimong called in a voice like a siren, at the same instant that Lady Kosch said, "Get away, you layabout!"

"I'm being attacked!" the Daimong cried. "They're attacking me!"

Martinez felt the situation begin a horrid, vertiginous slide out of control, as if he were sliding down a hill made entirely out of pebbles. More Daimong filled up the walk ahead of him, and he saw that the marching column had come to a halt. A host of eyes stared at him from beneath the banner condemning the Terran criminals. He took a breath and stepped forward, the cold autumn air rasping in his throat. He drew himself up to his considerable height and squared his broad shoulders.

"What do you want of me?" he said, in the voice with which he might address a compartment full of recruits.

The Daimong rubbed his arm. "You're a thief!" he said.

"And you're a drunk!" Martinez said. "And you're embarrassing your friends, so just quiet down."

There was silence. The drunken Daimong hesitated, as if he were considering for the first time whether he might in fact be an embarrassment. His friends also seemed willing to consider this same possibility.

Martinez turned to one of the other Daimong. "Take your friend away," he said quietly. "It's time he left."

It was impossible to read their immobile expressions, but for a moment he thought they might obey, and then a bottle came sailing out of the crowd. Martinez felt the breeze of its passage on the back of his neck, and then it hit the glass window of a shop. No mere bottle was going to break a shop window, so the bottle rebounded and hit Martinez on the ankle. He turned in the direction of the bottle thrower and saw the Lai-own who had first recognized him, and who stood pointing with his muzzle agape and triumph in his golden eyes.

Fur bristling, Sodak charged with her head down, hurtled into the Lai-own's narrow frame, and knocked him sprawling, then delivered a serious of savage kicks to the prone body. Hollow Lai-own bones cracked, and the Lai-own shrieked.

"They're attacking us!" cried the drunken Daimong in a voice of tortured metal. "Stop them!" He charged in, fists swinging.

Martinez's overcoat was hampering his arm, so he threw it over the Daimong's head, then seized the Daimong's arm and shoulder and, using the upper-body strength he'd honed as a racer, hurled him headfirst into the nearest building. Kelly, eyes wide, leaped out of the way as the Daimong hit the window. Using his fist like a hammer, Martinez clouted the

Daimong on the head as the drunk rebounded, then snatched the overcoat as he collapsed at the feet of his friends. His dead-flesh reek clung to the back of Martinez's throat.

"Back to the club," he said, as another bottle came blindly out of the crowd and smashed on the sidewalk. Martinez saw Lady Kosch about to launch herself at the Daimong chorus and put a hand on her arm to hold her back. "To the club," he repeated. He and Kosch and Kelly backed away.

Snarling in triumph, Sodak returned to the sidewalk and began to lead the party toward the club. Marchers surrounded the wounded Lai-own. Martinez saw grim expressions as the marchers recovered from the shock of Sodak's violence. Bottles and debris sailed through the air. Martinez batted away a bottle aimed at his head and heard it smash on the pavement.

The Daimong chorus hesitated behind the sprawled drunk, but then a group of young Daimong burst through them and charged. Two of them tripped over the drunk, and they came in more strung out than they intended. Martinez threw his overcoat over the first one, punched him in the body, then laid him out with a forearm to the face. The Daimong dead-flesh smell filled the air. Lady Kosch met her attacker head-on, her powerful arms hooking one body punch after another. Kelly fought a third, but any combat courses at the academy were long ago, and her lanky body was not built for street fights. She staggered back reeling from a blow to the face, and her assailant followed, shrugging off her wild punches. Martinez came in from his blind side with his shoulder low and hurled him into the plate-glass window of the shop to the right. Martinez then seized the Daimong's head in his two big fists and smashed it repeatedly into the glass until the Daimong went limp. He bent to snatch up his overcoat from the half-conscious form of his original opponent and looked for the next attacker, only to find that Lady Kosch had pushed her own attacker in the way of the next assailant. They collided, flailed, rebounded. Martinez kicked the nearest one in the hip and knocked him into his friend. They both fell sprawling.

Martinez and Kosch continued their retreat. Bottles smashed and bounded off the wall near them. Martinez turned to Kelly and saw her wiping blood off her face. She was pale, but she doubled her fists at the ends of her skinny arms, game for the next encounter but looking about as threatening as a child.

"Call the club," he told her. "Make sure the door is open for us. And then call the police."

Because where *were* they? A huge column of marchers like this, blocking cross-traffic for the better part of an hour, should have police shepherding them along their route.

At least they weren't being attacked by Torminel, all fangs, aggression, and thick protective fur.

He fended off a bottle, and he kept scanning the crowd for signs of another attack. Some of the Daimong picked themselves off the sidewalk, but they didn't seem eager to renew their assault. And then he heard someone rapping out orders in a tone of command.

"You three, get behind them. You lot, get ready. And the rest of you, keep up the aerial barrage."

Aerial barrage. A term unlikely to be employed by a civilian. He scanned the crowd and saw an elderly Torminel with thin, patchy brown fur, and a single fang overhanging her lower lip. Fleet medals hung on her vest, and there was a feral, cunning look in her glowing night-adapted eyes. A retired petty officer, he assumed.

The Torminel saw him looking at her, and her lips drew back in something that might have been either a snarl or a smile, but which Martinez read as a challenge. She knew just who he was, and how she planned to hurt him.

A bottle sailed over his head and smashed against the wall. He thought that perhaps he might want to convert that broken bottle into a weapon, but he didn't want the crowd to see him and be reminded that they'd be that much more dangerous if they stopped throwing bottles, and instead used them as clubs, or broke them and used them as knives.

Then he saw people rushing through the crowd carrying long staves they'd got from somewhere, and he realized the question of disarmament had already been settled. Covering his movement with his overcoat, he bent to pick up the broken bottle by the neck.

Four Fleet officers, he thought, *and nobody has a sidearm.*

"Better arm yourselves," he said. "I see big sticks out there."

The Torminel petty officer called for an increased barrage. There were few bottles left, but garbage filled the air, along with a trash receptacle that whooshed overhead and clanged against a storefront. The bobbing staves were coming closer, and Martinez realized that they were the poles the crowd had been using to carry signs.

"Now!" the Torminel cried. "Attack, attack!"

There was a rush of Daimong and a few Lai-own. Some swung staves. The dead-flesh smell was blended with the acid note of Lai-own. Martinez blinded an attacker with his overcoat and punched through it, reversing the bottle to use the end of the neck as a hammer. The attacker staggered back, but one of the staves hit Martinez on the neck, and for a second he felt every nerve in his body paralyzed as if by electric shock, his every brain cell flailing like a falling man pitching headfirst into a dark cellar—and then a wave of fury rose in him, and he dropped the bottle and the overcoat and seized the stave with both hands and kicked the Lai-own attacker away from his own weapon.

He hadn't done much brawling in his life, and so far he'd been depending on size and strength rather than skill; but he'd been a fencer at the academy and he had an idea how to use a polearm. He thrust it at the faces of the attackers around him, using his weight to bruise them and keep them from closing. They all drew back. He saw Kelly fighting with a Daimong on his right, and he swung the pole at the legs of the Daimong and knocked the attacker off his feet, then had his point back in the face of the next assailant before the attacker could react. He was able to keep a number of attackers at bay, because they weren't professionals and they weren't coordinated. Every time he saw one of them gather courage to attack, he'd thrust his staff at their eyes or chest and discourage them. People thrust their poles at him, but he was able to riposte, and he disarmed one startled Lai-own with a circular parry. When the stave fell to the ground, he kicked it behind him for Kelly or someone else to use.

Lady Kosch hurled one bleeding Lai-own into the pack, and then Martinez heard the voice of the Torminel petty officer above the roars of the crowd.

"You idiots! You're supposed to attack all at once!"

You didn't have *to point that out,* Martinez thought. One of the Daimong on his right seemed to have summoned his resolution and was readying himself to make an attack, and Martinez shifted his staff and jabbed him in the face. He hit the Daimong in an eye, and the attacker clutched the eye and fell back. A siren yowl rose from his immobile lips.

"All of you attack on my mark!" the petty officer shouted. "Three! Two! One! . . ."

On each number, Martinez jabbed at a different target. He could feel sweat or blood dripping down his face.

"Mark!"

Oh fucking damn, Martinez thought.

This time they actually *did* come more or less at once. Martinez shortened his grip on his stave so that he could fight with either end, and he slashed and stabbed right and left, the shock of his strikes running up his arms, but still he was borne back by the sheer weight of numbers. A stave smashed him in the face and again he felt that paralyzing shock that left his brain cells flailing. The breath was driven from his lungs as he was driven into the storefront behind him, and after that he was just a target for fists and feet, pinned against the wall by his own stave, hardly able to defend himself. He could taste his own blood. He felt his knees give way and he sagged, his arms raised to guard his face as the blows came in.

With luck, he thought, he'd be unconscious soon.

Then he heard a *squall,* the cry of a Torminel carnivore as it pounced, a nerve-shredding shriek intended to paralyze its prey. The scream worked as intended, freezing Martinez in place, and it seemed to freeze his attackers, too. Then they were battered away from him as another of their number was hurled into them like a bowling ball into a stack of pins. Martinez straightened and took his first free breath of cool night air in what seemed to be a hundred years.

Lady Kosch squalled again and pounced on one of the reeling Daimong, hugging him close. The Daimong gave a weirdly sonorous cry of pain and terror. Then there was a spray of red as Lady Kosch's fangs tore her victim's throat, and she spun him around to face his fellow attackers, showering them all with arterial blood.

The attackers fell back in horror. *"This is what awaits you, scum!"* Lady Kosch screamed. She continued to brandish the dying Daimong before her as she forged a path back to the Corona Club, stalking down the sidewalk as the crowd fell back before her. Sodak limped after in silence. Martinez, panting for breath, turned to follow and found Kelly unconscious at his feet. He let his stave fall and swept Kelly up in his arms, then gasped as bruised ribs protested.

Ti-car, dignified in his green uniform, opened the door of the club, and Sodak and Martinez entered. After the brawl in the street, the deep silence of the club and the lobby's immaculate, gleaming fixtures both carried a sense of unreality.

Lady Kosch alone remained outside, her eyes glowing with triumph. "This will teach you to threaten your betters, vermin!" she proclaimed, and kicked her bleeding victim toward his comrades. The Daimong fell to the pavement at their feet. Blood still pulsed from his torn throat. Then, snarling, Lady Kosch backed into the club. Ti-car closed and locked the door behind her.

"Have you called the police?" Martinez asked him.

"Yes, my lord. They said they would come."

"Turn off the lights in here. And better make sure the kitchen door is locked."

"Yes, my lord."

"Sodak, could you call for an ambulance? Tell them we'll need more than one."

"Yes." Sodak's voice seemed to come from half a dozen light-years away. "Yes, I'll do that."

Kelly's bloody head lolled against Martinez's shoulder. He carried her up the stairs to the lounge and laid her on one of the couches. Beneath the gore her skin was pale, and freckles stood out against her pallor. He had never noticed the freckles till now.

Breath whistled past her bloody lips. He checked for a pulse, found one, then lifted her eyelids. Both her pupils were vast, dark, empty pools.

Martinez needed to wash away the blood to continue his examination, and he went into the washroom to find a cloth. He turned on the light, saw himself in the mirror, and paused to view the damage. Cuts on his forehead and scalp bled freely. His knuckles were swollen. His lower lip had been cut, and one eye was swollen half shut. He moistened a towel and cleaned himself as well as he could, then soaked another towel in warm water and brought it out to Kelly. He cleaned her face gently, then took her head in his hands and carefully probed with his fingers to discover if there was any damage to the skull. Blood oozed onto his fingertips from the cuts. When he found nothing, relief filled him like a breath of wind.

But then his fingers worked around to the back of Kelly's head and his heart sank. There was a soft depression at the very back of her skull, and he could imagine all too well Kelly being knocked into the storefront and her head smashed into the unyielding wall.

He didn't want to probe further lest he drive shards of bone into Kelly's brain, so as gently as possible he laid her head back on the sofa. He rose, felt blood dripping down his forehead, and wiped it with his towel.

A tread sounded on the stairs, and he turned to see Ti-car enter the room. "I've locked all the doors, my lord." His golden eyes turned toward Kelly. "Is Lieutenant Kelly badly hurt?"

"Skull fracture. Did Sublieutenant Sodak call for an ambulance?"

"She did, my lord."

But the ambulances could only come if they could get through the crowd, and they might not come at all unless they could get a police escort. It was time to call the police again. Martinez was about to turn to his sleeve display when Ti-car spoke again.

"I have a first aid kit, my lord. Should I bring it?"

"Yes—wait. I don't suppose there's a firearm in the building?"

Ti-car hesitated. "I'm afraid not, my lord."

"How many staff are here now?"

"Besides myself, there's three kitchen staff, and Mock the waitron, so that's five—no, my lord, six, because Sekalog is still here. I just saw him closing the bar."

"Make sure they all know not to leave the building."

"Yes, my lord."

Martinez wiped away another trickle of warm blood. "Then bring the first aid kit."

He raised his left arm and triggered the sleeve display just as a crash sounded from the front of the building. He told the display to call the police as he left the lounge and went down the stairs to the ground floor. Sodak and Lady Kosch stood at the foot of the stairs, watching as members of the crowd smashed a waste container against one of the front windows.

"Don't worry," Martinez said. "That window's up to code. Nothing short of a bomb will break it."

Kosch looked over her shoulder at him. The fur around her mouth, and down her throat, was matted with blood. "Worried?" she said. "Hardly!" She bared her fangs. "The *impudence* of that rabble! If I only had a sidearm, I'd send the lot of them to the crematorium!"

Martinez did not reply. Lady Kosch's belligerence had almost certainly made the situation worse, but then that very belligerence had just saved him from a mob. Any comment would be superfluous.

He called the police on his sleeve display, and to his surprise was answered by a Naxid in the uniform of a corporal of the Urban Patrol. Martinez reported a riot in progress, with several people injured, one—a Fleet lieutenant—critically.

"We are aware of all that, my lord," said the Naxid. "But all our officers are deployed on traffic control, and we—"

"That means they're *right here,*" Martinez said. "If they're on traffic control, they're *already deployed in this area*. All they need to do is put a few squads together and—"

"Captain Klarvash is trying to do that," said the Naxid. "But control has broken down and it's very difficult."

Another crash sounded from the front window. "Do you hear that?" Martinez said. "We're under siege here. They're trying to break in."

"Captain Klarvash is doing his best, my lord."

"Let me speak to Captain Klarvash."

"That's not possible, my lord."

Klarvash was a Naxid name, and the corporal-dispatcher was another Naxid. Though Naxids were no longer permitted in the Fleet with its planet-searing weaponry, they still served in some of the security services, mostly on the grounds that they were better than other species at policing other Naxids. A demonstration this large had probably called in a lot of police from all sorts of districts, and apparently this Klarvash was in charge of them.

Martinez had killed a great many Naxids in the war, and he had to wonder if Klarvash and his dispatcher had any reason to resent it.

Lady Kosch snarled. "Who is that imbecile to refuse you?" she demanded. The Naxid corporal blinked his bright red eyes.

"I'm following procedure, my lord."

Martinez ended the call, then jumped as yet another

crash boomed out, strong enough to shake the entire building. Something in the next room clanged as it toppled from a shelf. Martinez looked out to see that the rioters had carried away a heavy iron bench from the nearest transit stop and were trying to ram it through the window. On the second strike a skull-shattering alarm bell began to clatter. Sodak put her hands over her ears.

The alarm might spur the police, Martinez thought. But probably not. And certainly it wasn't a deterrent to the rioters, who smashed the bench into the window again.

"Upstairs," Martinez said, and turned for the stairs. Sodak followed, but Lady Kosch remained, glaring out the windows at the attackers. Martinez had to shout over the alarm bell. "We'll hear them if they break in! We need to make plans!"

Kosch snarled at the rioters, then followed Martinez up the stairs. The sound of the alarm faded slightly. In the lounge, Martinez found Ti-car kneeling by Kelly, applying healing patches to Kelly's wounds.

"Be careful with her," Martinez said. "The back of her skull's been damaged. Don't touch her there."

"Yes, my lord."

Martinez knelt by Ti-car and helped him apply the bandages. Kelly's skin was clammy, and Martinez assumed she was in shock. He found a blanket in a cupboard, returned, and covered Kelly's body.

The building shook twice more to an assault, and then the crashes stopped. The alarm clattered on. Sodak, hands still over her ears, collapsed into a chair.

Then while Ti-car was applying fast-healers to Martinez's

head, he called Roland. An automated secretary answered, and Martinez told it that this was an emergency. Roland answered in a few seconds.

"What just happened?" he asked. He knew Martinez wouldn't call at this hour unless something startling had occurred.

Martinez outlined the situation. "You need to light a fire underneath Captain Klarvash," he said.

"I'll do better than that," Roland said, and then the orange end-stamp filled Martinez's sleeve display as Roland ended the call.

Lady Kosch had prowled down the corridor to the library overlooking the street in order to keep an eye on the attackers, and now she came back in a hurry.

"That bitch of a petty officer is haranguing them again," she said. "If only I had a rifle!"

Then there was another crash, this time in a somewhat higher timbre. Kosch dashed back out to the library, then dashed back. "They're ramming the *door* now," she said. "Will it hold?"

"The doors are steel," Ti-car said. "The glass in them is made from the same compound used for the windows. There are substantial bolts shot from the doors into the steel frame."

"The doors should hold for a while, then," Martinez said. An idea struck him, and as he turned to Ti-car he inadvertently tore a fast-healing patch from his scalp. He winced, but managed his question anyway. "The windows over the street can open, yes?"

"Yes, my lord." Ti-car was trying to reapply the patch.

"Get the staff up here. Tell them to bring whatever they can find to use as weapons."

"The kitchen staff can bring knives."

Martinez winced as Ti-car's fingers pressed the patch firmly to his scalp.

"Tell them to bring *all* the knives," he said.

A FEW MINUTES later they were assembled in the darkened library, watching the crowd mill in the gleam of the streetlights. The Torminel petty officer was prominent among them, urging the attackers on, sending parties running off on errands. Her night-adapted eyes glowed as she prowled among the rioters. A broad patch of blood was still visible on the pavement where the Daimong casualty had bled out, but the body had been carried out of sight.

The club's staff were gathered around Martinez: Ti-car the Lai-own maître d', the Daimong waitron Mock, the Terran chef, his Daimong sous-chef, and their Terran apprentice. Sekalog, the Cree bartender, was reopening the bar to provide bottles to be used as missiles.

The alarm bell continued to clatter downstairs. The building echoed to another ramming attack on the door.

Martinez had a couple carving knives stuck in his belt, and he felt faintly ridiculous, as if he'd just shown up at an elite cocktail party in the costume of a pirate.

"Who's good at throwing?" he asked. "Anyone taken up the Pitcher's Post in indoor fatugui? Or thrown the shot in lepper?"

There was no response. Martinez sighed, unbuttoned his tunic, and rotated his arm in hopes of warming his throwing muscles. Sekalog scurried into the room carrying a case of wine bottles.

"I hope you brought the cheap stuff," Martinez said. No one laughed.

Lady Kosch seized a bottle and hefted it approvingly. "I'm going to try to brain that fucking petty officer," she said.

"Bring more bottles," Martinez told Sekalog. He planned never to run out of ammunition again.

He, Kosch, and Sodak positioned themselves behind the three tall windows and triggered the panes. They were hinged in the middle and pivoted open, the lower halves of the panes opening out over the street, the upper halves tipping into the room. No one in the crowd seemed to take notice.

Martinez could see the Torminel petty officer plainly but doubted he could reach her with a bottle. The lower part of the windowpane was in the way, and he feared the bottle would bounce off. If the window had just opened like a door, he'd have had all the room he needed. But Lady Kosch was indefatigable.

"I'll have to throw sidearm," she said. Martinez decided he might as well follow her example and leaned to the right as he practiced a sidearm shot.

The building quaked as the improvised ram struck again.

"Are we ready?" Martinez said. "On my mark—three, two, one, *mark*!"

The three bottles winged out into the crowd. Martinez's grazed the window frame and whirled out of sight. The other two bottles spun like boomerangs in flight and landed short, detonating at the petty officer's feet. She looked up in shock as glass fragments sprayed her legs, and she bounded back out of range.

Martinez reached a hand behind him, and the Terran chef slapped a fresh bottle into his hand. He stepped closer to the window and fired his missile directly at the crowd trying to ram open the front doors. It struck a Daimong rioter directly on the shoulder, and he fell in a tangle of limbs. Bottles followed from Sodak and Kosch, and one more attacker fell sprawling.

Screams of rage rose from the crowd. Three more bottles were hurled onto the besiegers before they dropped the iron bench and scurried to safety, leaving one of their number lying on the pavement in a growing pool of red. The rest of the crowd formed a semicircle in front of the Corona Club, safely out of range.

"Cowards!" Kosch raged. "Filth!" She turned to Martinez. "We should get some brandy or whisky, and tie burning rags around the neck. Set the lot of them on fire!"

"I don't think we want to give them any ideas about fire," Martinez cautioned.

Kosch snarled, then stuck her head out the window. "Cowards!" she called again.

"*We're* not hiding!" The mocking voice came from the petty officer. "Come out and say hello!"

Martinez began to suspect he was now caught in the middle of a feud between a pair of Torminel, by far the most dangerous place to be in all the worlds under the Praxis. Still, he might be able to do a bit of damage to the alliances that the rioters had forged among themselves. He bent to look out the window. "Oh, you'll fight all right!" he called. "You'll fight to the last Daimong! You'll fight to the last Lai-own! But you won't do any fighting yourself!"

The petty officer brandished a fist. "I'll fight to the last *Terran*!" she screamed. An enormous roar of approval rolled up from the crowd, and Martinez saw fists and weapons brandished.

For a moment there was a stalemate filled only by the endless clatter of the alarm. Martinez took advantage of the opportunity to call Roland again. There was no answer, and Martinez assumed his brother was busy rounding up reinforcements. But then there was movement in the crowd, and Martinez could see the petty officer busy assembling parties of rioters. One group of a dozen or fifteen ran off to the right, and Martinez could see tools in their hands.

"I think they're going to try to break in the back of the building," he said. He turned to the sous-chef. "Could you go down the back stairs and let me know if they start trying to get in through the alley? And does anyone know if there's a window overlooking that back door?"

"Yes, my lord," said the chef. "A small one, off a landing on the stairs."

"Perhaps we'd better set up another defensive post there."

Sodak and the sous-chef went to the rear of the building, lugging two cases of wine. Martinez continued to look out the front. The rioters, he saw, had been reinforced by a group of Torminel, who would provide a tenacious, belligerent core around which further assaults could be launched.

Their glowing night-eyes moved through the crowd like little lamps. No Terran was in sight, though Martinez remembered seeing Terrans in the march. They knew better than to appear here, where they might fall victim to the mob.

Martinez hadn't seen Naxids connected with the march at all. Since the war they'd been discreet about appearing in public, even those—the vast majority—who'd had nothing to do with the rebellion.

But no, the Naxids, in the person of Captain Klarvash, were in charge of the response, and they, too, were standing aside.

Sekalog the bartender arrived with another case of wine, his winglike ears tuned toward the windows and the sound of the crowd. He put the case down with a clatter. Then he straightened, turning, one ear reaching toward the door behind him.

"They are behind us," he said. "They are attempting the back door."

"Are we responding?" Martinez asked.

Somehow the Cree's eyeless, purple-fleshed face gave the impression of careful attention. "We are trying to get the window open on the stairs landing," he said. "And that Torminel female out front is ordering up a barrage for the windows, followed by an attempt to pry the front door and windows open."

Well, Martinez thought, *that was comprehensive.* And Sekalog was managing to overhear this despite the sonic interference of the clanging alarm.

"When are they—" Martinez began.

"Now."

A yelling chorus rushed forward on the street, hurling bottles and bricks and knives at the defenders waiting behind the windows. Most of the weapons caromed off the building or the windows, but Martinez had to sidestep a heavy wrench as it tumbled toward his head. The defenders responded, hurling bottles among the incensed enemy, knocking a few down. The apprentice chef, who had stepped into Sodak's place at one of the windows, was hit in the elbow by a bottle and had to start throwing with her left arm.

Ti-car returned and had to shout over the blaring alarm and the shouts of the crowd. "They're trying to open the back door," he said, "but Sodak's repelling them."

"Make sure she has enough bottles," Martinez gasped, and hurled a magnum of champagne that exploded splendidly among the rioters.

The odor of spilled wine clogged the air. The missiles thinned as the attackers began to run low on ammunition, so another group of rioters, with crowbars, chisels, and axes, dashed forward to the building. The windowpanes had proved invulnerable to their attacks, and now they were going to try simply to pry the windows out of their frames. This, Martinez thought, stood a fair chance of success, and he hurled bottles down directly on the heads of the improvised assault engineers and did his best to dash their brains out. A water bottle bounced off his forehead without doing any damage, and in response he hurled a hearty wine from Cavado that dropped an attacker to the pavement.

His breath rasped in his lungs. He shook sweat from his

eyes. Throwing bottles was a lot more work than he'd ever imagined.

Still, he thought his defenders were doing well. The attackers were so busy fending off missiles that they were making very little progress breaking in.

And then there was a sharp crack, and his windowpane filled with stars. He dropped to the floor as another shot threw glass chips into the room.

"Down!" he said. All dropped to the floor except for Lady Kosch, who was in a frenzy, hurling bottle after bottle upon the attackers while cursing them without cease. Martinez gathered his legs under him while unease crept up his spine at the realization he was about to throw himself into the line of fire. He hurled himself forward and tackled Lady Kosch just as a pair of shots cracked through her window. She gave a guttural, furious shriek as he landed on top of her, and for a moment he was all too aware of her bared fangs a hand's width from his throat.

"One of them has a rifle," he said. *Which should be fucking obvious by now.* A roar from the crowd outside confirmed this, as the rioters now realized it wasn't the police shooting at them, but one of their own number adding to their firepower.

With a heave of her powerful body, Kosch rolled Martinez off her. "I know that," she said. "But he's too far away to fire with any accuracy."

More shots snapped through the windows, perforating the walls and ceiling and bringing down flakes of plaster. Sekalog came into the room on his knees, dragging a case of wine behind him.

"Probably a veteran of the Secret Army," Martinez said. *Or a Naxid cop,* he thought.

Kosch snarled. "How many more veterans are out there?"

"Veterans? I'll have to get Lady Sula to give them all a stern talking-to," Martinez said. He crawled back to his position and carefully rose to his feet on one side of the window, keeping the wall between himself and the shooter. He took a bottle of wine in his hand, took aim, and hurled it at one of the attackers. His arm was exposed only for an instant, but it was enough to produce a pair of bullets that flew through his window. A third bullet shattered the windowpane entirely.

"He seems to have plenty of ammunition," Martinez said. "Everyone be careful."

The defenders returned to their work and stood between the windows with their backs to the wall, throwing bottles onto the besiegers. The stance required for staying out of the line of fire was physically awkward and hampered throwing, and the view of the street was less useful. Martinez knew he was contributing less to the defense than he had been.

Several times the wall punched him in the back as it absorbed bullets from the shooter.

From below, there was a cracking noise, and then a rending shriek. The attackers had peeled away a part of the window frame, and the crowd awarded their success with a baying roar that sent a cold shiver up Martinez's back. The defenders were losing.

Martinez chucked a bottle in the direction from which the rending sounds originated, and then wiped sweat and blood from his face and reached for another.

"We've got to get out of here," he said. "We can't defend this place once they break in." He looked at the Terran apprentice chef. "Have you been in the cellar? Is there a way out, into tunnels or into the next building?"

"No," she said shortly. "No way out of the cellar." She had taken off her uniform jacket and revealed tattoos on wiry arms and shoulders. Her right elbow was bruised and swollen and she was tossing left-handed, and grunting with every throw.

"The stairs go all the way to the roof, yes?" Martinez said.

"Yes, we can get onto the roof. But there's no way off it once we get up there."

It seemed to Martinez that the door to the roof might be more defensible than any of the rooms in the club. He tried to recall whether the buildings on either side overlooked the club and could furnish a sniper's nest for the shooter, but he was exhausted, gasping for breath, and the blaring alarm was hammering his skull and short-circuiting his thoughts. The answer wouldn't materialize.

Martinez hurled another bottle down onto the attackers but was rewarded only with another rending shriek as another piece of the window frame was torn loose.

"Can we get over to the next building?" he asked.

"There is an alley behind and to the north," Ti-car said, bending out of the line of fire as he dragged another crate of wine into the room. "To the south, it might be possible to jump the gap."

Martinez hurled another bottle. "We've got to get Kelly over somehow," he panted.

Ti-car paused for thought. "Perhaps we could bridge the

gap." He turned to the waitron, Mock, who was handing bottles to the defenders. "Have we planks?"

"Back door," said Mock. "We have a ramp for carrying supplies to the kitchen."

"We shall bring it up," Ti-car said.

"Hurry," said Martinez.

Sekalog half crawled into the room with two crates of wine. Martinez turned to the Terran chef. "Relieve this woman," he said, nodding at the apprentice. Then, to the apprentice, he said, "Go up to the roof. Don't let anyone see you. See if it's possible to get to the next building."

The apprentice gave him a grateful look, then bent low and loped out of the room, holding her wounded arm close. The chef picked up a bottle, peered narrowly out the window, and launched his missile. A crash was followed by a torrent of abuse in a wounded, lisping Torminel voice.

Shots rattled out from the street, and bullets snapped through the windows. *Does that bastard have an unlimited supply of ammunition?* Martinez wondered. He heaved one bottle, gasped for breath, heaved another. Even Lady Kosch was nearing her limits, and no longer bothered to curse the enemy as she hurled bottle after bottle at them.

After some minutes Ti-car returned. "We got onto the roof," he said. "We've placed a ramp to the next building."

His words were echoed by another shriek of a part of the window frame being torn away. *The moment decisive,* Martinez thought.

"Keep up the fire," he told the others. "I'll get Kelly." He bent low and scurried out, then once in the corridor took

Ti-car by the arm. "We'll have to break into the next building," he said. "Can you get me some tools?"

"I'll see what I can do, my lord."

He went into the lounge and found it strangely peaceful and unreal. The soft gleam of the polished, paneled walls, the scent of the taswa-leather furniture, the gold racing trophies on their shelves. Kelly lay beneath her blanket and seemed unchanged. Her skin was clammy, but her breathing seemed regular.

Martinez considered for a moment while he caught his breath, then took Kelly's blanket and knotted two of the diagonal corners together, then hung the result over his neck and one shoulder, part sling and part hammock. He knelt by Kelly's couch, adjusted the two kitchen knives that were still in his belt, and carefully scooped Kelly into the sling, tugging it so it was wide enough to hold her hips and lanky body. He cradled the fractured head against his shoulder, got his feet under him, and stood. Pain crackled through his ribs, and he winced.

Kelly was lighter than he feared she'd be. Making sure not to crack her head on the doorframe, Martinez maneuvered into the hall. He walked to the back stairs and looked down at Sodak and the sous-chef, who were on the landing below him. Sodak was standing on a chair to give her the chance to fire bottles down from the small window on the landing, though there seemed to be no action at present.

"They're breaking in downstairs," Martinez told them. "We're going up to the roof. Sodak, help Ti-car bring tools to the roof. And you—" He gestured at the Daimong sous-chef.

"Nettruku, my lord."

"Nettruku, tell the people in the front room it's time to withdraw."

"Very good, my lord."

Martinez turned and went up the stairs. The door at the top was open, and Martinez was out of breath by the time he stepped out onto the roof's flat, spongy resinous surface. The stairs were part of a boxy structure that also held the mechanism for the club's elevator, and elsewhere the roof supported machinery for heating and cooling, and a water tower in the shape of a racing yacht standing on its tail. If they didn't hang over the parapets, he thought, the mob in the street wouldn't see them. Even watchers in the taller buildings nearby would have trouble seeing them at night, unless they were Torminel.

Martinez leaned, exhausted, on the doorframe and took long breaths of the cool night air. The clean taste was welcome after breathing the air in the library, heavy with the scent of sweat, spilled wine, and desperation.

The antimatter ring made a serene, perfect arc overhead. Pain shot through his ribs and his knees. He waited until Sodak and Ti-car arrived with boxes of tools.

"Can you lock the roof door once we're all here?" he asked.

"No, my lord," Ti-car said. "The door can never be locked from the inside lest it trap the victims of a fire."

"Have you got something that can wedge it?"

Sodak and Ti-car examined their tools, and Ti-car lifted out a pry bar with a wedge-shaped head. "We might try this. If we drove it in with sufficient force . . ."

Sodak lifted a large mallet. "This will do the job."

Martinez could only nod. Sekalog then came up the stairs in a rush, panting for breath, his purple skin almost invisible in the darkness. "Lady Kosch and the Terran gentlemen are firing a final volley," he said. "Everyone else will be up here soon."

Martinez didn't want to leave anyone behind, so he counted them all as they came up, remembering that Mock and the apprentice were already on the roof. But the numbers swam in his head, and he found himself repeatedly asking the others if everyone was here. Then there was a huge crash from the front of the building, followed by a roar of approval from the crowd, and Martinez concluded that one of the front windows had finally been torn away.

"Wedge the door," Martinez told Ti-car, and he led the others to the south side of the building, where Mock and the Terran apprentice had placed a pair of wide planks between the parapet of the club building and that of the next. The planks perched on their edges and barely bridged the gap, and Martinez was worried that one or both would slip and drop one of the party into the narrow gap between the buildings.

Another alarm was sounding from the other building, an alarm with a deeper baying tone, so possibly some windows had been broken there, too. A metallic battering came from behind Martinez, where Sodak and Ti-car were trying to jam the rooftop door.

While Martinez hesitated, Lady Kosch stepped onto one of the planks, and crossed in a half crouch. After the crossing, Mock and the apprentice adjusted the planks in case she'd shifted them slightly. Then Martinez stepped to the parapet, cradled Kelly's head with one hand, and held her body close with the other.

Martinez was a noted yacht captain, accustomed to extreme gravities or none at all, capable of whirling his boat in dizzying spirals or of grazing the atmosphere of planets. He was a stranger to vertigo. But still he was thankful that it was too dark for him to see the ground waiting below as he stepped onto the planks that bowed beneath his and Kelly's combined weight. His breath stopped in his throat, and he kept his eyes rigidly to the front as he walked. Two steps, three steps, four . . .

He didn't actually fall until he was all the way across and misjudged the drop off the parapet on the far side, and then Kosch was there to catch him before he dropped Kelly onto the roof and fell atop her. He breathed thanks to Lady Kosch and stepped out onto the neighboring roof, his head whirling.

The others came over quickly. Sodak and the Terran chef didn't like the looks of the planks, and instead leaped the gap, the chef landing with skinned knees as he misread his landing. "Pick up the planks," Martinez said. "We might need them for another crossing."

The party moved along the roof in the darkness, the nocturnal Torminel in the lead. The neighboring building was much larger and broader than the clubhouse, straddling the block from front to back, with retail space on the ground floor and offices above. The building's alarm groaned on. There were a pair of doors to the roof, both locked, and skylights gazed down at rooms of empty desks and office equipment. The Terran chef came back from scouting the parapet, his eyes agleam. In the darkness he loomed like a seasoned warrior, a carving knife in one hand and a cleaver in the other.

"Look—it's what we want," he said. "A tube to the next building over."

He led Martinez to a view of an enclosed pedestrian bridge connecting the east side of the building with the property across Gearing Street. "Once we get across that," he said, "we should be clear of all this mess." Because there were still people wandering the streets below, some probably trying to get away from the violence, but others clearly looking for trouble.

For the first time in a long while Martinez remembered Alikhan, who was in Martinez's car, supposedly awaiting him on Gearing Street. He looked down the street, but failed to see the car.

"Right," Martinez said. "Let's get into the building."

Tools were deployed to break through one of the roof doors, but the door proved resistant to the party's pry bars and hammers. "It might be easier to break through a skylight," Sodak said. "I can drop down, find the stairs, and let you all in."

The skylight was more vulnerable than the door, and it took only a few minutes to break its lock and wrench it open. Sodak wormed through the gap, hung at the end of her arms, then dropped onto someone's desk. Her arms windmilled for a moment, then she regained her balance, hopped off the desk, and prowled out of sight. The rest moved to the door to wait.

A few minutes passed. Pain flooded Martinez's ribs, knees, skull. He tried to listen for Kelly's breathing, but couldn't hear anything over the sound of the alarm.

He was standing next to the door when it opened, and in the light rising from the stairs saw that the Torminel stepping onto the roof wasn't Sodak. Without conscious thought Martinez snatched one of the carving knives from his belt and drove it under the Torminel's arm with all his strength. The Torminel shrieked and leaped away, wrenching the knife out of Martinez's hand, but the jump placed the intruder within the range of the Terran chef, who buried his cleaver in the Torminel's skull.

The next shriek came from Lady Kosch, who pounced onto the second Torminel running onto the roof, her knife driving repeatedly into her target. The Terran chef followed, his cleaver held high.

Martinez groped blindly for his other knife as combat erupted on the stairs. Screams resounded in the night, along with the crash of crude weapons striking the walls and the squalls of hunting Torminel. Martinez heard thumps as bodies were hurled down stairs or into walls. He found his second knife and drew it, then hesitated. He couldn't drag Kelly into a close-quarters knife fight.

Nettruku charged in, and then the Terran apprentice. There was a final scream, one that cut off with a horrific liquid sound, and then there was silence. Martinez cradled Kelly's head to keep it from hitting the edge of the door as he peered down the stairs at a scene of carnage.

Apparently the rioters, frustrated with their slow progress in breaking into the club, had sent a party into the building to gain the roof, cross over to the club, and attack the defenders from above, or open a door for their friends. The party hadn't got into the building as quickly as they'd hoped, or got lost once they got inside, and came up onto the roof later than they expected.

Bodies lay strewn on the stairs, and blood drained in thick, half-clotted waterfalls down the risers. The rioters' improvised weapons were scattered over the scene, pipes and knives and broken bottles. Lady Kosch stood at the bottom of the stairs covered in gore and leaned on the wall for support. Nettruku, the Terran chef, and Sodak were also present. Sodak's large eyes glowed in the light of the stairs.

"Come down," Sodak said. "It's safe now."

Martinez descended gingerly, cradling Kelly's body. The smell of warm blood caught in his throat. His heel slipped as he neared the bottom, and he sat down on the body of a staring Torminel. He felt warm flesh give way, then heard bones crack under his weight. He made a frantic attempt to rise, but with Kelly in his lap he couldn't manage it, and the chef had to help him to his feet.

"We couldn't let any of them get away," Lady Kosch said. "They'd have brought the whole mob down on us."

Sodak had come up from behind, Martinez realized, and blocked their retreat just as Kosch had launched her attack. The rioters were trapped, and they were so packed together their weapons were hampered.

The rest of the party came down the stairs, and tracking blood they went in search of the bridge over Gearing Street. Lady Kosch, Martinez saw, was swaying as she walked.

"Lady Kosch, are you hurt?" he asked.

"Not badly."

Kosch looked pale even through her fur. "Someone help her," Martinez said. Sodak hurried to her side and put one of Kosch's arms around her shoulder.

They were within sight of the bridge when Lady Kosch gave a sigh and slipped into unconsciousness. Her knife dropped from her hand and clattered on the floor. Sodak hung on and called for help, and Nettruku ran to her other side, and the two helped prop her up and supported her to the bridge.

Martinez's sleeve display chimed as he stepped onto the bridge, and he ordered it to answer. "We're on our way," said Roland. "Do you hear the sirens?"

"No," Martinez said.

"I'm in the car with the Minister of Police," Roland said. "I've also been talking to the Minister of Justice and the Minister of Security."

"We need ambulances, not ministers," Martinez said. "We've got two casualties."

"Ambulances are coming, too." Roland sounded insufferably smug. "Also crews from Empire Broadcasting, to record your heroic actions for history."

"We're not in the Corona Club any longer," Martinez said. "We're walking over a bridge into—" He peered out the window. "Into the Five Petal Market."

"Did you hear that, Minister?" Roland asked.

"I hear sirens now," Martinez said. He was in the middle of the pedestrian bridge and could look through windows to the street below, where people were beginning to scatter at the sound of approaching police. They'd had a lot of practice at scattering during the war, when Naxid convoys went out in search of hostages.

And sure enough, vehicles in the black and yellow colors of the Motor Patrol raced into sight and began spitting out Naxid police in helmets and armor, each carrying a weapon. Captain Klarvash, or someone like him, had finally come to the rescue.

The Naxids raced out of sight, toward the riot, scrambling on their four frantic legs. And then came the sound of concentrated rifle fire, as they made up for their belated appearance by beginning a massacre, just as they had so often during the war.

Naxids, Martinez knew, did not believe in warning shots.

Martinez was too exhausted to summon anything like surprise or outrage, and so he plodded after the party as they trudged down the bridge. Pain snarled through his ribs.

The ambulances arrived a few minutes later, but too late for Lady Kosch, who had drawn her last breath just as the sirens began to wail.

THE SCENT OF lilacs filled the hospital room. Kelly lay on her back surrounded by a sea of bouquets, her face colorless, her eyes closed, her breathing regular. Vitals were displayed on a screen over her head.

Her short fair hair had been shaved, and her bald head was naked on the pillow, with only a small bandage over the site of the surgery. After hours in the operating room, the bone shards had all been plucked from her brain, but in the three days since she had never risen to consciousness.

Coma. No one could say how long it would last. No one could say it wouldn't last forever.

Kelly's face bore a slightly pursed expression, as if on some level she realized she was in trouble.

The hospitals had been full after the riot. The Motor Patrol had killed or wounded nearly eighty people when they'd charged to the rescue, picking targets more or less at random, except for those who came tumbling out of the Corona Club, and who had been deliberately gunned down as they fled. These last Martinez did not mourn.

Once the mob had broken into the club they'd been outraged they hadn't found anyone to kill, so they looted the place and set it afire. Which resulted in more casualties, three who had been so intoxicated by stolen liquor that they'd passed out in the burning building, and two who'd been trapped by the flames on the stairs, unable to escape because Sodak and Ti-car had jammed the roof door.

The parts of the building that hadn't burned had been drenched in fire retardant, and the contents were a total loss. At least, Martinez thought, they'd put the wine cellar to good use.

Too, they had good insurance. They would rebuild.

If only the same could be said for the people who had died.

Martinez's orderly, Alikhan, had survived without harm. Once he'd arrived in his car and seen the crowd turn violent, he'd returned to the bar where he'd been meeting with his cronies and tried to turn them into a rescue force. But they'd been unable to obtain any firearms—which was lucky for them, since they would have been overwhelmed, or shot by the police. By the time they'd charged to the rescue waving bats and bottles, the riot was over and the gutters ran with blood. Alikhan and his friends had to drop their weapons and run, lest they be targeted as rioters themselves.

The retired petty officer who had organized the attack had been identified quickly: there simply weren't that many snaggletoothed, piebald Torminel petty officers in the Steadfast League. She had been arrested in her home and was now in the hands of the torturers until she gave up the names of whoever had issued her orders. The Minister of Police was confident that a mere petty officer couldn't have managed the attack on her own. Martinez didn't exactly agree, and had certainly come away from the siege with an idea of her competence, but nevertheless hoped she'd name Lady Tu-hon or Lord Tork.

He paced around Kelly's bed, then came to a sudden halt when a bolt of pain shot from his ribs. He pressed a hand over his side. None of his ribs had actually been broken, but the ligaments holding his rib cage together had been torn, and he now wore a binder under his shirt to hold everything together.

Martinez gasped, took a breath, and looked at Kelly. The doctors had told him it was all right to talk to her, in fact that the stimulation of a familiar voice might enhance her recovery. He didn't want to talk, however, because he knew that whatever he said, it would come out angry. Anger was what he felt now, a dull sullen throb at the back of his mind.

The crowd had wanted *him*. *Him*. They had wanted Terran Criminal Martinez, a member of the robber gang who had caused all their misfortunes.

Kelly was in a coma because she'd defended him. Lady

Kosch Altasz was dead. And neither of them should have been hurt, because he shouldn't have been attacked in the first place, because he was *not* Terran Criminal Martinez, he was a decorated Fleet officer and a celebrated yachtsman and he had never overthrown a bank in his life. He had *bet* on banks being overthrown, but he had nothing to do with their purchasing the time-bomb assets, ticking away in their vaults and ready to explode . . .

And now the Motor Patrol had gunned down dozens of citizens, and Martinez knew with absolute certainty that he would be blamed for it. As if he had given the Naxids the order to fire.

All of which he wanted to explain to Kelly, except that he was afraid he'd end up shouting.

He threw himself into a chair. Anger snapped in his skull like an angry dog. He made an effort to calm himself, and he looked at Kelly again, at the pale face on the pale pillow, and the anger poured out of him. Perhaps all she needed was someone to talk to her, and he was the man on the spot. Her family lived on Devajjo, months away in the Hone Reach, and he didn't even know if they'd received his message telling them of Kelly's injury.

Nobody but me, he thought. He took a breath.

"Well," he said, "let me tell you about my son, Gareth. He did something quite brilliant the other day . . ."

"THE STEADFAST LEAGUE has revealed itself," Sula said, "as a knife pointed at the heart of this assembly." Her gaze took in the half circle of the Convocation. Half the desks were empty, which was normal, but the faces of the convocates who had bothered to attend the session seemed more interested than was usual for them. "A distinguished lady convocate makes an unsubstantiated accusation in this chamber, and days later one of the accused is attacked by a mob, a mob the distinguished convocate supports with her money, and which is organized along military principles by redundant members of the Fleet."

She looked around the amphitheater again. More faces were turned toward her; more faces displayed interest. She wished she were not obliged to use the polite terms common in the Convocation, which for some reason was called "this assembly" instead of by its name. She also disliked being obliged to use "distinguished convocate" rather than "idiot bitch."

Sula brought her speech to its conclusion. "I should like to inquire of the government whether it is conducting an investigation of the Steadfast League, its financing, its leadership, and its political purpose."

She had not addressed her remarks to Lady Tu-hon, but Tu-hon was on her feet as soon as Sula sat down. As were Roland Martinez, Lord Chen, Lord Ngeni, his son Pierre Ngeni, and Oda Yoshitoshi.

The Lord Senior called on Roland and his allies first. Roland waxed indignant on the menace to his family, and the others mentioned the one Peer murdered, and a second in critical condition in a hospital. All united in a call for a thorough investigation.

By this point anger and impatience were radiating off Lady Tu-hon in waves. When Lord Saïd at last recognized her, she leaned forward as she spoke, as if she were about to launch herself at his throat.

"The Steadfast League has no political purpose, and it is not an army!" she proclaimed. "The League proclaims nothing but unity, loyalty to the empire, and devotion to the Praxis!" Her orange eyes gleamed. "If the League *were* an army, I assure you that the Terran criminals would already know it!"

Sula repressed a smile. Lord Saïd had not been oblivious to the threat that Lady Tu-hon posed to his administration, and there had been a minor backstage conspiracy between the Lord Senior and Roland to let Roland's faction speak first, in order to goad Lady Tu-hon into saying something impolitic.

Threatening members of the Convocation, Sula thought, probably counted.

Sula was, as always, uneasy in her alliance with the Martinez family. They were an ambitious, dedicated band of climbers, whose skillful ascent of the High City had left any number of their friends broken on the stones below. At least, she thought, she was working with Roland and not his brother, who seemed to specialize in bringing her misery.

It hadn't escaped Sula's attention that Gareth Martinez had survived the mob's attack perfectly well, to emerge glittering a few hours later on one of his sister's news programs, while two Corona Club teammates were delivered either to the hospital or to the morgue. If by some miracle he were made king, he'd climb to his throne atop a pyramid of his friends' skulls.

Tu-hon turned to the Lord Senior. "May I ask the Lord Senior and the ministers whether there already *is* an investigation of the incident at the Corona Club?"

Lord Saïd's face was impassive. "In the absence of the Minister of Justice, I will confirm that an investigation is under way."

"In that case," Tu-hon said, "why these calls for an investigation that is already in hand? We need only wait for the official results."

Now it was Sula's turn again. "My own question was aimed not at investigating the Corona Club incident, but at investigating the League itself. I intended to warn this assembly against a militarized extralegal organization engaged in unauthorized political activity." She treated herself to a thin smile. "And I speak as someone with experience in raising and training a secret army."

Which sent Lady Tu-hon off on another rant, which was more or less what Sula intended. She played no part in the debate that followed, but instead followed the players. Those who spoke in Roland's favor were all Terran, and the absence of Terrans was marked among those who supported Lady Tu-hon. The majority of the convocates present didn't speak at all, but that told Sula something else: that none of the other species thought the Terrans were worth defending.

We're already divided, Sula thought.

She was beginning to think that the time for the restrained, polite language of the Convocation was coming to an end.

She was beginning to wonder if Terrans might not be the new Yormaks.

"WELL, PRINCESS," SAID Naveen Patel, "it's not like we haven't noticed that the Steadfast League is starting to look like a menace."

Julien Bakshi took a drag on his cigarillo, coughed, then inhaled more smoke. "They're being urged to report lawbreakers to their superiors," he said. "And traitors and subversives, if they can find any."

Sula laughed. "Their superiors will spend so much time chasing down false leads," she said, "they'll never accomplish anything."

They had the back room at Julien's restaurant off Harmony Square, and the remains of a luncheon were scattered on immaculate white table linen. Julien tapped his cigarillo into an ashtray that had been placed at his elbow. "The League members are starting to throw their weight around. Three of them braced one of my bookmakers the other day."

Patel looked at him. "Which one?"

"Big Ngo."

"And what happened?"

Julien grinned. "What do you think? Ngo sent them to the hospital."

Patel laughed. "What did they *think* Ngo would do?"

"But in hospital they talked to the Patrol," Julien continued, "so Ngo is keeping out of sight."

Sula remembered Big Ngo from the Secret Army, a slab-sided enforcer who had served as Patel's bodyguard. She wasn't particularly surprised that he'd been able to handle himself in an attack.

"We can't all be Big Ngo," she said. "There will be other attacks, against people less able to defend themselves, and we should be ready for them."

Patel raised his coffee to his lips, then paused, his brows knit in thought. "What are you asking us to do, princess?" he asked. "I have a feeling you're not talking about just defending our, our thing, but defending—who? All Terrans?"

"If need be," said Sula.

Patel returned the coffee cup to its saucer without tasting it. He pursed his lips. "Exposing ourselves that way," he said. "Could be a problem."

"That sort of thing really isn't our remit," Julien said.

"Do you remember," Sula asked, "what we did to the Naxids in the war?"

They were silent. So relentless had been the attacks of the Secret Army that the Naxids had been driven into their own neighborhoods and only traveled out in guarded convoys.

"Most of the Naxids we killed weren't rebels," Sula said. "They weren't working for the rebel government, they weren't in the security forces. They were just *people*. We killed whoever we could catch, and the ones we could catch most easily were the ones with no defense at all."

Julien's pointed face was thoughtful. "You think it will come to that?"

"I think we should take care that it doesn't," Sula said. "We don't want attacks on Terrans to become common."

"You want us to retaliate for that business at the Corona Club?" Patel asked.

Sula felt her lips give a disdainful little twitch. "The Martinez family can look after themselves."

Julien jabbed his cigarillo into his ashtray. "Lots of people dead already in that one. The Naxids got a little of their own back, you ask me."

Patel took a sip of his coffee. "Here's another problem, princess," he said. "Terrans aren't the only people with military experience in this town. We made up thirty percent of the Secret Army at most. Which means, if it comes to it, our crews will be outnumbered at least two to one by people who have just as many guns and bombs as we do."

Following this depressing revelation, there was a moment of thoughtful silence. "We should start talking to those people. To the Secret Army veterans. And *you* should talk to the rest of the Commission. There's no benefit to the cliques if there's war in the streets that you don't control. That's how warlords get started, and from your perspective, warlords are your *rivals*."

Julien's lips gave a disapproving twist. "We may be getting ahead of ourselves," he said, "with this business about warlords."

Sula smiled. "I'm rehearsing your speech for the Commission."

"Though any kind of disturbance *would* be bad for business," Patel said. "With none of the banks making loans, people have to come to us for their money."

And pay fifty or a hundred percent interest, Sula thought.

"I'll see if I can produce a list of the League's officers and organizers," Sula said. "If we retaliate, we need to retaliate against the right people, and explain why we're doing it."

Julien searched in his velvet jacket for another cigarillo and failed to find it. He nervously tapped his rings on the edge of the table. "It's good to think about this, I suppose," he said. "And I'll do as you like and talk to Sagas and the others on the Commission. But I'm reluctant to go any further until the situation clarifies itself."

"Until another riot?" Sula asked.

Julien grimaced. "That would be clarification, yes."

"It might stop short of that," Sula admitted. "We can hope that Tu-hon's followers aren't as crazy as she is."

Though for herself, she was inclined to doubt it.

"HOW IS YOUR Lieutenant Kelly?" Roland asked.

"No change," said Martinez, resting his forearms on the bar. It had been fifteen days since the riot, and Kelly remained in her hospital room surrounded by dying lilacs. The only change in her condition was the stubble growing on her scalp. Martinez visited daily and chatted with her about his life, and when he ran out of anecdotes he read to her. He'd roped in other officers who knew her, like Sodak and Vonderheydte, so she'd have familiar voices around her much of the day.

It didn't seem to be helping.

There had been a trickle of arrests made since the riot, as those already in custody gave up the names of their comrades. But all the arrests had been of minor figures, and no one had named any of the higher-ups. No one involved in the investigation was talking.

Despite the rioters' growing casualty lists, to Martinez the whole affair felt like a defeat. And he wasn't used to defeat, or to the sense of helplessness that followed, and he found himself stalking down the corridors of his house, anger smoldering in his nerves, his big hands curled into fists. He remembered all too well the bloodbath on the stairs, the sneer of the snaggletoothed petty officer, the mindless seething violence of the crowd. He wanted to tear the memories to bits with his own hands.

Whatever violence the state exercised on his behalf, torturing and killing the rioters, it would not erase his anger, or his sense of humiliation. He'd had to flee, and he didn't like running away.

And now there was another emergency family meeting at the Martinez Palace, in Roland's study with dim autumn light glooming through the eye-shaped windows. Roland had come straight from the Convocation and was still in his red jacket. Roland unbuttoned his shirt collar, loosened his cravat, and walked behind the bar. "Drink?" he asked.

"Whatever you're having."

Roland poured Laredo whisky into crystal glasses and handed one to Martinez. He wore a slight air of distraction, as if he were thinking through a difficult problem.

Another damned defeat, Martinez thought, which his

brother would relate in his own good time. Rather than sift through his own dispirited thoughts, he tried to lighten the mood.

"My genius son, Gareth," he said, "used 'dysfunctional' and 'osmosis' in conversation today."

Roland scowled into his whisky. "My genius daughter, Girasole," he said, "would like to know in what conceivable context Gareth used 'osmosis.'"

Martinez shrugged. "In reference to the colligative properties of pressure across a semipermeable membrane. Naturally."

Roland nodded gloomily. "Of course."

Martinez inhaled the aroma of his whisky and felt a tingle across the fine hairs of his nasal cavities. "I don't suppose you're going to tell me what disaster has occasioned this meeting," he said.

"Not till everyone's here," Roland said. "It will be depressing enough going into it only once."

"My father-in-law won't be patron to Rol-mar, will he?"

Roland only looked at him.

"Who got Rol-mar instead?"

Roland swept his glass from the bar and carried it to one of his overstuffed chairs. "We'll talk about it when everyone gets here."

Vipsania and Walpurga arrived a few minutes later, found refreshments, and sat in the crepuscular light beneath a dim window. Not drinking but swirling the amber liquid in his glass, Roland related the substance of the report from the Committee for Planetary Settlement. Though the report was full of compliments to Lord Chen, the committee had decided that the patron of Rol-mar would be the Daimong patrician Lord Gonihu.

"Who is he, exactly?" Martinez said.

"Very old, very grand," Vipsania reported. "He keeps company so exclusive that I'm not sure any of us would ever have seen him."

"He has that Nayanid-style palace on the Boulevard of the Praxis," Walpurga added. "The one with the alternating courses of black and white stone."

"The place that looks like a layer cake," Martinez said.

"That's the one."

"Hideous and pretentious at the same time. I've wondered who had the bad taste to live there."

"Lord Gonihu's represented in Convocation by his grandson Lord Pyte Gonihu," Roland said. "Lord Convocate Pyte condescended to call upon me this afternoon, just after the committee issued its report, and he informed me that it would not be necessary for the Chee Company or Meridian to tender any bids as contractor or planning authority."

Martinez ground his teeth. "It's going to cost them a fortune to ship in new contractors. You *did* explain that, didn't you?"

"I did. But apparently Lord Gonihu has a fortune to spare."

"Or thinks he does."

Vipsania's brows contracted. "Who's behind this?"

Roland shrugged. "The Gonihu clan has not taken a position on the Terran criminals," he said. "They're not part of the Steadfast League, though that may be because some of the principals are too unrefined for Lord Gonihu's taste." He made an equivocal gesture with one hand. "As are *we,* for that matter."

"Are the only workers allowed on his planet from the Peer elite?" Martinez asked. "How is he going to find only acceptable people to work for him?"

Roland made an angry gesture with one hand. "I don't know how some of our smaller subcontractors will survive this." His eyes glanced over at his siblings. "If any of you are planning any rebuilding or redecorating, maybe you can employ them. It won't be work on the same scale as settling a planet, but it might make a difference."

"I need to rebuild the Corona Club," Martinez said. "Though the insurance company is delaying payment until the police report is filed."

"Whatever you all can do," Roland said.

"I can call Lord Chen again," Martinez said. "Lord Gonihu would probably talk to him, since they probably claim descent from the same ultimate globule of primary protoplasm, or whatever."

Roland managed something like a smile. "We would appreciate that very much, thank you."

"Otherwise, can we outflank them somehow?" Martinez asked. "Gonihu might not want us, but can we work through the Planetary Settlement Committee or someone else to make sure we're a part of the picture?"

"Unlikely," Roland said. "I will do my best, however." He looked at his siblings again. "I think we may have to concede defeat with as much grace as we can," he said. "We can shift all the contractors to Chee or Parkhurst, but that's half the empire away, and it's going to cost us. It's going to cost more than it's worth to ship a lot of our equipment home." He looked at his brother. "Gareth, we're going to need someone with experience in logistics. I hope you'll be able to contribute."

"I'm not a logistician, but I'll do what I can," Martinez said. "But if we have to leave, I recommend scorched-earth tactics."

Roland gave him a warning look. "I *have* cautioned you about applying military solutions to political problems."

"I'm not saying scatter bombs or booby traps around. But we leave nothing behind," Martinez said. "My guess is that Lord Gonihu's expecting a windfall. You said yourself it makes economic sense to abandon a lot of our equipment—well, my advice is *not to do it*. Take *everything*. Leave them with roofless buildings and half-built infrastructure. Leave the breakwaters half built and hope the cities flood, leave the crops to rot in the fields. We own anything that Lady Gruum hasn't paid for, so we take all that with us—and the things she *did* pay for, we leave in the rain with the windows open."

"That would be emotionally satisfying, I admit," Roland said. "But how much do you really want to spend to achieve that satisfaction?"

"If the equipment costs too much to ship, destroy it. Burn the buses, sink the barges with the trucks parked on them, drive the trains off a bridge. If we have to leave so much as a toilet behind, fill it with concrete."

He looked from his brother to his sisters and back, and they all seemed to be probing the idea with what seemed to be cautious pleasure. The satisfaction might only be emotional, as Roland had said, but it was still satisfaction.

"We might be making unnecessary enemies," Roland said.

"We already *have* enemies. We'll be teaching them not to screw with us. Just as we taught Lord Minno and his friends not to manipulate our stock prices."

Roland decided to concede. "I'll be in touch with the managers, and see what we can do."

LORD CHEN PAID a call upon Lord Gonihu and was received with polite, immaculate condescension. Lord Chen argued Roland's case and was turned down flat. Lord Gonihu appointed a nephew as general manager of Rol-mar, and the nephew set about forming a company. Clearly Lord Gonihu intended to keep as much in the family as possible.

What no one had anticipated was that the situation would be taken out of the hands of the managers, the Martinez clan, Lord Gonihu, and his nephew. When the first draft of Roland's complex evacuation plan was transmitted to Rol-mar, the workers flat refused to carry it out.

They'd had plenty of time to make their plans. They had traveled to Rol-mar to build settlements and live in them, and that's precisely what they intended to do. They weren't interested in Roland's shipping them to another world, and they certainly weren't interested in falling in with Lord Gonihu's plans, whatever those were. They took command of their own fate—and, in addition, an entire new world.

They didn't stop work. They weren't on strike. They just went on building their own communities quite independent of anyone else's plans. A few of the managers joined them, and the rest cast up their hands in despair and flocked to the elevators for evacuation.

Roland had no leverage over the workers save a threat to withhold their pay, which in time he did. But once he made that decision, he had no power over the workers at all, and they seemed not to need the money, having instead the possession of an entire world. There were plenty of supplies left, including years' worth of antimatter for generating electricity, which had been kept high above the world, in the terminals of the skyhooks, until the workers went up the elevators and secured it for themselves. Then they went on using Meridian's equipment as if they owned it, a fact that made Roland snarl.

There were more than three hundred thousand workers on the planet. It would take an army to stop them, and the empire had no army—only the Fleet. Lord Gonihu would not be permitted to raise an army of his own, for fear he might use it to challenge the government. And in any case, the workers weren't offering violence—in fact they were working at their jobs quite peacefully. Who would an army shoot at? Who would the police arrest? No one was in rebellion.

Roland failed utterly in his long-distance negotiations with the workers, and in frustration he asked his brother if he would travel to Rol-mar and negotiate in person.

"What could *I* do?" Martinez asked.

"Be *useful* for a change," Roland snarled. "You can get together with Nikki Severin—he's returned to the system, yes?"

"I'd like to see Nikki," Martinez said, "but tell me what I'm supposed to accomplish there, and I'll consider going."

At that moment Roland was too harassed and angry to

offer a plausible, or even a coherent, scheme; and so Martinez was left wondering just *what* he could achieve, and how he could do it. Go down to the planet, grab workers by the elbow, and tell them how wonderful life would be on Chee?

Still, by the next day he had almost talked himself into the trip to Rol-mar, when he got a call from Roland.

"The Commandery's decided to send a cruiser to Rol-mar," he said.

"A cruiser?" It took Martinez a moment to process the information. "You mean a cruiser from the *Fleet*?"

"Yes," Roland said, "the *Beacon*."

"*Beacon*'s a Daimong ship," Martinez said. "Who's commanding her?"

"Lord Oh Derinuus."

Martinez searched for a memory and failed to find it. "I don't know him."

Roland offered a brief laugh. "It probably doesn't matter," he said. "What can a cruiser do?"

Martinez was on the verge of laughing himself, when a sudden realization caught him by surprise, and he felt a cold, sick feeling in the pit of his stomach.

"What a cruiser can do," he said, "is annihilate a rebellion."

CHAPTER 13

"Depressurize and withdraw boarding tube," said Shushanik Severin. "Crew to secure for zero gravity."

"Yes, Lord Captain." This from Pilot First Class Liu.

"Maneuvering thrusters gimbaled," said Warrant Officer Falyaz. "Pressure at thruster heads nominal." The shrill zero-gee warning rang out, and then there came Falyaz's redundant announcement, "Zero-gravity warning sounded."

"Boarding tube retracting," said Liu. Then, "Boarding tube secured. Outside connectors sealed. Outside electrical power withdrawn. Ship is at one hundred percent internal power."

"Main engines gimbaled," said Falyaz. "Gimbal test successful. Engines standing by."

Severin checked the heads-up display on the inside of his helmet. There was no traffic in the area, and therefore no chance of collision.

"Launch," he said.

The pilot pressed two buttons, the docking clamps released, and Severin began to float in his restraints as *Expedition* drifted away from the elevator terminal. The docks were always positioned just at escape velocity, so that any ships would sail away from Rol-mar, not fall toward it.

As Pilot Liu accelerated away from the terminal with short bursts of the thrusters, Severin triggered the virtual display and Rol-mar expanded before his eyes, as if it were painted on the interior of his skull. Blue oceans, swirling white clouds, green-and-brown mainland, silver winding rivers . . . from this distance there was no sign whatever of habitation. The foreshortened elevator terminal hung in space before him, its exterior painted in bright geometric patterns to aid pilots in finding their way to the right berth. Its edges were marked by jigsaw crenellations, designed so that new modules, or new counterweights, could be slotted into place as necessary.

Severin felt tugs at his inner ear as Liu oriented *Expedition* onto its new heading, which meant that *Expedition* was far enough from the terminal to ignite its antimatter torches. Severin took himself out of virtual and looked at his displays.

"Ready for orbital injection, my lord," Liu said.

"Sound acceleration warning."

Another, deeper alarm clattered through the ship. "Warning sounded."

"Engines," said Severin, "fire on Miss Liu's mark."

Falyaz confirmed. Liu gave her countdown and the cruiser's big engines fired, punching Severin back into his couch and sending his acceleration cage swaying on its gimbals.

Pilot Liu placed *Expedition* in a higher orbit, not quite geostationary, drifting slowly over the surface of the planet below. The engines cut, and the crew floated again in zero gravity.

Severin switched to virtual again and looked through the hull toward Rol-mar Wormhole One, where he saw the bright deceleration flare of *Beacon,* coming ever closer. The flare had been visible for days, and the cruiser was on course to enter Rol-mar orbit in something like thirty-seven hours.

He frowned as he looked at the flare, and he wondered again how he was going to approach the problem that *Beacon* and its captain represented.

SEVERIN AND *EXPEDITION* had been on exploration duty for almost a year. Rol-mar itself was a world discovered only years before, and its system contained two newly discovered wormholes that had the potential to lead to even more useful, undiscovered worlds.

Rol-mar Wormhole Two had led to a star orbited only by seven gas giants and bands of stony rubble—apparently the tidal stresses of so many giant worlds had torn apart any rocky planets before they'd formed. The rubble might be of interest to mining firms, and possibly a survey would one day be conducted, but Severin's job was to locate habitable worlds, not mineral deposits. His sensing team discovered a wormhole on the far side of the system, and Severin took *Expedition* through it. There he found a binary system bathed in the ferocious radiation of *two* giant blue-white stars. It was impossible for life to exist in such a massive storm of high-velocity particles, so Severin, glad of *Expedition*'s comprehensive radiation shielding, turned around and began the long voyage back to Rol-mar Wormhole Two, and from there to Wormhole Three.

Wormhole Three led to a system with a roaster world, a gas giant actually orbiting within the corona of its primary, careening along with a "year" of only 1.4 days. This was the first such world seen close-up, so *Expedition*'s science team spent a month studying it before the ship continued into another wormhole. This one led to a barren system, a white dwarf surrounded by rocky planets with only the most tenuous of atmospheres, completely uninhabitable.

By this point *Expedition* had been gone for ten months and food supplies were running low, so Severin laid a course for Rol-mar. After entering the system, he sent his formal report, asked Exploration Service headquarters for instructions, and sent off greetings to everyone he'd left behind. Because he knew Martinez would be interested, he included in his message to Gareth Martinez his report of the trip and much of the data, along with spectacular video of the roaster world.

Ten days later a reply arrived from Martinez, explaining the unique situation on Rol-mar and strongly suggesting that *Expedition* arrive on the scene before *Beacon.* So Severin began drilling the crew in tactical problems involving single-ship combat and reduced his deceleration burn, arriving at Rol-mar a comfortable two days before *Beacon* transited Wormhole One.

The Exploration Service had gone into a long decline after the Shaa had decided their empire had grown to its limits and ceased looking for new worlds, but the Naxid War had proved a boon to the near-moribund service. Severin himself, a mere warrant officer commanding nothing more than an unarmed lifeboat, had distinguished himself at Protipanu;

and the larger Service vessels had taken part in combat. More importantly, the Exploration Service had got a share of wartime shipbuilding funds, and the result was newer and larger ships, equipped not only for exploration but for war. By now the Exploration Service had a sizable little fleet, for all that its ships were usually deployed alone on missions taking them far from home. To keep its crew comfortable during its extended missions, *Expedition* was large for a light cruiser, with twenty-eight missile tubes, a full set of antimissile batteries, and a sensor array more advanced than any in the Fleet, with a large science team trained to use it.

The Exploration Service had been unfashionable for centuries, officered by members of a few Peer families for whom such service was a long-standing tradition. Most Peers preferred the Fleet, with its pomp, its rigid traditions, its glamorous social hierarchy, and its glittering squadrons that traveled from world to world as if on parade. The wartime expansion of the Service required new officers, and the few Peers in the Service were not enough. Severin, a commoner, had risen to captain on what he liked to think were his own merits, and in the emergency other experienced warrant and petty officers had received their commissions. The Peers had flooded in as well, but by the time they were graduated from the academies the commoners had not only received commissions but were pleased to wield seniority over their social betters. Only two of Severin's four lieutenants were Peers. With their missions taking them away for long periods, and with fewer aristocrats, the Service was considerably less formal than the Fleet; and Severin spent most of his time on the ship in jumpsuits or sweats, and only buttoned himself into his formal blue jacket when making video reports, conducting an inspection, or convening a disciplinary board.

Not that he'd needed to devote a lot of time to ship's discipline. *Expedition* was a contented ship, doing exactly the sort of thing people joined the Exploration Service to do. Even the miscreants who made wine from kitchen scraps, or ran a dice game in one of the holds, made their own contribution to the ship's happiness. If the captain's closet was full of puppets and bits of scenery, that was entirely his own business.

But even in the Service, a captain still carried the authority of an absolute tyrant when he wanted to, and he had no need to justify his extra drills. What he worried about was that the drills might, ere long, prove necessary.

SEVERIN EXAMINED THE problem of *Beacon* with slow care, as if he were probing a missing tooth with his tongue; and then he put on a clean shirt along with his blue jacket and his medals, sat at the desk in his office, and recorded a message to Captain Derinuus. He identified himself and his ship, of which he had no doubt Derinuus was already aware, and offered to host Derinuus and his officers at a dinner. He received his reply within the hour.

"My officers and I will be pleased to accept your gracious invitation," Derinuus said. "I hope I may beg your indulgence concerning the timing, as first it will be necessary to deal with the rebellion on the planet's surface."

Severin viewed the message several times, hoping to gain an understanding of how Derinuus planned to handle the rebellion, but he found himself unable to read the gray frozen Daimong face with its round black-on-black eyes and the gaping, motionless mouth with its rigid bony lips. The resonant Daimong voice was pitched in a neutral tone.

In the absence of context, Severin thought, it was all too easy to assume the worst. He decided to send another message.

"I hope our dinner won't be too long delayed," he said. "If you have received instructions from the Convocation concerning Rol-mar, I will be honored to offer my assistance and that of my ship. *Expedition* has just undocked from the elevator terminal, and I've spoken with several of the officials on the terminal concerning the situation on the planet. I would be happy to brief you on the latest developments, should you require more information."

In retrospect Severin felt this message was hardly his best and did little but show his own desperation. He could hope that Derinuus would find him as unreadable as Severin had found the Daimong captain.

He spent the next half hour viewing Derinuus's service record, but he found that as unenlightening as everything else. Derinuus had been promoted to lieutenant-captain during the war and given a frigate, but the end of his shakedown cruise coincided with the end of the war, so Derinuus saw no action. In due course he'd been promoted to junior captain and given *Beacon* and had been on his way to join the Fourth Fleet at Harzapid when diverted to Rol-mar. His going straight from one ship to another suggested he had a patron in the service, but there was no indication who that patron might be.

So far as Severin could tell, it was a complete coincidence that he was here at all.

Severin's frustrating search through the records was interrupted by a response from Derinuus.

"Your offer of assistance is noted, and you have my thanks, but it's hardly necessary. The question is only whether the planet remains in rebellion, and I will make that determination on arrival."

Severin stared at the blank gray Daimong face and felt his heart sink. He looked at the chronometer at his desk and realized that *Beacon* would enter orbit in less than thirty-three hours.

He spent the next hour viewing regulations and ordinances regarding civil disorder, then sent messages to his four lieutenants asking them to come to his dining room. He then had his steward make coffee and tea and bring fried dumplings that filled the room with the sharp scent of garlic.

Expedition was a new ship that broadcast its newness: clean fresh paint, undented metal trim, flooring not yet worn by thousands of shoes. Severin hadn't personalized the ship's decor as did other captains, with their special hand-painted tiles, exotic wood trim, eye-catching color schemes, and artwork—for one thing, he wasn't rich, and he had to stay within the budget the Exploration Service had provided. He had made a virtue of necessity and adopted the clean lines of the Devis mode, with simple white and dark geometric shapes broken here and there by abstract bits of color. Instead of paintings or etchings or tile, he filled his own personal space with video screens showing a rotating series of astronomical scenes: the torus-shaped wormhole at Protipanu Two; the lacy bloodred Maw looming over Protipanu's small white sun; the four giant stars in their fatal spiral around the supermassive black hole at the center of the galaxy.

Astronomical scenes were also prominent in Severin's dining room. It was large enough to seat eight if people were careful not to scrape the walls, but he had only four guests and Severin was able to order the table to swallow one of its leaves and permit his guests plenty of elbow room. The table, chairs, and other furniture were smart enough to cling to the floor when gravity was absent, and the chairs were smart enough to adjust themselves to their guests. Which was lucky for the premiere lieutenant, Lord Chungsun Cleghorne, who was very short, and whose chair boosted him to eye level with the others.

Severin sipped the fragrant green cloud that was his tea, then placed the cup back in its saucer and began the meeting.

"I'm looking for your counsel and, I hope, your cooperation," he said. "We have a situation developing between the planet and the *Beacon*."

With that, he replaced the astronomical art on one of his screens and played the messages he'd sent to Derinuus, and the Daimong's replies.

"What do we think of that?" he asked.

Lord Chungsun frowned at the screen. "So will we be having guests for dinner or not?" he asked.

There was a moment of silence. "I believe," said Second

Lieutenant Cressida Toupal, "the captain wanted our thoughts on whether or not there's going to be a massacre on Rol-mar."

"Can we see the messages again?" said the Third. "I can't read Daimong faces at all."

Severin played the videos again. There was an uncomfortable silence afterward, broken only by the sound of the Fourth pouring herself more coffee.

"I think Lord Oh is determined to make a name for himself," said Toupal. "Vijana got a promotion and the thanks of the Convocation for putting down the Yormaks, and all the Naxid War heroes are ahead of Lord Oh in seniority and achieving promotion." She tossed her curly hair. "*Kill rebels, get a prize.* It's a simple equation."

Lord Chungsun frowned again and touched his mustache. "Well," he said, "they *are* in rebellion down there."

"The Naxids and the Yormaks *attacked* us!" Toupal said. "The people on Rol-mar haven't attacked anyone, and they don't have any weapons."

"I'd think it would be a matter for the police," said the Third. "Not for missiles with antimatter warheads, which is what *Beacon*'s got."

Severin looked at the screen with its frozen face of Derinuus. "The question is whether Lord Oh has instructions from the Convocation to bombard the settlers from orbit," he said. "If he does, then the word of the Convocation is all the justification he needs. But if he *doesn't* have an order from the Convocation to kill citizens of the empire, then we're left with another question—are we obliged to intervene to protect those citizens?"

The discussion that followed was prolonged, and—on the part of Lieutenant Toupal—heated. Severin called onto the display relevant texts from the law and regulations, which served mainly to confuse the matter. Finally Severin brought an end to the debate.

"It's ultimately my decision," he said. "I don't know yet what I'm going to do, because I don't know what Captain Derinuus intends." He looked from one of his officers to the other. "However," he said, "I'd like to know whether, if I find it necessary to act in defense of the settlers, I can count on your support."

Lord Chungsun looked at him in blank surprise. "You're the captain, my lord. Of course I'll support you."

Officers were normally referred to as "my lord" whether or not they happened to be Peers, and Severin had always found it both strange and encouraging to be called a lord by an actual Peer. He was granted an equivalence with the elite of the empire, but the equivalence was both conditional and temporary, and he never knew how to value it.

At the moment, though, its value was quite high. "Thank you, Lord Chungsun," he said.

Once the premiere showed his support, the other officers fell quickly into agreement.

"Well, then," said Severin. "Let's refresh our cups, and I'll call up the tactical display. We'll try to see if we can work out a way to handle this problem that doesn't involve bloodshed."

***BEACON* ENDED ITS** deceleration burn and fell into orbit on schedule. Severin placed *Expedition* a respectful distance behind *Beacon,* as if to support Derinuus, and instructed Pilot Liu to keep *Beacon* within line of sight.

Derinuus began his broadcast within minutes of taking up station.

"I am Captain Lord Oh Derinuus of the cruiser *Beacon,* and I have been sent to resolve the situation on Rol-mar. There can be no dispute that the planet is in a state of rebellion. I have but one message: if the rebels do not return to their obedience by 14:01 hours tomorrow, and surrender unconditionally, they will be annihilated."

The message was repeated every few minutes for the next hour. Severin watched the expressionless gray face deliver the bloodthirsty message three times and stared into black-on-black eyes that looked like pits extending into the darkness of Derinuus's skull. The exquisite subtlety of which the Daimong vocal apparatus was capable was not in evidence, and Derinuus's tone was harsh and bombastic. Severin put on his blue uniform coat and asked to speak to Derinuus directly—now that *Beacon* was within less than a light-second they could have an actual conversation rather than send messages back and forth.

"Yes, Lord Captain?" Derinuus said. "I hope this will not take long—we are very busy here."

"You have promised to annihilate the settlers," Severin said.

"To annihilate the *rebels,*" Derinuus corrected.

"As you like," Severin said. "What I would like to know, Lord Captain, is whether this *annihilation* has been authorized by the Convocation."

Unwinking light shone in the unwinking eyes. "Authorization was not necessary. I am an officer of the Fleet with a duty to eradicate the enemies of the Praxis, and I will carry out that duty as I see fit."

"Is your intended action authorized by the Fleet, then? By Lord Tork?"

There was a slight hesitation before Derinuus's answer. "My authorization may be found in imperial law and in Fleet regulations. At such a distance from the Commandery, I can hardly await their decision on every urgent matter."

"But, Lord Captain, you *could* have," said Severin. "You spent *days* in your deceleration burn, and there was more than enough time for a query to reach the Commandery and return. Did you make such a query?"

"It was unnecessary." Flatly. "I was sent here on special assignment to deal with the situation. Implicit was the understanding that I may act as I see fit against rebels, otherwise there was no point in sending me at all."

Kill rebels, get a prize. It's a simple equation.

"Captain," said Severin, "calling them 'rebels' may be stretching the term. They are not in arms against the government. They have offered no violence, and they have no store of weapons."

"They defy their superiors. That is rebellion in any meaningful sense of the term, and rebellion is forbidden by the Praxis."

"Captain, you plan to use missiles against the settlements?"

"Of course."

"In addition to loss of life," Severin said, "there will be

enormous property damage. Property that doesn't belong to the rebels, but to Lady Gruum, or Lord Gonihu, or the contractors who had to abandon their equipment on the planet."

"Property damage will be minimized," said Derinuus. "We will remove the tungsten jackets from the warheads, so there will be no fireballs. The missiles will be used as radiation weapons only."

Thus producing long and agonizing deaths for your victims, Severin thought.

"There will still be shock waves, and substantial property damage," he said. "And what of the bases of the elevators? The skyhooks aren't private property, they are owned by the government and under imperial administration."

Derinuus's answer was serene. "I will begin the bombardment with settlements other than those beneath the elevators. But if submission is not forthcoming, I will not hesitate to risk imperial property."

Severin had used up his arguments, and he was finding himself exhausted by futility. "Thank you for your frank admissions, Lord Captain," he said. "I will take up no more of your time."

He ended the conversation and hoped that the word *admissions* might cause Derinuus to wonder if his transmission could be used as evidence against him in some future legal proceeding.

Though probably he would not.

As Severin unbuttoned the collar of his uniform jacket, a solution suddenly swarmed into his mind—not the solution to Derinuus or Rol-mar, but a lingering plot problem in one of his puppet projects. How would Lord Sphere react when he discovered that his mistress, the woman known as the Comador Vampire, had attracted the attentions of his rival, Lord Belletrain-Hoxley-Chalmonderly-Rix-Rax-Drax? He would of course contact the Doyenne, Lady Arbitrage, who would restrain Lord Belletrain-Hoxley-Chalmonderly-Rix-Rax-Drax via the as-yet-unrevealed hold she had over him.

Strange that this resolution should come out of the completely unrelated conversation with Lord Oh Derinuus. Perhaps he had been subconsciously wishing that Lady Arbitrage would arrive at Rol-mar to take charge of the situation.

Oh well. At least *something* had been resolved.

Wearily, he called up the tactical display and contacted his lieutenants for another meeting.

SEVERIN SENT A report to Gareth Martinez even though he knew whatever action he took would be over long before Martinez could view it. If Severin were killed, he hoped Martinez and his family could at least use the report to blacken Derinuus's name.

Over the following twenty hours Severin was witness to Rol-mar's idiosyncratic reaction to Derinuus's ultimatum, a contradictory combination of panic, defiance, and indifference. Messages of individual surrender were sent from the planet's surface, though since those who submitted were still living among large numbers of rebels, their surrender was hardly likely to spare their lives. The sensor crew reported seaworthy vessels heading to sea, no doubt in hopes of being over the horizon by the time the bombs went off. Vehicles struck off into the interior, probably in the same hope. A few thousand people, most with children, tried to flee up the elevators into orbit. Ships cast off from the elevator terminal and were doing their best to get as far away from the planet as possible. Since most of the ships had been intended to evacuate Rol-mar's settlers, this effectively stranded even those who wanted to get away.

Others on Rol-mar sent a series of truculent, obscene, or insulting messages. It had to be said that Severin's favorite was "Do your worst, you pie-eyed dwarf," proudly signed by "Mahmouf Ahmet, former rigger, *Corona*."

One of Martinez's protégés, no doubt.

Most of the settlers seemed to be doing nothing at all. They had grown used to disregarding the orders of higher authority, so they continued to ignore instructions and went about their business.

Severin sent his crew to action stations an hour before Derinuus's ultimatum was due to expire: all crew in their vac suits and strapped into acceleration cages, damage control robots deployed to areas of maximum vulnerability, and Lord Chungsun, the premiere, at his station in Auxiliary Control ready to take command if Severin and the Command room crew were killed.

Severin took a long breath of air scented with the odor of his suit seals, then took his captain's key from the elastic band around his wrist and inserted it in his weapons board. "Lieutenant Toupal," he said, "prepare to turn your key on my mark." He shifted to the command channel and called Lord

Chungsun in Auxiliary Control, then had the premiere insert his own key.

Expedition's planet-crushing weaponry could only be used if three of its five officers agreed, thus making it impossible for a mad captain to start a war on his own. Though all he'd need, Severin knew, were a couple subordinates who were just as mad as he was.

"On my mark," Severin repeated. Suddenly his mouth was dry. "Three, two, one, *mark*."

He turned the key and his weapons board lit up. *This is really happening,* he thought.

"Power up point-defense lasers," he said to Toupal, who was staffing the main weapons board along with a warrant officer. "Power laser range-finders. This is not a drill."

"Powering lasers, my lord. This is not a drill."

"Charge missiles in battery one with antimatter. This is not a drill."

"Battery one missiles charging, Lord Captain. This is not a drill."

"Stand by."

More lights shone on Severin's weapons board. "Track any missiles fired from *Beacon,*" he said. "Prepare to destroy them on my order. This is not a drill."

"Yes, Lord Captain. Not a drill."

Severin contacted the chief engineer and made certain that the engines were ready to fire when called upon, and then there was nothing to do but wait. Minutes crept by, marked only by the soft sigh of air circulation in Severin's suit and the murmur of his own heart. To ease the suspense, he tried to work on plot problems for his puppet theater.

When the broadcast came from Derinuus, it almost came as a relief.

"As I have not received proper submission from the rebels on Rol-mar," Derinuus said, "I will begin the cleansing of the planet." His voice sounded like metal clanging. It rose to a peak of exultation. "*Long live the Praxis!*" he cried.

Two missiles launched immediately, carried away from *Beacon* on chemical rockets. Severin watched their track on his tactical display and saw their antimatter engines ignite once they'd reached a safe distance from the Fleet cruiser.

"Light up those missiles," Severin said. "Stand by to bring them down."

"Range-finder operation nominal. Standing by, Lord Captain."

Severin watched digit counters flashing as they tracked the missiles' rapidly receding range. When he calculated their destruction would be unlikely to injure *Beacon* or *Expedition,* he gave the order to fire the point-defense lasers.

"Missiles destroyed, Lord Captain." It happened about that fast. In Severin's display he saw vast blooming radio clouds standing like a white-hot wall between himself and the planet.

"Pilot," he said. "Enact preprogrammed course. Engines, fire engines. Signals, get me Captain Derinuus."

Expedition kicked him in the spine as the main engines ignited. His acceleration cage swung on its gimbals. A tiny Derinuus head appeared on his communications display.

"*What do you mean by this outrage?*" In his passion Derinuus had lost control of his vocal apparatus and his voice sounded like a wheel squeaking. Severin hoped his own voice would show a little more composure, though he wouldn't have bet on it.

"I can't allow you to kill citizens of the empire entirely on your own initiative," Severin said. "There have been no arrests, no trials, no findings. Your action was illegal."

"You're siding with the rebels!"

"No," Severin said. "I suggest instead that we refer the matter to higher authority. If your action is endorsed by the government, I will stand aside."

"That will take *days*!"

Severin tried to project serenity and confidence. "We have time," he said.

The engines shut off and suddenly everyone was weightless again. There was a shimmer in Severin's inner ear as Pilot First Class Liu began to pitch the ship end over end so that she could fire a brief deceleration burn to place *Expedition* alongside Derinuus's cruiser.

"You will suffer retribution for this!" Derinuus had regained control of his voice, and his words created a harsh harmony in the air. "I'll blast you to atoms!"

"No, you won't." Severin thrust out one arm and held out two fingers, as if he were poking Derinuus right between his lidless eyes. Because he'd expected to be engaged in conversation with Derinuus for this period, he'd arranged to give a series of hand signals to the Command crew to tell them what he wanted. Toupal responded sotto voce: "Yes, Lord Captain."

The point-defense lasers lashed out in a preprogrammed series of bursts, targeting *Beacon*'s own laser turrets. *Expedition*'s records contained a complete set of *Beacon*'s plans, its weapons crew knew exactly where the turrets were placed, and at this range Toupal and her lasers couldn't possibly miss. Only *Beacon*'s lasers on the far side of the ship, where *Expedition* couldn't reach them, were spared destruction.

Expedition's engines fired again, a few seconds of very hard gees that caught Severin by surprise and knocked the breath from his lungs. At the end of the burn, *Expedition* was neatly paired with *Beacon,* courses and speeds matched, *Beacon* caught between *Expedition* and the planet below.

Severin didn't know where Derinuus stood in the tactical debate that had gone on in the Fleet—whether he was one of Tork's traditionalists or supported Martinez's innovations—but he knew that in the present situation none of that mattered. All existing tactics were based on opposing ships, whole squadrons or fleets, approaching from out of range and into the danger zone. No one had ever assumed that an action would begin with the ships nearly within spitting range of each other.

Beacon was pinned. If it fired a missile, at this close range the missile would be tracked and destroyed before it could lock on to *Expedition*. All lasers that bore on *Expedition* had been rendered useless. It might be possible to replace or repair them, but that would take time, and *Expedition*'s sensor crew would see it happening and lasers would blast the turret all over again.

Severin drew in a breath while Derinuus's voice yowled in

his ears. "You have attacked an imperial vessel! You will die for your treasonous action!"

Blah-blah-blah, Severin thought. "That's up to a court to decide," he said. "There's nothing you can do. If you'll only stop and think—"

The orange end-stamp appeared on Severin's communication display, and he realized that Derinuus had cut communications. He turned his eyes to the tactical display while another eddy shimmered through his inner ear, as Liu yawed *Expedition* around so that it was pointed in the same direction as *Beacon* and could match the other cruiser's movements.

Liu was in the midst of this maneuver when *Beacon* responded to Severin's provocation. Its main engines ignited, it rolled ship to present its undamaged lasers, and it fired a missile . . .

And then it vanished in an eruption of gamma rays, pi-mesons, and neutrons, the by-products of antimatter annihilation. Every sensor on *Expedition* was burned to a crisp, the point-defense lasers were wiped out, and every exterior antenna was scoured from the ship.

If *Expedition*'s defensive lasers had been set on manual operation, the missile could have been tracked by Toupal or her assistant, then blown up when it was at a safer distance; but the lasers had been set on automatic to follow the preprogrammed attack on *Beacon*'s turrets, and when the missile fired, it had been tracked and destroyed within a half second of its launch. *Beacon* had fired an antiship missile with a tungsten jacket, and the cruiser was immediately engulfed in a fireball that destroyed it and set off the rest of the antihydrogen ammunition and fuel.

So massive was the explosion that the weight of neutrons and gamma rays actually slapped *Expedition* with enough force to give it a shove. Severin felt the lurch as all his exterior displays went blank, and then he heard the cheep of a radiation alarm and his displays beeped an alert that the hull temperature had risen to a dangerous level. Damage lights began to flash.

"Damage control," he began, lost track, then had to start again. "Damage control, report as soon as you have information."

I told him to think, he thought. *He didn't.*

"Medical, break out antiradiation medication," he said. He turned to Warrant Officer Falyaz. "Engines," he said, "if you think it's safe, fire and get us to a cooler part of this cloud."

As Falyaz began a cautious acceleration, Severin looked at the stunned faces of his crew, and at the temperature alerts. *Expedition* was in the middle of a vast radioactive fireball. But that, he thought, was nothing compared to the fireball awaiting him when he returned to base.

I think I may be in trouble, he thought.

CHAPTER 14

The Matrix Bookstore on Lapis Street in the High City was widely acknowledged as a cultural treasure, three stories tall, with bookshelves that stretched from floor to ceiling and were surrounded by lacy wrought-iron balconies. There was an area for rare books and manuscripts, another area for maps, another area for vintage software. An annex held printers that could assemble an otherwise unavailable work at short notice, though in practice these were used mainly for government documents. The bookstore had been in its current location for twelve hundred years, since it had moved from its earlier location in the Lower Town.

Sula had prowled the bookstore herself, looking for and browsing through old Terran books that dated from before the conquest. She couldn't read the dead languages, so she chose her purchases largely for aesthetic reasons—if she liked the paper, binding, type, and production, she might consider taking it home. Sometimes the scent of the pages or the leather covers made up her mind, sometimes the illustrations. If she could find a translation to aid her comprehension, so much the better.

But many of her purchases were books of artwork or photographs. Sula enjoyed turning the pages and dreaming her way through the cultures of old Earth, with their ancient buildings, primitive technology, and extraordinary and unwieldy fashions. Farthingales? Stovepipe hats? T-shirts with advertising on them? There was something to be said for modern civilization after all.

But now she wasn't looking for an old book, but a new one. Today was the debut of Ming Lin's book, *The Cosgrove Legacy*, her history of the financial crisis, published by a company owned by Lady Koridun. Because Lin had been fully committed to working for Sula while at the same time finishing her dissertation, her editor had hired a Lai-own journalist, Ko-don, to serve as coauthor. The collaboration had been fraught, as Lin complained that Ko-don insisted on simplifying the story and using unspecialized language that other economists might find unprofessional or uninformed—but fortunately Ming Lin was so preoccupied with her other work that she was unable to turn a popular history into a dry, balanced, scholarly work amply hedged with footnotes and caveats.

In its final form, *The Cosgrove Legacy* displayed a certain schizophrenia. In addition to the book itself, there was another volume of documentation, for the most part available as an electronic file, though the printers in the annex would create and bind a copy if a purchaser desired. If sufficiently stimulated by Ko-don's narrative of sharpers, dupes, and cretinous bank officials, the reader could plunge deep into the figures, and if so inclined, they could do their own math and add up the numbers themselves. Not, Sula supposed, that anyone would.

Nervous censors had sliced large sections out of the book, sections mainly having to do with the disgrace of well-connected public figures, or some of the same figures offering quotes that made them seem like idiots. Sula had intervened personally and pointed out that all the quotes were from recordings, public records, and official announcements, and that the time to censor them was long past. The censors bristled and restored the text, then eased their feelings by cutting some minor passages, and Ko-don—who was used to dealing with censors in his capacity as a journalist—had created artful paraphrases that managed to convey the same ideas in more measured language.

Ming Lin had to be talked out of wearing her scholar's robe for her authorial debut, and Sula had bullied her into purchasing a silk crepe dress by Chesko, a designer she used herself when obliged to wear something other than a uniform. Lin complained about the expense, but Sula reminded her that she was no longer on a student's budget, but that of a renowned author.

For such she had become. Reviews had been laudatory. The advance orders for *The Cosgrove Legacy* were enormous, and copies were being printed or readied for download throughout the empire. In part this was because the book was the first work to examine the financial crisis in any kind of detail, let alone with the kind of insider knowledge to which Lin had access; and in part because of a massive publicity campaign by the publisher executives, who knew perfectly well what kind of blockbuster was on their hands.

The publisher, Brio, had been encouraged in its campaign by its owner, Lady Koridun, who had begun to benefit from Ming Lin's financial advice. Certain politicians might also have been instrumental in making sure the book received a degree of support, along with positive reviews. *The Cosgrove Legacy* was the only counternarrative available against Lady Tu-hon's claim that the financial collapse was the result of a band of Terran criminal conspirators in league with a corrupt administration, and people like the Lord Senior, Lord Chen, and the Martinez family recognized that the book could be a weapon to deploy against their enemies.

And so a line formed outside the Matrix Bookstore that stretched far down Lapis Street, drinks and cakes were circulated by waitrons in the store and on the sidewalk, and a Cree band played popular tunes from a little stage more accustomed to hosting the ramblings of drunken poets. Ming Lin, flushed and dazzled by her own success, sat behind a vast desk of arculé wood that was piled high with her books. Her coauthor sat next to her and seemed slightly distracted, as if he were of two minds about becoming so public a figure. Journalists who grew too popular could become a threat to powerful people and might have to tread carefully.

Sula, wearing a nondescript gray civilian suit to avoid attracting attention—though still with a pistol tucked into the small of her back under her jacket—stood on one of the wrought-iron balconies with Lady Koridun and watched the proceedings with pleasure. Her servants Shawna Spence and

Gavin Macnamara, also discreetly armed, wandered the floor of the bookstore. The siege of the Corona Club had been followed by a series of apparently random attacks on Terrans, and even though none of these attacks had taken place in the High City, Sula wanted to make sure Ming Lin would be safe from any fanatics bent on punishing her species. *The Cosgrove Legacy* was both readable and sensational, and it not only refuted but *demolished* all the claims made by the Steadfast League. Therefore it might make Lin and Ko-don targets.

Not that the Terrans had been exclusively victims. All League members caught in the Corona Club riot and not already shot down by the police had been executed. After the random attacks began, Julien Bakshi and Naveen Patel had organized retaliatory strikes outside of Terran neighborhoods, all aimed at League members who had gone on record as being opposed to the Terran criminals. Some had acquired guards for themselves, but that just increased the number of targets. The Bogo Boys were very good at what they did.

The Bogos handed out nothing worse than beatings and threats, and no one had actually been killed since the Corona Club siege, but probably it was only a matter of time.

Sula's chief frustration was that none of the League's leaders had been implicated in any of the violence. Either the rioters were all very good at holding out under interrogation or torture, or the riot had truly been spontaneous.

Or, Sula thought, the leaders were very careful about how orders reached their subordinates.

"I think it's charming," Sula said. She looked down at the long line waiting for Ming Lin's signature, and the waitrons circulating with snacks and drinks. "You've done a lovely job with the reception."

"I didn't make the arrangements myself," said Lady Koridun. "The publicity staff at Brio did the work, and they have experience."

"I detect your hand in the choice of music," Sula said. "I saw that band at your garden party last summer." Her hand comm offered a discreet chime. She ignored it.

Lady Koridun's blue eyes glowed. "I made a suggestion, that's all."

A suggestion that her subordinates would disregard at their peril, Sula knew, especially in light of the Koriduns' reputation for violence and insanity.

"The band makes it more an event," Sula said. Her hand comm chimed again. She took it from her pocket, saw that the call was from Lamey, and dropped the comm back in her pocket.

"Is it important?" Lady Koridun asked.

"The call? I don't think so." And then there was a slightly different chime, this one signaling the arrival of a message, and Sula surrendered, took out her comm, and told it to play.

Lamey's face appeared distorted in the display, and there was a sheen on his skin that made it seem as if he were sweating. His voice was harsh, parts of the words clipped.

"Earthgirl, you need to look at the feed from the Convocation. *Right now!* I'm not joking, this is important!"

Sula looked at Koridun. "Sorry, I suppose I'd better look at the feed."

"What's happening?"

"No idea." But she hadn't seen Lamey so agitated, certainly not since he'd appeared, with his braided trousers, in her apartment in the Petty Mount.

So she wouldn't disturb Ming Lin's event, Sula walked down the catwalk toward the back of the store as she called up the Convocation feed. It wasn't available on any of the public channels, which meant a closed session. Sula gave her password and Lady Gruum appeared on the screen, immaculate in a black gown with white tokens of mourning pinned to her sloping shoulders. Her sonorous Daimong voice bore the sobbing overtones of high tragedy.

"The Terran criminals have prevented Rol-mar's return to order!" she cried. "As a result of this treachery, over two hundred Daimong were killed by a crew of Terran butchers!" Her voice rose to a dramatic quaver. "I demand justice! Justice for the martyred Captain Derinuus and his heroic crew!"

"What the hell?" Sula muttered. She knew no Captain Derinuus, let alone his heroic crew.

She looked at the news feeds and found nothing. She returned to the Convocation feed and, over the next fifteen minutes or so, managed to piece the story together. Derinuus and his *Beacon* had been sent to Rol-mar to suppress a mutiny among its inhabitants, and then got blown up by Shushanik Severin and his Exploration Service cruiser.

Sula barely knew Severin, who was a Martinez protégé; but she knew he had a good reputation and had a few years ago saved Chee from annihilation. She hardly thought that Severin was a piratical rebel who went around obliterating Fleet cruisers for his own amusement.

As the Lord Senior pointed out in the discussion that followed Gruum's speech, Severin had volunteered to take his cruiser to Harzapid, where the Fourth Fleet was based, and where he and his crew would submit to whatever investigation was demanded by the authorities. He and *Expedition* were not in a state of mutiny. When Severin arrived at a base, there would be a thorough inquiry, and if there had been a crime, the criminals would be punished. Until then, any claims of conspiracy, murder, or demands for vengeance would be premature. Justice would be done.

"When has this administration ever done justice?" Lady Gruum wailed, her vibrato throbbing through the video screen. "Criminals walk free in the streets of the High City! Mutineers have seized an entire planet and are defended by warships!"

Sula looked at Lady Koridun, who was watching the video over Sula's shoulder. "Captain Severin's actions saved the settlers that Lady Gruum herself sent to Rol-mar," Sula said. "Many are her clients. Even if her company's bankrupt, I'm sure she still owns property on the planet, and Severin's saved that, too. Lady Gruum seems to have forgotten all that."

Koridun's blue eyes glowed with concern. "What does that mean?"

"It means she's not the least bit interested in justice," Sula said. "She only wants to punish the people she views as her enemies."

The blue eyes widened. "Are you among them?"

Sula laughed. "I'd be proud if I were," she said. And then she felt the laughter die, and she felt the pistol in the small of her back and was acutely aware of its weight. Suddenly the day seemed old and gray and full of shadows.

"Lady Gruum is delusional," she said. "I've seen it on the Committee of Honor, in Peers who have lost their money and who think it's going to come flooding back if only . . ." She searched for words. "If only enough people die," she said.

MAURICE, LORD CHEN sat in a quiet corner of the Convocation's lounge, finished his second glass of mig brandy, and considered ordering a third. It was the day before Solstice Recess, and for Lord Chen the adjournment couldn't come soon enough. He was heartily sick of his fellow convocates and the revolting turmoil they were creating. Accusations, counteraccusations, conspiracies, venom and shouting, all to the drumbeat of the rising and apparently unstoppable violence in the Lower Town—unstoppable, because whenever the police intervened, the violence increased rather than diminished. Bullets and executions didn't seem to be a solution.

Worse, the conflict in the Convocation pitted him against members of his own class. Lady Gruum's ancestors were as distinguished as Lord Chen's own, and her faction included some of the most distinguished members of the Convocation. Lord Chen, on the other hand, was being driven closer to the Martinez family as they helped to organize support for the Lord Senior and the government.

And last, his own affairs demanded more and more of his attention. His fortune was dependent on shipping, particularly in the Hone Reach, and if Lady Tu-hon achieved her goal of shifting the tax burden back to the merchants, the business he'd spent the last eight years rescuing could be again in jeopardy. He'd already had to halt a number of shipbuilding projects, all cargo carriers, and had instead concentrated on building enormous passenger ships intended to carry emigrants to the newly opened worlds. But with Rol-mar in a state of mutiny, even *that* business now seemed risky.

He decided to order a third brandy. He signaled the waitron, and then he saw a young Terran in Fleet uniform approaching him. The man had a lieutenant's rank, dark brown skin, hair shorn close to the scalp, and the red triangular collar tabs of the staff officer.

"My apologies, Lord Convocate," he said with a bow. "I'm to convey Lord Ivan Snow's compliments and tell you that he hopes he may see you directly."

"Does he?" Lord Chen murmured in surprise. Lord Ivan Snow was the Inspector General of the Fleet, and the head of its military police as well as the Investigative Service that pursued criminals within the military. He had held the office since before the Naxid War and had seemed one of those officers so thoroughly lodged in his position as to be immovable. Like Lord Tork, he would hold his office as long as he wanted, or till death claimed him.

But however immovable Lord Ivan might be, Chen had never had, or required, a private meeting with him. The Lord Inspector had reported to the Fleet Control Board every so often, and that had been that.

"*Now,* if you please, my lord," said the young man.

Brandy seethed along with surprise in Lord Chen's brain.

"Yes," he decided. "Yes, I will oblige his lordship." However inconvenient the summons, at least it would delay his return to the wrangling on the Convocation.

He rose from his booth just as the waitron arrived with his third brandy balanced on a stained-glass salver. Lord Chen paused for a moment, then picked up the brandy and swallowed it. Fumes stung his sinuses. "Lead on," he said, his voice husky, his throat half aflame.

To his surprise the staff officer led Lord Chen clean out of the Convocation and to a waiting automobile. The door rolled up, and the staff officer stood by to respectfully help Lord Chen into the vehicle.

Lord Chen paused with his hand on the doorframe. "I'm sorry," he said. "I don't know your name."

"Ratna, my lord."

"You aren't coming along, Lieutenant Ratna?"

"I have another errand, my lord."

Lord Chen nodded and seated himself. The scent of the aesa-leather seats suffused his senses. The door rolled down and the car sped off down the Boulevard of the Praxis, traveling in silence on electric motors. There was scarcely any vibration. The driver was behind an opaqued screen and Lord Chen could see only a Terran silhouette in the typical brimless flat cap worn by chauffeurs. Just short of the Garden of Scents, the car turned onto a side street and drew to a stop in front of the Nicotiana Smoking Club, a venerable institution that required, for membership, at least one grandparent having been admitted as a member. Two of Lord Chen's grandparents had belonged, but Chen had never developed much of a taste for tobacco, let alone hashish, and had never applied for membership, though he'd been present now and again as a guest.

The door rolled up, and a young Terran man appeared to help Lord Chen from the car. He wore civilian clothes, but there was something unmistakably military about his carriage, and he led Lord Chen through the green coppered doors into the club. It was a comfortable place, brass and dark wood, with alcoves and small rooms for the sake of privacy. Wooden locker doors lined the walls, each holding a humidor or a pipe belonging to a member. The porter, an elderly Terran with a fringe of hair straggling around his bald head, nodded as Lord Chen entered, but did not ask him to sign the guest book.

The club had a deep ingrained tobacco scent, loam and hay and saddle leather all blended together. Chen's guide led him to a room in back, knocked quietly on a recessed door, then opened it without waiting for a reply.

In the room Lord Inspector Snow reclined on a divan, his hawklike face coldly majestic in the illumination of a globular overhead light. He wore a rich purple velvet smoking jacket with a monogram and the club badge on the breast pocket. Before him on a low table was a hookah with two mouthpieces, its reservoir made of beautifully colored blown glass and its marble bowl carved in the shape of a lotus flower.

"Thank you for coming, Lord Chen," he said in a sandpaper voice. "Please have a seat, and join me if you like."

"Thank you, no, I'm not much of a smoker." Lord Chen unbuttoned his wine-red jacket and sat on another divan across from the Lord Inspector. Alcohol fumes whirled in his head. He wished he hadn't ordered the third brandy.

Lord Ivan reached out to touch the bowl, and electronics gently ignited the tobacco. He took one of the amber mouthpieces in his hand. "Did anyone see you leave?" he asked.

"Lots of people saw me," said Lord Chen. "I doubt I raised anyone's curiosity."

"Very good, then."

The Lord Inspector smoked. The pipe bubbled pleasantly and then released into the room an improbably sweet, cloying floral scent. Something like burnt molasses seemed to grip the back of Chen's throat, and he tried not to sneeze. He found the divan uncomfortable and he wished he were back in the Convocation lounge drinking his third brandy in peace. Or maybe his fourth.

"How can I help you, Lord Fleetcom?" he said finally.

Lord Ivan lowered the mouthpiece and blew out an impressively large cloud of sweet smoke, then fixed Lord Chen with a calculating gaze. "Were you aware of the meeting of the Fleet Control Board this morning?" he asked.

Lord Chen blinked. "I knew of no such meeting." He had been a member of the Fleet Control Board since the war, and he would naturally have been informed if the board met.

Lord Ivan nodded. "You and Fleet Commander Pezzini were both excluded," he said.

Lord Chen was puzzled. He and Pezzini were hardly allies, since Pezzini was one of those who loathed Gareth Martinez with a passion and supported the Supreme Commander in practically everything.

"Why?" he began, and then realization dawned. "Oh."

"*Oh,* indeed," said the Lord Inspector. He seemed bitterly amused. "The two Terran members of the board were kept away. The other seven met privately."

The brandy fumes cleared from Lord Chen's mind as if blown away by an arctic breeze. "This was Lord Tork's decision?" he asked.

"Of course."

"What is he planning?"

"The Supreme Commander was alarmed by Captain Severin's actions at Rol-mar. He fears that Terran officers of the Fleet may imitate the Naxid revolt and stage a mutiny."

Lord Chen gave a laugh of derision, and then another, more alarming thought intruded. "Does he have any evidence?"

Lord Ivan's smile was savage. "Beyond one of his cruisers being blown up along with two hundred members of his own species? No."

"What did the meeting decide?"

"At some convenient date, all Terran ships are to be occupied and disarmed. When Lord Tork decides the danger has passed, the Terran crews will be allowed back aboard their ships."

Lord Chen absorbed this with his full attention. Relays seemed to be opening and closing in his mind, *click clack clack,* leading from one irretrievable conclusion to the next.

"Is there a tentative date?"

"Lord Tork is working with his staff to berth as many Terran squadrons as possible at bases where they can be taken.

Once Tork has made his dispositions, the Terran ships will be at his mercy."

Chen felt his heart lurch against his ribs. "And then what? Detentions, interrogations?"

"I think those are inevitable."

"And if the interrogations produce false confessions?"

"They may be designed to do exactly that."

Lord Chen pondered this, the relays in his mind still going *clack clack clack,* while Ivan Snow, his hawklike face opaque, picked up the mouthpiece of the hookah and inhaled. The hookah bubbled, Lord Ivan exhaled. Sweet tobacco haze clouded the air.

"How do you know this?" Lord Chen asked finally.

"An informer. I have a partial transcript of the meeting, should you care to see it."

"Your informer is not a Terran?"

Snow offered a tight-lipped smile. "No Terrans were at the meeting."

So that meant at least one non-Terran was outraged by the board's attempt to seize—seize what? Supreme power? Because they had to carry this scheme out without the knowledge of the government, or at least the Lord Senior.

"What should I do?" he asked. "Inform the Lord Senior? Raise the issue in Convocation?"

"Not yet," said Ivan Snow. "We don't know the date, no orders have been sent, and at present Lord Tork and his friends can simply deny everything."

"And you'll know when the orders are sent?"

"I have friends in the Commandery who work in Operations Command. The orders would be transmitted through Operations, and I will know the hour the message is sent and have a decoded transcription within minutes." He inhaled tobacco, exhaled a sweet cloud, coughed. "But we should send our own messages, yes?"

"I have no access to Operations Command, my lord. I can send no messages to the Fleet."

Snow pointed at Lord Chen with the amber mouthpiece of his pipe. "You should not *send* messages. You can't do it safely. You should *take* messages, in person to a safe location, and deliver them verbally. I suggest you start by passing a message to your son-in-law."

"Gareth?" Lord Chen blinked. "He has no command. What can he do?"

"Flee," said Ivan Snow. "He should flee to your sister at Harzapid. And he should take as many officers with him as he can."

Lord Chen considered this, then nodded. "Michi doesn't command the Fourth Fleet, just the base and dockyards."

Snow's gaze was cold. "She can *take* command of the Fourth Fleet," he said. "She will have to. And once she does, she will need experienced officers."

Chen looked at the Lord Inspector and felt his heart begin to founder. "You don't think we can stop this."

"I don't absolutely know that we can. So we need another plan. We can't leave the human race absolutely without a defense."

"Civil war."

"Civil war *again*." Ivan Snow sighed, then drew in more tobacco. "I can send messages to your sister that should be safe. In the meantime, I suggest you speak to Captain Martinez as soon as you can. Harzapid is three months away, and much can happen in that time."

CHAPTER 15

The sound of Terza's harp floated through the palace from the music room. Martinez walked toward the sound blindly, his mind aswim in something like a storming sea. Part of his brain saw nothing but horrors, the Corona Club filling with bodies, the stairs running with blood, friends fighting and dying while Martinez himself stood helpless, unable to prevent the slaughter. Another part of his brain was making lists—lists of routes, of officers, of supplies. A third was working on a more abstract level, conceptualizing fleet tactics to be employed when heavily outnumbered. That last process was going on entirely on its own, and he was aware of it only when some small insight bubbled to the surface of the crashing waves that seemed to fill his head.

He walked into the music room and saw Terza with her harp, her long black hair pinned back, her agile fingers plucking at the strings, and he realized that now she lived in a different world than he, a world in which war and treachery and annihilation were far, far away, and not looming right on the doorstep.

Martinez walked into the music room and sat heavily on a couch. Terza remained focused on her music, though he knew by a slight shift in the angle of her eyebrows that she was aware of his presence. The music flowed on, glissandos alternating with fingernail attacks. Singing chords echoed from the geometric Devis-style roof beams. Terza was an expert harpist and often played in a chamber ensemble made up of her friends.

It's starting again, he thought.

Except that it was worse this time. During the Naxid War the majority of Naxids remained loyal, and when the ringleaders were killed or committed suicide, Naxids were ejected from the Fleet and some of the security agencies, but otherwise permitted to go about their lives unmolested.

But now it seemed that all Terrans were being judged guilty of crimes that no one had so much as defined. Perhaps, Martinez thought, the Convocation shouldn't have been so eager to congratulate Lord Mehrang on his bloody suppression of the Yormak Rebellion. The Yormaks had been reduced to a few refugees penned up on reserves, and no one knew if they would survive as a species.

Annihilating an entire species, Martinez thought, might have set entirely the wrong precedent. Particularly since his own species might be the next to be eliminated.

The piece came to an end in a great swash of glimmering sound. Terza paused to let the last echoes fade, then looked up. "What's wrong?"

Martinez only blinked at her.

"Is it Lieutenant Kelly? Has something happened to her?"

"No."

Good, Martinez thought. He had managed to utter a single syllable. He could only improve from here.

He gave the words all his concentration, and spoke. "I just had a meeting with your father. It's very bad news."

Terza turned off her harp, shifted it from her shoulder, rose, and joined Martinez on the couch, landing with a swirl of silk skirts and the heart notes of vetiver. Intelligent concern shone in her dark eyes. She took his hand.

"In your own time," she said.

In his own time he told her, stumbling a bit here and there. "So Maurice thinks we should become refugees," he concluded, "then mutineers."

"It's that bad?"

"Apparently." Martinez took a breath. "I'm one of the Terran criminals, after all. I shouldn't be caught here when things come apart."

In silence, her eyes inward, Terza pondered for a moment. "Who else knows?" she said finally.

"I'm the only one Maurice has told."

"Does your brother know?"

Martinez considered the question. "I don't think so. Certainly he hasn't told me anything."

"He's a Terran criminal as well. So are your sisters. If you're going to run, they should come as well."

"I'm supposed to take officers with me to Harzapid, to crew Michi's ships. I've been . . . making a list."

Her warm hand shifted in his. "I hope I'm on that list. Along with the children."

His breath caught in his throat. A surge of pure inchoate emotion prickled the hairs on Martinez's arms.

He looked at her. When he could manage words, he said, "Are you positive you want to do this?"

She had been in mourning for her fiancé, Richard Li, when Roland had strong-armed her father into agreeing to let her marry Martinez. Martinez himself had been in shock after the shattering of his relationship with Sula. The development had been so sudden that there were still white mourning threads in Terza's hair during the public announcement of their engagement.

He had sworn to himself that he would treat her with all the courtesy and regard that a husband owed his wife, and for the most part he had succeeded. If his thoughts sometimes strayed to Sula, to her golden hair and emerald-green eyes and the pale skin that could flush so easily with passion, it was not his fault. He behaved toward Terza as if his own passion had been directed always toward her.

But he could not help but wonder if she, too, had made a similar resolution. If each of them was playing a part, then what was the marriage but a fragile structure like Young Gareth's cardboard castle, knocked flat by the first careless blunder?

"Last time," she said, "you were off on a warship, and I was pregnant, and I couldn't be with you even though I wanted to. But now we're going to be refugees, and if that's going to happen we should be refugees together."

The words had stopped up his throat again, so Martinez took Terza in his arms and held her against him. Her vetiver perfume whirled in his head.

"I'm glad we'll be together," he managed finally.

We should be refugees together. It was the strongest possible affirmation of Terza's commitment to their marriage.

How can I possibly deserve this? he asked himself.

But then he knew immediately that he didn't deserve it at all and drew back. Terza took his hand again.

"Roland has the family yacht docked on the ring," Terza said. "Do you know how many passengers can fit aboard?"

"A dozen or so in comfort." He offered a faint smile. "The junior officers can sleep on the floor and on the tables."

"Lots of playmates for Chai-chai."

And then a thought struck him, and he laughed.

"We don't need Roland's boat!" he said. "We've got *Corona*!" He laughed again at the thought of the yacht carrier flying his refugees to Harzapid in complete luxury. "We can put a hundred passengers on board if we need to."

Amusement touched Terza's lips. "And if we're bored, we can stage yacht races."

He looked at her. "I suppose we can *hope* the cruise is boring, yes?"

She looked away. "Yes," she said. "I suppose we can."

Martinez glanced again at the brass plugs on the walls, each marking a bullet fired in anger. Until a few hours ago, they had been an interesting item of decor, but now they seemed an omen.

SULA LEFT THE Nicotiana Smoking Club and took her first welcome taste of fresh air. *Hope I can get the smoke out of these clothes,* she thought. She walked away from the club brushing at the sleeves of her jacket, and taking one grateful gulp of air after another.

She was going to need a shower.

She was so offended at Lord Inspector Snow's trapping her in a room filled with tobacco smoke that it took a while for his message to sink into her mind. Ships being moved to where they could be captured and disarmed. Trials and torture. The human race labeled as criminals and rendered defenseless.

There is no situation so terrible, she decided, *that Tork can't make it worse.*

She wondered if it could be called mutiny if it were the head of the Fleet leading it.

And then, as she walked toward the Garden of Scents, her old wartime reflexes suddenly invaded her perceptions, the habits she'd acquired while hiding underground during the Naxid occupation, when she was known as the White Ghost. Sula found herself making abrupt, random turns at intersections, covertly examining the other pedestrians on the street, looking in shop windows in order to use the reflection to check for anyone tailing her, and keeping a mental tally of automobiles and small trucks to note if they kept reappearing. She had just been enrolled in a conspiracy that the authorities would find subversive, and there was no way she could know that Lord Ivan Snow hadn't already been denounced or discovered, and that anyone meeting him would be incriminating herself. If she were being followed, she might have to sprint for safety, something that would be difficult insofar as she was one of the most recognizable Terrans on the planet.

No one seemed to be keeping her under observation, though. Which was no guarantee that she wasn't, but it was enough to allow her to walk to the funicular, descend to the Lower Town, and from there walk to the Petty Mount and her home. The instincts of the White Ghost remained alert as she walked, and it was the White Ghost, rising to consciousness, who began a series of calculations that she continued once she arrived, and while she was taking her shower.

The first thing she did after showering and changing clothes was to log on to the Records Office through the back door she had built during the Naxid War. She hadn't had occasion to use it since the war, and she wasn't sure it would still be there, but the Records Office computer hadn't been upgraded or altered, and Sula began to create new identities for herself, as well as for Spence and Macnamara.

Time to put Action Team 491 back in commission, she thought.

Macnamara walked into her study when she was thus engaged and asked if she'd like a pot of tea.

"Yes, thank you," she said. "By the way, we're going to have to go underground for a while. I'll have your new identity ready in a few minutes."

There was only the briefest hesitation before Macnamara's reply. "Yes, my lady. Shall I inform Spence?"

"Yes. And start to consider how and what we're going to pack. Necessities only, I'm afraid."

"Right away, my lady."

Sula paused for a moment to appreciate Macnamara's virtues. He was a fine shot with rifle or pistol, reasonably competent in the kitchen, and sufficiently anonymous to disappear into a crowd. He was a little overprotective, certainly, but he would do his best with every assignment, either shadowing a target, serving a cocktail, or burying a dead Koridun. And, more importantly, keeping his mouth shut about the latter.

While Sula was busy with the Records Office computer, she could feel the White Ghost active in some other level of her consciousness. So when she finally finished crafting the new identities, she found herself busy checking means of getting to Harzapid and the Fourth Fleet. There would be no passenger vessels traveling directly to Harzapid for some time, but a huge immigrant ship was leaving Zanshaa's ring for Chee after embarking thousands of new settlers. While it stopped at Zarafan to take on more passengers, Sula and her party could transfer to another, smaller cargo-passenger vessel heading for Harzapid. The immigrant ship would be leaving in six days. That gave her a deadline.

Next Sula followed the list the White Ghost had made and began looking up officers who might be available for a very long trip out of town. At the head of the list were Haz, Giove, and Ikuhara, lieutenants from Sula's last command, *Confidence*. They had been contaminated by their association with Sula and had been unemployed since the war. Haz, she remembered, had got promoted to lieutenant-captain due to family influence, but he'd never got a command, and now he was here with the others, kicking at the doors of the Commandery looking for a job.

She looked for other old acquaintances and found Senior Captain Linz, who had commanded a frigate in Sula's Light Squadron Seventeen. She had been promoted after the war and commanded a cruiser but was now an inspector of replacement parts and foodstuffs destined for Fleet bases and ships—hardly the most stimulating of assignments.

Sula began making calls. A reunion of the officers of *Confidence* was definitely in the cards.

"WHAT," SULA ASKED, "would be the effects on the economy of another war?"

Ming Lin looked at Sula in concern. "What sort of war?" she asked.

"Let's be optimistic and say it's somewhat smaller than the last one."

Sula and Lin were having one of their regular meetings, over tea, in Sula's office. Lin wore her student's gown and managed not to look even remotely like a successful author.

The Convocation was not in session, and most convocates were away, but their offices were still open and handling routine business. The fundamental prisonlike gloom of Sula's inner office had been relieved with flowers and gleaming porcelain, and Sula was amused that Lin's rose-pink hair was echoed by a display of dianthus and hibiscus blooming behind her on a shelf.

The clove-like scent of the dianthus complemented the aroma of the tea, which had a subtle taste of almond that survived even when diluted by Sula's usual dollop of cane syrup. Sula sipped her tea deliberately while Lin considered Sula's question. When Lin spoke, her voice was cautious.

"Would there be, for example, battles and raids involving the Fleet?"

"Let's say there are."

Lin nodded, more to herself than to Sula. "Civic disruption on the surfaces of planets?" she asked.

"We've already got that."

"It could get worse," Lin said.

Sula nodded. "It probably will," she said.

"If warships get blown up," Lin said, "they will have to be replaced. Shipyards and shipbuilders will get contracts. And there will be more contracts for supplies, replacement parts, and so on. Shipyards are almost at a standstill now, because nobody knows how hard Tu-hon's tax will fall on commerce, or when, or if it will at all—so if you expect their business to pick up, they'd be a good investment now."

"Yes."

"But of course if the shipyards are destroyed in the war," Lin continued, "your investment will be destroyed as well."

Sula sipped her tea and nodded.

"Large government expenditures will benefit certain industries and supply chains and will supply a boost to the economy—but really, if the spending is confined to the Fleet, it won't create that much wealth across the board. And if the Fleet is interdicting commerce between worlds, and destroying ships and supplies, that will significantly hamper any recovery. So you might consider investing in some rather basic things, like food, food packaging, and food distribution, because people will need food whether there's a war or not." She raised her cup of tea to her lips, then lowered it. "And, you know, *water*. Because people need that, too."

During the Naxid War, Sula had bought stocks of chocolate and coffee, items that she knew would become scarce on Zanshaa. Buying into ordinary food suppliers had not occurred to her.

"Thank you," she said.

Again Ming Lin raised her cup, then let it fall again. It rattled in the saucer.

"My lady," she said carefully, "do you know something I don't?"

Sula looked at her. "I believe I just told you."

The cup rattled in the saucer again. Lin put the saucer on the side table with a trembling hand.

"Do you know when it's going to start?" she said.

Sula put her own saucer down and leaned back in her office chair. Pneumatics sighed.

"I advise you to leave Zanshaa. A promotional tour for your book, say."

Lin blinked. "I can't afford that."

"I'll pay for it," Sula said.

"I—" Lin raised a hand to her throat. "When? Because I'm supposed to defend my dissertation."

"When?"

"Something like twenty days from now."

"You'll have to leave before that, if you're going."

Lin's dark eyes began to search the shadowy corners of the room, as if she could find an answer there. "I don't know," she said.

Sula let the breath sigh from her lungs as she considered her words. "If it helps you make up your mind, you should remember that you're a known associate of one of the Terran criminals, and that you've written a book that contradicts the story that Gruum and Tu-hon are spreading about the causes of the decline." She restrained a savage laugh. "They might well decide you need silencing, one way or another."

Ming Lin straightened in her chair, her spine erect. "It seems I have little choice."

"I'll make the arrangements," Sula said. "You should pack, and you shouldn't tell anyone you're going away. Once we've left Zanshaa, you can send your regrets to your dissertation committee."

Lin offered a rueful smile. "They may not forgive me."

"They will have more important things not to forgive," Sula said.

Lin's look darkened as she puzzled that out, then she shook her head. "When am I leaving, then?"

"I'll let you know. And you may trust that the message will come at the last possible second."

Lin reached for her saucer. "I suppose that if I am going underground," she said, "I'll be safest going with you."

Sula sipped at her own tea, found it cold, put it down. "I'm sorry if I surprised you," she said. "Sometimes I forget that not everyone has been expecting this for years."

Lin seemed puzzled. "Years? How long exactly?"

"Since the end of the last war, in the Year of the Praxis 12,483. I remember telling Gare—telling Captain Martinez that we'd be at war again within six years. I seem to have been overpessimistic by three years."

Lin seemed intrigued. "Why did you think there'd be another war? The Naxids were beaten pretty comprehensively."

"Because we still have a government that could permit something like the Naxid War in the first place." Sula warmed her cup with tea from the pot. "They have no way to prevent a conflict from starting." She stirred more cane syrup into her cup. "The convocates were set up in the Convocation to follow policy set by the Great Masters, not make policy themselves," she said. "They were reasonably good at that, that and sucking up to the Shaa. But they're not good at making decisions, or questioning themselves, or coping with changed circumstances. They've been hopeless at dealing with the economic crisis, and they've allowed something like the Steadfast League to spread right under their noses." She spread her hands. "So—we'll be on the run soon."

Lin nodded, her expression bleak.

"Be sure to pack something nice to wear," Sula said. "We'll be going first class."

Lin stared at her. "Wars seem to have improved since I fought in the last one."

Sula sipped her tea and smiled. "At least the accommodation will be better."

THE REUNION OF *Confidence*'s wardroom took place at Julien Bakshi's restaurant. Sula was known there, and the maître d' welcomed her and showed her into the private room she'd booked. The Cree chef hustled in to explain the latest features of the menu. As the afternoon progressed, it was difficult chasing off the highly attentive staff so that Sula could deliver her message.

Rebecca Giove was her usual kinetic self, and the perpetually youthful Pavel Ikuhara had grown a little mustache in hopes of looking more mature. It wasn't working. The big surprise, however, was in discovering that her former premiere lieutenant, Lord Alan Haz, was now Lady Alana. This sort of transformation was uncommon among the Peers, who worried that it might interfere with their primary duty of reproduction, but apparently Lady Alana had sufficient resources and independence to flout tradition.

The metamorphosis was clearly a work in progress. Lord Alan had been a big, square, hearty young man, with a robust manner, a commanding baritone, and an exquisite set of tailored uniforms. Lady Alana's dress sense remained, for her Chesko frock was elegance itself and artfully de-emphasized her mesomorphic frame; but the personality that had seemed natural had now become studied, and the voice a mere whisper until she forgot herself, and the baritone boomed out over the table. In her tall heels, she towered over everyone else in the room.

Sula waited until the meal was over, and brandies and coffee had been delivered, before she told the others why she'd brought them together.

"It's time for us to leave Zanshaa," she finished, speaking into the stunned silence. "We're going to be needed elsewhere."

"Where?" asked Giove.

"You don't need to know that now. But you'll each be traveling under another identity, just in case anyone is looking for groups of Fleet officers moving from one place to another."

Lady Alana stared at the table, her expression troubled. "I don't know if I dare go."

Sula looked at her. "Why not?"

"I've got a wife and three children in Zanshaa City. I can't leave them behind, not with things as they are."

So apparently Haz *had* done his reproductive duty before beginning his conversion. And he'd remained married through the transformation, which Sula was inclined to think was unusual.

"Can your family come with you?" Sula asked.

"Yes, but—" Haz searched for words. "The children are small. I don't think they'll be able to travel under cover identities. They won't remember who they're supposed to be."

"In that case," said Sula, "you and they can travel under your own names. A single officer shipping with her family is unlikely to set off alarms. Just remember that you don't know any of the rest of us."

Lady Alana still looked worried, but she nodded. "That seems possible," she said.

Sula gave Ikuhara and Giove envelopes with their new

identities, prepared ahead of time. "Memorize all the details," she said. "Do not bring any other form of identification."

"Very good, my lady!" said Giove. She sounded as excited as a child running free after a day at school.

"Another thing," Sula said. "Are there any other officers we might contact? We need people we can absolutely trust, officers who can leave at a moment's notice, and who will be useful in combat—no glits, no high decorative Peers—we'll need *fighters*."

"Do you know Naaz Vijana?" Giove said. "They promoted him after Esley, and promised him a cruiser, but the ship's not been built yet. I think a subcontractor went bankrupt, or something."

Vijana, Sula remembered, had been the officer who had obliterated the Yormak Rebellion. Ruthless, she supposed, and a proven fighter, but his combat experience was hardly conventional.

Though maybe an unconventional fighter was exactly who they needed.

"Should you contact him?" Sula asked. "Or should I?" Giove said that she would do it.

Lady Alana mentioned a lieutenant who had served in one of the other Terran ships in Sula's squadron and volunteered to contact him.

Ikuhara touched his sparse mustache. "Are we looking only for officers? Maitland and Markios are both living on the ring, and currently unassigned."

Warrant Officer Maitland was a sensor specialist, and

Markios, Engineer First Class, had been in charge of the engine station in *Confidence*'s Command center.

"Very good," Sula said. "We'll need experienced specialists."

"I'll have to go to the ring to contact them."

"As soon as possible, then." She looked at the clock on her sleeve display. "If you'll pardon me," she said, "I have another appointment." She looked from one to another. "Pack and be ready to leave on a few hours' notice. Don't tell *anyone* what's about to happen, not unless he's one of the people we discussed." She looked at Lady Alana. "Don't tell your family anything, Lady Elcap. Just tell them you've got an assignment and they have to depart immediately."

"They may not understand," Lady Alana said.

"Understanding isn't important," Sula said. "What's important is that we all leave when we can."

She went from the private dining room to Julien Bakshi's private office on the second floor. Julien had just arrived—he was practically nocturnal—and his bodyguards knew Sula and let her enter. Julien had been fighting the war for weeks, his Bogo Boys ambushing members of the Steadfast League, and sometimes being ambushed in return.

He accepted Sula's news with a nod. "We'll be getting weapons out of storage, then," he said. "I suppose we might have to arm half the Terrans in Zanshaa City."

"I'll see you when we take the city again," Sula said.

They embraced. His hair pomade had a repellent fruity scent, and it took an effort of will for Sula to hold him close.

From Harmony Square she went to the High City and Sidney's Superior Firearms. Sidney welcomed her into his basement firing range, a place that smelled of both propellant and Sidney's hashish. Sidney looked more like a dying man than ever, but his mustachios were waxed at a jaunty angle, and he offered her a lemonade and gave her a metal stool to sit on while he fired up his pipe. He coughed, hacked, drew in more smoke. Sula told him what was happening.

"You can come with us," Sula told him. "We might be able to use a weapons designer. But if you stay, I hope you'll be able to assist the Terran Secret Army that will be starting."

Sidney was surprised. "Me? Leave the planet?"

"Why not?"

"The only person in my family ever to leave Zanshaa was my son. And he was killed in the war."

Which had motivated Sidney to help Sula's Secret Army during the fighting on Zanshaa. After his son's death, Sidney had been suicidal, offering firearms that could be traced straight to him; but Sula had found him too useful to sacrifice and used him instead to design cheap, easily assembled weapons suitable for her amateur fighters.

"Do what you like," Sula said. Even secondhand, the hashish was making her head spin. "But you have to make up your mind now."

"Well," he said. His pupils were wide as platters. "I'll have to let my manager know that I'll be out of touch for a while."

"Tell him you've gone hunting."

He laughed, and then the laugh broke down into a wheeze. He spat into a handkerchief, but then he swabbed his chin, straightened, and grinned. "Another world?" he said. "If not now, when?"

She handed him an envelope with his new identity and gave him instructions. "If you can," she said, "you should bring some weapons with you. Suitably packed, because you won't be allowed to carry."

The grin broadened. "I think I know just the thing."

Sula nodded. "I'm sure you do."

WEAPONS WERE STILL on her mind the next day, when Sula was in her parlor trying to work out a way to fit an automatic weapon into a credenza. The secret compartment at the back wasn't long enough to hold the barrel, even after she'd disassembled it, and she hated to leave the weapon behind.

"Let me look at it, my lady," said Macnamara. He was a fair carpenter, and during the war had built secret compartments into the furniture found in their safe houses. Each apartment had been a small arsenal of firearms, grenades, explosives, and detonators.

In the back of Sula's mind was the thought that they might have to take command of their transport. Sula had checked the policy of the shipping company, and civilians—which Sula and her friends would pretend to be—were not allowed to carry firearms on the ship. Any weapons would have to be placed in a labeled container and given to the purser for storage. Sula hoped that weapons would be unnecessary, but she didn't want to trust to the mercies of the purser; and so she'd thought of shipping some of Macnamara's special furniture as well. If they couldn't get into the purser's stores, through either compassion or bribery, they might be allowed into the hold to break the weapons free.

She wondered if she was being paranoid, then reminded herself that paranoia had kept her alive so far.

The air was scented with gun oil. On the floor was a container that Spence and Macnamara had retrieved from one of Action Team 491's storage units. The equipment had been stored during the Naxid War, and though the weapons and armor should have been turned in at the end of hostilities, Sula had decided against it.

The tradition of paranoia was hard to break.

The container was open, which was unfortunate when Lady Koridun walked in along with Ming Lin. Sula had been expecting Lin—she was arriving to pick up her tickets for the transport—but apparently Lin had met Lady Koridun on the way and hadn't been able to brush her off.

Lady Koridun's blue nocturnal eyes opened wide and seemed to glow like lamps. Wordlessly she viewed the rifles, the grenades, the bricks of explosive scattered over the table.

Ming Lin's face filled with appalled surprise. "Oh, hello!" she said. "I ran into Lady Koridun in the lobby!"

Surrounded by firearms, Sula thought, and not one of them was loaded. She straightened from her crouch behind the credenza and measured her distance to the nearest magazine.

"We're . . . taking inventory," she said.

A false, brittle brightness entered Lin's voice. "Is all that left over from the war? You've got a lot of souvenirs!"

Lady Koridun's eyes shifted from the weapons to Sula. "I wondered why Miss Lin canceled her video appearance next week," she said slowly. "Now I suppose I know. You're all running away, aren't you?"

She had killed so many Koriduns, Sula thought, one more shouldn't matter. She was trying to work out how to do it, decide whether Koridun would stand still while she loaded a magazine, or whether she'd have to just beat Koridun to death with a gun butt.

"How can I help?" Lady Koridun asked.

Sula was so surprised that she had no real response. "I'm sorry?"

"You're fleeing, but you're taking weapons with you. You're going to start a war against Tu-hon and Tork and the rest. And I want to help."

Lady Koridun's tone was so reasonable and full of enthusiasm that it took a moment for Sula to formulate a response.

"Well," she said, "you might not want to be so closely associated with Terrans right now."

"Why should I care about that absurd claptrap?" Lady Koridun said. "Tork and Lady Gruum and so on are just *wrong.* You've been right about *everything,* and they're out to punish you." Her blue eyes gleamed. "I'll do all I can! I'll bring all my clients into the war on your side!"

"That may be a little premature," Sula cautioned.

"Hah!" said Koridun. "Tell me what I need to do, and I'll do it. But I *will* get to run away with you, won't I? It'll be so exciting!"

Sula had found Lady Koridun's hero worship trying in the past, but now she was beginning to understand its uses.

"Well," she said. "Let's talk about that."

IN THE END there were eighteen of them, officers, cadets, and enlisted, plus Lady Alana's family. Lady Koridun traveled supreme class in a vast suite decorated in eight shades of cream, while Ming Lin was in first class, her suite adjacent to that of the Haz family.

Lady Koridun had a lady's maid with her, another Torminel who knew nothing of the purpose of the journey. Koridun was supposed to be traveling to Harzapid in order to take charge of a publisher she'd bought there. Ming Lin was along to do an author tour.

Sula, under her new name of Tamara Bycke, was supposed to be a consultant helping Koridun with her acquisition. Shawna Spence was installed as Ming Lin's servant, and the rest of the Fleet officers and enlisted were either more consultants, more servants, or immigrants leaving Zanshaa. Most traveled second class—Sula shared a room with Spence, as she had during the war. She didn't mind second class—at least it was better than immigrant class.

For they traveled on an enormous immigrant ship bound for Chee via Zarafan and Laredo, its four giant engines capped by what looked like a silver mushroom-shaped half dome. There were thousands of voyagers aboard, all bound for their new lives, and nobody questioned the cover identities of Sula's party. It was easy to disappear into the crowd, and Sula—with contact lenses and a wig disguising her signature green eyes and blond hair—enjoyed anonymity. She drank tea in the lounge, worked her mathematical puzzles, and tried to think as little as possible about events on Zanshaa.

She was less pleased that the ship was the *Marcus Martinez,* named after the paterfamilias of the Martinez family—Clan Martinez owned the ship and had built it in their own shipyards at Laredo. Lord Martinez was shipping all these immigrants to a planet under his own patronage.

Before she'd left, Sula had told everyone she would be vacationing on Zanshaa's southern hemisphere, at Lady Koridun's country estate. She figured no one would be likely to travel all that distance to discover whether or not she was there.

One of the options for video entertainment was a simulation of nearby space, and she noticed the big yacht carrier *Corona* leaving Zanshaa's ring three days after the immigrant ship, after which it shaped its course directly toward Harzapid. There was speculation in the media concerning the yachting tactics that would supposedly be developed during the voyage. *Trust Martinez,* Sula thought, *to run for his life in a way guaranteed to make himself seem important and grand.*

Corona would probably arrive at their mutual destination ahead of Sula, who would have to detour by way of Zarafan.

Sula kept a watch for warships tracking outgoing vessels, but none seemed interested.

During the war, Fleet elements had traveled from Zarafan to Zanshaa in ten days under massive acceleration, but the immigrant ship, accelerating more gently, took thirty-two days to make the same journey. Sula and her party disembarked from *Marcus Martinez* straight onto *Striver,* a cargo-passenger vessel considerably smaller than the vast immigrant ship. There was room for only a hundred passengers, and while there was nothing as crowded as immigrant class, neither was there anything as grand as supreme class. Lady Koridun moved into the vacant owner's suite, which was the best on the ship; and Ming Lin managed with a suite half the size of the one on the *Martinez*. Sula and Spence moved from a cabin with double beds to one with bunks.

Sula took the top.

The difference between first and second class was strictly the size of the room: there was no lounge reserved for the higher classes, and all the public spaces, including the restaurant, were used in common. There was no table service in the restaurant, but instead a buffet—and worse, high-caste passengers might think, was that crew dined along with passengers instead of being kept out of sight.

This was fine with Sula until, mere hours before departure, she saw uniformed Torminel come crowding through the passenger entry port into the common room, and she recognized the black tunics of the Legion of Diligence, the fanatical upholders of the Praxis who had dedicated their careers to the eradication of dissidence and rebellion.

CHAPTER 16

Once Martinez passed on Lord Chen's message to Roland, a different organizing principle took hold. Martinez had been concerned with escaping with his family and enough officers to make a difference in any subsequent battle, but Roland's intentions were more dynastic. Walpurga, Roland decided, would take the family yacht home to Laredo, taking with her Vipsania's children; Roland's daughter, Girasole; and Martinez's daughter, Yaling.

"In case we're annihilated at Harzapid," Roland said, "we each need an heir in Laredo, to carry on our work."

"You always maintain the most cheerful outlook," Martinez said, and then he felt a wave of surprise. "*You're* going to Harzapid?" he said.

"Assuming I'm welcome on *Corona,*" Roland said. "It won't just be fighting at Harzapid—there will of necessity be a political element in what we're doing. And I'll handle that."

I'll handle that. Roland's words, oozing confidence, obliterated any possible objection.

Such a jolly family vacation, Martinez thought. *I wonder if Vipsania's bringing a camera crew.*

Lord Chen would stay, despite the danger. So would Vipsania's husband, Lord Oda Yoshitoshi, to provide opposition to Tork in the Convocation.

Martinez had reasonable success recruiting officers. Since those who had worked most closely with him in the war had been denied a posting by Lord Tork, many were on Zanshaa looking for employment. Martinez hadn't told all of them where they were going and why, just hinted there might be a confidential mission for which they'd be suited. Chandra Prasad, Sabir Mersenne, and Ahmad Husayn from *Illustrious;* Vonderheydte and Elissa Dalkeith from Martinez's first command, the frigate *Corona;* and Martinez's friend Lieutenant-Captain Ari Abacha, who joined the expedition with his hairdresser and his personal bartender in tow.

A special case was Lieutenant Garcia, who had escaped promotion not because she was too closely associated with Martinez, but because she had managed to miss the war completely. She'd been second lieutenant of *Corona* under Fahd Tarafah and had been captured along with most of the crew during the opening hours of the war. She'd spent the war in a prison camp on Magaria, her service patrons had been killed in battle, and thousands of officers with genuine war experience had been promoted over her head. Her own career had been frozen. Yet, on her last day of freedom, she had slipped her lieutenant's key to Martinez, which allowed Martinez to unlock *Corona*'s weaponry and make his escape from the enemy, and Martinez always felt he owed her a debt of gratitude. She had been so desperate for employment that she'd volunteered before Martinez got halfway through his recruitment speech.

Each of the recruits was given leave to suggest others who might be willing to join the expedition. Those recruits were given no information at all, only that Captain Martinez wanted them for duty that was hazardous and extremely secret. Martinez was gratified to know that his prestige in the service was such that nine junior officers joined knowing nothing more than this.

Nor was Martinez the only person recruiting pilgrims. Roland brought Hector Braga along, for reasons that seemed obscure. All Martinez could imagine was that whatever Roland and Braga were planning, they were planning it together.

Deep sadness flooded him when he thought of Kelly, still lying in a coma in her hospital room. The escape from Zanshaa to a chaotic situation at Harzapid was the sort of thing she would have very much enjoyed.

He couldn't take her with them, but Martinez decided he didn't want Kelly remaining helpless in Zanshaa when the conflict started. He arranged for her to be transferred to a hospital well away from the capital.

Martinez had contacted all the Terran officers he knew and could find, all save one—the one he'd need the most, but also the one he most dreaded.

Three times, he'd found himself in her orbit. Three times, she'd run away.

He cringed at the thought of speaking with her again. Yet he wanted nothing more.

But he knew the meeting was inevitable, and so he let Alikhan drive him to the Petty Mount.

HIS MOUTH WAS dry as he arrived at Sula's building, and he felt a touch of vertigo swim through his senses.

He had never ceased to dream about Sula. The flashing green eyes, the silver-gilt hair, the straight-backed hauteur that dissolved to passion in bed.

At the end of the war he had made a decision, or perhaps the decision had been made for him. To be with Sula he had been willing to risk the wrath of Terza and her powerful father; the anger of his brother, Roland; and the scorn of strangers; but when the moment came he had found himself disarmed by his child. The infant had been born at his father's home on Laredo and brought for months across the empire to be placed in his arms at the very moment he returned to his home in Zanshaa.

When he had looked up from the wonder of Young Gareth's eyes, Sula had been gone.

But now he had come to ask her to join him on the flight to Harzapid, and his nerves jangled as he looked up at her building.

There had been snow overnight, but the morning had brought the melt, and when Martinez left the car he stepped into a small stream running at the curb. He felt an uncomfortable moisture creeping through the seams of his shoe.

A uniformed Terran doorman opened the door for him, and he stepped into the lobby's warmth. Another uniformed man waited behind a curved desk, and Martinez detected the impersonal sweep of the man's eyes, eyes that grew more interested when they detected the bulge of Martinez's sidearm under his overcoat.

"May I help you, sir?" the second man said.

Martinez began to speak, found the words jammed in his throat, then cleared his throat and spoke again. "I'm Captain Martinez. I hope to see Lady Sula."

"Lady Sula is not in residence," the man said. "She's spending the holiday as a guest of Lady Koridun."

"Ah. Thank you." Lady Koridun headed a prominent Torminel family, and Martinez could hardly chase Sula down at a Torminel Peer's estate to warn her that a group of non-Terrans was planning to seize power.

He would have to tell Roland or Lord Chen to pass the word to Sula another way.

"Do you wish to leave a message?" the man asked.

"Just that I called on her."

Martinez turned, and the doorman kindly opened the door for him. On his way out, he saw the weapon lying heavy in the doorman's overcoat pocket.

Carrying firearms, he decided, was very much the new fashion.

THE VOYAGE OUTWARD from Zanshaa combined aspects of a vacation, a country house outing, and a sports training camp.

Water bubbled from the fountains and waterfalls, the dining room echoed with conversation and laughter at mealtimes, and officers punished themselves pushing weights in the gym, building the muscle that would help them stand the heavy acceleration that battle might bring. Young Gareth played in the ponds and fountains, chased the rare fish, and had to be locked out of the racing yachts after he spilled apple juice on *Laredo*'s control panel.

All this was too strenuous for Ari Abacha, who preferred reclining with a cocktail while watching sports on video. He exerted himself to the extent of starting a sports book, and from his chaise longue in the lounge took bets on everything from lighumane to football.

Corona flew under the direction of a reduced crew augmented by the Fleet officers. Captain Sor-tan and the other non-Terrans had been furloughed with full pay, and First Officer Anderson, a Fleet veteran, was now in command. The Terran chef who had fought so well in the Corona Club riot now reigned in the kitchens.

Officially the *Corona* was on a mission to audition new captains for the yacht races, and so Fleet officers were allowed the use of the yachts that rode piggyback on the carrier's hull. Races and gymkhanas were improvised. Martinez watched the races carefully. He and Michi Chen might have to promote some of these officers to command warships, and the tactics employed in a race might be the only evidence of their suitability.

Chandra Prasad turned out to be the most successful of the new racers. Martinez was not surprised, as she'd been a very gifted tactical officer under Michi Chen, and he was grateful that she had found something to occupy her restless spirit.

Terza had brought her harp, and others had brought instruments, and so there were sessions that were too informal to be called "concerts," but too organized to be viewed as complete improvisations.

As if she had been reading his mind, Vipsania had arrived with a camera crew and was producing a documentary on the phony yacht trials and the various candidates. *To be introduced into evidence at my court-martial,* Martinez thought. *To demonstrate our innocence.*

As if that would work.

There was only one real surprise in the first few days, and that happened on the third day when Martinez saw Lieutenant Vonderheydte walking to dinner with a young woman on his arm. He recognized the pale bouncing curls and the spray of freckles over the snub nose and bowed as she approached.

"I wasn't aware you were aboard, my lady."

The laugh of Lady Marietta Li sounded like the trill of an exotic bird. "Von and I are running away together," she said.

Poor Lord Durward, Martinez thought. Then it occurred to him to look on the bright side—maybe Lord Durward could divorce Marietta and marry his first wife all over again.

He fixed Vonderheydte with a stern look. "You failed to inform me you were bringing a . . . *companion.*"

Vonderheydte offered a weak smile. "We're in love, my lord. And this time it's the real thing."

This was not the first time he'd heard Vonderheydte

proclaim one of his affaires the real thing. Reality seemed unusually transient where Vonderheydte's love life was concerned.

Which, for that matter, applied to Lady Marietta as well. At least she seemed to have good taste in officers, if Vonderheydte and Nikki Severin were anything to judge by.

"This journey is all too likely to become the *real thing* before it's over," he said. "For Lady Marietta's sake, you'd better hope it doesn't."

Vonderheydte at least had the decency to blush before Marietta gave another exotic-bird trill and led him away.

Martinez decided it was time the passengers got more serious about being in the military, and he told everyone to don their uniforms and do their best to pretend they were on a warship. To this end, he made a point of censoring all communication from the ship. Officially this was to prevent anyone from blabbing about the brilliant new racing techniques *Corona* was developing, but he wanted to make sure that no one made a slip or tried to tip off a friend.

Roland and Hector Braga spent a lot of time sending coded messages to their allies in Zanshaa, and Vipsania likewise remained busy with her media empire, spinning the news to the support of her family and Terrans generally. Martinez didn't censor *their* messages—in fact he didn't dare. He knew how conflicts with his formidable siblings turned out.

But still, after *Corona* passed through Zanshaa Wormhole Eight into a series of other systems, and as the weeks wore into months, there was too much free time, and too much of it was spent listening to the news and the dread, thudding drumbeat of disintegration, suspicion, and violence that was engulfing the empire.

Corona passed through Chijimo's system, where a full-blown regatta was staged to impress their peaceful character on any observers. Twelve days after leaving the Chijimo system came a message from Zanshaa, eyes only to Martinez, using the code that Lord Chen had provided him. The message consisted only of a single date.

"Eleven days from now," Martinez said, in a family conference in his suite. "That's when Lord Tork plans to disarm all Terran ships."

Terza said nothing, but calculation was visible somewhere behind her dark eyes. Roland looked at the piece of paper with the decoded message, and he nodded.

"And there's nothing we can do," he said. "Not here. Not halfway to Harzapid, far away from any elements of the Fleet."

Martinez spread his hands. "And that's just the problem. We're helpless. All we can do is wait and hope that Michi knows how to organize a mutiny."

WHEN SHE SAW the black uniforms of the Legion, Sula knew she was about to be arrested, and the White Ghost, seizing control of her mind, planned the route to the purser's office to break out her firearms . . . but then she noticed that the members of the Legion were carrying identical shoulder bags, which were not weapon shaped, and that some were carrying shopping bags with personal items bought on Zarafan's ring. They didn't look as if they were about to arrest anyone: they stood in an orderly group, and stewards arrived to take them to their cabins.

They weren't here to apprehend anyone, then—they were here to travel to a new posting. At Harzapid, Sula assumed.

There were more than forty of them, a whole company. And they would be sharing accommodation on the *Striver* with Sula and her rebel officers.

Her pulse still racing in response to the jolt of adrenaline she'd just experienced, Sula forced herself to move casually as she rose from her corner booth and began a stroll out of the room. She needed to alert her people to the presence of the Legion. She didn't want anyone jumping to the same conclusion she had, and either running or going for a weapon.

This voyage was going to be far more complicated than she had intended.

"MISS BYCKE," SAID Captain Lord Naaz Vijana, "may I join you?"

"If you like," said Sula. "I'm sorry, but I've forgotten your name."

"Kaanan Koti, miss." Vijana had just arrived from the buffet with his tray, which he placed on the table opposite Sula. Like Sula, he'd chosen the stewed Hone-bar phoenix and dumplings, which was about the most reliable item on the rather limited menu.

Sula was missing her Cree chef. Without knowing it, she seemed to have developed a refined palate.

Vijana arranged his napkin on his lap, which allowed him

to look to his right to see Lady Koridun dining with Lord Arrun Safista, the commander of the Legion contingent on the *Striver.* The two had a table to themselves, and Lord Arrun's servant stood within hailing distance, ready to freshen their drinks or bring them another item from the buffet.

"How's Koridun doing?" Vijana asked.

Sula rubbed the pad of scar tissue on her right thumb. "We're not arrested *yet,*" she said.

Lord Arrun, as one of the two Torminel Peers on *Striver,* had shown a purposeful, businesslike interest in the other Peer. In fact he was so narrowly focused on her that he ignored everyone else and monopolized Lady Koridun at meals and social functions. Lady Koridun would normally be far above Lord Arrun in Peer society, but here they were isolated on a ship for months, and Lord Arrun was giving romance every conceivable chance to blossom. Lady Koridun, after all, was young and presumably impressionable, and Lord Arrun was mature, confident, and on the hunt. The possibility of failure seemed not to have entered his head.

Lady Koridun had told Sula that she'd resigned herself to a long voyage and was considering feigning illness.

Of course with the Torminel, there was always the option of violence. But if Koridun picked up Lord Arrun and hurled him headfirst into a bulkhead, he might view it as a form of flirtation.

"Lady Koridun told me that Lord Arrun has arrested any number of fascinating thieves and subversives," Sula said.

Amusement crossed Vijana's pointed face. "That must make for delightful dinnertime conversation," he said.

"At least the lord commander isn't looking at *us,*" Sula said. She gave Lord Arrun a glance. "I've been researching the Legion of Diligence," she said. "There aren't that many of them, you know, but they make up for lack of numbers by fanaticism and ferocity. Sending an entire company on a two-and-a-half-month trip to Harzapid is unusual."

Vijana's black eyes turned hard, and for a moment Sula saw the ruthless officer who had so efficiently slaughtered rebellious Yormaks. "You think they're going for a reason," he said.

"Someone decided they're needed there."

"You think that someone might have got wind that Lady Michi is plotting a—" He cleared his throat and dabbed at his mouth with his napkin. Two members of the Legion walked by carrying their supper trays, their large nocturnal eyes scanning the room. Sula examined the sidearms they wore on their belts.

The Torminel passed. "I think all sorts of things are possible," Sula said.

"It's occurred to me," Vijana began, then stroked his upper lip where, till recently, he'd worn a pencil mustache. When Sula had built him the Kaanan Koti identity, she'd looked at his photo, decided she didn't like the mustache, and removed it. Vijana had been forced to conform, and shave. Now he was forever stroking his lip, a gesture that amused Sula every single time she saw it.

"It's occurred to me to wonder," he started again, "what happens if Lady Michi opens the, the *business* before we arrive. Once the Fourth Fleet is in her hands, what do you think is going to happen on board *Striver*?"

"It depends on whether anybody tells Lord Arrun and his men that something's happened."

"Do you have a plan to prevent their finding out?"

"Not yet." Sula considered. "It occurred to me there might be a fire in the comm center."

Vijana shivered. A fire anywhere on a spacecraft was a terrifying prospect.

"And if Lord Arrun isn't prevented from finding out?" he said.

"I can't think he'd take on the Fourth Fleet by himself," said Sula. "I imagine he'll order *Striver* to turn around and return to Zarafan."

Vijana looked at her levelly. "And to prevent that we'd have to take the ship ourselves."

"Indeed."

"Do you have a plan for that?"

"Not yet."

They fell silent as two passengers joined them at their table, an elderly Torminel couple on their way to visit family in Harzapid. The coppery scent of warm blood drifted from their plates. Sula and Vijana devoted their attention to their stew for a minute or two, and then Vijana looked up.

"How have you been amusing yourself, Miss Bycke?"

"Working puzzles, Mister Koti. And helping Lady Koridun with her business plans."

Vijana offered a charming smile. "Perhaps you'd like to join me this evening for a game of cards."

"Cards?" Sula said. "What sort of stakes?"

Vijana waved a hand. "Whatever sort you like. I'm happy to oblige you."

"I've seen you play in the lounge with some of the other passengers. Judging by the stacks of tiles on the table, I'd guess the stakes were pretty high."

Vijana shrugged. "We can play for lower stakes, if you like. I don't know how many of the others would join us, however . . . We might have to play alone."

Ah. Hah, Sula thought. Perhaps Lady Koridun was not the only person in the restaurant with a persistent admirer.

Carefully she considered Naaz Vijana in the light of this surmise. With his alert face, his caramel skin, the long black eyelashes that framed his dark eyes, and his absurd mustache shaved, he was not unpresentable. He was smart and a fighter and seemed aware of possibilities that existed outside the sphere of normality for Peers. As a distraction from impending war and its impending horrors, he had much to recommend him.

But she was also focused on the problem at hand, and so a distraction probably wasn't what she needed. The White Ghost was in her head, quietly planning mayhem, and a card game might pull the White Ghost away from her proper business.

"I think I'm not in the mood for cards tonight," she said. "I'm really not much for gambling."

"You don't gamble, and you don't drink," Vijana said. "Don't you have any vices at all?"

I kill Koriduns, Sula thought. She felt her lips pull back in a smile that was perhaps too much of a snarl.

"Perhaps we can indulge in vice some other time," she said.

"I'll look forward," said Vijana. He seemed a little pleased with himself.

Sula sipped her sparkling water and took another glance at Lord Arrun as he chatted with Lady Koridun.

The White Ghost was already trying to work out a way to kill him.

SHAWNA SPENCE HELD up a large tube of topical pain relief gel. "Before we left I filled the tube with a semiliquid plastic explosive," she said. "I've also filled several bottles of skin lotion and some packages of nutrient bars. Glycerin is a primary ingredient in lotions and some foods, and on an X-ray the explosive looks just like glycerin, so we got it through security and onto the ship." She lowered the gel tube. "I also have the raw materials for detonators, the same type created by Mister Sidney as propellant for his rifles."

"I'll make all the detonators you want," said Sidney.

"The explosives may be useful," said Alana Haz. "But they're not really antipersonnel weapons. And we have to overcome twice our numbers, and they have sidearms, and we don't." She corrected herself. "Well, *you* don't. Since I'm traveling as a Fleet officer, I was permitted to retain mine."

"That," said Sula, "might make you a target, if the Legion is ordered to arrest any Terran Fleet officers."

Sula, Spence, Macnamara, Sidney, Haz, Giove, Ikuhara, and Vijana were in Lady Koridun's suite, gathered around her dining table. Koridun's lady's maid had been given an evening's holiday and provided with some money to throw into the ship's gambling machines. Drinks were scattered around the table, along with comm units containing the phony business plan for Lady Koridun's alleged publishing investment, in case the servant returned early.

Lady Koridun herself was with Lord Arrun Safista, at a screening of the new Dr. An-ku mystery. She had promised to keep him busy for the whole evening, and Sula had been impressed by her willing sacrifice.

"It's not just the Legion we have to worry about," Vijana said. "We've got to seize the Command center, the engine room controls, and anyplace else from which control of the ship can be managed. We've got to contain the ship's officers, or at least the ones who aren't Terran."

"The third officer is Terran," said Giove. "And he's ex-Fleet, so he may be on our side in the end."

"Engineer Markios can handle the engines," Sula said. "Any number of us could command the ship if we needed to. The Legion of Diligence has to be our main target, because they can offer resistance and retake the ship if we're careless."

There followed a discussion of how to dispose of the Legion, including bombing their rooms, stationing gunmen just outside their cabins to mow them down as they came out, or simply knocking them off as they wandered about the ship in the course of an afternoon.

"Kill them at supper," Vijana said. "They all sit together for the most part, and mostly eat at the same time. Those elsewhere can be hunted down once we've disposed of the rest."

"There will be other people eating in the restaurant," said Ikuhara. "We don't want casualties among the bystanders."

"It will terrify them," said Vijana. "Terrified people are much less likely to give us trouble."

Sula looked at Vijana, and the man who had killed half a million Yormaks looked back at her, his expression mild.

"Let's try to get them all there," she said. "Maybe Lady Koridun can host a special dinner to honor the Legion."

A proper Torminel feast, Sula thought, *plenty of blood and raw flesh.*

Macnamara looked up from his glass of fruit juice. "What do we kill them *with*?" he asked. "All our weapons are held by the purser or hidden in crates in the hold. We've got to get access before we can do anything."

"The purser is a Daimong," Sidney said. "But his assistant is a Terran." Since he'd been aboard ship his smoking was confined to a single lounge reserved for that purpose, and his consumption of hashish had been somewhat reduced. So had his constant coughing. His voice remained hoarse, but at least he wasn't wheezing all the time.

"How do we get to that person?" Sula asked. "And who can let us into the hold?"

Spence held up the bottle of pain relief gel. "We can blow open the hatch," she said.

"Let's try other remedies first," Sula said. "We don't want the Legion to storm into the hold and find us fumbling with a container of disassembled weapons."

Vijana frowned. "And once we get firearms, where do we *put* them? With this one exception, all our cabins are small, and an attendant cleans them daily. What's an attendant going to do if he finds a dozen rifles stacked in the closet next to grenades and detonators?"

"Tell them we're cleaning our own rooms?" Macnamara wondered.

Well, Sula thought, *we'll worry about that when we get the guns.*

CHAPTER 17

Captain Lord Jeremy Foote held his arms over his head as the two riggers dropped the upper half of his vac suit down over his body. Enveloped in the shroud, Foote found himself in a dark, enclosed space that smelled of disinfectant and suit seals. Once they made sure that Foote's arms were properly in the sleeves, the riggers pulled the upper half down atop the lower part, already installed, and began to mate the two halves of the suit. In so doing they had to shove one of his legs into a more appropriate position.

Normally Foote would have resented being manhandled by a pair of enlisted apes, but his mind was busy with other matters.

I don't see a choice, he thought.

His Light Squadron Eight had been traveling in company with Cruiser Squadron Four and Light Squadron Eleven, together known as Force Orghoder, after their senior squadron commander, Lord Sori Orghoder. Lord Sori, a nephew of the Lord Orghoder who had presided over the yacht race at Vandrith, had fought under Lady Sula at Second Magaria and later at Naxas, and had been a celebrated yachtsman both before and after the war. An officer noted for dash, breeding, bravery, and intelligence, he was the sort of officer whom Foote would have been pleased to serve under.

And now it looked as if Foote was going to have to kill him.

I don't see a choice, he thought again.

AS PART OF the Commandery's plan to keep Fleet units shuttling about in order to prevent collusion and rebellion, Force Orghoder had been on a tour of the outer reaches of the empire. The last port of call had been Laredo, where the officers had been feted by Lord and Lady Martinez, the parents of Gareth Martinez. Foote had been disappointed—not by the hospitality, which was lavish, but by the fact that Lord Martinez hadn't turned out to be a bumpkin with dung on his feet and a straw up his nose, which was what he had hoped.

The Martinez family always managed to find some way to defy expectations. It was one of the things Foote disliked about them.

Force Orghoder had been within hours of departure when a sublieutenant of the Military Constabulary came aboard *Vigilance* with a message for Captain Foote's eyes only. Once she and Foote were alone, she informed him that the message was personal from Lord Ivan Snow, the Inspector General of the Fleet. The message was ciphered, but the sublieutenant conveniently provided a hand comm able to read it.

"Do you know what's in it?" Foote asked.

"No, Lord Captain."

Foote viewed the sublieutenant with the eye of a connoisseur. She was young and reasonably attractive, with smooth sienna skin and eyes of a vivid green. He considered the possibility that she might prove a compliant partner for the next few hours, before *Vigilant* was scheduled to depart Laredo's ring.

"Well," he said, "sit down and have a glass of wine, and I'll read the message."

The message made him forget all about the woman sitting next to him. The Lord Inspector informed him of Tork's plan to disarm the Terran elements of the Fleet. Apparently Lord Sori had not yet been informed of the plan, which envisaged Foote's squadron being confronted and disarmed by the other two sometime on the return journey to Zanshaa. More ciphered communiques would be forthcoming, so Foote was to retain the hand comm and keep it in his safe, but if necessary he should try to escape along with his squadron to Harzapid and the Fourth Fleet.

Foote stood, and he looked at the sublieutenant, who had made herself comfortable in a chair with her glass of wine. She looked up at him for a lazy moment, then realized the atmosphere of the room had changed. She put down her wine and rose to her feet.

"I think that will be all, Lieutenant," Foote said.

The sublieutenant braced to attention. "Shall I send a reply, Lord Captain?"

"No," Foote said. He'd handle that himself. "Let me call someone to escort you off the ship."

"My lord." Leaving her glass on his desk, the sublieutenant made a proper military turn and left his office. Foote sank into his chair again, alone with the dark thoughts that swirled in his skull.

An hour later, he realized he'd forgotten to call for the sublieutenant's escort, but when he looked into the corridor, she was gone, having presumably seen herself off.

A pity. Another time, and they might have had some fun.

A PAIR OF metallic clicks announced that the riggers had drawn on Foote's gloves. "Shall I attach your helmet, Lord Captain?"

No choice.

"No, I'll carry it. You'd better get in your own suits, the drill will begin in just a few minutes."

"Yes, Lord Captain."

Foote tucked his helmet under his arm, left his quarters, and took the belt elevator two levels to Command, buried in the heart of the ship. He walked through the hatch, and the third lieutenant said, "Captain is in Command!"

"I am in Command," Foote agreed.

Foote listened to a brief status update as he replaced the third lieutenant in the commander's acceleration cage. All was as it should be: nothing had changed since the last watch, except that Foote and his squadron had moved a few hours closer to their fate. The oval room, with its couches in their cages, each at different stations, had fallen silent, waiting for the captain to speak, or otherwise indicate his mood. Sometimes he enjoyed conversation with the other officers, usually about sports. Other times he preferred silence, and the Command crew had learned to be sensitive to his frame of mind. Foote looked at the chronometer on his display, stowed his helmet in the mesh bag intended for miscellaneous bits of gear, and then said, "Sound general quarters."

A tone began to bleat from the ship's speakers. It was a tone deliberately calculated to set the nerves on edge and was impossible to ignore.

Vigilant moved efficiently to a state of readiness. The officers' servants, or assigned enlisted, came into the room with the Command crew's vac suits, helped them dress, then went to their own action stations. The departments began to report their state of readiness, and lights began to glow on Foote's displays.

"All personnel to take their prep shots," Foote ordered. He reached into one of the compartments on his couch and drew out a med injector. He dialed the dosage, pressed the injector to his neck, and triggered it. The drug entered his carotid with a hiss and would help prevent stroke and keep his circulatory system supple for high accelerations.

"Signals," he said, "messages to Eighth Squadron's captains. 'Captain Foote's compliments, and he requests your company for dinner tomorrow, 14:01 hours. Signed, Foote, etc.'"

The warrant officer on the signals board repeated the message, then sent it. Replies began arriving, all affirmative.

The message to the other captains seemed straightforward but was in fact a code. The invitation to dinner was a request to report: the affirmative answers told him that the other ships in his squadron had gone to general quarters.

He couldn't ask the question directly without the risk of being overheard by the other ships of Force Orghoder. And he couldn't send the messages in cipher, because then Junior Squadron Commander Orghoder might wonder why Foote's Command were sending ciphered messages to one another.

I see no choice, Foote thought.

WHEN HE'D RECEIVED that first message from Lord Inspector Snow, Foote had considered informing his other captains, then either fleeing or fighting a battle right there at Laredo, destroying the other ships of Force Orghoder. But then he considered that a premature action might compromise other Terran-commanded ships in the Fleet, and that he should hope that some kind of political solution would be found before Tork actually issued his order to disarm the Terran ships. If he went into action while a solution was on the verge of being worked out, Foote would become a more infamous mutineer even than Taggart of the *Verity.*

So Light Squadron Eight had departed Laredo along with the other ships of Force Orghoder and began an acceleration toward Zanshaa. Since Force Orghoder wasn't in a hurry to get anywhere, there was no heavy acceleration after the first hours, and the time was spent in drills, exercises, inspections, and friendly visits of officers from one ship to another.

Foote had invited his captains and their premieres to dinner one night, after a message from Lord Inspector Snow informed him that Orghoder had received his orders from the Commandery. His officers were all Peers and drawn from the highest-ranked Peer families in the Fleet. One was the daughter of superior officers who had aided Foote's ascent and had been taken aboard so that he could repay the favors by advancing her in the service; and his premiere and second lieutenant belonged to families who might get him his promotion to squadron commander. Each of these arrangements had been made years ahead of time. Foote's officers formed a glittering company at the table, all in tailored full dress uniforms with the tall collar and the two rows of silver buttons, each perfectly groomed by the hairdressers and cosmeticians they employed as servants.

Captain Foote made certain that the food and wine were worthy of the company. His chef had trained at Baldpate in the Petty Mount, then worked under the famous Cree chef Tillat at his restaurant in the High City. Snatching him as a private chef on *Vigilant* had been quite a coup, and one that had cost a lot of money, but as a single bite of his eskatar pie shimmered on his tongue, Foote knew that the expense was worth it.

After the final remove, Foote told the servants to leave the room, made sure the doors were locked, and told his guests about Lord Tork's plan.

"I don't believe it is desirable to leave the Terran species completely defenseless," he said. "So what can we do?"

They offered one suggestion after another, but each proved impractical. In the end, the bleakest solution stared them in the face.

Foote looked down at his table, the elegant linen, the porcelain with the Foote crest, the crystal wine goblets, all tangible symbols of his position, his heritage, his wealth. Everything that made him a Peer, the member of an ancient, privileged family who had never committed a mutinous or revolutionary act in its history.

"So," he said carefully, "I see no other choice."

Foote and his officers met regularly to make plans and search for new solutions, but two months into their voyage, when a ciphered message from the Lord Inspector told Foote the date for Tork's coup de main, he looked at Force Orghoder's planned course and saw a problem.

Lord Inspector Snow's plan called for Foote to somehow escape Orghoder's other two squadrons and flee to Harzapid and the Fourth Fleet. There were two ways to accomplish this, the fastest being to alter course at Zarafan by swinging around its sun, accelerate through Zarafan Wormhole Four, and jump through a series of eight wormhole gates to Harzapid. The problem with this was that two additional squadrons were based on Zarafan, one Torminel and the other Daimong, and either one of them outgunned Foote's light squadron. Both together would bring a swift and decisive end to Foote's odyssey.

That left Foote with the second option, which would mean breaking away early, at Colamote, the system just before Zarafan. From Colamote he could take a series of five wormhole gates to Toley, where he could rejoin the route from Zarafan to Harzapid. It would mean a longer journey through more wormhole gates, and there was still a chance of being intercepted by the two squadrons from Zarafan, but it was the safest route by far.

But altering course at Colamote meant starting the conflict prematurely. To slingshot around Colamote's sun, he'd have to make his move a good six days before the planned date for Tork's strike. If any message were sent out of Colamote, it would travel at the speed of light to Zanshaa within a couple of days—and if the message reached Tork, the Supreme Commander might launch his own strike early, and that might doom the Terran squadrons of the Home Fleet.

Ultimately, Foote decided that he couldn't be responsible for whatever happened with the Home Fleet, and so he and his captains made their own plans, and he sent a ciphered message to Lord Inspector Snow informing him of his decision.

No choice.

LIGHTS GLOWED ALL the way across Foote's status board. All his captains indicated they were at quarters. *Vigilant* was ready, and so was the rest of Light Squadron Eight.

Foote felt strangely light-headed. His heart seemed to lurch into a new rhythm every few seconds. The hands that manipulated his displays felt as if they belonged to someone else.

He'd never experienced this sensation in a yacht race, or during combat in the Naxid War. Then he'd been confident, analytical, his various options racing through his brain at what seemed to be the speed of light.

Now he felt unsure, even though he knew perfectly well what he had to do.

Take action, he thought. *Action will force my mind to obey my will.* Foote triggered the ship's public address system.

"All crew, attention," he said. "This is Lord Captain Foote." He licked his lips with a suddenly dry tongue. "I regret that I must inform you of certain impending ac-actions in the Fleet." For some reason he had stammered. He charged on.

"Because of political developments in the capital," he said, "Supreme Commander Tork has issued orders that all Terran-crewed ships in the Fleet are to be boarded and disarmed. This illegal action will take place throughout the empire in six days' time."

The officers in Command were already aware of this, but it was news to the cadets and warrant officers who sat at most of Command's action stations. He could see them exchange glances, their eyes wide.

Despite the cooling units in his suit, lakes of sweat seemed to have sprung into existence under Foote's arms. More sweat soaked his back.

"I and the officers of Squadron Eight have agreed that we will refuse any attempt to board or disarm us," he said. "Terrans should not be left without a means of defense. We don't want to end up like the Yormaks."

We don't want to end up like the Yormaks. Foote hadn't considered that aspect until now. He wondered if the annihilation of an entire species was normal now.

Not if he had anything to say about it, it wasn't.

He felt that his confidence and delivery improved as he spoke. Simply explaining the situation aloud made its logic clear, and he spoke his final words with conviction.

"Obey your officers, do your duty, and we will resist Lord Tork's illegal order and preserve the freedom of the Terran species. This is Lord Captain Foote, acting in the name of the Praxis." He turned off the public address system and spoke immediately to the crew in Command. He didn't want to give them time to think, only to react.

"Weapons, charge batteries one and two with antimatter. This is not a drill. Power point-defense lasers. This is not a drill."

The third lieutenant, who shared the weapons board with a warrant officer, acknowledged and bent to her work.

"Batteries one and two charged with antimatter," she reported. "Point-defense lasers charging. This is not a drill."

"Let me know when the—"

"Defense lasers charged, Lord Captain."

Foote frowned. He didn't like being interrupted, and his tone made his disapproval clear. "Weapons, this is not a drill. Have you programmed your missiles with targeting information?"

"Yes, my lord."

"Ready point-defense weapons to shoot down incoming missiles. This is not a drill."

The targets had been chosen well ahead of time, in conferences with Foote's other captains. Force Orghoder was traveling in three packs, each squadron loosely grouped around its flagship, each oriented so that any likely course change wouldn't result in their being bathed in the fiery radioactive tail of another ship. Sori Orghoder's heavy squadron was in the lead, and the other light squadron in the rear, with Foote sandwiched between them, a situation that put Foote at a disadvantage—a *deliberate* disadvantage, Foote assumed, since the formation had been ordered a couple days ago, after a series of maneuvers that had disarranged the original order, which had Foote at the rear.

Light Squadron Eight had eight ships, and the other two squadrons seventeen between them. Each of Squadron Eight's ships was targeting three of the others with two missiles apiece, which Foote hoped would provide sufficient redundancy.

"This is not a drill," Foote said. "Prepare to fire on my mark." He put a gloved hand on the acceleration cage and spun his couch to face the signals board.

"Signals," he said, "message to the squadron: 'Transmit birthday wishes in eleven seconds. Signed, Foote.'"

"Yes, Lord Captain." There was a moment's delay, and then, "Message transmitted, Lord Captain."

Foote started a digit counter on his command board. "Weapons," he said, "this is not a drill. Fire on my mark." He looked at the digit counter. "Six, seven, eight, nine, ten, *mark*."

Foote felt no change in the ship as his six missiles fired, but lights shifted color on his weapons display board, and he gave his next order without waiting for a report from the third officer.

"Engines, rotate ship to heading two hundred twenty degrees by forty-three degrees relative."

"Missiles clear of the tubes," the third lieutenant reported doggedly. "Traveling normally on chemical rockets."

Foote's inner ear shimmered as *Vigilant* rotated to its new heading. His acceleration cage swiveled as the ship spun around it. *Vigilant* had been decelerating at one gravity, and now it was aimed in a completely different direction.

"Missiles fired from all ships in Squadron Eight," said the cadet at the sensor station. His voice shivered with dread, and he was barely audible. The third lieutenant was more emphatic.

"All missiles report antimatter engines alight. All missiles tracking to target."

"We are on our new heading, Lord Captain," said the warrant officer from the engine station.

"Engines," Foote said, "increase acceleration to twelve gravities for nineteen seconds. Then five gravities."

"Yes, my lord."

Increased gravities slammed Foote into his couch, and his cage swung to its dead point as the gravities piled on. He grunted as if someone had just punched him in the solar plexus. His suit closed on his arms and legs to keep blood from draining out of his body and brain. He fought for breath, his vision going dark. Consciousness seemed to drain away as if his mind were pouring like a waterfall out of his skull. Yet, at the end of the nineteen seconds' acceleration, he thought he hadn't completely lost consciousness, and he congratulated himself on retaining his yacht captain's reflexes.

At five gravities' acceleration Foote's awareness returned slowly, and his vision remained dark. Fortunately his instrument boards were brightly lit, and they stood out against the murk of his conscious mind.

"Detonations!" called the third lieutenant. "Radiation spikes!"

The cadet at the sensor station spoke, but at insufficient volume to penetrate Foote's leaden awareness. In irritation, he reached out against gravity to his own sensor board, tilted it so he could better view it, and saw nothing but vast, rapidly expanding fireballs, each of them completely opaque to his sensors. He could see his own squadron, though, still burning on their prearranged heading.

Foote kept the high acceleration as the expanding, now attenuated clouds enveloped his ship, and his view of the universe narrowed to the immediate vicinity of *Vigilant*. He fought for breath against five gravities, grunting every few seconds as his abdominal muscles forced out air.

Over time the radioactive cloud cooled, and his own ships were all he could see.

Wonder and relief sang through Foote's nerves. "Signals, message to squadron to reduce acceleration to one gravity."

He'd just destroyed seventeen ships. He'd killed his own commander, and thousands of officers and crew. Despite their orders to act against Foote, they hadn't considered the possibility that Foote might attack first, and that had doomed them all.

Foote's muscles eased along with the force of gravity. Blood surged into his brain, and the darkness cleared from his vision.

"Secure from general quarters," he said. "Navigation, plot a course to Harzapid by way of Wormhole Two."

"Yes, Lord Captain."

A course to Harzapid, Foote thought. And it would be Footeforce that would be racing on to the Fourth Fleet. They could scarcely be called Light Squadron Eight when they were no longer in the Fleet.

"My lord," said someone on the signals board. "We have two casualties. Recruit Nang and Weaponer Second Class Quispe. Apparent strokes during acceleration, and they're being taken to the medical section."

Foote was annoyed. He didn't know Nang and Quispe by name and probably wouldn't know their faces. He preferred to keep his interactions with the enlisted to a minimum.

His concerns had always been elsewhere.

Foote could hope that no one in the system had been looking in his direction during the brief battle. If no one noticed the bright flashes in the darkness, or wondered about the series of radiation pulses that signified the destruction of seventeen ships, then he might be able to make a clean escape. If someone reported the slaughter and the two squadrons at Zarafan were alerted to intercept him, then there could be another battle before very long.

Foote deliberately stretched his arms and legs. Cold sweat had pooled between his back and the suit, and he shivered.

He'd started a war, he realized, Terrans against everyone else.

He'd better figure out a way to win it.

CHAPTER 18

Winter rain, half sleet, rattled against the skylight. The day was dark, and dark shadows lurked in the Lord Senior's office. There was a woody scent in the air, like sandalwood. Tapestries and brasses glowed softly in the subdued lighting. Maurice, Lord Chen rose as Lord Fleet Commander Pezzini entered the room.

"Hello, Pezzini," Lord Chen said.

"Chen," said Pezzini.

Lord Chen and Pezzini weren't friends, but they served together as the only Terran members of the Fleet Control Board. The board was divided between politicians and professional serving officers, and Pezzini was one of the latter. He wore full dress, bright silver buttons winking against the dark green tunic, and his gray hair was perfectly waved and shaped, clearly by expert hands.

Lord Chen had also dressed formally, in his wine-red convocate's jacket, and his shirt collar buttoned practically to his chin. He'd had a few glasses of mig brandy before he'd set out, and now he was feeling overheated. He tugged at his collar to release some of the heat, and at that moment Lord Saïd entered, majestic with his wand of office and his scarlet brocade cloak. His large dark eyes were intent.

"My lords," he said. "I am told that Lord Tork has just arrived from the Commandery."

"Very good," said Pezzini. He smoothed the front of his tunic. The Lord Senior stood behind his desk, the others flanking him, waiting in silence and sandalwood scent, all dressed formally for the formal duty that united them.

A chime from Saïd's secretary announced Tork's arrival in the outer office. Saïd told the secretary to send him in.

As he entered, the Supreme Commander studied the trio with his round, expressionless black eyes. His cadaverous gray face was incapable of expression, but his walk was brisk and animated, and he carried his Golden Orb. Saïd and Lord Chen were already standing, but as an officer Lord Pezzini braced to attention, his chin lifted, his throat bared. Lord Tork walked to stand before Lord Saïd's desk, then braced in the presence of the Lord Senior.

"I believe we may all stand at ease," said Saïd. Tork and Pezzini relaxed. Lord Saïd studied Tork for a moment, then indicated Lord Chen and Pezzini.

"These lords have approached me with a complaint," he said. "It appears there have been secret meetings of the Fleet Control Board from which they have been excluded."

Lord Tork's melodious voice insinuated itself into the room. "It was my decision to act in the interests of caution, and to avoid involving anyone who might be connected with the Terran criminals."

Lord Pezzini gave a snarl. "You call us *criminals*?"

Tork's response was instant. "Absolutely not, my lord!" he said. "But I do not know all your friends. And Lord Chen—" His black round button eyes turned to Chen. "Lord Chen has married his daughter to a man connected with criminal interests, one who has profited by the financial crisis, and who—"

Lord Chen roared in anger. "That is not only a lie, that is *insane*!"

Tork's voice rose to goblet-shattering power. He raised the Orb like a truncheon and brandished it. "Captain Martinez is a *rebel*! He is a *dangerous innovator*! He is a *threat to the Praxis*! It will be my personal pleasure to disgrace him and to break him in rank, and if I can't execute him, I will send him back to that pathetic provincial world he comes from, where he can crawl back into the mud with the rest of his parvenu family!"

"You bullying shit!" Chen shouted as alcohol flamed through his veins. It had not escaped his attention that he had thought of Martinez and his family in these terms himself, but to hear these sentiments from another sent him into a rage. He looked on Lord Saïd's desk for a weapon to smash Tork in his frozen gray face.

The Lord Senior's copper wand dropped atop Lord Chen's arm just as he reached for a heavy bronze bust of one of Lord Saïd's ancestors. Saïd turned to Tork.

"Perhaps we may discuss your strange vendetta at another time," he said. He used the voice that he employed in cutting off debate in Convocation, and his words rang with authority. "Let us return for the moment to these secret meetings. What was discussed at these meetings that was so dangerous that no Terran could attend?"

"Fleet deployments," Tork said.

Lord Saïd cocked his head. His beaky nose pointed at Tork like an unsheathed sword. "Fleet deployments? What was so secret about these deployments that it had to be kept from the Terran members of the Control Board?"

Tork did not reply, and so the Lord Senior answered for him. "Deployments designed to make the Terran ships vulnerable? Along with plans to board the Terran ships and disarm them?"

Melody had returned to Tork's voice. "Precautionary measures only," he said. "After Severin made his unprovoked attack on *Beacon,* I thought it best to be certain that the violence would not be repeated."

"By storming armed warships?" Pezzini said. "And you intend to *prevent* shooting this way?"

"Do you plan interrogations?" Lord Chen said. "Detentions? Torture?"

"The Military Constabulary will be authorized to investigate whether the officers have been corrupted," said Tork, "and if any conspiracy is discovered, it will be referred to the Office of the Judge Martial for prosecution."

"You have no evidence!" Pezzini said. "You intend to create it!"

"On the contrary," said Tork. His voice had turned to an impatient bark. "There is already ample evidence of rebellion and conspiracy. I intend not to start a war, but to prevent one by making a rebellion impossible."

Lord Saïd spoke with cold precision. "The Praxis mandates equality for all species living beneath its peace. Yet you defy the Praxis by acting against Terrans only."

A metallic clangor entered Tork's words. "If you had uncovered evidence of the Naxid conspiracy before their rebellion began, my lord, wouldn't you have acted against them?"

"I wouldn't have skulked around like a cowardly sneak!" Pezzini said. "Your Terran conspiracy is the delusion of an unbalanced mind!"

Tork turned to Pezzini, and Lord Chen flinched as a strange, threatening insect buzz issued from Tork's cavernous, immobile mouth. Saïd interrupted before Tork could speak.

"Lord Supreme Commander," he said, "these actions of yours are insupportable, and your concealing them from my office, and from your colleagues who have proved their loyalty countless times during the war, shows an alarming lack of prudence. With regret I must ask for your resignation."

Tork looked at Saïd with his cold black eyes. "You don't have the votes," he said.

Lord Saïd seemed a little surprised at this. "I do not need votes to replace you," he said.

"You might dismiss me," Tork said, "but the Convocation would vote to reinstall me immediately, once they hear my report, which is that the Terran rebellion *has already started.*"

The last words boomed out like a rolling barrage. Tork raised the Golden Orb and once again brandished it. "Word arrived less than an hour ago that a Terran squadron commanded by Captain Lord Jeremy Foote has opened fire on the other ships of Force Orghoder and *wiped them out.*"

Lord Chen stared, his breath bottled up in his throat. "That can't be true," he murmured.

"Seventeen ships," Tork said. "Over four thousand crew. Blown to bits in a surprise attack at Colamote. Do you still claim there is no evidence of conspiracy?"

Lord Chen was speechless. The Convocation would be screaming with rage once they found out about Force Orghoder. Lady Gruum, Lady Tu-hon, and all their allies would be in a fury to wipe out anyone they claimed to be a conspirator.

He rather thought that he might be somewhere at the head of the list.

"Is this interview over, Lord Saïd?" asked Tork.

"You will send me the information about Force Orghoder," said Lord Saïd.

"Yes, my lord." Tork braced and left.

Lord Chen stared at the door as it closed behind the Supreme Commander. He was as breathless as if he'd just run the length of the Boulevard of the Praxis.

Saïd gave a long sigh. Lord Chen looked at him, and he saw the Lord Senior crumple, as if he were in a tightening vise. Saïd sagged into his chair. His elaborate red cloak seemed to drag him down like a great weight. His skin had turned gray.

"I don't know if I can survive this," he said, apparently to himself.

Lord Chen looked at Pezzini. "None of us might," he said.

CHAPTER 19

Martinez walked in the direction of the lounge, thinking perhaps to ask Ari Abacha's bartender to make him something cold and fizzy to accompany a sandwich. He'd just been in the ship's gym lifting weights until he ached from his neck to his arches, and he felt he could do with some calories, not to mention relaxation. Seven days remained before Tork's coup, and he had nothing to do but organize activities that would prove irrelevant no matter what happened at Harzapid or Zanshaa.

He was considering his sandwich—crispy bread, cheese melted perfectly over shaved breast meat from a Hone-bar phoenix—and then he heard raised voices from the lounge.

"You *worthless,*" Chandra Prasad shouted from inside, "you *lazy,* you *utterly supine* waste of protein! What excuse do you give yourself even for *breathing,* you hapless, useless, fumble-witted—"

Without thought Martinez pivoted on his heel and began walking away. He had been through enough scenes with Chandra himself to never want to be in the vicinity of one ever again.

He decided he'd have Alikhan bring him a sandwich in his quarters.

Chandra's voice pursued him. "I don't even know why I bother to *insult* you!" she said. "No useful idea could possibly enter that impenetrably thick skull of yours!" And then she gave a snarl, a sound all too reminiscent of a Torminel in a fight. The snarl was followed by a crash of broken glass, and Chandra stormed past Martinez, red metallic hair swinging, her pointed chin high. As she passed Martinez, she glared at him over her shoulder, as if he were somehow responsible for the state of affairs, and then she stomped on. Martinez slowed, considered again the matter of his sandwich, and then turned back toward the lounge.

There he found Ari Abacha stretched on his chaise longue, his cocktail in his hand. His bartender was fussing over him, wiping drink off his face and uniform. Smashed glassware ground under the bartender's feet.

"What was that about?" Martinez asked.

Abacha looked at him wide-eyed. "I haven't the faintest idea, Gare," he said. "Though I believe I may be correct in my surmise that Lieutenant Prasad and I are no longer a twosome."

Twosome? Martinez thought. He took a chair, placed it outside the splash zone, and sat. "How did you get involved with her in the first place?"

Abacha shrugged. "The way these things always happen. She seemed a very exciting girl, delightful really, full of spirit and vitality. And then—" He waved a hand. "Boom! Suddenly, *this*." He sighed. "I would offer you a cocktail, Gare, but Chandra seems to have smashed the pitcher."

The bartender dropped towels on the spatter and went for a broom.

"Is she involved with anyone else?" Martinez asked. He hoped she was, because that lessened the chance that she might take a sudden swerve in his direction.

"No idea."

"Captain Martinez." Lieutenant Garcia's voice came on the public address system. "Captain Martinez, please come to the communications suite."

Martinez rose to his feet. There were very few reasons why anyone would be sending him a message.

"I'll try to come back for that drink," he said.

On a warship the communications center would have consisted of a single console in Command, but on *Corona* the center was a spacious room filled with displays, keyboards, cameras, and ergonomic chairs adaptable to any species under the Praxis. A tank full of brightly colored fish occupied an entire wall and filled the room with a faint briny scent. The room was designed for a large group of racers, crew, and guests to remain in touch with those they left behind, to send and receive text and video messages, and for journalists and broadcasters to send race results to their headquarters.

At the moment the only occupant was the small dark-skinned figure of Lieutenant Garcia, her wiry hair jammed under her billed cap. Members of the *Corona* expedition had less reason to send messages than most. Half were not supposed to be on board at all, and the rest were subject to Martinez's censorship. Whoever stood a communications watch on *Corona* was guaranteed a lonely few hours.

Garcia jumped from her chair and braced to attention as Martinez entered.

"You called?" he said, and Garcia held out a data foil.

"I put the message on this. It was clearly for you, my lord."

Which meant the message was in the code that Lord Chen had given him. Martinez felt a hum of anticipation in his nerves. He thanked Garcia and went to his suite, where he took out a special hand comm and inserted the data foil. He went through several layers of security, giving his thumbprint and a series of passwords, and then called up the decoder.

The message appeared in plaintext on his screen, and his heart surged into a higher gear.

"It's begun," he said, a few minutes later, over the public address system. "Seventy-eight Terran ships of the Home Fleet have departed Zanshaa's ring and are accelerating at high gees away from the capital. I assume they're heading for Harzapid but I don't know that for certain. I also do not know if they're being pursued."

Martinez paused and tried to sort out his thoughts. "I assume this means that a political solution to the crisis has failed," he said. "While I'm sure politicians will continue to do their best, we should prepare ourselves for the likelihood that the situation will be solved only by force."

Having run out of words, Martinez ended the communication. Lieutenant Garcia gazed at him solemnly from behind her desk.

"What do we do now?" she asked.

"Hope for the best," Martinez said. Because hope was all he and the rest of the *Corona* passengers could do. A solution favorable to the Terran mutineers would only be found if Michi Chen succeeded in seizing the fleet at Harzapid. And from Harzapid he'd heard nothing.

"I was wondering," Garcia said, "if we should disable the ship's transponder. That would make it harder to track us."

"They can track us by our engine flares," Martinez said. "We're going to be accelerating or decelerating the entire journey. Anyone with a radiation detector, or even a telescope, could find us."

"Yes, my lord," said Garcia.

"And it might attract attention if our transponder suddenly cut out. Right now we have no idea they're looking at us."

"Yes, my lord."

Though if they *were,* Martinez thought, they could find *Corona* easily enough. And that was a disturbing realization.

DESPITE SULA'S APPREHENSIONS, *Striver* flew on for a month and a half with nothing to remark save tedium. The only person who failed to succumb to monotony was Lord Arrun Safista, who continued his relentless pursuit of Lady Koridun despite her conspicuous lack of encouragement.

Members of Sula's party began to make friends with the crew, particularly the Terran third officer, the assistant purser, and anyone with access to the cargo holds. Sidney, who was willing to share his hashish, became popular with the crew. Tetrahydrocannabinol and bribery assured access to the holds, and it wasn't too long before sidearms and some detonators were smuggled out.

Everyone strapped into their beds while *Striver* cut its engines, spun around, and began its deceleration toward Harzapid, still over a month away. Despite the tide of anger and violence shown on the news programs, there was no sign that the tranquil life of the ship would soon alter.

This changed when Sula received a coded message from Lord Ivan Snow informing her that Tork's coup was scheduled to take place in nine days. "We move a day ahead of Tork," Sula told her crew. It gave them a goal to work toward, and Sula made lists of supplies to be acquired over the last days. Lady Koridun, pleased at the thought of finally ridding herself of Lord Arrun, offered to host a dinner for the Legion of Diligence on that day.

Lady Koridun was so utterly gleeful when she contemplated the slaughter of her suitor that Sula became supremely grateful that Koridun had never discovered who had killed her brother and cousins.

Thus it came as a surprise when the Legion took the ship, and not Sula. The announcement came at suppertime, when half those on the ship were sitting in the restaurant, staring in dull disappointment at the predictable meal from the buffet that had failed for weeks to provide anything like novelty. Sula shared one of the long tables with Giove and Vijana, and Lady Koridun sat with Ming Lin. Sula was surprised that Lord Arrun wasn't sitting opposite Koridun, trying to make himself pleasant, or at least available. Then, over the public address system, came the voice of Fau-tan, *Striver*'s Lai-own captain.

"I regret to inform you," said Fau-tan, "that Captain Safista of the Legion of Diligence tells me that *Striver* has been requisitioned by the government for emergency duty. The Legion is now in command of the ship, and we all, passengers and crew, are obliged to follow their instructions."

Sula stared at Giove and Vijana while calculations spun through her head. *Hide,* an inner voice urged, *find a place in the hold and stay there until . . .* until what? There *was* no hiding place on *Striver.* Another voice told her to head for her cabin, find the pistol she'd secured there, and shoot the first member of the Legion she met.

"I'm sorry to have to say that our current course puts us in some danger from rebellious elements within this region of the empire," Fau-tan continued. "Accordingly, we will be increasing our deceleration and will return to Zarafan as soon as we can safely do so. We will be going to two gravities' deceleration starting at 25:01 and will continue at two gravities until 07:01 tomorrow, when we will take a break of a few hours in order to enjoy the first meal of the day. Please take steps to secure your families and yourselves in your beds before increased gravities begin.

"I apologize on behalf of your crew, and the On-dau Company, for this interruption in your schedule. Rest assured that these steps are all taken for your safety, and that the Legion of Diligence assures me that you will be able to resume your journey as soon as the current emergency is over."

"Current emergency," Sula repeated, her mind spinning. She'd seen nothing in the news broadcasts. She needed more information.

"My cabin," she told the others, and rose from the meal she'd barely tasted.

Nothing concerning any emergency was mentioned on any news broadcasts. Giove, Vijana, Spence, and Macnamara were soon crowding the cabin, all needing to know what had just happened.

"I don't think they're going to arrest us," Sula said. "They'd do that *first,* before they made any announcements. They don't know who we are, and we shouldn't give them any reason to suspect us. Whatever they're doing, it's got to be in reaction to something happening outside the ship."

"Fleet Commander Chen!" Giove said, waving a hand. "She must have taken the Fourth Fleet! That's why they're turning us away from Harzapid!"

"If that's the case," Sula said, "she moved very early, for word to travel all the way to Zanshaa and orders to Safista to come back."

"We don't know what pressures she was under," Vijana said. "Circumstances may have compelled her."

Spence threw out her hands. "None of that matters. What do *we* do?"

"Exactly what we planned," Sula said. "We're going to have to move during the periods of normal gravity."

Vijana shook his head. "I disagree," he said. "Under high acceleration the Legion's going to be confined to quarters, in their beds. *That's* when we kill them."

Sula was considering this when there was a knock on the cabin door. Sula called to ask who it was, halfway convinced it was time to reach for the pistol she'd hidden in her bags, but then she heard Lady Alana's voice, and opened the door. Lady Alana shouldered her way into the small cabin, tall on her heels, chagrin radiating from her face. "They've taken my sidearm," she said. "Came to my door, polite as you please, and asked me for it. They gave it to the purser, and they tell me it will be returned to me when we reach our destination."

"Well," said Sula. "How very civilized."

Vijana's eyes darkened. "Civilization's not for us any longer," he said. "We'll have to be the barbarians now."

***CORONA* NEVER RECEIVED** another message from Zanshaa, but it was able to eavesdrop on news broadcasts, which denounced the Home Fleet Terrans with a completeness that told Martinez that the mutineers had got clean away. Two days later came the news of Foote's destruction of seventeen ships, followed by official outrage and vows of vengeance. At the same time came the news that Lord Saïd had stepped aside—"temporarily"—as Lord Senior in order to recover the health he had lost in years of service to the empire. The Convocation duly elected Lady Gruum as Acting Lady Senior.

Lord Saïd, it seemed, still had too much prestige to be removed from office altogether. Martinez hoped that the new government wouldn't kill him and then announce he'd died of age and illness. Still, they seemed to have given themselves that option.

Lady Gruum saw no need for deceit when it came to Lord Ivan Snow, head of the Investigative Service. The Inspector General, along with several of his aides, had been arrested and executed, for "conspiracy on behalf of the Terran criminals."

Lord Chen hadn't been mentioned in any news reports, nor had Vipsania's husband, Oda Yoshitoshi. If they'd been arrested, it had been done very quietly. Whatever had happened, Chen hadn't managed to send a message to Martinez or to his daughter, Terza.

One appointment gave Martinez wry amusement: Lady Tu-hon had been appointed to the Ministry of Right and Dominion, the department that provided civilian support to the Fleet. She was now in charge of the military, and of prosecuting the Terran criminals with warships and antimatter bombs—though if she had her way with tax policy, he wondered how exactly she intended to pay for the war she'd had such a hand in starting.

Perhaps Lord Minno would know. Lady Gruum's banker, the Cree who participated in pump-and-dump schemes, had been appointed Minister of Finance. It was breathtaking to consider the sort of mischief he could do now that he was in charge of the government's money.

Martinez wondered what he'd started with that bet he'd talked Minno into accepting.

The news seemed to have less censorship than usual, possibly as a result of disorganization in the new government, and the news was encouraging. The Terran squadrons in the Second Fleet at Magaria had also made a getaway, but they wouldn't be turning up in Harzapid anytime soon. The direct route passed through Zanshaa, where the rebel squadrons would be destroyed by the Home Fleet. The alternative was a lengthy chain of wormholes, mostly in barren systems, that would take over half a year to traverse. Michi Chen couldn't expect them to arrive anytime soon.

The Terran squadrons of the Third Fleet at Felarus were in a very different situation. They were on the far side of the wormhole map from Harzapid and had no hope of fleeing there unmolested. All routes led through either Zanshaa or Magaria. So Senior Squadron Commander Nguyen, the ranking Terran, simply sealed himself and his crews in their ships and announced that any Third Fleet warship departing the ring station without his permission would be fired on. Even though Nguyen would lose any fight that followed, the Third Fleet would be shattered, very likely along with Felarus's ring. Nguyen had succeeded in neutralizing a force more than twice the size of his own. For this he had Martinez's admiration, the more so because the Third Fleet was under the command of Lord Pa Do-faq, formerly Martinez's superior. Martinez knew that Do-faq was a first-rate commander, and he was grateful that Nguyen had kept him out of the fight.

The odds were bad enough as it was.

CHAPTER 20

Taking the ship from the Legion was going to be harder than Sula expected. Guards were placed in Command, in Engine Control, and at the entrance to the hold. Torminel in black uniforms prowled the corridors in pairs. Sula set her crew to finding out when the shifts changed, so that she could prepare her countercoup.

It was Pavel Ikuhara who found out the cause of the Legion's strike, from *Striver*'s third lieutenant. "It was Captain Foote," he said, during one of their meetings, this one in Ming Lin's cabin. "His squadron attacked two others at Colamote and wiped them out. He's running toward Harzapid, and the two squadrons we saw at Zarafan are moving to intercept."

A disgusted note escaped Sula's throat. "That idiot Jeremy Foote started the war early!" she said. "And those Zarafan squadrons aren't just chasing *him,* they're on *our* tail. They're going to overrun us if we're not careful."

"Maybe not," Ikuhara said. "Lord Arrun ordered an alteration of our course, so we're going to miss the next wormhole transit altogether. We'll do our whole deceleration in *this* system before our return to Zarafan."

"When were we scheduled to transit the wormhole?"

"In nine days or so."

"Then we have a deadline," Sula said, and then she shook her head. "But why wait? We have a plan, don't we?" She took a breath. "Let's do it tomorrow."

SULA ASSIGNED VIJANA to lead Sidney, Rebecca Giove, and Ikuhara to the purser's office to retrieve some of the party's firearms. She and Ming Lin would approach those guarding the hold and put them out of the way, with Haz, Macnamara, Spence, and three others as backup once the guards were disposed of. She considered having them all advance on the guards at once, but then decided a mob of Terrans charging out of the elevator, or the stairs, would be more likely to convince the guards to call for help than a pair of nonthreatening Terran females.

Lady Koridun would be in the restaurant in the company of her suitor, who—now that his command of the ship had become routine—had resumed his relentless pursuit of the Koridun fortune. If an alarm was transmitted to Lord Arrun, Koridun would know, and she would try to alert Sula to the problem.

"Are we sure the purser's office doesn't have security cameras?" Vijana asked.

"We've not been inside," Sula said, and then, "Oh, hell."

"What's the matter?"

"I just remembered there's a security desk in Command." Before the Legion had taken the ship, Sula had asked Lady Koridun to petition *Striver*'s captain for a tour of Command, and he'd been happy to grant the request of a prominent clan head. Sula and Giove had gone along and had kept the captain and officers occupied answering questions while Koridun had taken a series of photographs.

Sula got her comm unit and paged through the photos until she found one of the security desk, an unoccupied console brilliant with video feeds from elsewhere in the ship. "We didn't pay much attention because the console was unoccupied," she said, "and the officers seemed to be ignoring it. But you can bet there's a Legion recruit sitting at that console now."

"We'll have to take Command first," said Vijana. "We can't hope to do anything else with those cameras looking at us."

"Right," said Sula. "We postpone our plan by one day."

Damn.

In the end she decided to lead the Command storming party herself, and to make the attack toward the end of the midday break and shift change, when *Striver* was burning at one gee, but ten or fifteen minutes before gravities were scheduled to increase. Anyone not on duty would be getting to their couches for the next period of hard deceleration.

Command was key to the rest, and she had to make sure it was done right. She took eight of her eighteen recruits, including Macnamara and Sidney, the best shots; Ikuhara, who could control the ship once it was taken; and Ming Lin, who had experience in the war as a bomb delivery system. She took only eight because the whole party had only eight firearms.

Command rested between *Striver*'s crew and passenger sections, more or less in the middle of the habited sections of the ship. On the level above were the passenger entry port, a common room, and the purser's office. Below were three levels of crew quarters. Leaving the elevator, visitors were presented with a bulkhead, and recessed into it a locked door, a camera, and a speaker. An airtight hatch would drop across the recess to seal the bulkhead in a decompression emergency, but normally the hatch was open.

She didn't know what to expect when the elevator doors opened, because she hadn't dared scout Command level since the Legion had taken the ship. The Legion was composed of professional paranoids, and someone sticking her head out to view whether the airtight hatch had been sealed, or whether the door was guarded, might have been considered worthy of an investigation.

So Sula had to prepare for *everything*. A bomb big enough to blow open the airtight hatch, a bomb necessarily large enough to damage a lot more than the hatch. Enough guns to take care of whatever guards might be standing around. And enough of a civilian appearance to seem innocent, at least to someone who wasn't a member of the Legion.

The day of Sula's strike, she waited until the crew and the Legion had changed shifts, then assembled her storming party in the passenger quarters. All were dressed inconspicuously except for Lady Alana Haz, who had decided to wear viridian Fleet undress. She loomed above everyone in her tall heels, which she seemed to view as part of her uniform.

Sula's eight stepped into the elevator, and a tsunami of adrenaline jolted Sula the second the elevator doors closed. It took a fierce act of will to simply stand there, and not leap or bounce or shriek. She shuddered as a sudden chill swept her body. She could feel gooseflesh prickling her skin, and her teeth wanted to chatter. She reached for the pistol in her pocket and gripped it in a fist of iron.

The doors opened, and Sula found herself looking at a Torminel guard at a range of perhaps three paces. The Torminel was viewing her with polite attention.

"Excuse me," Sula said, and took a single step to the left, unmasking Sidney with a drawn weapon. Sidney shot the guard multiple times with a pistol equipped with a homemade sound suppressor that he'd brought with him in a sample case. The noise was surprisingly loud, and in the elevator deafening, but the sound was so distorted it was not immediately recognizable as a gunshot.

The Torminel collapsed. "Ming," Sula said, and Ming Lin ran out of the elevator toward the door.

The airtight hatch, thankfully, was open. No hidden guard opened fire from ambush. Ming Lin slapped a container of Spence's pain relief gel on the Command door, secured it with tape, and readied the preinstalled detonator. The rest of the party took positions on either side of the recessed door, hands over their ears, and Ming Lin triggered the detonator mechanism, stepped out of the recess, and flattened herself against the wall.

"Three," she said, "two—"

The explosion came before she could say "one," homemade detonators not being known for their reliability. There was a second crash as the door, blown off its hinges, smashed into something in Command. Sula drew her gun and ran for the door through the acid reek of explosive. The adrenaline that burned through her veins rejoiced that she was finally in motion.

The Command crew were staring either at the door, which had flown across the room and crushed a video display, or at the empty doorframe. The design of the room was elegant, a white diamond-checked floor with pale green walls and elegantly styled instrument consoles. Sula saw *Striver*'s Daimong first officer in his white uniform jacket, a Legion recruit sitting at the security station, a Legion officer rising from a chair, and other crew members sitting at their stations. Nobody was reaching for a weapon, and Sula realized they didn't realize they were being attacked—they thought the explosion was the result of some kind of horrific malfunction . . .

Sula pointed her pistol at the Legion officer and began to fire. She wasn't the only one: within two seconds half a dozen pistols began to bark. Crew members froze at their stations or dived for cover.

The two black-clad Torminel sagged dead in their chairs, astonishment fading from their large nocturnal eyes. Sula's ears rang in the sudden silence. The air stank of propellant and explosive and blood. Adrenaline urged Sula to keep pulling the trigger, but she pointed the pistol at the ceiling and forced herself to calmly survey the room.

"Everyone stand away from your consoles, please," she said. "I am Caroline the Lady Sula and *Striver* is now under Fleet command."

She realized that she wasn't exactly recognizable in her disguise, and so she drew off the dark wig and threw it on the deck, revealing her pale blond hair cut short. The crew rose to their feet, hands raised. They seemed more interested in her gun than in her hair, and Sula decided she may as well leave the contact lenses in her eyes.

"Whoever's handling signals, just step to the wall." She didn't want anyone sending out a distress call or a message to Lord Arrun. "All hand comms on the floor, and push them toward me. If you have a sleeve display, I want you to take off your jacket."

She turned toward Ikuhara and saw that Ming Lin and Alana Haz were very sensibly collecting the equipment belts from the dead Torminel, which included their pistols, restraints, stun batons, and comm units. Vijana was dragging the door guard into the room. Sidney loaded his pipe, lit it, and inhaled. Apparently he'd decided that no one had the authority to tell him not to.

"I'm leaving you in charge here," Sula told Ikuhara. "Close the airtight hatch once we're gone, and don't open it unless you hear from one of us."

"Yes, Lady Captain." Ikuhara looked over the silent room, the staring, stunned crew. "Shall I put us back on course for the wormhole?"

"May as well," Sula said. A hashish scent filled the air, and Sula repressed the urge to sneeze. She called the other members of her group to meet in the stairwell one deck above them, on the level of the common room. She left Maitland and another petty officer in Command with Ikuhara, then led the rest to the elevator. Everyone tucked their weapons away. Sidney sucked on his pipe.

Two stairwells, Red and Green, with stairs of bare metal strongly braced against accelerations, connected all the levels of the ship, though not all doors would open to everyone. Sula's collaborators met in the stairwell in a creeping fog of hashish smoke. The three new pistols were passed out. Sula told Vijana to wait six or eight minutes before going for the purser's store, then led her re-formed group of eight down four levels.

She was glad to be in fresher air and took several deliberate breaths to calm the storm in her nerves. She was going to walk out of the stairwell door with Ming Lin, turn right down a curved corridor, and surprise the pair of Torminel guarding the cargo hold. She and Lin would then shoot them—or, if there were unexpected complications, the other five would join the engagement.

But when she pushed the door open, not two but *four* black-clad Torminel stood directly in front of her. The two guards on the previous shift had apparently stayed to chat with their comrades.

Sula could think of nothing to do but shoot. She got her weapon clear and fired into the nearest target, but on her right, Lady Alana's weapon snagged on her pocket, and by the time she got it clear a Torminel knocked it from her hand and went for her throat.

Nerve-paralyzing Torminel squalls rent the air. The recruit Sula had shot didn't fall but seized her gun hand and yanked her forward, practically off her feet. She tried to turn her pistol toward her target and took a wild shot, and then the Torminel clouted her on the side of her head, and she stumbled. Gunshots hammered the air. Something wrenched at her hand and she lost her pistol. Then she was hit on the head again and fell to the beige carpet with a Torminel landing hard on top of her.

She looked up at the snarling face within inches of her own. The Torminel's black-and-cream fur stood on end and his head resembled a horrifying puffball with two enormous dark eyes and a snarling scarlet mouth. Panic flared in Sula. She punched at the face as she tried to writhe out from under the recruit's weight. The Torminel clawed at her face, and then his fangs dived for her throat. She managed to get a forearm between them and tried to lever his head away from her, but his jaws opened and he clamped down on her forearm. Pain galvanized her and she squirmed and kicked and punched with her free hand. Nothing seemed to work. His weight on her made it hard to breathe. The Torminel's hot breath reeked of carrion.

And then the recruit's body went limp, and the jaws relaxed on Sula's arm. Sula blinked up at Alana Haz, who stood astride the Torminel, and who then seized him by his collar and rolled him off Sula.

Sula saw, as Haz pulled the recruit away, that Alana had killed the Torminel by driving one of her high heels into his brain. *Wasn't expecting that,* Sula thought.

I'm guessing neither was the Torminel.

She gasped for breath, looked around, and saw that the four Torminel were dead, while Macnamara and Shawna Spence were busy looting them of their weapons. Ming Lin was streaming blood from a broken nose. Engineer Markios sat against the back of the elevator, looking dazed but otherwise unhurt. None of the Terrans seemed beyond repair.

"Come out, please," said Lady Alana. "We need to get you to safety." Sula turned her head to see a Lai-own engineer looking out his cabin door.

Of course there would be crew on this level, Sula realized. Those working other shifts might be in their rooms sleeping, or going about their own business.

"Come out, please," said Alana. "Everyone, please. We're going to put you in the hold until this is over."

Sula sat up and felt her head swim. Something warm ran down the side of her face where the Torminel had clawed her. Sula waited for the storm in her head to grow quiet, then rose to her feet and reached in a pocket for a handkerchief. Torn muscles in her forearm ached where the fangs had ripped them.

She found and retrieved her pistol, checked the magazine, put the magazine back in. These actions were simple and automatic, and she felt bits of the world fall into place as she performed the simple, undemanding movements.

"Come out, please," called Lady Alana once more.

Sula stretched her jaw muscles, managed to form words. "Move the bodies back into the stairwell," she said. It might reduce the terror of the civilians.

Her hand comm chimed, and Sula answered when she saw it was Ikuhara. "The security desk here has been getting calls about a gunfight," he said. "We've told them to stay quiet and remain in their cabins."

"If they're all on this deck, tell them it's over, and they should come out. The Fleet is going to evacuate them to a safe place."

"Yes, my lady."

The Torminel were dragged away, leaving bloody smears on the pale deck. Lady Alana, limping along with one bare foot, took charge of the off-duty crew.

"We're going to put you in the hold till this is over," she said to a new group. "You'll be safe there."

Maybe it was the Fleet uniform that gave Alana Haz the authority to bring the off-duty crew shuffling toward the hold. Maybe it was the confident baritone voice. Whatever it was, it worked, and Sula was grateful.

The corridors in the passenger section were wood-paneled, or mirrored, or had paintings or photos. Here on the decks inhabited only by crew, the walls were plain beige composite, now somewhat marred by bullet holes and blood spatter.

Farther along the curving corridor was the actual entrance to the hold, a large cargo elevator capable of carrying supplies from the hold to inhabited sections of the ship. Sula called the seven unarmed members of her group, who were standing in reserve, and told them to come down the stairs to their level.

In the meantime, Alana Haz and Shawna Spence shuttled the off-duty crew down to the hold, and by the time the elevator returned, Sula had been joined by her remaining seven Terrans. Along the way they'd passed the four dead Torminel piled in the stairwell, the blood smears on the deck, the bullet wounds in the walls. When they arrived, they found Sula dabbing blood from her face and Ming Lin with her broken nose, and by that point they were grim. Though they'd all served in the Fleet during the war, none of them had trained for the kind of personal close-quarters combat that had just erupted, and they looked as if they were mentally girding themselves for a new kind of war.

Once they'd arrived, Sula called every elevator to her floor, then locked them in place by using their emergency cutoff switches, further disabling them by jamming open their doors with furniture taken from the crew cabins. If the Legion sent reinforcements to this deck, they'd have to go by stairs.

Sula took the new arrivals to the holds. These were fourteen decks deep, most levels completely filled with containers, but the cases and trunks belonging to the passengers were in a separate area, walled off behind a locked grille. One of the crew knew the combination to the gate, and Sula led her party to pull her furniture out of crates and then the hidden weapons out of the furniture.

A fair amount of ingenuity had gone into hiding Sula's arsenal, but that meant all the guns had been broken down into their constituent parts, so as not to look so much like guns. Which meant they required reassembly. Sula took it upon herself to put together the Sidney Mark One, a small homemade submachine gun that Sidney had designed during the last war. It was a crude weapon and far from perfect, but Sula had retained hers throughout the campaign for Zanshaa City. Sula's was the first such weapon ever made, and she'd hung it on the wall of her office on *Confident,* then later in her apartment.

Despite the Sidney's drawbacks, Sula reminded herself that it was a far more deadly and impressive weapon than anything the Legion of Diligence was carrying.

She'd just finished threading the tube stock onto her gun when her hand comm chimed. She answered and heard Vijana speaking over a series of gunshot booms.

"We've run into trouble," he said.

"Where are you?"

"In the purser's office. But we can't get out, there are Legion all over the place."

More booms. Sula recognized the sound of a shotgun, a sensible weapon in the close confines of the ship.

"What happened?" she asked.

"Sidney asked the purser for access to his stores, but the purser wouldn't allow it once he realized Sidney wanted to check his firearms. So I stuck a pistol in his back and told him to open his stores, and he panicked and began to yell for help. I had to knock him out, but half a dozen people heard him and—" There was the sound of a crash, and more booms.

"Anyway," he concluded. "We're trapped in here. But we have good cover and better weapons than they do, so they're not coming in."

"Where are the Torminel?" She tried to build a picture of the purser's office and the common area in her mind.

"We've killed a couple," Vijana said. "Some of the live ones are in the common area, behind the furniture. Some in the gift shop across the way. Some in the stairway on my right, and others in the corridor on the left somewhere—I can't be sure without getting my head blown off."

Sula closed her eyes, built a picture, and thought she understood what was happening. "We'll be there as soon as we can get organized. But right now I need to call Ikuhara."

When she got Ikuhara, she told him to get the security station to see what was going on in the common room and purser's stores. Ikuhara ordered Maitland at the security station to locate the proper video feeds, but he also had another issue.

"The ship's captain is outside Command," he told her. "He's demanding to be let in."

"Does the camera work? Does it show he's alone?"

"He seems to be."

"Then let him in. He can do less damage as a hostage than free and wandering around giving the Legion advice."

"I'll do that, but now Maitland's got the video up from the common room." Sula heard Ikuhara's sudden intake of breath. "It's a mess there! What went wrong?"

"Can you tell me where the Legion is?"

"There are about a dozen on Stairwell Red, looking through the door into the common room. Another eight or ten have passed through Stairwell Green and into a corridor that leads to the common room from there. It looks like both are keeping Vijana's group pinned down in the purser's area. There are ten or so in the common area, but there may be more because the cameras don't cover all of it."

"Right," Sula said. "Fairly soon now I'm going to ask you to cut the engines, so we'll go weightless. Then I'm going to ask you to start the engines again under high acceleration. Understand?"

"How high?"

"Let's say three gravities for ten seconds, then two until I tell you to stop."

"Very good, Lady Captain." He hesitated a few seconds, then spoke. "Should I ring the warning for zero gee, and then for acceleration? We could have a lot of injuries among the passengers if we do this without warning."

"No," Sula said. "We can't let the Legion know what we're doing."

"Yes, my lady."

The passengers will have to take their chances, Sula thought. She glanced up to see Lady Alana Haz looking at her.

"My wife," she said. "My children. They have no experience of zero gee, and they won't have warning of high acceleration." She pressed her lips together in apprehension.

"They're in their cabin, aren't they?"

"Yes, of course."

"They won't have far to fall," Sula said.

"Can I send them a warning?"

Sula wondered whether the Legion had any way to intercept her communication and decided that with Ikuhara established in Command, they didn't.

"Be quick," she said.

She looked over her group of twelve. Macnamara and

Alana Haz were armed with semiautomatic carbines, and Spence with another Sidney Mark One. The others at least had pistols.

In addition, Spence and Ming Lin were carrying explosives and grenades. Sula's group was still outnumbered over two to one, but Sula was beginning to feel a trickle of optimism.

Storming an enemy-held position, like Zanshaa High City or *Striver*'s common room, was turning out to be Sula's specialty.

SULA LED HER group back to the crew levels, then up Stairwell Green to the passenger entrance deck. She peered through the port in the stairwell door and saw the black-clad backs of at least ten Torminel, all crouched on the corridor's thick umber-colored carpet with weapons in their hands, the lead officer peering around the corner into the common room and the entrance to the purser's quarters. No one was shooting. The battle seemed to have died down.

"Macnamara," Sula said, "contact Vijana on your comm. Tell him that in a minute or so we're going to need them to start firing. And tell them shortly after that I'm cutting the engines, and they need to be in a place where they won't drift up into the line of fire. And after *that,* heavy gravities."

"Yes, my lady."

While Macnamara was making his call, Sula called Ikuhara and told him to prepare for zero gravity.

"I had to call Engine Control and tell them to strap in,"

Ikuhara said. "They asked what was up, and I told them there was no time."

"Good," Sula said. "Stand by." She turned to her group. "Macnamara, Haz, I want you in the doorway with your weapons. I need everyone to anchor themselves against zero gravity. And when the engines ignite again, we'll be at three gravities, so make sure you don't float too high, or over anything too sharp."

The stairs were bare metal, with open air between each stairstep, and there were strong guardrails braced against high accelerations, so there would be little problem finding something to hang on to or brace against during a period of zero gravity. The problem would come later, under high acceleration, when the alloy edges of the stairsteps would cut into flesh and bone.

It would only be for a few seconds, Sula thought. People would survive.

A bigger problem would be anchoring Macnamara and Alana Haz in the doorway. Sula put them prone on the landing just behind the door, with Spence and Markios braced against the guardrail to either side, each with one hand clasped firmly around their belts.

"Choose your targets," Sula said. "No wild shooting, we don't have that much ammunition." And then, to Macnamara, "Tell Ikuhara to stand by." And then, into her hand comm, "Vijana, you can start the shooting."

There followed the great boom of a shotgun, heard clearly through the door, followed by rifle shots, followed by a massive answer of pistol shots, presumably from the Legion. Sula looked through the port on the door to see the Torminel tensing in the corridor, as their leader leaned around the corner to aim in the direction of the purser's station.

Moving as lightly as possible, Sula pulled open the corridor door—Haz wedged it open with an elbow—and then Sula linked arms with Spence and called to Ikuhara to cut the engines.

Even though she knew it was coming, weightlessness still seemed a surprise. Sula's inner ear swam as she began to drift away from the landing. The metal stair creaked and snapped as weight came off it. And the Torminel began to drift away from the floor as they frantically scrambled for handholds. There weren't many for them to grab, though, only a few door handles leading to storerooms or offices.

"Fire," Sula said, and Macnamara and Haz began what was, in effect, an execution.

The Fleet trained their personnel in zero gravity.

Apparently the Legion of Diligence did not.

The Legion recruits' movements grew more frantic as they realized they were being fired on, and that they were helpless to save themselves. They clutched at each other, shrieked, squalled, raved. A few fired wild shots, but recoil sent them into a slow, helpless tumble. Furred bodies bounced off the walls, the deck, the ceiling. Blood trailed through the air, forming perfect spheres.

Sula waited until Macnamara and Haz ran out of bullets and reloaded. She could see movement among the floating

Torminel, but she couldn't tell if they were moving on their own or drifting with the breeze. She waited for Macnamara to take a few careful shots, then called for resumed gravity.

The metal landing came up very fast and hit Sula with three times her own body weight. Stars flashed behind her eyes. Metal stairs and railings groaned. Her mouth tasted of copper. She blinked the growing darkness from her vision and turned her head—she couldn't quite *lift* it—to look toward the Torminel, who had come crashing down on the deck in a rain of their own blood.

She gasped air for the time the heavy gees lasted. Then her weight returned to normal, and she rose to a kneeling position. Only one of the Torminel tried to rise, and Macnamara took deliberate aim and shot him.

Macnamara, star of the Fleet combat course. To think, before joining the Fleet, he had been a shepherd.

The scent of blood eddied toward her, and Sula felt her stomach clench. She'd lived through violence, but nothing this close-up and intimate, not on this scale. Not shooting helpless people hanging in midair and landing in a lake of spattering scarlet. She felt nightmares swarming nearby, circling her, trying to break into her mind, and she turned away from the sight in the corridor. She clenched her fist on the metal guardrail and gave her orders.

Sula assigned Haz, Ming Lin, and two others to advance down the corridor. "Don't engage the Legion unless they attack you," she told them, "or if they try to rush the purser's office. Wait for me to come at them from the other side, and bear in mind that we're going to lose gravity again in a few minutes."

Haz and her party advanced down the corridor, examining the Torminel carefully to make sure they were as dead as they looked. Each pistol was collected and stuffed into pockets and belts.

There were two shots as Legion survivors were executed. Sula didn't look.

She heard no shooting from the common room. Zero gees followed by everyone crashing to the deck in three gravities had stunned all parties into silence.

Sula felt warm liquid trickling down her cheek. Smashing into the landing had opened the cuts on her face.

She led her group up two decks on Green, then along a curving corridor to Stairwell Red. She peered cautiously around the door, then looked down two decks and saw members of the Legion on the landing and the stairs leading to the common room. From what little she could see they were in some disorder, not having quite recovered from her trick with acceleration.

Time to do it again. Red seemed to pulse on the extremities of her vision, but Sula managed to brace herself on the landing, her leg hooked through the guardrail. Spence settled herself in next to her, and Macnamara hooked an arm through the same rail, his rifle at the ready. Everyone else secured themselves to something solid, or to each other.

Spence prepared a bomb and handed Sula a grenade.

The next few seconds throbbed in time with Sula's heartbeat. She raised her hand comm and told Ikuhara to cut the engines again.

She heard shouts and growls from the Torminel as they began to float. She turned to Spence and nodded.

Spence triggered the timer on her bomb and tossed it, in slow motion, toward the Torminel. She and Sula leaned back over the landing as soon as the bomb was released.

Three, Sula counted to herself, *two, one.* A well-designed detonator, for once.

The bomb blast was far beyond what Sula had expected. She flapped like a flag in the wind as hot waves of concussion bounded and rebounded in the confined space of the stairwell, but she kept her knee locked on the guardrail and managed not to get thrown into a wall.

Metal shrapnel flew past, clinked on the metal stair. The stair shuddered and groaned. Torminel shrieked and squalled.

Sula pulled herself toward the guardrail again, looked down. Several of the Torminel had been blown off the landing and were swimming through the air, trying to reach a handhold. Others were trying to rescue them. They were all shouting and screaming at once, but they had all been deafened and no one heard.

Sula set her grenade for three seconds and launched it, again in slow motion, toward the target, then pushed herself away from the stairwell.

The sound was much less impressive than Spence's bomb, but its fury was demonstrated by the rattle of shrapnel flying up and down the stairwell. The screams echoing up the stairs took on a panicked timbre.

"Three gees," Sula told Ikuhara, and a few seconds later gravity threw her on her back and knocked the breath out of her. The gridded metal surface of the landing imprinted itself on her flesh. She stared at the landing above her and took one breath after another and listened to the shrieks of Torminel falling nearly twenty decks to the bottom of the stairs. The metal stairsteps crackled and clanged in high gee. She wondered if Spence's bomb had torn something free.

Then the weight came off Sula's chest, and she dragged herself to her feet. She swayed, or perhaps the staircase did, as she readied her Sidney Mark One. "Macnamara," she gasped. "Give us cover. The rest of you, follow me."

Her party couldn't follow at once, because they took some time to recover from being flattened by gravity. Eventually they were all on their feet, weapons in their hands, and following Sula down the stairs while Macnamara leaned out over the rail, his rifle pointing down, and shot at any target that displayed itself.

Sula swiped at the blood running down her face, then went down two flights to the next deck, then another length of stairs, and turned the corner carefully, deep in a crouch. The Legion recruits were fully visible on the landing below, huddled away from the guardrail and Macnamara's fire. Some were wounded, and all were half stunned. Sula went down on one knee, brought the Sidney up to her shoulder, aimed, and pulled the trigger.

The chatter of automatic fire must have been terrifying to the Torminel armed only with pistols. She heard screams and cries, saw Torminel fall and the bright sparks of rounds hitting the guardrail or whining off the composite wall. Shots came back, but none found her.

She fell back to reload, and Spence stepped up with her own Sidney. As the second gun opened up, Sula heard a collective moan of fear and terror from the Torminel survivors. Then more screams. Then the sound of panicked flailing.

Spence emptied her magazine, and Sula took her place only to see a pair of terrified Legion recruits break free of the others and stagger through the door into the common room. Since the belligerence of Torminel was legendary, she found herself surprised by this display of terror. She signaled to those above her.

"Move up! I'll cover!"

The others rattled down the swaying stairs, their weapons pointed toward the black mass of Legion recruits on the landing below. No shots came in reply.

The only firing came from Sula's party, finishing off any Torminel still alive.

Macnamara came down the stairs and helped Sula to her feet. Sula didn't go all the way to the landing—she didn't want to get near the blood-soaked pile of limp, warm bodies—and so she detailed two people to hold the door and everyone else to shift the bodies out of the way. While Torminel were being dragged and rolled down the stairs, Sula called first Alana Haz, then Vijana, to let them know to join in when shooting started.

Sula took a breath, walked across the blood-smeared landing, and prepared herself for what she hoped was the last slaughter of the day.

The one-sided fight started with Ming Lin throwing a bomb into the middle of the common room, followed by a grenade lofted in underhand by Spence, so that it would go off near the ceiling and rain shrapnel down on the people below. Then Macnamara and Sula stood on opposite sides of the door and began firing.

What remained of the Legion sheltered behind the furniture and benches in the common room. With Vijana and Giove firing at them from the front, and Haz and Sula on either flank, they had no way of protecting themselves from the fire, and they were slaughtered. A few fled into the gift shop at the far end of the common room, but another of Lin's bombs was tossed in the door and blew the windows out from the inside. A fire started in the clothing racks, and that triggered a rain of pale green fire suppressant. A cautious advance sloshed toward the gift shop and discovered that no one inside was left alive, including the hapless Lai-own female who had been working in the shop when the fight had started.

Sula told Ikuhara to shut off the fire suppressant, which he managed after a few minutes fumbling through menus. Sula cautiously entered the common room and saw Haz and Vijana advancing toward her. Haz's wig had come askew, but it looked jaunty tilted on the side of her head, and she wore it like a panache. "Where's Safista?" Sula said. "Has anyone seen his body?"

Haz attempted a laugh. "Maybe he's too busy courting Lady Koridun to have noticed what we were up to."

"Maybe he—" Sula's nerves jolted as Vijana fired two shots. Sula spun and saw that he had just executed two wounded Torminel with his pistol.

Vijana saw her look and raised his eyebrows. "What?" he said. "They're just animals."

"Battle's over," said Sula.

"Tell that to Sidney. They shot him."

Sula snarled. "You might have mentioned that earlier," she said. She hurried past the purser's desk, half shattered by bullets, and into the series of offices and storerooms beyond. Sidney seemed asleep, propped up behind a desk with one of his fine custom shotguns in his lap. His curled mustachios stood out against a face drained of color, and someone's mustard-colored jacket was pressed to his side. The jacket was turning red.

Sula dropped to one knee and took Sidney's hand. His eyes opened, and he tried to smile.

"You don't look so good, either," he said in a whispering voice, and then he coughed for a while. Fine red drops spattered from his mouth and dropped down his chin.

Sula carefully took a hold of the jacket to draw it away and examine the wound. "May I?" she said.

"Don't," Sidney said. "There's air coming in and out."

She got out her hand comm and called Ikuhara. "Page the ship's doctor to the purser's station," she said. "We have a casualty."

"Yes, my lady."

"The doctor's Torminel," Vijana said from behind her. "She may not—"

"She *will,*" said Sula. She turned to face him. "How did this happen?"

Vijana shrugged. "He's never been in zero gee before. He made a wrong move and drifted out into plain sight. Rebecca was pulling him to safety when one of the Legion got off a shot."

"I want a smoke," said Sidney.

Sula looked at him. "I don't think so."

He winked at her. "Worth a try," he said.

Vijana checked his pistol. "There are still a couple guards in Engine Control," he said. "And Safista's still on the loose."

"No. You stay here."

She dropped next to Sidney again, took his hand, and told him she'd be right back. Then she left the purser's offices and went into the common room. Dead Legion bodies and broken furniture lay under gelatinous fire retardant. The air was a chemical stew, explosives and retardant and death, and it turned Sula's stomach.

Sula sent Alana Haz with six others to Engine Control. "Don't shoot them if they don't resist," she said.

"We don't have enough personnel to guard them," Vijana said.

"Go," Sula said to Haz. She turned to Vijana. "I'm not in the mood for more massacres today," she said.

"You'll get used to them. It's us or them."

Sula glared at him. "You're *distracting* me," she said. "If there's going to be more killing, it's going to be on *my* order, not yours."

Vijana considered this for a half second, and then braced. "Yes, my lady," he said.

"We may have to send parties for Safista." And then she remembered what Haz had said and thought that he really *might* be with Lady Koridun. She spoke a query into her hand comm, and the comm turned it into text and sent it to Koridun.

The reply came. SAFISTA WITH ME IN RESTAURANT.

Sula collected Spence and Macnamara and Giove, and they went to Staircase Green and up to the restaurant level, where they cautiously entered the restaurant to find Lady Koridun sitting on a table with a pistol propped in one hand and a cocktail in the other. Lord Arrun Safista lay dead on the floor, his limbs splayed. Sula halted in the doorway.

Lady Koridun's fangs flashed. "You should see your faces!" she said. Delight danced in her large blue eyes.

Sula lowered her Mark One and absorbed the scene. "What happened?" she managed.

"He was going to follow the rest of his company down to the common room as soon as he could raise his guards in Command. I didn't want him trying to take Command back, and since he'd sent everyone else away I threw him headfirst into a bulkhead and then strangled him with my belt." She raised her cocktail. Methanol simmered dangerously behind greenish glass. "I'm finally rid of him! I'm celebrating!"

Sula's head whirled. Koridun's face took on an expression of concern. "Are you hurt?" she said.

"I got scratched and bit. Nothing serious."

"We eat raw meat, you know," Koridun said. "You should get a shot so you don't get infected."

"I'll do that." Sula made another attempt to find sense in this situation. "You're lucky it was us who came here," she said. "If someone else saw an armed Torminel, they might shoot."

Lady Koridun put the pistol down on the table. "There," she said. "Now I'm harmless."

Sula hardly thought so. Koridun picked up a hand comm.

"This is Safista's," she said. "I've been sending out false messages, saying that the fighting is a mistake and that everyone should hold their fire."

Sula took a moment to absorb this. "Good work," she said. "Have any messages come in from people we've missed?"

"Not in the last ten minutes or so."

Sula took the hand comm and looked at it. "Maybe you should go to your suite," she said. "I'll join you later once things are settled."

Koridun waved her cocktail glass. "I'll make another drink first," she said.

Sula sent out a message to any of Safista's recruits who had managed to survive the massacre to report to the hatch outside Command, then told Ikuhara to let her know if anyone showed up. She and her group returned to the purser's offices. The Torminel doctor had arrived and was looking at Sidney.

"He'll need surgery," she said. "I'll need two people to take him to sick bay on a stretcher and help me prep. I'll have to look up the procedure, because I don't know it that well."

"Whatever you need," Sula said. After she detailed two of her group to go with the doctor to bring the stretcher, she knelt next to Sidney. The blood-soaked jacket had been taken away, and his shirt cut off: a pale blue temporary bandage sealed the wound. From the ashen look of his face there seemed not an ounce of blood left in him. She took his hand. His eyes opened narrowly and regarded her.

"You should have let me smoke," he said, and died.

WORKING WITH AN air of quiet competence, and operating under Macnamara's wary eye, the Torminel doctor repaired the cut on Sula's forehead. She bandaged the fang wounds and gave the shot against infection. The doctor then performed a septoplasty on Ming Lin's broken nose, and for the next few hours treated sprains and broken bones that the wild shifts in gee had inflicted on crew and passengers. The crew that had been evacuated—"for their safety"—to the hold had been thrown around badly in the large hold spaces, and few had come through without injury. They would have been safer in their own cabins.

The two Legion recruits in Engine Control had surrendered without trouble and had been locked in a small second-class cabin and placed under guard. No more Legion members were found on the ship.

Sula wanted nothing more to do with dead bodies or blood and absented herself from the cleanup. Crew carried the Legion bodies to the hold and put them in a shipping container for disposal later. Sidney and the Lai-own vendor from the gift shop were put in body bags—the ship actually carried a few—and were stored in the freezer. Fire retardant was mopped up from the common room and from the ruin of the gift shop.

The Terran assistant purser was put in charge of his department. Firearms were distributed among the Terrans or locked away. Because paranoia was never far from Sula's mind, Spence and Macnamara were put in charge of feeding the Terrans, so that *Striver*'s crew wouldn't poison them.

The food wasn't necessarily better, but it became less predictable, and that was an improvement.

While the crew were deployed carrying away bodies and swabbing away the blood, Sula planned the next stages of the journey. The journey to the next wormhole gate was supposed to take seven days, but Sula decided to do it in four. Accordingly, as soon as *Striver* was cleaned and secured, she ordered everyone aboard into their beds or into acceleration couches, cut the engines, pitched the ship over, and began accelerating for the wormhole at three gravities.

Three gravities, she decided, wasn't too punishing if you were prepared. But it also meant you had to fight for every breath, and you had to be careful when you moved. You couldn't commit sabotage or plan rebellion when under high acceleration, and when gees were cut so that you could use the toilet or take a meal, you were too tired to do anything else. If the crew or *Striver*'s captain had any intention of retaking the ship, Sula was going to make certain they wouldn't have the energy.

When *Striver* passed through the wormhole into the Toley system, she disabled the ship's transponder. With its antimatter torch blazing against the interstellar night, *Striver* couldn't go completely dark, but at least it could stop advertising the fact that it wasn't where it had been ordered to be.

Toley was a system of gas giants and asteroids, barren of habitable worlds; but it was also a crossroads, with one wormhole leading eventually to Harzapid, another to Colamote, and another to Zarafan. Foote's squadron was in a race with the two squadrons from Zarafan to arrive at Toley first, and *Striver* had to keep ahead of them or get caught up in a battle it had no way of winning.

Because of the three strands of traffic meeting at Toley, the system was filled with spacecraft, and no one paid *Striver* any attention. Sula was amused to see that the yacht carrier *Corona* was sailing on at least ten days ahead of *Striver.* Martinez was still parading through system after system, with his transponder pinging away, announcing his presence to anyone who cared to look for him.

Well, Sula thought, *if trouble comes, maybe it will find Martinez before it finds me.*

CHAPTER 21

After her coup, Sula kept the second-class room she shared with Spence. She used the room only for sleeping when she wasn't on duty, and the punishing schedule of accelerations made the pleasures of first class inaccessible anyway.

So Spence was on the bunk below when Sula woke screaming and clawing for the pistol under her pillow. Three gravities had torn tears out of her eyes and tracked them down her face. She felt the fading touch of hands on her throat. Her forearm, where the Torminel had bitten her, throbbed with pain. The scent of blood filled her senses.

"My lady!" Spence called. "My lady! It's only a dream!"

Sula gave a gasp and let gravities push her back into the bed. The dream faded, and she struggled for words.

"It's been a long time since I had one of those dreams."

"Me too."

"Not since I was on Terra." And her mind, then, had regularly replayed the bloody scene of Ermina Vaswani dying in her arms, and Tari Koridun's snarl as she tried to tear out Sula's throat.

"I had forgotten what war was like," said Spence.

Sula thought about that and decided that Spence was right. What Sula needed to do was *become even more paranoid.*

Lord Mehrang, Vijana, and others had nearly wiped out the Yormaks, and they'd been richly rewarded for their actions.

Maybe, she thought, Lady Tu-hon and her clique were intending to reward themselves in a similar way. Make the Terrans disappear, or a lot of them anyway, then redistribute their wealth.

Wholesale murder might be Lady Tu-hon's way of recovering any fortunes lost in the economic debacle.

SULA CUT ACCELERATION entirely just before the next wormhole transit, having decided to enter the Contorsi system dark until she could complete an inventory of the ships in the system and assess them for threats. Transports appeared, and little mining settlements. And *Corona* with its transponder pinging away like a songbird.

And mere minutes behind and closing the distance fast, a warship.

A cold shimmer went up her spine as she realized that trouble had found Martinez, and that he and his merry band of yacht pilots were about to be faced with an enemy they couldn't fight.

If we stay dark, Sula thought, *maybe they won't see us.*

Maybe, she thought, they would be satisfied with killing Martinez and leave *Striver* alone.

CORONA **HAD ENTERED** the system of Contorsi, a small, pale yellow sun. None of the eleven planets were inhabited, but many of their satellites were being exploited for mineral resources, water, gases, or chemicals. *Corona* was en route from Contorsi Wormhole Two to Wormhole Three when a bright engine flare appeared from the direction of Wormhole One.

Corona was still twenty-five days from Harzapid and was decelerating at 1.2 gravities, hard enough to make a significant difference in transit time without overly inconveniencing the passengers, who grew used to carrying 20 percent more weight. Three of the racing yachts were hurling themselves into maneuvers with much higher gravities, as their captains trained for war. A racing yacht was very like a Fleet pinnace, a small boat with a big engine, and training in a yacht was the best way of preparing crew for the stresses of battle.

The message came as soon as it could, given that the newcomer had to find *Corona* in the system before delivering its dispatch. Vipsania, already in the communications suite, viewed it, then summoned Roland and Martinez for a replay.

The Lai-own captain glittered in her viridian dress uniform with its double row of silver buttons. She spoke quickly and formally, fixing the camera with her golden eyes. "Carrier *Corona,* I am Captain An-sol of the cruiser *Conformance.* I order you to continue your current course and maintain your current rate of deceleration. *Conformance* will maneuver to a rendezvous, and you will be boarded and searched." The orange end-stamp filled the screen.

"Well," Roland said. He frowned at the screen. "That was perfectly clear. And unexpected."

Martinez looked at Roland in silent fury. *At least your daughter isn't here.* Whatever happened to *Conformance,* Young Gareth would be a witness.

To the execution of his father, very possibly.

Vipsania replayed An-sol's message, then viewed the Lai-own captain's frozen image on the screen. "She put on a full dress uniform for a message of only a few seconds," she said. "Call that a compliment to Gareth—she'd hardly put on full dress to send a message to some civilian captain."

"She knows we're on board, then," said Roland.

It wouldn't be hard to find out, Martinez thought. There would be records of who came up the skyhook to Zanshaa's antimatter ring, and video of people moving on the docks. And since the Martinez family had all been named Terran criminals, people in the security services might have been keeping track of them anyway.

"I'll call Captain Anderson," Martinez said, "and have him tell *Conformance* that we will comply with their directives."

He did so. Pneumatics sighed as Vipsania lowered herself, and her 20 percent extra weight, into one of the office chairs. "What do you know about this Captain An-sol?"

"A protégée of Squadron Commander Esh-draq," Martinez said. "Was his first officer in the *Judge Solomon* during the war. I've met her a few times, but we're not friends."

"Is there anyone we can"—Roland searched for words—"*approach* to bring pressure on her?"

"Esh-draq, possibly, but he's serving under Do-faq in the Third Fleet at Felarus, and it would take ten or twelve days to get a message to there and back."

Martinez could see hard calculation cascading somewhere behind Roland's eyes. "And *Conformance* will catch up to us sooner than that?"

"I haven't plotted our courses, but I'm going to assume so."

"Why don't you make the plot, and we'll consider other alternatives."

Martinez seated himself at a terminal and called up a navigation display. *Corona* didn't have the sensor suite of a warship, let alone a trained crew to operate it, and for that reason hadn't been tracking *Conformance,* or for that matter any other vessel in the system. Martinez didn't have much data on the cruiser's movements, so he called up a multispectrum telescope and told it to track the cruiser. While he waited for new data to appear, an idea struck him, and he realized his mind had been quietly working on another problem altogether.

"I can tell you what this means," he said. "It means that Michi's succeeded in taking the Fourth Fleet. Or most of it, anyway."

Vipsania and Roland looked at him in surprise. "Yes?" Roland said.

Even as stories of rebellion and mutiny had flooded the news services, there had been no word from Harzapid. Amid all the ranting, riots, and denunciation, and with so many stories of mutiny at other Fleet posts, the Fourth Fleet hadn't been mentioned at all—Harzapid seemed to be a singularity in the new government's story, a black hole from which no information emerged. As the days passed Martinez had found himself itching to use Lord Chen's code to contact Michi Chen, but he'd always argued himself out of it. If the situation was delicate, he didn't want to give the opposition evidence that Fleet Commander Chen was in contact with conspirators.

But now it seemed clear. "If the Fourth Fleet were under government control," he said, "we'd fly right into their arms, so there would be no need to send *Conformance* after us. But *Conformance* was sent after us precisely *because* our welcome at Harzapid would be friendly. The government is trying to keep Harzapid from getting reinforcements. I'm sure they looked at their tracking data and saw *Corona,* and then they wouldn't have to do too much work to guess who's aboard."

"That's encouraging, I suppose," Roland said, his eyes fixed on the screen frozen with An-sol's image. "But I'm guessing you don't expect that Michi's going to charge to our rescue with a couple dozen warships."

"I'm not counting on it," Martinez said. "She may not know where we are, depending on whether the government's cut communication with Harzapid."

"In the last war," Vipsania said, "the government and the Naxids were in communication all the time."

"But that didn't mean that you and I could chat with the Naxid high command," Martinez said. "All messages from unauthorized personnel stopped at the censors, or at the wormhole relay stations." And he sighed. "We might as well send a coded message to Michi now. It probably won't go through, but it's not likely to do us more harm than has already been done."

Roland nodded. "If she's our only hope of rescue, then do it."

They watched while Martinez coded the message on his hand comm and sent it to the relay station this side of Contorsi Wormhole Three. In the silence that followed, Roland looked at the comm unit in his brother's hand.

"You need to get rid of that before *Conformance* arrives," he said. "If they find that code on you, that's evidence."

"I know," Martinez said. He'd chuck the hand comm out a port and let it be burned to atoms by *Corona*'s radioactive tail.

Vipsania had been staring with a fierce expression at the exotic fish, as if they were an enemy she planned to overcome. "What if we run?" she asked. "Turn the ship around and start piling on acceleration?"

"A carrier isn't built to stand the kind of acceleration you'd see in a warship," Martinez said. "And even if we could accelerate at the same rate as *Conformance,* we can't outrun a missile."

"And there's no way to knock the missile down?"

Martinez spread his hands. "With what?"

Roland cleared his throat. "I don't suppose we could build a laser?"

"Again—with what? It would have to be a damned powerful laser, and there'd have to be some way of mounting and aiming it, and tracking the incoming missile, and even if we blow up the missile, *Conformance* has thirty missile launchers and plenty of reloads . . ."

There was a dark, morose moment of silence. "Any other ideas?" Martinez said. He could stick knives in his belt, as he had at the Corona Club riot, and maneuver the carrier to try to take *Conformance* by boarding. *That* would surprise

Captain An-sol, and then she'd burst out in coarse laughter and fire the missile that would end his pirate days once and for all.

There was a chime from the navigation display, and Martinez turned to find that it had gathered enough data on *Conformance*'s speed and trajectory to make a prediction about its future movements. Laying the plot against that of *Corona,* he saw that the cruiser would intercept the carrier in three to three and a half days, depending on how close An-sol chose to fly past the star Contorsi when making a course change. *Corona* would fly past Contorsi a few hours earlier and intended to use a gravity assist and a burst of acceleration to put her on a direct course for escaping the system at Wormhole Three.

Not that this plan was even viable now.

He looked at the plot, and suddenly his despair vanished and was replaced with a growing sense of wonder. He saw how he might save *Corona*.

Or get everyone killed, including his wife and son.

He decided not to mention his revelation, at least for now.

MARTINEZ WALKED INTO his suite and found Terza waiting for him on a chaise. She rose to greet him, elegant in an ankle-length dress of midnight-colored jersey, as if she were about to go to a formal reception—and that, he remembered, was what she had intended, before the appearance of *Conformance* had smashed everyone's plans. She'd made arrangements to play her harp during a cocktail party hosted by Ari Abacha.

Now the party would be replaced by a very sober meeting of all officers to discuss their options for somehow fending off *Conformance.*

He approached, embraced, and kissed her cheek. Vetiver, the heart notes of her perfume, smoothed his senses. "Where's Chai-chai?" he asked.

"Drawing lessons with Lieutenant Garcia." Young Gareth had been taken out of his school at midterm, and his parents and a series of volunteers were making sure his education progressed on schedule. Martinez had done his part—at lunch he'd been pleased to hear his son use the word *deracinate.*

"It's good Chai-chai's elsewhere, because—" His mouth turned dry. "We need to talk."

Her jersey dress rustled as she took him by the hand and led him to a sofa. He looked at her face, lovely, framed by the black waterfall of hair, her impeccable serenity marred only by a slight hint of concern.

Martinez was still sorting through his ideas when Terza spoke. "You're afraid of being arrested," she said.

"I'm *worried* about being arrested," he said. "I'm *worried* about being executed. What I'm *afraid* of is interrogation." He tightened his hands around hers. "No one knows whether they'll hold up under torture," he said. "I could name your father. I could name Lord Oda, or Vipsania, or anyone. I could name *you.*"

She absorbed this, and he saw himself reflected in her dark eyes. "You haven't done anything illegal."

"That's why they'll have to make something up, and force

me to admit to it." He shook his head. "The best solution might be for Roland and me to commit suicide before we're boarded. That way they might leave you alone."

"No." The word wasn't spoken in shock, or surprise, but as a confirmed resolution, as if she'd thought this out well ahead of time. "No. We won't consider that. If we have life, we have a chance."

"I could kill us all," Martinez said. Again he saw in his mind the solution that had flooded his thoughts as he looked at the navigation plot. "I could kill us all in more ways than one."

Something like a smile briefly touched the corners of Terza's mouth, as if he were confirming something she had already known. "You have a plan," she said.

"Yes," he said. "But it's very dangerous. If it goes amiss, Captain An-sol could decide to fire a missile, and we'd be defenseless against it."

This time, when the slight smile appeared, it lasted a little more than a fraction of a second. "A missile strike is very sure, and very quick," she said. "It's better than suicide, and it's better than torture." She took his arm, rested her cheek against his shoulder, and looked up at him. Her body's warmth prickled his cheek. "And we'll be together."

Her courage took his breath away. She had been bred to rule an empire, and here she was, at the very tail end of hope, willing to roll fortune's dice and let them fall where they may. If it was a performance, it was brilliant. If she had given him a glimpse of her true self, it was even more impressive.

Martinez put his arm around her. "Yes," he said. "Whatever happens, we'll be together."

THE OFFICERS' MEETING was held in the pilots' ready room, near the shuttle docks, a clean white space with clean white tables and chairs, a white counter with snacks and beverages served in clean white tableware, and excellent video and holographic displays, fortunately in a wider variety of color. When Martinez entered, he saw Chandra Prasad and Sabir Mersenne in an animated conversation at one of the tables, while a glum Ari Abacha sat by himself at another table contemplating a cup of coffee. Vonderheydte stood at a holographic display of *Corona*'s decks, making mysterious marks at various intersections. He saw Martinez arrive and braced to attention.

"Captain on deck!" he called. The others braced.

"As you were," Martinez said. He looked at Vonderheydte's marks on the *Corona* schematic. "What is this?"

"Resisting any attempts to board, Lord Captain," Vonderheydte said. He pointed to the marks he'd been making on the display. "We can block certain corridors to channel the boarders into kill zones covered by our small arms, or booby-trapped with homemade explosives."

Martinez viewed the schematic with interest. Vonderheydte seemed to have made an excellent start on his project, if it weren't for the rather large factor he'd omitted from his calculations.

"Don't you think an antimatter missile might trump all that?" Martinez asked.

Vonderheydte shrugged. "We work with what we've got, Lord Captain."

"I suppose we do." Martinez went to the café and got a cup

of coffee and a pastry made fresh that morning, topped with cream and dotted with raspberries. By the time he'd finished his pastry, Garcia, Husayn, and Dalkeith had arrived, completing *Corona*'s roster of Fleet officers. Martinez walked to an unused display and faced the others.

"If I may have your attention," he said. The officers straightened to a more alert posture, all save Ari Abacha, who continued to stare at his cold, half-empty coffee cup. Martinez looked from one to the next.

"Lieutenant Vonderheydte just said that we fight with what we've got," he said. "*Conformance* has missiles armed with antihydrogen. We have antihydrogen as well, but it's confined to *Corona*'s propulsion units and to the yachts." He spread his hands. "We don't lack explosive punch, we lack a means of delivery." He stood square to his audience and tried to maintain a posture of absolute confidence as he spoke the next words. "Therefore I thought I'd call you here today to discuss turning one of the yachts into a missile, and using it to destroy *Conformance*. Any ideas?"

For a moment they just stared at him, all but Abacha, who absorbed the idea into his solitary, all-encompassing gloom without changing expression.

"Lord Captain," said Sabir Mersenne. He was a plump man, with yellow-brown skin and short crisp hair that came down his forehead in a widow's peak. His attitude was normally jovial, but Martinez's idea had sent him into a state of alarm. "Lord Captain, they'll see it coming, and they'll blow it up."

"We'll hide it," Martinez said. "We're scheduled to perform a deceleration burn around the star Contorsi in three and a half days. *Conformance* will do its own burn around the star later that day. We'll hide our improvised missile behind the star, then send it on an intercept course."

On their faces he saw brief flares of hope, followed by looks that seemed more thoughtful, more troubled, as they mentally calculated trajectories and probabilities.

"We'll work out the details of that later," Martinez said. "But right now I'd like to discover if we can actually turn one of the yachts into a weapon with a proper warhead."

Mersenne still seemed dubious. On *Illustrious* he'd been the propulsion officer, and antimatter drives were his specialty. "The yachts' power comes from the Howe DM-5 unit," he said. "It's a very old, very reliable design. But—"

Chandra Prasad jumped to her feet. "If we try to breach containment, the Howe will kill us!" she said. "The unit is protected by diamond/graphene armor and operated by an autonomous program that can't be altered without a visit to the factory. If the program detects any threat to the integrity of the containment vessel, it will respond with a controlled radiation burst. Our equipment will be destroyed, the operators will be irradiated if not killed outright, and if we use *enough* power to try to break containment, the resulting explosion might well destroy *Corona*."

"I know," Martinez said. He forced a smile onto his face. "That's why we've got to work out a way of getting around it."

"Lord Captain," said Mersenne, "it's not as if people haven't *thought* about this sort of thing. If rebels or terrorists could get their hands on antihydrogen, they could destroy a *city*. But it's never happened." He waved a hand. "Because units like the Howe DM-5 were designed not only to prevent such misuse, but to *kill anyone who tried it*."

"I admit it's a challenge," Martinez said, then mentally gave himself an award for understatement. "But what other ideas do we have?"

The response was silence. Martinez turned to the video display and put up a schematic of his own yacht's engine compartment. "This is my *Laredo*," he said. "And this is what we've got to work with."

Chandra stepped closer to the display and gave the image a ferocious look, as if she were trying to obliterate the problem by sheer force of will. "How can we reach the software?" she said.

"Some kind of proprietary coupling available at the factory," Mersenne said. "And if you jury-rig a coupling, you still have layers of security to dive through, and if you fail, you get fried."

Martinez was getting a little tired of Mersenne's insistence that his idea was a nonstarter.

"I have an idea, Lord Captain," said Lord Ahmad Husayn. He was a blade-thin man with a pencil-thin mustache and had been a weapons specialist on the *Illustrious*. "Not about the power source, but the triggering mechanism. We're going to need to rig a proximity fuse of some sort to make sure that the weapon goes off when it's supposed to. If we ever find out a way to create a warhead, we're going to want it to go off at the right time."

Martinez was deeply relieved that someone had offered a useful idea. "Very good," he said. "Let's look at the problem."

Husayn called up a display and began a sketch, while Martinez and Vonderheydte watched with interest. Garcia and Elissa Dalkeith joined Mersenne and began a discussion in low tones. Chandra continued to stare furiously at the schematic of *Laredo*'s engine bay.

Ari Abacha continued to gaze at his coffee. Then, sighing heavily, he rose to his feet, walked to the coffee dispenser, and filled his cup. He walked carefully, as if his feet pained him. He put a pastry in the microwave oven, warmed it, then took the plate as he began a return to his seat. As he passed Martinez, he muttered, "Just go around it."

"Sorry?" Martinez said.

"The DM-5 is armored. Don't go *through* the armor, go *around* it."

Martinez was bewildered. "Go around it *how*?"

Abacha only shook his head, then shuffled back to his table. But Mersenne had heard, and he turned around, his eyes wide.

"Quantum tunneling?" he said.

His words hung in the air for a moment, and then Chandra turned from the display. "The cladding on the DM-5 is too thick," she snarled. "Quantum tunneling works on far too tiny a scale—you can't jump a barrier that wide."

She was right, damn it.

"Good idea, though," Martinez said. "We're on the right track. A conventional approach won't work for us. As Lieutenant Mersenne has pointed out, all that's been anticipated."

Lieutenant-Captain Elissa Dalkeith raised a hand.

"Yes, Lady Elcap?" Martinez said.

Martinez was still surprised nearly every time by Dalkeith's voice, which had the high pitch and lisping tones of a child. "It seems to me that the DM-5's software is our problem," she said. "We have to breach containment faster than the software can react."

"And the software operates at the speed of light," Husayn said. "So what can we use—a great big laser?"

Dalkeith pushed gray strands back from her forehead. "We already use defensive lasers to destroy missiles," she said. "Why can't we do the same here?"

Vonderheydte looked blank. "Do we *have* a laser large enough to destroy a missile? This is a civilian ship."

So far as Martinez knew there were no powerful lasers on board, but he was willing for the sake of argument to assume that such a laser could be cobbled together.

"Let's for the moment assume we've got a laser of sufficient power," he said. "What happens if we use it?"

"We can't put it at sufficient distance to be safe," said Garcia. "It'll be right there in the engine bay, and within a tiny fraction of a second of it firing on the container, there will be a release of energy sufficient to destroy the laser, *and* the engine bay, *and* the yacht as well."

"But the container will remain intact," Martinez said. "As will *Conformance*."

Garcia shrugged. "I'm afraid so, Lord Captain."

Oh well, Martinez thought. *We didn't have the laser anyway.*

"A big damn mortar," Vonderheydte said. "Fire a great shaped charge at point-blank range. Breach the cladding, flood the container with plasma, the plasma will melt the chips and set them off."

"I'm afraid not," said Mersenne. "The container is covered with sensors, and the software possesses enough situational awareness to detect when a projectile is on its way. There will be a release of energy sufficient to destroy the projectile."

"Stick to the electromagnetic spectrum," Martinez said. "We've got to be faster than the software."

"The antihydrogen's in silicon chips," Dalkeith said in her lisping voice. "Held by a charge of static electricity. What can destabilize that, and quickly?"

"A blast of gamma rays," Husayn said, as if reading from a mental list. "X-rays. Any kind of ionizing radiation, really."

"No," Garcia said. She swiped a strand of her bushy hair out of her eye. "The other end of the spectrum. But we'd need a colossal burst."

Martinez felt he needed clarification. "A burst of what, exactly?"

Garcia blinked, then turned toward the snack counter and silently pointed at the microwave oven.

"There," she said. "That's what you want, only a million times more powerful."

"Where do we get the power?" Dalkeith asked.

Garcia gave a little laugh. "Well," she said, "we've got more than one yacht, don't we?"

"WHAT'S THE MATTER, Ari?" Martinez asked as they left the ready room. "You seem . . . less than invigorated."

Now that he'd set things in motion, Martinez was feeling utterly reawakened. He'd created teams to deal with aspects of the problem: Garcia, Mersenne, and Dalkeith to breach the DM-5's cladding, Husayn and Vonderheydte to work out the fusing, and Chandra Prasad to work out ways to bypass *Laredo*'s safety mechanisms, the mechanisms that might prevent the boat from doing exactly what Martinez intended to do with it.

Ari Abacha had volunteered for none of the groups and had abandoned his coffee and pastry and shuffled out of the ready room as soon as the others had begun working at their tasks. Martinez had followed and intercepted Abacha in the corridor.

"Less than invigorated?" Abacha repeated. "Well, I suppose I am."

"Is it the business with Chandra?" Martinez asked. "You'll get over that quickly—take my word, as someone with experience. There will be plenty of girls on Harzapid."

Abacha touched his perfectly groomed mustache. "Chandra? Oh, possibly, that's a part of it." He sighed. "I'm suddenly feeling very old, Gare."

"But you're not old. You're only a couple years older than me."

Abacha paused and passed a hand over his balding forehead. "I think I'm in mourning for my world," he said. "It's all gone, isn't it? Or going?" He turned to Martinez, his dark eyes looking past Martinez into a shadowy future. "From now on it's all battle and killing and looting, and us trying to turn a device that provides power and light into a *bomb*. That's all we have to look forward to, isn't it? Until the last one of us stands on a heap of corpses and proclaims himself king?"

"We don't have kings," Martinez said. Amid his infinite surprise it was the only response he could manage.

Abacha's eyes shifted from the indefinite future to focus on Martinez. "We *will,*" he said. "Whatever they call themselves, Megalords or Supreme Commanders or Sublime Potentates, they'll be kings." He touched Martinez's arm with his knuckles. "You're suited to this new world. You'll do well—you'll build all the bombs you want. You might be king yourself. Or Roland. Or maybe you'll cut each other's throats over it." He blinked and touched Martinez's arm again. "Sorry, Gare. That was uncalled for."

"I'm not offended." Martinez was far too surprised to be hurt, surprised not only at the bleak view of future history that Abacha had presented, but at a side of Abacha he'd never seen before. So far as he knew his friend's attention had never extended beyond the good life, beyond drink and good company, pretty women and sport.

Abacha's eyes glistened. "I'm going to drink some of *Corona*'s excellent liquor now, Gare," he said. "I'm going to mourn the world that's dead." He turned away and began to walk down the corridor. "Join me later if you want."

Martinez watched him shamble away, then returned to the ready room to help his officers build a missile.

MARTINEZ SAT IN the custom seat of his simulator, lights and displays surrounding him in a semicircle, a fan purring somewhere behind his head. Chandra's voice came out of the speakers.

"I've disabled the code where I could find it," she said, "but I'm not convinced I've located everything."

"You could run the simulation yourself," Martinez said.

"I'd rather you do it." Irritation showed in her voice. "You're the damned yachtsman. You know which buttons to push."

Martinez was in place to help remove recent innovations intended to preserve the pilot's life. After Captain Blitsharts had gone spiraling off into the dark under full acceleration with his dead hand on the throttle, another element had been added to the software that allowed a third party to take command of the boat and return it safely to its berth. Martinez would use that to provide guidance to *Laredo* once it detached from *Corona*. The only problem was a second element of the new safety program, which flat forbade Martinez to accelerate the boat at a rate that would kill a human.

Martinez had assigned Chandra to the duty of altering the software because she had a diabolical talent for corrupting code and turning it to her own purposes. On Martinez's last command, *Illustrious,* he'd discovered that Chandra had given herself database superuser privileges and rewritten her own personnel evaluation to make it more flattering.

Top marks for ambition, Martinez thought, as well as subversion. It was high time that she used her powers for good.

A tuneless, breathy whistle came from the speakers. As she worked, Chandra voiced whatever tune was running through her head. This might take some time.

Martinez relaxed into the acceleration couch that had been custom-molded around his body. Except that he had been wearing a vac suit at the time, as he would have in *Laredo,* and now that he was in his Fleet uniform, he fell into the couch as if it were an overlarge bathtub. At least the simulator had a pleasant smell, some kind of citrus-scented disinfectant, whereas fully suited in *Laredo* he could smell only his own suit seals.

The breathy tune came to an end. "All right, Gareth," Chandra said. "Launch when ready."

Martinez took the controls and shoved the throttle all the way forward. His couch shifted on its pneumatic supports to provide a convincing and somewhat exhilarating simulation of acceleration—the difference being that if the boost had been genuine, Martinez would have been mashed flat, and unconscious within a matter of seconds. Instead he watched the gauge that marked the gee force that he would have endured had his journey not been simulated, and then watched as the engine cut out at 21.3 gravities, in response to a programmed safety feature that Chandra had missed.

"Right," he heard Chandra mutter. Then, "I found it. It'll take me an hour or two to make sure I can disable it without also removing something we need."

"Very good," Martinez said. "Page me when you need me." He hoisted himself out of the simulator and went down the stairs to the boat deck. There *Laredo* sat amid a scattering of components deemed no longer necessary: the acceleration couch, radiation shielding, much of the life support. The access hatches to the engine compartment were all open, and

Garcia and Mersenne were involved in a discussion concerning how to attach new hardware to the DM-5 fuel source. Dalkeith watched while jotting notes into her hand comm.

"Get close enough," Mersenne said, "and it'll perceive it as a threat."

"It'll give us a warning tone if the Howe doesn't perceive the threat as imminent," Garcia said. "That'll give us a good idea how close we can get."

"At some point the warning tone turns into hard radiation," Mersenne said. "Do you know where that point is? Because I don't."

Martinez saw that Dalkeith was standing on a drop cloth, and that she shared the drop cloth with magnetrons, waveguides, capacitors, diodes, and high-capacity transformers, all looted over the cook's objections from the large, industrial-sized microwave ovens in *Corona*'s kitchens. She looked up as Martinez approached. "I'm generating some theoretical maximums," she said in her child's voice. "If we set up a proper magnetron array, we can generate a surprisingly large microwave burst before everything burns out."

"How surprisingly large?"

Dalkeith showed him the calculations on her hand comm display. They *were* surprisingly large.

"What's the range?"

"That depends. A microwave oven is a steel box that reflects the microwaves and contributes to heating the target, but we won't have time for the microwaves to reflect even once. We'll get a fraction of a second before either we succeed or the Howe unit destroys our array. So I'd like to do some experiments and find out exactly what the ideal range might be."

"Carry on," Martinez said.

Alikhan entered with a tray of cups and a vacuum flask of coffee. Martinez thanked him and poured himself a cup.

Garcia and Mersenne, in the meantime, had come to some kind of agreement to resolve their problem through experiments, and he urged them to coordinate their trials with those of Dalkeith.

"You know," Martinez said, "if this works, we can't tell anyone."

Garcia looked up at him from her crouch near the scavenged electronics.

"We don't want anyone to know this is even possible," Martinez said. "So if we succeed, we have to hold this a complete secret. We don't want to show terrorists a way to blow up cities."

Dalkeith seemed relieved. "Thank you, Lord Captain," she said. "That had worried me, also."

Carrying his coffee, Martinez then went in search of Husayn, whom he found in the ready room.

Husayn, designing the proximity fuse, had the easiest task of all, because racing necessitated an impressive sensor array for *Laredo,* and all that was necessary was to define which sensor inputs would trigger the explosion. Husayn had essentially finished his work, but still needed to check it.

Martinez rolled his shoulders, undid a button on his tunic, and allowed a feeling of satisfaction to roll over him. The technical issues were being addressed and the project had a chance of success. He decided to go for a stroll to clear his head.

He took the elevator up to the dining hall with its spectacular waterfall. The air was filled with the tang of the sea. Crew were setting up the tables for supper, laying out crystal and porcelain. He saw Young Gareth standing on the lip of the fountain, staring down at the bright fish beneath the rippling water and touching a stylus to an oversized hand comm. He waved the stylus in greeting as Martinez approached.

"Hello, progenitor!" he said. "I'm trying to draw the fish, but it's hard. I wish Lieutenant Garcia were here to help."

"She'll be free in a few days," Martinez said. *If we aren't all dead.*

"Are you working?" Young Gareth asked. "You're all so busy all of a sudden."

"My day has been good," Martinez said. "I'm blithe, perhaps even jocund."

Young Gareth was impressed. "Jocund? Really?"

"Yes," Martinez said. He plucked at the knees of his trousers and knelt by his son. "Now why don't you show me your picture?"

TWO DAYS LATER, Martinez was back in the *Laredo* simulator, the hatch closed, the fan behind his head humming. He wore a virtual reality rig, and so a virtual navigation plot seemed to float in the air in front of him, with the yacht's virtual controls just beyond.

He didn't actually need to be in the simulator, but he preferred to be alone.

The weight of expectation was growing too heavy for company.

He breathed in the scent of citrus, and of gun oil. He had taken his sidearm into the simulator with him.

Corona was swiftly approaching the small yellow star Contorsi. Captain Anderson had asked *Conformance* for permission to do a course correction burn around Contorsi to place them on track for Wormhole Three, and *Conformance* had responded in the affirmative. The burn would have been the expected thing.

So far, so routine.

Martinez knew that *Conformance* would be doing its own burn around the small yellow sun to fall into *Corona*'s wake, but he couldn't predict its track for certain. It might swing wide so as not to pile on too many gravities, but Martinez was inclined to think of Captain An-sol as the sort of smart, efficient officer who would welcome the opportunity for testing her ship and crew with a precise hard-gee burn.

But because he couldn't be certain, his intended course for *Laredo* was a compromise, accelerating at a rate that would kill any human passenger, and intersecting a number of courses that seemed plausible for *Conformance*.

"Three minutes to course correction." Vonderheydte's voice came over the speaker.

"Acknowledged," Martinez said. He really hadn't needed the reminder—he had one eye on the chronometer.

Everyone on the ship was strapped into an acceleration

couch for the burn. The fountain and waterfall had been drained, and all the fish and water tanks were secured for higher gravities. The crystal and porcelain had been placed in intelligent storage units that would provide them with exactly the amount of support necessary to survive any plausible acceleration.

"One minute."

He could feel eddies in his inner ear telling him that *Corona* was yawing slightly, more precisely aligning the engine for the burn.

"Fifty-one seconds." Half a Shaa minute.

Martinez enabled the automatic controls and kept his eyes on the plot.

"Nineteen seconds."

At zero the engines increased their burn, and Martinez felt gravities increase. He took strong, deliberate breaths. Darkness pulsed at the edges of his vision. *Corona,* the ship, now traversed the actual corona of the sun, drawing a burning line through the outer envelope of the star. And then, as the sun passed between *Corona* and *Conformance,* he saw the signal that *Laredo* was away, its track separating from *Corona* until it reached a safe distance and its own powerful engine could ignite. Martinez's eyes shifted to the virtual cockpit as he watched displays shift to the telemetry coming in from *Laredo.*

The pressure on his chest gradually eased as *Corona* flashed past Contorsi. *Laredo* was decelerating at a furious rate, the gees building—*six, nine, fifteen.* He knew that the jury-rigged system in the engine compartment had been braced against such accelerations, but he felt worry gnaw at him. Something could break loose, some wiring come undone . . . *twenty, twenty-two.* Always keeping the star between *Conformance* and the yacht.

Nothing went wrong, and the yacht continued along its programmed course. Martinez felt his anxiety decrease by what seemed a microscopic amount. There were still so many places where it could go wrong.

In a half circle around *Laredo*'s antimatter container was the jury-rigged array of microwave emitters, all ready to be powered by another Howe container scavenged from Captain Kelly's racing yacht. If any of the improvised gear broke under the stress of acceleration, the mission would fail.

If *Laredo*'s guidance failed, or contained an error, the mission would fail with it.

If *Conformance* chose an unconventional path around the sun, and *Laredo* failed to intercept, the mission would fail.

If the improvised proximity fuse didn't perform as expected, the mission would fail.

When the proximity alert gave the signal, the DM-5 scavenged from Kelly's yacht would fire a great burst of energy through the microwave array. If the DM-5 failed to trigger, or if it had been hooked improperly into the system, or if it flooded the microwave array with too much energy and blew it apart, the mission would fail.

The microwave array aimed at *Laredo*'s DM-5 might not work, or it might be misaligned. In which case the mission would fail.

And last, if the microwave burst was insufficient to destabilize the antihydrogen chips in the DM-5, then the DM-5 would assume it was under attack and release enough radiation to wreck *Laredo*. There would be no enormous release of energy, and the mission would fail.

But if everything went *right,* a strong overload current would destabilize the chips, and the antihydrogen flakes would hit the silicon wall and all their energy would be released at once. Which would be enough to destabilize the antimatter in Kelly's power unit, and the two would go off together.

And then, if *Conformance* was within range of the blast, it would be destroyed, and the mission would succeed.

It would be the better part of an hour before *Conformance* began its own burn, and during that time Martinez stayed in the simulator while anxiety gnawed at his insides, and he played every failure mode over and over again in his mind. He could smell the sweat that was soaking his armpits and dousing his back.

He looked at the pistol he'd brought into the simulator with him. If the improvised missile failed, he thought he might record a few last messages to his family, and then kill himself before *Conformance* caught up with them.

Assuming, of course, he could actually pull the trigger. He could use radiation weapons to destroy ships and their crews between the stars, but he didn't know whether he had the nerve to put the gun to his head.

He watched as *Conformance* vanished behind Contorsi and reappeared a few seconds later, its engine pointed directly at *Corona* and burning brilliant white. He had to keep reminding himself that what he was watching had happened nearly four minutes ago, and that whatever was going to happen had already happened.

Laredo was no longer decelerating, but accelerating along its intercepting course. And then there was another white flare, and Martinez felt his heart stop.

The confirmation was in the radiation counter, a double spike—the two Howe units on *Laredo* going up simultaneously, and then a tiny fraction of a second later all the fuel on *Conformance* detonating, creating a nova flare that for a brief instant burned brighter than the star, a flare that marked the death of a ship and its nearly three hundred crew.

Martinez felt his heart lurch into motion. He let out the breath he didn't know he'd been holding, and took in air.

"Well," he said aloud. "Now we really *are* the Terran criminals."

CHAPTER 22

Sula stared at the monitor in *Striver*'s Command as *Conformance* burned bright as a star, and then transformed into a bubble of hot expanding plasma.

How in hell . . . ? Sula wondered. *Corona* was a civilian ship. It was *defenseless.*

Yet somehow Martinez seemed to have developed the ability to explode enemy warships by remote control.

A useful trick, she decided.

"Pitch over the ship," Sula ordered. "We're going to start our deceleration. Maintain our course for the wormhole, and sound the warning for engine start."

As the alert rang through the ship, Sula considered sending Martinez a message of congratulations, then decided against it.

It would only make him more smug.

TWENTY-TWO DAYS LATER *Corona* transited into the Harzapid system, and Martinez sent a coded message to Michi Chen. Seventeen hours later, he received a reply.

Michi's video showed her tired and aged, her bangs gray now, her face jaundiced and drawn. Her uniform tunic was buttoned up to her throat, as if she were warding off infection.

"You're very welcome to the Fourth Fleet, Captain Martinez," she said. "I'm glad you've arrived, because we have a lot to talk about."

AFTER TWENTY-NINE MORE days of brutal deceleration, *Striver* finally docked at Harzapid's ring. Most of the ships of the Fourth Fleet were moored around her, though two Terran squadrons were already in orbit around the system's star, preparing to defend the system against attackers.

Sula had spent days in consultation with Michi Chen since entering the Harzapid system, and most of her group of officers and enlisted had already received their new assignments. Michi had taken the non-Terran vessels by surprise, captured and disarmed the officers and crew, and was now converting the ships to Terran use as quickly as she could.

In the last few hours before docking, *Striver* had reduced acceleration, and Sula had taken a long, lingering shower and put on clean clothes. After the heavy gees, her body was a mass of cramp and pain, and it pitched a little to the right as she walked.

She would schedule a massage as soon as she could and hope it could relieve some of her aches.

But first there were formalities. No sooner had *Striver* docked than Fleet crew came aboard to take possession and relieve Sula of her responsibilities. The two captive Legion recruits were marched away to detention on the station. Sula picked up her Sidney Mark One and led her party down to the common room, and out the passenger access hatch.

Only Alana Haz was in uniform, because she was the only passenger traveling as a Fleet officer. The rest wore civilian gear and were accompanied by Lady Koridun, who startled in a glittering Chesko gown accessorized with Lord Arrun Safista's gun belt and sidearm. Free of heavy gravities, Koridun was practically skipping as she danced through the hatch, and her blue eyes glowed with delight as she looked forward to the sequel to her adventure.

Sula was aware of the sensational picture they made, the fighters carrying their rifles, their Sidneys, their shotguns and pistols. Victors in a merciless, close-quarters battle with a fanatical enemy. Hard-fighting veterans of a war that had barely started.

Sula stiffened as she saw the reception party: Michi Chen, Gareth and Roland and Vipsania Martinez, Nikki Severin in his blue uniform, and assorted Martinez clients and underlings. Lord Durward Li's stray wife, laughing and dressed in canary yellow and with her arm linked with that of a small fair-haired officer.

And Lamey. *Lamey.* She would have been surprised, if she weren't so tired.

At least Terza Chen hadn't turned up with the Martinez brats.

The group waiting at the end of the gangway were not just a welcoming committee, they were a political faction. They had come to draw Sula to their rebellion, to the embrace of their glittering, rising family, to make use of her skills and talents to smash their enemies and clear a path for them to rise.

Whatever might happen to Sula in the coming conflict, she knew Gareth Martinez would somehow end up looking good.

Well. Maybe she could find a way to carve out a faction of her own, along with a share of the glory.

Sula straightened as she approached the Martinez group, and she thought of a derivoo singer who broadcast defiance while staring into the hungry jaws of inexorable fate. Of choices made, choices spurned, consequences endured. Of the triumph of her plan for taking *Striver,* and of waking up night after night with her senses flooded by the smell of blood and a shriek bottled in her throat.

She walked up to Michi Chen and braced at the salute, her chin high.

"Lady Fleetcom," she said. "Here I am."

A NOTE ON THE CALENDAR

The Shaa "year" is, so far as anyone knows, an arbitrary period of time unconnected with the orbit of any planet, or the measurement of anything in the natural world. It consists of 0.84 Earth years, or 306.6 Earth days. Caroline Sula, twenty-three in Shaa measure, is twenty by the reckoning of old Earth.

Planets within the empire of the Shaa have their own local calendar by which they chart the local year and seasons. But all official business is conducted in reference to the imperial calendar rather than the local.

The Shaa year is divided into equally arbitrary units that demonstrate the Shaa love for prime numbers. The Shaa year is divided into eleven months of 27.9 Earth days each, and each month is divided into 23 Shaa days, each 1.21 Earth days. The Shaa day is divided into 29 hours, each of 59.98 Earth minutes; and the hours are divided into 53 minutes, each 67.9 Earth seconds long. A Shaa minute consists of 101 seconds, each of 0.67 Earth seconds.

There is no Shaa equivalent of the "week," though many planets have such a period in their own local calendars.

Measurements of time in this work, unless otherwise noted, are exclusively in Shaa measure. Readers may take comfort in the fact that, though the Shaa day is a little longer than Earth's twenty-four-hour day, the hours and minutes are roughly equivalent.

ABOUT THE AUTHOR

Courtesy of the author

Walter Jon Williams has been nominated repeatedly for every major science fiction award. He lives near Albuquerque, New Mexico, with his wife.

ALSO BY
WALTER JON WILLIAMS

DREAD EMPIRE'S FALL: THE PRAXIS

"Space opera the way it ought to be [...] Bujold and Weber, bend the knee; interstellar adventure has a new king, and his name is Walter Jon Williams." —George R.R. Martin

A young Terran naval officer, Lt. Gareth Martinez is the first to recognize the insidious plot of the Naxid—the powerful, warlike insectoid society that was enslaved before all others—to replace the masters' despotic rule with their own. Martinez and Caroline Sula, a pilot whose beautiful face conceals a deadly secret, are now the last hope for freedom—as the interstellar battle begins against a merciless foe whose only perfect truth is annihilation.

DREAD EMPIRE'S FALL: THE SUNDERING

"A spectacular far-future space opera." —*Locus*

Following *The Praxis*, Walter Jon Williams' critically-acclaimed mix of space opera and military science fiction, the conflict grows for the fate of humanity...and the universe.

THE ACCIDENTAL WAR

"Williams's prose is distinguished by a no-nonsense confidence." —*New York Times*

Blending fast-paced military science fiction and space opera, the first volume in a dynamic trilogy from the *New York Times* bestselling author of *The Praxis*, set in the universe of his popular and critically acclaimed Dread Empire's Fall series—a tale of blood, courage, adventure and battle in which the fate of an empire rests in the hands of a cadre of desperate exiles.